The ISLAND of TIME

The Journal of Randy Carr

Matthew DeBettencourt

TATE PUBLISHING & *Enterprises*

This title is also available as a Tate Out Loud product. Visit www.tatepublishing.com for more information.

Published by Tate Publishing & Enterprises, LLC
127 E. Trade Center Terrace | Mustang, Oklahoma 73064 USA
1.888.361.9473 | www.tatepublishing.com

Tate Publishing is committed to excellence in the publishing industry. The company reflects the philosophy established by the founders, based on Psalm 68:11,
"The Lord gave the word and great was the company of those who published it."

Cover design & interior design by Elizabeth A. Mason
Illustrations by Genevieve Stotler

Published in the United States of America

ISBN: 978-1-60604-647-0
1. Youth & Children: Youth Interest: Teen Fiction
2. Juvenile Fiction: Science Fiction, Fantasy & Magic
08.09.17

To Billy, Amy, Jakub,
and Michael Paul

Table of Contents

Part One

Part Two

Part Three

Part Four

Prologue

Ever since the studies of European mathematician Albert Einstein, scientists have studied the relationship between space and time. His theory of the earth's time passing more quickly than time in space has been disproved with research associated with the Space Program Agreement between the United States and the Russian Republic. And although this side of the theory, the exploration of space, has been thoroughly explored and researched even by sending one space station outside of the Milky Way, *time* is another story.

American and Russian scientists have been on the cutting edge of the leading technologies and the most efficient scientific researches and breakthroughs, from curing virtually any physical and mental ailments to creating inhabitable atmospheres in the most hostile and ethereal environments.

The American researchers worked with Western European scientists to develop continuous and abundant electrical energy through wind-powered plants. With the aid of American finances, the Japanese instituted the first Oceanic Colonies in 2237. There have been twenty independent colonies since the 2300s, each birthed from separate Surface Nations. Beyond that, the Americans and the Russians have had Moon Colony programs running simultaneously but independently, and both proved successful. The Russians were online first, something the Americans can't publicly admit, but they were truly the first colony to begin generating their own atmospheric bubble.

Time was simply the only science to remain science fiction by the time Taran Flint was born. It was simply an impenetrable barrier. No machine or device manufactured by man had the ability to travel to a dimension or occupy the space in a former reality that had already come to pass. It was the past, and it will be the future. There was nothing except the present, and there was certainly no means by which to leave it.

Scientists at the Thompson Foundation of Time have, since 2335, implied research based primarily on time travel, but their efforts have so far been in vain. Knowing full well that traveling through a space outside of our atmosphere wouldn't substantiate travel into the future, the time and space relation was abandoned. They worked off of the theories and research that had accumulated from millions of studies about velocity equivalence, radiatomic inhibitors, and even molecular reversal in the past four hundred years. All of these previous theories had failed, but as the leader, Patrick Thompson believed there had to have been flaws. Though the information seemed flawless, there must have been miscalculation in live tests.

One of Thompson's branches, however, has had an exciting breakthrough. This branch, led by a man named Taran Flint, works out of Thompson's headquarters in the Karz Centre in downtown Detroit. This discovery, Thompson believes, will make his time traveling dream a reality.

Karz Corporation was founded by one of Thompson's ancestors over two hundred years ago. When they first started out in business, they had developed the first hydroleum powered engine. Though the hydroleum engine was replaced only twenty or so years later by the polar engine, it wasn't a loss for Karz. The polar engine was a design of theirs as well, more difficult to create, but more finely tuned. Polar engines are still in use today, superb because of their durability—a polar engine has no moving parts. Furthermore, most vehicles with polar engines are hovercrafts as well, leaving little to no wear on the vehicle.

Consequently, the purpose of this book is not to study the technological advancements made up until Taran Flint's birth, but to witness the effect his research has on his own future—past, as it were. Taran is among hundreds of scientists in the Karz facility that are working on their own theories and methods of time travel. But he is the lucky *one* to stumble upon it.

Over the last few months, Taran had designed a technology that even he had trouble believing could actually function. The machine he'd built failed on every test he'd run with his assistants. It continued to fail after every tweak, every adjustment, big or small. Finally, a late night test performed one night had a remarkable result. With the help of a mysterious technical expert from the east coast, Flint was able to transport himself and his assistant through time.

His story, beginning in 2348 AD, is much different than that of our own lives. In the twenty-fourth century, space isn't an obstacle, and the former United States has taken more countries "under its wing." Now named the United Nations of the Americas, it stretches from Alaska to Chile, leaving only the Northern Territories of Canada—the northeastern area of twenty-first century Canada—independent from the UNA, as well as Haiti, Columbia, and Brazil.

Many forms of entertainment have remained, and people still trifle over antiques and cultures of the past. People still pass time with games and such. Of course, technology has also been put to practical uses. It has enhanced security for many residences. Even the poorest parts of town have automatic doors. Nuclear power is a primary power source in all but the poorest nations. Even the African and Antarctic nations have full electrical power.

Taran's hometown is Detroit, in the original state of Michigan. The states' boundaries remained the same over the centuries, even after the UNA formed. Detroit was an exception compared to other large American cities (aside from New York, which was always an exception). It was also, like New York City, divided into four boroughs, namely Northern, Southern, Eastern, and Western Detroit. But recently, Michigan has been having some economic trouble from the Great Lansing Stock Exchange Crash in early February of 2348. This led to another businessman coming to Detroit who raised its economy significantly with donations and business. This business, Brick Industries Corporation, gave Michigan's top company, the Karz Corporation, some competition.

Part One

The Sundaes' Investigation

Chapter 1

Over the rolling hills and expansive plains of the area were bright blue skies and fluffy, white plumes of clouds. In the center of this picturesque landscape, there stood a grand cityscape, piercing the sky. Along the main road of that city, there stood several gray buildings that reached up toward the soft clouds. One particular building that stood apart from the rest was a black-framed building with numerous windows. A lit sign near its summit read "KARZ" in dark green.

Inside this office building were many individual offices, each on different floors divided for different research and development purposes. All of the offices bore the same semblances to that of one particular office on the ninth floor. Across the hall of this office, there sat a young woman named Miss Dawn Vañia, often called "Vanilla" because of her association with a detective practice, Strawberry Sundae Investigations. She was waiting patiently for her fiancé to come out.

Dawn had naturally blond hair brushed back in a ponytail. She wore a gray overcoat trimmed to the shape of her body, similar to how the average businesswoman of her day would dress. She had beauty that needed no makeup, but nevertheless, today she wore bright red lipstick and light blue eye shadow, as was her custom.

She had left her book in the car, anticipating that this wouldn't be a very long wait. All she knew was that her fiancé had asked her to swing by his workplace after she was finished with her day at the Sundaes office in Northern Detroit.

She had been waiting very patiently, but she soon began to tap her foot on the soft carpeted floor, more a nervous habit than it was impatience. That was when she suddenly heard the sounds of electricity crackling come from the room and saw a bright blue flash come from the door's glazed window. She rose to open the door, but remembering it was locked, sat back down.

Now she was concerned. Her mind went wild with thoughts of what may have happened. She figured she'd have heard a scream if something had gone wrong. *A little morbid, don't you think?* She was worried just the same; she was a very nervous type, for a detective.

It was hard to believe, even for her close friends, that she'd become a detective. She had an anxious personality in middle school that followed her through high school and college. And even though her teenage experiences with her detective friends had her solving the dramatic neighborhood capers that troubled her suburban locality, she had still been unable to shake her fearful and tense paranoia.

Soon she couldn't hear any sound from the office, which built so much anxiety in her that she felt she almost couldn't take it.

Waiting in the hall, she wondered what was going on behind the glazed door. What could her twenty-eight-year-old fiancé be doing that required such secrecy? They were just another couple in urban Detroit. The only excitement she saw was when her agency picked up a cold case file all but forgotten by the officials. How could Taran Flint be involved with top secret projects? Until now it had all been rhetoric, but it was finally becoming real. This was her first real visit to the Karz building that didn't stop at the lobby doors. All these thoughts piqued her curiosity, making the wait even more suspenseful.

The suspense passed as quickly as it came, however, when Taran Flint and his employer, Mr. Thompson, opened the door and stepped out, talking. Her fiancé was an inventor for the Karz Corporation, a company that originally designed engines and later on, designs for automobiles and practical hovercrafts, hence the name Karz. Soon after it began to invent and manufacture different gadgets and devices, making Karz the household name it was today.

Mr. Thompson was a tall man. He wore a black overcoat over a red collared shirt. He had a bushy black mustache and neatly combed black hair. Taran was quite the opposite; he was thinner than Thompson and had sandy brown hair. He wore a gray suit over a white collared shirt and a blue necktie.

Thompson eyed Dawn as he walked out of the office. His demeanor always intimidated her. He seemed to know that he was better, and he felt justified in flaunting it. Thompson knew that kind of silent manipulation would help him remain in control at all times.

"Congratulations, Mr. Flint," Mr. Thompson said. "You've earned this new position. If everything goes well tomorrow, I'll make you chairman of the new division, and I'll have you begin our Time Crew projects immediately."

Taran shook his boss' hand. He was quite a sight compared to the hefty Thompson. If Dawn didn't know any better, anyone might have thought Thompson's hand would have crushed Taran's. Taran wasn't lanky, nor was he weak, but he was small. His shoulders weren't broad or threatening, as

Thompson's were. He was athletic, but had more of a runner's form than a linebacker's.

"Did you hear that, honey?" He hugged Dawn tightly.

"Yes. Congratulations," Dawn replied. She had done what she could to support him and his work since he had begun designing the equipment that Mr. Thompson was yet to approve. In fact, she and Taran had planned to set the date for their wedding to be as soon as possible after he finished the project. "Are you coming home now?"

"Yes, I just have to tie up a couple loose ends," Taran answered, smiling. "I'll see you there."

Taran's apartment was in the same building as Dawn's. He had arranged for his apartment to be right next door after they got engaged. Now, both of their rooms were on the second floor. Taran's old apartment had been two floors above hers.

Dawn pushed the down button for the elevator that was next to the office. While she waited, Taran kissed her and told her he would be home in about half an hour.

"Don't be too late!" Dawn warned. She blew a kiss to him as the elevator door closed.

"Bye," Taran said softly.

Chapter 2

As Dawn left the office building, her compact videophone, CVP for short, began to ring. It had been clipped to her suit pocket. It was strictly for use between her and the Sundaes, the freelance detective agency she and her friends found themselves creating after they finished college. So, anticipating more trouble with the case she was presently trying to decipher, she braced herself. She took the CVP from her pocket and pressed the screen.

"Hello?"

The face on the phone was that of Diane Stroby. She was the leader of the Sundaes, code-named "Strawberry." She had short, bright red hair with bangs that sometimes fell into her eyes.

"Fudge wanted to know what you had planned for tonight," Strawberry said. Danielle Fudge, code-named "Fudge" for obvious reasons, was the acting secretary for the Sundaes' agency. "I told her to call you, but you know that would be too complicated for her." She drew in a deep breath. "So, what are you doing tonight, Vanilla?"

"I'm making dinner for Taran and me," she answered.

"Oh, him again, huh?" Strawberry scoffed. "I'm telling you, he's bad news, Dawn." Strawberry had only met Taran Flint a few times during the years Dawn had been going out with him. Though she and Dawn were good friends, she preferred to keep love and relationships separate from her work fraternizations, which would include the other Sundaes.

Besides, as small as Taran was, Strawberry couldn't take him down. She was borderline anorexic and didn't spend much of her time eating the foods that nominally inspired her investigatory staff. However, she had quite an appetite for chocolate, but only when she was feeling depressed. With a sanguine personality like her own, though, there was plenty of time she wouldn't waste eating.

"You remember what happened with Doris's fiancé, the 'handyman'?"

Strawberry attempted once again to deter her friend's love for this man. "When she went on that business cruise, and she found that rat with Felicia Hayes?"

"Yeah, yeah, yeah," Dawn said. She shook her head. "Well, I'm not Doris, and Taran Flint isn't Tom Faraday. I don't even know why we're discussing this again!" She stopped to gather her thoughts.

She transferred the call to audio only as she began to walk across the busy parking lot. "Well, anyway, he finished his project, and I wanted to make something special tonight. All I need to do is go shopping for some of the stuff first."

"You didn't go shopping yet?" Strawberry gasped. *I've got an excuse to come over and protect her from him*, she thought. Instead, she said, "Well, you go shopping, and the girls and I will be at your house to help prepare. See ya!"

Dawn heard a click. She hung up, shaking her head once again. She peered over at her car and realized it was in fact the only hovercraft in the Karz parking lot that was not a Karz make. She simply had to laugh as she got in and started it up.

As she drove to the grocery store, she thought about what to make. She knew Taran liked steak and chicken, but she wanted something different. It was close to Christmas time, so she decided not to make a ham or turkey; they were overly used during this season.

When she arrived at the store, she made her way to the butcher's section.

"I know the perfect thing." The comment was made to no one in particular as Dawn scooped up two packages of pork loin chops. "Diane's aunt had a wonderful recipe I wanted to try out."

The nearby customer didn't seem to care, though Dawn looked directly at her with the latter statement.

On the way to get Italian-style dressing, she picked up a bushel of the largest Maine potatoes. She'd need that much, assuming the Sundaes would probably invite themselves to eat while they were there. She put them all in a shopping basket and found the express lane.

Joe Young was her registrar. Young's Grocer was a local store, which Joe's father had owned for as long as he could remember. Dawn was a regular customer, so he'd gotten to know her fairly well in conversations at check out, as well as small talk when they passed in the neighborhood.

Joe immediately noticed the food Dawn was putting on the conveyer belt. Looking up at her, he said, "Taran finally finished his project, I presume. You're making a celebratory dinner, and your colleagues decided to join you, right?"

Dawn simply smiled. "You always start conversations this way, don't you?" Without waiting for an answer, she added, "And, yes, I'm making a special dinner. But, my boss is kind of edgy about Taran, so she just found another way to look after me."

"Pork chops and baked potatoes, right?" He rang up the two items.

"Yes—" she gasped. "Oh, I forgot—"

"Right here." Joe pulled up a pint of sour cream from below the counter. "So, you said he's supposed to marry you after this project of his, right? So why don't you guys live together by now?"

"Oh, that's a long story," Dawn began. "It was actually what he preferred to maintain the secrecy of his work, which I got accustomed to anyway. And you know how my friends can be."

"Just from the stories you tell me."

"Yeah, well, they don't care too much for Taran anyway, and they have a code about the boyfriend thing, especially since one of us moved in with this Tom Faraday guy. Needless to say, that relationship didn't go over well." She rambled on, "Diane doesn't want what happened to Doris to happen to me." She looked down at her groceries and gasped again. "Oh! I have to go back to the produce aisle—"

"For this?" he asked. "And these?" He lifted up a grocery bag with fresh onions, scallions, and butter inside.

Dawn just chuckled.

"Well, you're one of the few who don't send androids out to do this kind of dirty work," Joe said. "You know, the lame tasks people get so irritable over doing like shopping, and, well, menial tasks such as that of a cashier."

"Your dad doesn't trust androids, Joe?"

"Yeah, that's something our two families have always had in common," Joe answered. "I mean, I'm with you. I think they'd be a big help and everything, but—" Joe handed the plastic bag to Dawn. "Life would lose a lot of its quaint charms."

"Charms?"

"Well, like this." Joe motioned toward himself and his favorite, beautiful customer.

"I'll see you around, Joe." She smiled. She picked up her groceries and started out the door. "Oh, and thanks."

Chapter 3

DAWN MADE IT HOME to find her friends in her small kitchen. Two of them were leaning against a tall, black refrigerating unit, called an R.U. Another was sitting down at the table while two more were searching through the cupboards. Finally, Strawberry was tossing a salad in a large plastic bowl. Ignoring them, Dawn put her groceries on the table in one corner and laid them out on the smooth, hardwood surface.

"I fired up the grill for you, Vanilla," Strawberry said. The grill was built into the counter next to the stovetop. The lava rocks inside were lit, and the flames were licking just below the grill's surface. "So, you want to try Aunt Dottie's pork chop recipe, eh?" She started to search through the bags. As she did, she mumbled, "Oh good, Joe remembered the sour cream," but it wasn't loud enough for Dawn to hear.

"Yes, actually—"

"Did you get salad?" asked Fudge, the woman sitting down at the table. She had her dark brown hair tied back in a ponytail like Dawn's. Most of her clothes tended to be red, but her favorite color was green. She was the most health conscious of the Sundaes. The others said she was just a health nut.

"Well—"

"I didn't think so," she said, interrupting Dawn. "I brought a big bowl of tossed salad. It goes great with pork, or so I hear." She immediately changed her tone to an accusation. "You knew I was doing diet research for my job at Brick Industries. Of course, I knew you wouldn't take the initiative to buy me salad fixings, so Strawberry is over there tossing it with olive oil, cherry tomatoes, cucumbers, and black olives."

"Oh yeah, it was the whole 'nothing with the letter p diet,' right?" Dawn quipped.

Fudge sighed. "No, I'm done with that theory." She was always experimenting with new theories for her part-time job at Brick Industries. She could never quite find the right diet for herself, so she got a corporation to do it for her and pay her in the process. "Mr. Brick got some bogus information in the letter tips."

"No kidding," Dawn scoffed.

Ignoring the comment, Fudge continued, "The new one I'm doing is a study based on times of the day affecting the types of foods you eat, etc. Blah. I'm in the 'protein during the day, carbs at night' group."

"Do you think that's healthy?"

"Oh, Vanilla—" Denise Caramiel began.

Strawberry led five other primary detectives with Dawn. This included Fudge, Denise "Caramel" Caramiel, Donna "Butterscotch" Terscosh, Debbie "Chocolate" Shock-Lot, and Delores "Cream" Crém. They always worked together, going out in pairs much of the time.

"Yes, Caramel?" Dawn asked impatiently.

"I drank the last of your iced tea. I hope that's all right," Caramel said.

One by one, her comrades carried on with indistinct conversation as Dawn prepared the meal. It was a small apartment, so the sound filled the kitchen. She was trying desperately to ignore them without seeming to do so.

Strawberry kept mentioning how turkey or ham would have been more fitting for the holiday season. Cream carried on about the wax fruit in the basket that made up the centerpiece of the table and how she met somebody that knew someone who worked for a company that recently bought out a wax factory that specialized in assembling fruit baskets.

Chocolate and Butterscotch were off to the side arranging plans for a party that was coming up soon. They were the inseparable pair of detectives. They did everything together: investigations, research, travel, and so on. They and Vanilla were the original Sundaes under Strawberry when the agency was started. The four of them had been solving cases together since high school.

Very annoyed from the commotion, Vanilla finally suggested that they go and watch the 3-DV while she made supper. She told them she worked better without distractions. Strawberry, the only one who was helping anyway, stayed in the kitchen. She began to slice the potatoes part way down the center for the baked potatoes. The others left reluctantly, and each took a spot in the small living room between the entrance of the apartment and the kitchen.

"I didn't mean to cause any trouble, Dawn," Strawberry said quietly. "We should probably just leave you alone with Taran for dinner. It's just that—there's something fishy about him. Something's not right."

"Don't worry about me," Dawn replied. "I'll be fine. It's just another day in the life of Dawn and Taran. The only exception is that he can take his focus off work after today and get more involved in our relationship."

This was the moment Strawberry knew she would overtly cringe at, which forced her to look slightly away. "Well, you know how it is, girls. You win some, you lose some."

Fudge spoke up, "Yeah, but who knows, maybe this Mrs. Sundae thing won't be half bad. But technically, she'd be a Flint after this supposed marriage."

This sparked another conversation over the validity of her name being involved with the Sundaes. Dawn knew it was just background noise, no real threat to anything cosmically important in her microcosmic universe. She simply smiled and continued preparing the pork chops.

She let them soak in a marinade she made out of the minced onions and Italian salad dressing. She and Strawberry then wrapped eight potatoes in aluminum foil and placed them on the grill. Each potato had a small pad of butter wedged in the cuts Strawberry had made.

Strawberry then watched the potatoes while Dawn put the chops in the R.U. At this point, Caramel came in to get drinks for the others.

"What do you have to drink in here, Vanilla?" Caramel asked. "Oh, I'll look myself." She walked over to the R.U. and reached in for the new pitcher of iced tea that sat on the top shelf next to the milk. "Oh, she must have made more."

"That's for supper, Caramel," Dawn told her.

"Okay, fine. I'll take some milk," she replied reluctantly. She then poured five glasses of milk and brought them into the living room two at a time. When she came back for her own, she stayed in the kitchen. Strawberry had walked over to the table to talk to Dawn. Realizing the potatoes would burn if left unattended, Caramel stood near the grill and used tongs to rotate them, revealing the charcoal-black surface of the foil beneath them.

"So when are you gonna get one of them HTVs, Vanilla? You're the only person I know that insists on watching TV using the old 3-D LiteWave method," Caramel said. "The new holographic images are so lifelike. The progression scans aren't as noticeable as the thing you got in there."

"I like my TV just the way it is, Caramel." Dawn walked over to the R.U. to take the scallions out. "I personally haven't noticed that big of a difference in performance. Taran has an HTV, after all, and I actually like mine better."

Meanwhile, Strawberry watched as Dawn chopped up the scallions into very small rings. "Those chops won't be done by the time Taran gets here unless they start cooking soon. Do you want me to take them out?"

"Yes, thank you," Dawn answered. "They haven't been soaking for very long, but I'm sure it's enough for some flavor."

Strawberry brought the chops over to the hot grill. "The chops didn't have long enough to really marinate, but we can still use this dressing mixture for a sauce. Just heat it up," she said.

"That's what I said." Dawn looked over at her.

"Did you?" was her sarcastic response, along with the smirk that crept onto her face.

Caramel took the potatoes off of the grill and put them on a platter. Strawberry then placed a couple chops on the grill. The grill immediately made a sizzling sound, and smoke began to rise from the pork chop. She was only able to fit five chops on the small grilling surface. She then brushed them each lightly with the marinade. Fudge readied another platter for the chops and placed it next to the grill.

Chapter 4

AFTER A LONG FORTY-FIVE minutes—during which time Caramel, Dawn, and Strawberry cooked twelve pork chops, made an Italian dressing sauce, set the table, and kept the potatoes warm in the oven—there was a knock on the door. Dawn checked her kitchen surveillance screen.

The surveillance camera that she had installed was standard equipment for safety reasons. It was mandatory for condominiums, apartment complexes, and hotels to have cameras outside the door, while the inner cameras, in most UNA states, were optional.

State laws also determined mandating personal property cameras. Local police departments monitored the outer door cameras automatically, and inner cameras were at tenant or owner's consent. All of the cameras were accessible to the tenant and could transmit the signal to any modern HTV or 3-DV set via remote. That way, personal security was assured. That same remote could also unlock the door or doors leading into the building and turn off the inner cameras.

"You're late, Taran!" Dawn called from the kitchen. "Hurry up," she then said softly to Strawberry. "Get the food on the table, and then get everyone to wash their hands!"

"Come on, babe, let me in!" Taran said into the intercom. "I left my cards in the office."

"Go away!" she responded.

Taran smirked. "Dawn Vañia, open this door right now."

"Do you have the ring?"

Taran could only laugh. "Yeah, I picked it up at the vendor down on Parker Ave. You know, the Spanish guy with the one eye. He gave me a great deal, but I had to sell your little brother to get the last fifty bucks."

Since she'd had enough time to hide her friends, she pressed a button on the keypad. The door slid open.

"You sold Mikey? My parents are finally free?"

"I was kidding," Taran said. "I wouldn't do them that favor."

The Sundaes were in a separate room at the moment, washing their hands. "Done straightening up at the office, Taran?" Dawn asked. She led him toward the living room, away from where she assumed the Sundaes were.

"Yes, we finished cleaning up," he answered. "Why was your keypad locked?"

"Oh, did I lock it?" She shrugged.

"Oh, well," he said. "Anyway, we also moved the machine to another location. That is, for the test tomorrow." As he talked, the Sundaes snuck into Dawn's bedroom and out a window. "Of course, Thompson didn't want my assistant to leave it on again, so he assigned him to another department during the testing."

The two of them sat down on the sofa. As Taran talked, Dawn could barely hear the Sundaes as they climbed onto the fire escape. They then crept down the spiral staircase and found their way to the front door of the building. They let themselves in and climbed up the staircase to the second floor. Then they rang Dawn's doorbell.

"Who could that be?" she asked.

"I'll see who it is and get rid of them."

Taran proceeded to the door as Dawn wearily checked her bedroom, but it was now empty. Her friends had flown the coop; she knew they'd be back, of course. They wouldn't leave her alone with Taran for two minutes. *It's probably them at the door.*

Taran opened the door to see Strawberry standing there, alone. "Oh, hello, D... D... umm... Danielle?" he greeted her.

"It's Diane, but don't worry, I won't hold it against you," she said in a gruff tone as she let herself in. She proceeded toward the kitchen.

"Sorry about that," he said, scratching the back of his head. "We're kind of in the middle of something here."

"I just wanted to talk to Dawn about preparations for the Christmas party coming up," Strawberry told him. "She had a bunch of stuff I was supposed to pick up either today or tomorrow to bring to my house."

"She's in the kitchen." Taran began to follow her when he heard a knock at the door. "I'll get that. Excuse me."

He opened the door and found Debbie and Donna talking to each other. Assuming he would have better luck guessing which topping they represented, Taran attempted to address them in that manner instead. "Caramel, Butterscotch, what a pleasant surprise!"

"It's Chocolate and Butterscotch," Debbie corrected him. "And we came to talk to Dawn about a trouble spot we've been having in our case," she said in a rude manner.

Chocolate was the tallest of the Sundaes, towering over Butterscotch by about seven inches. They looked goofy together with Chocolate's short brown hair and thin features. Butterscotch was of more rounded proportions, and though her dirty blond hair was longer than Debbie's, it was only shoulder length.

"All right, Dawn's that way," Taran said, pointing to the kitchen. "Funny thing, though, we're trying to—" He stopped as they brushed right by him. He looked out the door and down the dark green hall in both directions, anticipating more visiting "D-women" with edible nicknames. Seeing no one, he shut the door and walked over to the kitchen. But before long, the doorbell rang again.

He stopped in his tracks and turned toward the door, now irritated but admittedly amused. He walked quickly, opening the door in time to see Cream and Caramel. "What a coincidence, D… girls," Taran stammered. He knew he'd be wrong, so he was better off not guessing.

"Diane and the others are here, too." He ushered them in, knowing all too well they were going to barge in regardless of what his action was.

Looking into the hall, Taran turned his head to the right in time to see the last Sundae, Fudge, walking toward him. She took her position next to the others in the kitchen.

"Surprise!" the Sundaes shouted.

Taran acted as surprised as possible, but it was difficult. After all, he knew they were up to something. He'd seen a glimpse of them when he came into the apartment in the first place. He became more suspicious when he found nearly all of them in the same room. "Oh, wow!" he exclaimed. "What's this for?"

"Congratulations, Taran," Strawberry said with an enthusiasm she apparently fought to express. "We heard about your recent… thing, and we are so excited!"

"That's… umm… terrific?" Taran said, looking over at his fiancée. "Oh, you didn't plan any type of party, did you?" Taran asked her.

"No, we didn't have the time to plan any big party," Dawn admitted. "But we did make Aunt Dottie's famous pork chops and baked potatoes!"

"Great," he said. He lacked enthusiasm, but for a different reason than Strawberry.

Everyone sat down at the dining room table except for Dawn and Taran, who poured everyone a drink. Bringing each of the girls iced tea, two glasses at a time, Taran realized that he wasn't going to get too much rest until his "guests" left.

When he finally sat down, he was at one end of the table with Dawn on his left. All of the Sundaes dug right in, but Taran toyed with his potatoes for a while. Seated around him in a clockwise order from Dawn, there was Caramel, Fudge, Strawberry, Chocolate, Butterscotch, and Cream.

"You know what happened today, Vanilla?" Strawberry was trying to get a conversation rolling. "The evidence we found proved that the body was not actually in the study when he was killed. Unfortunately, though, we've found so many weapon possibilities that it's getting pretty tough."

"We can't figure which weapon it is," Fudge added. "The weapons found in the building wouldn't have made a wound like his. We're going to go back later on and try and finish this off."

"It was probably Colonel Mustard in the library with the dagger," Taran said sarcastically. He presumed the Sundaes were discussing a tough case to crack. "It usually is. I mean, I always end up with a scenario similar to that." He looked over jokingly at Caramel. "Or the hall." He sipped some iced tea.

"*I'm* Colonel Mustard, and besides, we narrowed it down to either Miss Scarlet or Professor Plum, thank you very much," Caramel quipped. "Maybe next time, you'll investigate the case before you go pointing fingers at the Colonel."

"Sorry, I was just joking," Taran said in defense. "I thought you were talking about a real case."

"I was," she answered coldly, teasing him. All of the Sundaes started to laugh softly. "Oh, don't worry about it, Taran. Anyway," she said while looking at Dawn, "we did find out that the unidentified victim wasn't killed in the room where we found him. It also isn't clear what type of blade killed him. We only know he was stabbed."

Dawn nodded.

"Unidentified victim?" Taran queried.

"Yes. You see, he's not in the UNA government files," Cream explained. "That's the one thing that makes this case so strange. His retina scan, finger prints, dental records, none of these match any of the files, which date back nearly one hundred and fifty years—"

"So the only explanation," Chocolate continued, "would be that he's from a foreign region or nation, possibly the GU. They're one of the few European nations that aren't yet required to share citizen files with UNA databases."

"The German Union?" Cream scoffed. "Don't make me laugh. This guy was an American. I should know; I wrote up the report. He was a young American male, brown hair, brown eyes, five-foot-eight, 132 pounds. He was possibly of Irish descent, but he didn't match in their system either."

"He may be from the Northeastern Territory of Canada," Dawn suggested.

"We've already planned to send Sherri up there to get into their database and investigate their population files, remember?"

Sherri Marsh was the agency's independent investigator and the public face of the Sundaes. She had joined the girls a few years prior when they began taking on high-profile cases. To top it all off, Sherri worked alone and was more willing to do the traveling abroad.

"But still," Butterscotch added, "a middle-aged American—maybe Canadian—murdered in a big city like Detroit, and nobody can identify him? This is including a UNA computer system of every legal citizen since 2198!"

"What was his profession?" Taran asked.

"Well, we aren't sure. He was found in the upstairs apartment off an antique shop right next to the Owner's Auction Block," Dawn said. "Actually, I spoke with Mr. Owner, and it seems he tends to auction off a lot of antiques from there."

"But get back to the victim," Taran said. "Did he work for either of the businesses?"

"Don Forge, the antique shop owner, says he'd never seen him before," Chocolate said. "And Mr. Owner had said the same thing. Apparently, the apartment was owned by Mr. Forge, and he was planning on showing it to prospective tenants. That was when they found the body."

"Well, that place won't be rented out soon," said Caramel.

"Anyway, it's a little bit ironic, actually," Strawberry added. "Most of the more expensive antiques that Forge possesses are ancient swords, like the one from Captain Luke Blackbeard."

"Blackbeard, eh?" Taran said. He remembered hearing about him in history classes all through school. He was supposedly the most notorious pirate before his last voyage ended with his ship's disappearance. "That belongs in a museum or something."

"Oh, yeah! That reminds me," said Strawberry. "One place we haven't checked yet is the antique store. After supper, I was going to have Chocolate and Butterscotch go down to the police office and get a search warrant for tomorrow. We need to get an inventory of all of the items bought and sold within the last few weeks, and we need to double check Forge's physical inventory with the documented stuff. It's possible that the weapon was stolen right from his wares."

"Okie dokie," Butterscotch answered, stuffing the last bit of her potato into her mouth. "Could you pass the salad?"

Chocolate gave Butterscotch the bowl of salad and took another potato. "As far as that sword goes, I took a trip to the antique store a while back." She stuck a chunk of potato in her mouth and continued, chewing all the while.

"The certificate names Blackbeard as the originator of the sword, but that's slightly misleading."

"What do you mean, Debbie?" Dawn asked.

"I mean, it's authentic, I'm sure." Her mouth was now empty. "But we're not talking the same Blackbeard that *most* of us are familiar with. In the 1800s, there was a copycat treasure hunter that adopted the nickname from the Captain of *Queen Anne's Revenge*."

"So it isn't Blackbeard's sword?" Dawn frowned.

"Well, not *the* Captain Blackbeard," she noted. "The original Blackbeard lived about a hundred years before Luke Carver, whose sword Don claims to have. Carver, *our* Blackbeard, spent two years pillaging Atlantic island villages and American ports before his disappearance in the late 1830s. He simply used the notorious name for its dominating presence."

"Oh." Disappointment was distinct in Dawn's voice.

"He *was* a real pirate. In fact, the last time he was documented to have been seen was a port in St. Augustine. Sailors there claimed he was searching for a ship and crew. With an 'inherited' map to buried gold, he presumably left port with the Twin Captains of *Atlantic Gemini*."

"Of course," Butterscotch muttered.

"Now *that's* a pirate!" Dawn exclaimed. "Treasure maps and buried gold!"

"Now that we've had our history lesson..." Strawberry turned to Delores. "Cream, I know you were up pretty late searching around town for possible leads in the surrounding apartments, and I appreciate that. So don't worry about getting up early tomorrow. We'll manage the inventory when we get together in the morning. You can meet up with us whenever."

Cream nodded with excitement as she finished off her baked potato.

Chocolate swallowed the last bit of her pork chop. "I'm stuffed," she said, wiping her mouth with her napkin. She rose from the table and put her dishes in the sink. "I'll go warm up the car, Butterscotch. Thanks for the dinner, Vanilla. It was nice to see you again, Taran."

"Yeah, see you later," Taran replied. *Take the others with you, please*, he thought.

"See you tomorrow, Vanilla."

Chocolate left the building through the back entrance, where she had parked her car. She started it and waited for Butterscotch. While sitting there, she clicked on her Brick's TVP, a customized videophone built into her car, and dialed an all too familiar number. She watched the screen as it rang.

A woman's face soon appeared. She had long, bright red hair and soft blue eyes.

"Hello?" the woman said, but her motions weren't like a human's. She moved her mouth mechanically. Her voice was womanly but monotone. Furthermore, her eyes never moved; they stared off in one direction that seemed to be at about Chocolate's shoulder.

"Hi, Sherri. I—" Chocolate began, but the woman interrupted her.

"I'm sorry, but I can't come to the phone right now. If you'd like to leave a message, wait for the tone." Sherri continued to stare until the screen blacked out. There was a high-pitched beep.

"Oh, come on, Sherri, this is your Sundae's cell phone! For crying out loud!"

Sherri's face came back on the screen. "Will you hurry up? I'm pretty sure this is a long distance call, so unless you feel like wasting your time, not to mention your money—"

Now the woman was batting her eyelashes as she normally would and flipped her hair back as she always did. Chocolate was positive that Sherri was pulling her leg now.

"Sherri," she began. "Strawberry wants you to go to the NTC again so you can come up with the evidence that we—"

"Hey, hey. I ain't… I mean… oh! I blew my cover again." Sherri hung her head. "I'm sorry. I can't do it anymore."

"Don't worry, it's not the end of the world," Chocolate reassured her.

"Really? I always imagined that my entire purpose in life was to act as an answering machine operator for the next thirty-four years." Sherri sighed. "I guess I was wrong…" she said, her voice trailing off. "Whew! I never wanted to do that in the first place."

"So, will you go to NTC for us?"

"Of course! I love to travel, especially up north." Sherri paused. "Wait, that depends on where I'm going. What city, exactly?"

"The capital," Chocolate answered. "We need you to tap into the database in the NTC and find a file on someone."

"And he's Canadian?"

"We don't know. We only know what he looks like. We have his fingerprints, retina scan, and dental records," Chocolate explained. "But none of those match anyone in the UNA computer system."

"You have all of the unique information any one person possesses, and yet you still don't know who it is? Nothing?" Sherri exclaimed. "So you want me to go to Ottawa and see if he's a citizen. All right, I'll meet you at the office in about ten minutes. Bring the case file with you."

"All right." Chocolate smiled. "Bye!" The screen went black just as Butterscotch emerged from the apartment complex and started toward the car.

"I'm all set to go. Are you ready, Butterscotch?"

"Ready," Butterscotch affirmed. Chocolate went around to the passenger side. They both got in, and Butterscotch headed north toward headquarters.

Taran and Dawn walked down the hall with Cream a few minutes later. She had been assigned to get plenty of sleep that night and decided to get a head start. Taran stopped at the doorway as she continued to her car. "See ya later, Cream." He waved.

"Hey, Whip, wait." Dawn liked to call her "Whip" instead of "Cream" because it sounded funny. She caught up to her at the door to the stairwell.

"What's up, Dawn?" Cream turned to her. She brushed back her very light blond hair, tucking it behind her ears. When she tilted her head, however, it fell back over her shoulder again.

Dawn looked back at her fiancé and realized what she had to say could wait. "I need to see you at the office after Taran leaves tomorrow," Dawn explained. "Alone."

"About what time?"

"Noon."

"All right," Cream replied. She yawned. "I'll see you tomorrow, then."

"You okay to drive?" Dawn asked. "You should auto-droid it."

"Dawn Vañia suggests the android?" She gasped. "Are you sure *you* got enough sleep?"

Dawn laughed, turning back to the apartment where the others—Caramel, Strawberry, and Fudge—were being ushered out by Taran. "I wonder what we'll find at the shop after we get the warrant," she wondered aloud.

"What are *we* going to do?" Caramel asked Strawberry, halfway down the hall.

"Well," Dawn began to answer instead. Her eyes met Taran's as he helped Fudge with her coat. "You should probably investigate at the Auction Block to see if Mr. Owner sold a sword with a saber's design to it."

"You're still sticking to that saber theory of yours, huh?" Strawberry said. "Taran, you know, this girl of yours is obsessed with ancient sabers. One day she'll learn about another sword prominent in its own time, like a katana or a cutlass, and investigate its entire history, too."

"I wouldn't get obsessed with a katana," Dawn scoffed. She sarcastically added, "But tell me more about this… cutlass." She stopped and then shook her head. "Anyway, the only reason I believe a saber was used is because of the shape of the wound and how I presume he bled. We'll only know for sure after a coroner's report comes in."

"Anyway, Caramel, you and Fudge can check with Mr. Owner about any swords he might have sold recently," Strawberry suggested. Mr. Owner ran Owner's Auction Block, and Don Forge ran the antique store, Forge's Antiques. "Forge may have possibly omitted the sword we're looking for in his inventory if Mr. Owner had sold it on his block. Just check with Mr. Owner's records."

"Mr. Owner might actually still have the sword in his possession," Caramel added.

"That's true, too," Strawberry said. "So, the two of you can handle that." She nodded. "Dawn, you just need to be at the office in the morning. I have the report that the Detroit Police detective made about the case. I'd like you to read over it tomorrow."

"All right," Dawn answered. "Tomorrow."

Chapter 5

Chocolate and Butterscotch entered the tall, relatively new police office building. The building had the shape of an "L." The shorter of the two wings of the building was the department for issuing warrants, permits, and lawsuits. That's where the Sundaes needed to go. Once inside, Secretary Droid SY-19 greeted them from behind her station. She was one of the latest models that looked, sounded, and even acted like a real human.

"I detect your heart rate to be approximately double that of your resting pace," SY-19 told Chocolate. "It is as if you are suffering from overwhelming anxiety. Or is it ambition, Miss Chocolate?"

So she didn't act exactly like a human, but at least she addressed Debbie with a nickname instead of her first name, number, and age like the older androids did. *That* was the latest innovation: recognized slang associations.

"There's nothing wrong," Chocolate told SY-19. "We're just investigating what happened to a murder victim that was found on downtown Central Street. We need to get a search warrant for Forge's Antique Store."

With the economic trouble that Michigan had been suffering from lately, Detroit had been forced to cut budgets significantly to keep things running. One such part of the budget was investigative funding. The Detroit Police Force no longer funded, or even trained, its own detectives, leaving a lot of investigations to freelance detectives and private investigators. It prompted business for agencies like Strawberry Sundaes Investigations. Still, by law, they had to obtain permits and warrants through the police offices. That is what Chocolate and Butterscotch thought they were getting into by calling on Mr. Stone, the head of the investigative staff and the only paid official in that department.

"You don't have an appointment, so I will initiate a meeting for you." Behind the desk, SY-19 began to plug away at something on the touchboard. A few moments later, she addressed the Sundaes again.

"Everything is in order, you can wait just inside this door." The android led them to a sliding door on the far wall. "He will be with you shortly."

"Thanks," Chocolate answered. She and Butterscotch approached the door as SY-19 opened it. As it slid open, a buzz of voices flowed out from within the room. Chocolate's eyes went wide and her jaw dropped. "Oh my—"

"After the recent budget cuts, many of the officers have been transferred, and many of the 'pen pushers' are covering the shifts of the patrol officers," SY-19 explained. "That is because the androids programmed to patrol much of downtown Detroit have been cut from the force due to our lack of funds. Furthermore, Mr. Stone's office has been moved back to the West Wing since the reconstruction has been completed."

"But isn't this the East Wing?" Chocolate pointed into the hall.

"That is correct."

Butterscotch added, "And they're all…"

"I am afraid so." SY-19 peered into the room with them for another horrifying glance. The long hallway was completely filled with people standing in line who had surprisingly controlled, yet apparently annoyed, demeanors. As SY-19 had implied, they were all in line to see Mr. Stone.

SY-19 left the two standing in the doorway as she returned to her desk. Chocolate and Butterscotch tried to focus on the paintings, the ceiling tiles, *anything* to avoid looking at the staggered lines of people. There were two lines. One was along the left wall, and one was along the right. There was also a door to the left of Butterscotch.

Chocolate then noticed one of the women in line. She was at the end of the right side line, and she was motioning for them to come over. When they joined her, she immediately asked, "What are you girls in for?"

"We're investigating a murder trial," Chocolate explained. "We need a search warrant "

"Oh. You're in the wrong line, then."

"We are?" Butterscotch said optimistically. "So, what, we don't go in that line, do we?"

"Oh, no. Of course not."

"Really?" she sounded relieved, but Chocolate just listened.

"You guys go where that man went," the woman said, pointing to the door. "You go down there."

"What?" Chocolate shouted. They reluctantly went down to the basement.

Meanwhile, as Butterscotch and Chocolate waited in the basement to see Mr.

Stone, the other three Sundaes, Caramel, Strawberry, and Fudge, left Dawn's apartment.

"Bye!" Dawn called down the hall. As she shut the door, Taran started searching for his coat. Dawn walked into the living room and picked up the randomly placed empty glasses. She brought them out into the kitchen along with the half-eaten bowl of popcorn that Caramel had made. "What are you looking for?" she asked Taran.

"My jacket," he answered. He peered under the dinner table with no luck. "I have to get some sleep before my test run tomorrow."

"What exactly does the machine do?" Dawn stacked the empty dinner plates on the table before carrying them to the sink. She ran the water briefly to rinse the dishes and wash her hands.

"Essentially, it sends a person through a time warp," Taran explained. "The machine basically transports people 'through time and space.' It doesn't really involve space travel, but that's what they say."

"You mean it works like in those stories about Tim Cruise going through time and capturing time bandits?" Dawn asked. The idea intrigued her. She could remember reading the entire collection of the *Tim Cruise: Defender of Time* series. She had all six books, and she even had the rip-off books that were published after the author, Art Brown, died.

"The primary difference here is that this is real," Taran corrected.

"Yeah, but come on, how hard could it be?"

"It's very dangerous, Dawn," he replied. His voice remained grim. "It's all theoretical and has been tested to a very short limit. This machine could quite possibly still have some bugs in it."

"Well, I'll see you after tomorrow's testing then," Dawn said with excitement. She walked over to kiss him.

Taran stepped back. "Why after? Where are you going to be?"

"I have to work," she answered. "Didn't you hear us talking about the work we have to get done at the office tomorrow?"

"So you're not going to be at the launch?"

"No, I have to follow up on the new evidence in our case," Dawn explained again. "I have to go in early, review the police report, and search the—"

"But I want you to be at the launch."

"I want to be there too, but I can't," she tried to explain. "I'll see you after—"

"How can you be so naïve about this?"

Dawn gasped. "If you think it's so dangerous, why are you testing it yourself instead of using a monkey or something?"

Taran sat down on the sofa. "Listen, Dawn, I'm only telling you this because you're my wife—well, you're going to be. But this is top secret stuff. You can't blab to your friends, not to Darlene—"

"Diane."

"Whatever." Taran shook his head. "Donna, Diane, Danielle, Darlene—"

"There *is* no Darlene."

"Dawn, just listen."

"I was only joking, honey." Dawn sat down next to him and put her arm around his shoulders. "What is it?"

"You remember when I was working later than usual? Your parents came. We were supposed to meet with them, but I didn't make it."

"Yeah, it was two nights ago. Of course I remember," Dawn answered. "Don't worry about it. Oh, and Mikey says hi."

"Well, the reason I didn't make it was because… well, it worked."

"What worked?" Dawn straightened up.

"The machine. It worked."

"You went through time?"

"Yeah, sort of."

"What do you mean, 'sort of'?"

"Well, it was me and Dr. Brown. We were finishing programming the hardware that she designed into the machine, and—"

"Dr. Brown… was he the one with the two kids?"

"No, Dr.—"

"Oh, is that the one whose wife—"

"No."

"I don't think you ever mentioned him before, then."

"*Her*," Taran said, correcting Dawn. "And she just signed onto the project through another leading company last week. She had a surprisingly long list of impressive credentials, the likes of which only I could compare. Needless to say, Thompson put her on the project with me right away. She is incredible."

Dawn hesitated to say anything, but she was annoyed. Taran didn't notice.

"Anyway, like I was saying, she initiated a test run by the end of the night. She set the destination and time herself, so I wasn't even aware of where we were headed. She said she had Thompson's authorization. I had the return code already, so I was sure we could get back if we had any kind of emergency," he explained. "Turns out it wasn't enough."

"What do you mean?" Dawn asked.

"Well, there was some kind of miscalculation, I think, because somewhere along the line, the entire machine shook violently. Before I knew it, I was unconscious. I don't know how long I was out, but when I came to, I was still in the machine, sitting on a beach. But she was gone."

"She?" Dawn muttered, more to herself than anyone else. The disappearance of a co-worker was overcast by the fact that her fiancé had been working with a woman.

"I searched all around the machine," he said frantically, reliving the moments. "I went as far as I could into the jungle without losing sight of the beach. I waited as long as I could. I had to get back to Detroit; I couldn't wait any longer for Dr. Brown, under the circumstances."

"Why didn't you tell me about her?"

"What do you mean?" Taran tried to remember the credentials of the associate he barely knew. "She's a specialist in her field, I guess. She graduated from Miami Technical Institute. She was responsible for our first successful test; she made several adjustments that—"

"I'm not talking about that, Taran." She crossed her arms.

"What are you… no, babe, that's ridiculous," he said when he realized what she'd been implying. He shook his head in disbelief. "There is nothing going on between me and Sandy."

"Sandy?" she repeated.

"Yeah, Sandy Brown." Taran was getting impatient. "The *only* thing between us is my hair color. It's actually a big joke with her."

"Taran, you never told me about this woman," Dawn said.

"Did I really have to?"

Dawn didn't answer.

"Babe," Taran said, leaning in to kiss her.

She pulled away and stood up.

"There's nothing for you to worry about," he said, getting up to follow her into the kitchen. "All I have to do tomorrow is go back to when and where Sand—Dr. Brown programmed the machine to take us and bring her back safely."

"So you're not really testing the machine tomorrow," Dawn stated. "Another lie," she said under her breath.

"Dawn, I thought you understood the priority I have to put on the secrecy of this project," Taran said. "I made that very clear when we first got engaged. That's why we haven't gotten married yet, you know that. I don't want this to get in the way of us, but I don't want to risk a broken marriage by going ahead with this operation after you've made that kind of commitment to me."

"So that's why you spent late nights with this Sandy?" Dawn argued. "To save our 'pending' marriage?" This situation reminded her all too much of Tom Faraday.

"You know that's crazy, Dawn," Taran answered. "Just leave her out of this; she's nobody." He looked directly at her now. "You have to trust me."

Dawn looked down. She didn't feel she had a choice, really. She did have to trust him. They had known each other for nearly seven years and been committed to each other for six. If she couldn't trust that, whom could she trust?

"Well, what do you have to do?" She returned his stare with much softer eyes.

Taran grimaced, realizing he couldn't omit the truth like he had in the past, and said, "I have a log of the codes Dr. Brown programmed into the control console. All I have to do is re-enter the codes, and I'll be sent to the exact time and place we arrived at originally. Assuming she made it, she will perceive that I just arrived alongside her as I should have the first time. No harm done."

"And why haven't you done this already?" Dawn asked.

"Because we had to decrypt the codes, and I had a time fixing the miscalculation that caused the first incident."

"And what if she isn't there?"

"She'd have to be," Taran concluded. "Otherwise, she was somehow lost in time."

"Shouldn't there be a way to find her from the present? That way, you'd know exactly where she is?"

"Presently, there is no way to track people through time," he explained. "However, Dr. White and her husband are working on something to that effect. Even so, I don't know how safe this trip is going to be for me. Nothing's guaranteed."

"So what's so dangerous?"

"I don't mean that it's dangerous. It's just… risky," Taran answered. "This isn't like shuttling to the moon. This doesn't happen everyday. I have to plan for any contingency. I mean, since there's already been one incident, who can say there can't be another?" He paused. "It's possible I won't even be able to come back."

"Oh, come on," Dawn tried to reassure him. "I've supported your work since we met. I didn't know exactly what for because it had to stay top secret or whatever, but I've seen you work on schematics and diagrams. I've seen you put your heart and entire life into this machine. I have complete confidence in your machine's capabilities."

Taran sighed. "You've got a lot of faith in me, girl."

Dawn smiled. "Yeah. Yeah, I do."

"I just hope it's not misguided," he added.

"Taran, don't say that," Dawn said. "You're gonna be fine."

Chapter 6

THE COLD DAMPNESS AND eerie feeling of most basements would cause Chocolate to freak out, but this basement seemed well taken care of. Actually, it *was* well taken care of. The walls and decorations were identical to that of the first floor and lobby. It was very lively and bright. No one would guess it was the basement except for the fact that there were no windows. The two Sundaes were still in the back of the line, but the line had been drastically reduced. However, it wasn't because all those people had been in to see Mr. Stone. It was because they had been sick of standing, sitting, or pacing around in line. Chocolate and Butterscotch had now been in line for an hour and a half.

By now, the line was finally halfway down the hall, where chairs stood on the opposite wall. Chocolate sat in one of those while Butterscotch chatted with people ahead of her, one of whom was the man in black who had preceded them down to the basement. A woman was with him now. She was in her mid-thirties, wearing a red blouse and skirt. She introduced herself as Gloria Deo. She and the man, Harold Angel, were working on a case where the murder victim was an accountant of theirs who had recently retired.

"So, Gloria," Butterscotch began, "what do you suspect is the killer's motive?"

"Well, Harry and I have found out that the victim, Mr. Rueben Milton, had dozens of cases of tax evasion and three tax fraud accusations," she explained. She turned to Harry.

"Yeah, I'm not sure how we're gonna get our money back for this!" Harry joked. "All of the money in Milton's hundreds of accounts has been tied up. Good thing I didn't trust him with my big money."

"Yeah," Butterscotch said. She laughed. *Just shoot me now. Nothing's worse than two detectives that can't take a hint.* She looked over at Chocolate who returned a look saying, "you did it to yourself." *I know. Why can't I just stop talking to strangers altogether?*

Gloria whispered something to her partner and turned back to Butterscotch. "Excuse me, Donna, could you save our spot? We've been here since this morning, and we need something to eat. Want something?"

"Coffee would be great. Thanks," Butterscotch answered. *That is, thank God you're leaving me alone for five minutes.* "You're too kind, and I'd love to keep your spot for you."

"Thanks."

Gloria and Harry left the line quickly. With them went some other people annoyed by the long wait. Now, Butterscotch was only one flight of stairs from Mr. Stone's desk. Chocolate got up and caught up to Butterscotch.

"Where did that couple go?" she asked.

"They went to get coffee 'cause they've been in line all day," Butterscotch told her. "You wouldn't believe the dribble those guys are filled with. Bad enough they pounced on a potential Sundae case..."

The line was moving more swiftly now. "Oh, someone else must have come on duty to help Mr. Stone," Butterscotch said.

"Or they're telling everyone to leave," Chocolate replied.

"Oh, now, let's not get our hopes up." Butterscotch laughed.

The line was moving quickly now. As Chocolate and Butterscotch turned the corner, just as Chocolate had guessed, people were being directed out through the side doors by two police officers in front of Mr. Stone's office door. Butterscotch recognized one of the officers as Crystal Gates, a lieutenant on the Detroit Police Force who had just transferred from New York. The other was Officer Raymond Caldor, a ten-year veteran of the DPF.

Caldor was often an easy man to persuade—though Butterscotch would never tell his wife—so she thought about trying to get through them directly. However, she was told Crystal was a stickler for the most absurdly bendable of rules, so squabbling about it with her would be futile.

"I'm not leaving without a warrant!" Butterscotch whispered. Knowing she couldn't convince Lt. Gates to make an exception for her, she desperately began to search for an alternate route. She looked around herself and then back at the hallway. "We have to get to... Mr. Stone... there!" She spotted a vent for the heating ducts. "I knew it was around here somewhere."

The two Sundaes slipped away from the line and pried the grate off of the ventilation duct. They furtively crawled inside. Chocolate struggled to replace the grate at the beginning of the tight tunnel.

"I don't remember this vent being so small," Butterscotch said. She was right behind Chocolate. She was referring to when they used to sneak through the vents to see Mr. Stone as teenage detectives.

"Yeah, well, we were a lot smaller then," Chocolate reminded her. "Do you remember the way to his office?" She was straining to squeeze through the ducts herself, wondering even more how Butterscotch was making it.

"It should be right after the next left turn up here." Butterscotch groaned. "I need to get back on one of Fudge's diets..."

"There it is." The vent came to a tunnel, which ended at another grate. Chocolate peered out and spotted an older man sitting behind a desk saying something to two people leaving the room, a man and a woman. The man was an officer she had seen on patrol many times in the building. The woman looked vaguely familiar, but from so far away, the grate impaired Chocolate's vision of her. The woman quickly looked away from Stone and exited the room, followed by the officer.

"He's alone," Chocolate informed Butterscotch. "Now we can safely talk to Mr. Stone."

Butterscotch sighed quietly. She lowered her voice and poked Chocolate. "Let's try to sneak up on him." Butterscotch recollected her experience as a teenager and smiled.

"Oh, come on," Chocolate scoffed. But she too longed to do the same once again. It felt nostalgic, so she acquiesced. "All right, let's do it. I'll open the grate slowly and quietly."

She used a screwdriver to unhitch the grate and carefully lifted it off of the frame. She tied a short rope from her purse onto the grate and lowered it to the soft, carpeted floor. She then dropped herself as softly and slowly as possible onto the carpet and knelt at the foot of the wall. She waved for Butterscotch to follow her down and helped her climb to the floor. They sneaked up behind the officer, who was busy with his work. Butterscotch crept up further than Chocolate did; she got right behind him and hovered over his shoulder. From there she could see him signing a warrant that was issued to a Sherri Marsh.

"Sherri got here?" she shouted.

"Ahh!" Mr. Stone jumped. He turned to see the two Sundaes staring back at him. "Oh, it's only you two. What are you guys doing here? Did you—" he said, looking up at the grinning Butterscotch. "Oh you did, didn't you? You climbed through the vents again."

"Yes, we did," Chocolate said proudly.

"You girls don't think you're getting too old for this?" It was a phrase they'd heard Mr. Stone say a hundred times before. And it was always followed by the phrase, "Do I have to call your parents?" He probably would have this time, too, because their parents' phone numbers were still tacked to the bulletin board across the room.

Butterscotch ignored his smart remarks and got down to business. "Mr.

Stone, when did Sherri come in and request a search warrant?" she asked. She sat in the chair across from his large desk. Chocolate sat down as well.

"Actually, she was in here a couple minutes ago. She was the last one," Mr. Stone explained. "She got a search warrant for Don Forge's Antique Shop. And call me André, not Mr. Stone; you girls aren't kids anymore."

"So, she must be at the antique shop," Butterscotch deduced. "But how did she know the details of the case?"

Chocolate hummed quietly and looked around at the ceiling and walls of the room. "Okay, all right!" she suddenly cried. "I told Sherri to investigate and get files in NTC. I didn't know she'd get a jumpstart on us and go the antique shop!"

"Well, it doesn't matter now," Butterscotch said. "Now we just have to get to the antique shop while Sherri's still there."

"Yeah, she's expecting you," Mr. Stone mentioned. "She said Chocolate may be 'chasing' her, so she left a message with me." He fished through his top drawer and pulled out an envelope. "Chocolate" was scribbled on it in cursive in blue ink.

"Thanks." Chocolate took the envelope and led Butterscotch quickly out of the room, this time through the door. "See ya later, and tell Chief Palmer I said hi!" She quickly shut the door. "Listen," she said, turning to Butterscotch, "We've got to hurry and get to Sherri."

"She's probably been there and finished searching by now," Butterscotch added. "Let's go."

Chocolate and Butterscotch raced down the now vacant steps where people had been crowded around to see the police officer. They ran as fast as possible to Butterscotch's car. As soon as Chocolate got in, they sped off toward the antique shop.

Gloria and Harry, who had decided to camp out next to the police station that night in order to be first in line, could barely make out the blurs of the women who had jumped in their vehicle.

"Chocolate," Butterscotch said as she drove, "why did you call Sherri? This was our assignment. Vanilla wanted her to go to NTC, not the antique shop."

"I didn't tell Sherri anything about the case except that the victim was unidentified," Chocolate informed her. "I just told her to meet me at Headquarters—oh no!"

"You see," Butterscotch said. "While we were at the police station, Sherri probably waited so long that she went in, found our case files, and decided to get in on the action." She paused. "But how did she get ahead of us in line?"

"She probably bought her way through," said Chocolate as she parked the car.

Chapter 7

The building in which the antique shop was found was shorter than most of the other buildings on the street, standing at four stories tall. In the darkness, Chocolate and Butterscotch could clearly see the lights illumined on the second floor above Forge's Antiques. A silhouette soon passed by a window. Chocolate eyed the windows as she got out of the car.

They walked up to the building and knocked on the door. A short man with bushy eyebrows and a bushy mustache came out of his office. Through the dark window, Chocolate could see the man advance to the door.

"Get your badge out," Chocolate whispered to her partner.

"Why?"

"Because he won't let us in without the proper authority," Chocolate said quickly. "Shh! He's coming!"

"I'm sorry, ma'am," the man said as he cracked the door open. "We're closed now. We close at eight."

"Sir, we are on a criminal investigation about the murder in the second floor apartment," Butterscotch explained to the nervous man. She flashed her badge quickly, and it dropped to the floor just inside the door. Butterscotch hesitated to pick it up as Don, the mustached man, let the door open completely. She lowered to pick it up at the same time as Don, bumping her head into his and causing him to lean back.

"Oh, I'm so sorry," Don said. "I'll get the badge."

"No!" Chocolate said quickly. "Well, I mean, no, thank you. I'll get it. Thank you anyway." She picked up the badge. She handed it to Butterscotch and nudged her gently in the side.

They squeezed by Don and ran up the stairs.

"Excuse me, girls." The proprietor rubbed his forehead tenderly. "Do you have a warrant?"

The pair stopped on the same middle step and turned back to their host. Butterscotch peered at her partner hopelessly. "What now, genius?"

"Sherri's up there."

"How do you know?" Butterscotch whispered back.

"I saw *some*body in the window, probably her." She addressed Don next. "We're with Miss Marsh. We're supposed to meet with her."

"Oh." Don nodded. "Is she *still* up there? She didn't mention anyone else on their way…" He shrugged, rubbing his head again. "Well, no sense me wasting your time. The room is a mess up there; just be careful."

They sneaked up the stairs and opened the apartment door quietly. It was one of the few hinged doors left in Detroit—most doors power slid for security reasons. Don Forge wanted his antique shop to remain as much like the original building as could legally be; it had been built over three hundred years ago, making it the oldest building in Detroit.

The air inside was stale and dry.

Butterscotch held back the urge to cough, fighting the tickling in her throat. "Fug," she whispered.

Eyes wide, Chocolate turned to her partner. "What did you say?" she replied softly.

"I'm talking about the air in this room. It hasn't been used in years, I think," she explained. "Stale air is called fug." She paused. "What did you think I said?"

"Oh, never mind," Chocolate said. Now it was her turn to ponder the word. "I always thought fug was that foamy stuff on top of freshly made hot chocolate."

Ignoring the remark as immaterial, Butterscotch continued her perusal of the room. It seemed it had been built hundreds of years ago and then left to fester.

The only renovations were the newly reinforced walls and the sliding front entrance. In the darkness, they could just make out a hunched figure in the center of the room. It appeared to take no heed of the women's whispers. They stealthily crept toward the figure, who appeared to be searching for something on the floor. They tapped its shoulders, but the decoy collapsed in a pile of rags.

"Huh?" Butterscotch cocked her head to one side. She cringed as she felt cold metal press against her throbbing temple.

Next, she heard a woman's voice in a flawless but false German dialect. "Steigen langsam!" Butterscotch and Chocolate rose carefully. The only thing that was running through Chocolate's head was that the unidentified victim may have been a GU spy after all and had to be bumped off. Going through

Butterscotch's head was the fact that they had eaten a terrible last meal. It hadn't been that good; she had just been nice.

"Drehen Sie sich herum, beide von Ihnen!" the woman commanded.

They turned around.

They quickly recognized the petite redhead holding the pistol. Her bright blue eyes nearly glowed in the dim light, and her clothes were not that of a German officer.

"Sherri!" Butterscotch cried. "You had me going for a second there. I thought you were a GU spy!"

"Are you crazy?" Sherri scoffed. "You actually think the Sundaes would be lucky enough to get entangled with spies from the GU? Don't fool yourself. Like this victim was the target of a GU hit? Yeah, right." Sherri looked at her sideways.

"He could be if he fled from the GU," Chocolate suggested. "Then they may be responsible for killing him. He could have been a spy on assignment for the GU who was discovered. That may be why he hasn't been identified."

"That's a brilliant deduction," Sherri said, sounding impressed. "But it's way off. You can't speculate; you have to investigate." She moved to the outline made by the police. "The body, as I'm sure you already discovered, was placed here long after he died. I started to search through this room just before you guys came."

The small room was covered in a thin blanket of dust except for the spot where the body had lain. The tops of the chests, bureaus, and dressers were clear from dust as well. There were also sheets draped over the upholstery. Chocolate was confused as to how long the victim had lived there.

"I don't think," Chocolate said as she searched, "that the victim even lived here." She pulled what seemed to be a clean sheet off of one particular chest. She strained to lift up the chest's cover. Butterscotch knelt down to assist her. The loud creaking startled Sherri, who was searching through a roll-top desk in the corner of the room.

"You're absolutely right," Sherri informed her. "I talked to Don before I started searching up here. He claims there hasn't been a tenant up here in over nine years." She walked over to where the others were searching. "I don't know if you could tell, but the second floor of this building isn't exactly up to code."

Chocolate looked up and around the room. The windows were broken glass, two-paned windows with plywood nailed over them outside. The only two doors, aside from the door to the stairs leading out of the room, were unhinged, and the paint was peeling. "You're right."

"Did you find anything interesting?" Sherri asked, changing the subject.

"Oh my, yes, Sherri!" Chocolate exclaimed. "Look at this." She held up credit cards, identification cards, and personal effects. "Some of these things must be fake, or maybe really old." She held up a couple credit cards. "What kind of a visa comes in a card form like that?"

"That isn't a visa, Chocolate," Butterscotch corrected her. "That's a Visa credit card."

"It's the kind immigrants used to use?"

Butterscotch rolled her eyes. "No, Visa was a credit card company between the twentieth and twenty-first centuries. That was before people discovered the American Express as the master card.

Sherri smirked. "That was a good pun."

"You could say it was a 'capital one,'" Butterscotch said.

"I don't get it." Chocolate looked over at her.

"You wouldn't," Butterscotch said, walking over to her partner.

Sherri hurried over and shuffled through the cards, trying to remember the victim's face in order to make some sort of a match. She couldn't find a single card out of the pile, which had several names and pictures, that matched the victim's face. "Well, maybe you were right. He could've been a spy, and these were his targets. Why else would he have cards belonging to other people?" She then read some of the names aloud. "Steven Carter, Coty Clark, Donald Reynolds, Harold Angel, Gloria Deo, Kelley—"

Butterscotch stopped Sherri. "Wait."

"What is it?" Chocolate asked.

"What were those last two names, Sherri?" Butterscotch took the cards from her. "Aha! Gloria Deo and Harold Angel. Those are the two detectives I met in line at the police station."

"What?" Chocolate exclaimed. "Butterscotch, are you sure?" She tipped the cards toward herself and nodded. "Yeah, you're right. That's the two who went to get the—"

"The coffee!" they both shouted.

"What?" Sherri urged.

"I'll tell you on the way back to the police station," Butterscotch said. She dragged Sherri down the stairs and out the door.

"Bye, girls," Don said, waving. He turned and shrugged when he didn't get a response. He then muttered something and returned to his personal bedroom behind the service counter.

Chapter 8

Butterscotch's car sped down the side-winding road until it came to the urban area. The car slowed down, and Butterscotch recognized the two figures still sitting on the curb in front of the police station. She parked the car by the curb a few yards away from them. She walked up to Gloria and Harold with Chocolate behind her. Sherri stayed and leaned up against the car.

"Gloria," Butterscotch began.

She looked up; she had been looking down, presumably thinking. "Oh, Donna, you're back!" Gloria smiled. "I brought your coffee. I'm sorry, it's probably cold. I thought you guys would've returned sooner." She reached behind her and picked up a four-cup carrier with two coffees in it.

Butterscotch took the coffees and gave one to her partner. "So what are you guys doing now?"

"We're waiting for the police station to open up again," Harold declared. "You see, if we're here first, he'll see us first, and we'll never have to wait in line again. You can join us if you want."

"But, it's," Butterscotch said, looking at her wristwatch, "eleven o'clock at night. You guys can go home, get some rest, and come back to the police station really early. You know, at four or something."

"No, you see, that's what we planned to do last night," Harold explained. "We stayed here until ten o'clock the night before, got some sleep, and came back a couple hours before the first officer was supposed to come in. There was already a long line of people."

"Okay," Butterscotch said, "if you insist."

Sherri was getting impatient. She approached Butterscotch. "All right, enough chit-chat. Donna, show them what we found in our investigation."

"Okay, okay," Butterscotch said, reaching into her pocket and taking out the cards. "I know this will sound like a weird lead, but we found these in a trunk at the scene of the crime we're investigating." She handed the cards to Gloria.

Gloria gasped as she saw her likeness on one of the cards. "W… Where did you get these again?"

"On the second floor of Don's Antique Shop," Chocolate answered.

"That's strange," Gloria replied. "I've never been there. And I've never seen this card before. Like I told you in line earlier, I'm working on a case that led us here; we're new to Detroit."

"And who took this horrible picture of me?" Harold added. "I've never seen it before in my life. And if I had, I'd have burned it by now. Look, my hair's a mess! And my shirt, look at the collar—"

"Harry, it's going to be okay," Gloria said to shut him up. "They're just pictures."

"So you don't know anything about these?" Butterscotch asked. "Or anything about the victim? Any idea how he'd have an ID card with your information?" She took the card back and continued. "After all, this information is accurate. Deo, Gloria. Brown hair, brown eyes, 5' 11," 132 pounds."

"Not that I know of," Gloria answered. "Unless ***you*** know anything about the cards?" She peered at Harold accusingly.

"Listen, as far as I know, I know nothing about those," Harry said in defense. He looked toward Chocolate. "But, hey, if I find out if I do know anything, I'll be sure to call you up right away."

Butterscotch wrote her VP number on a piece of paper and gave it to Harold. "All right, we have to leave now. Will you guys need anything, pizza, food, sleeping bags, a tent, a life?"

When the three detectives got back to the antique shop, Don quickly let them in and left them alone. He went into his back room, and the girls ran up the stairs. They then returned to their investigation of the room. Butterscotch tossed the cards onto a side table and continued searching the trunk.

She found several other items, some she couldn't even identify. "This guy kept some strange things. What is all this?"

Chocolate was wandering around the room. Since her two friends were going through the only searchable furniture in the room, she was stuck looking under the bed and pretending to examine the walls. *How boring*, she thought.

At length, Sherri finally pried open the roll top desk. She searched carefully through the brittle, discolored papers that were piled sloppily inside. There were tax forms, foreign electoral signs, medical records, and notebook papers. Sherri carefully sifted through the ancient materials, and then suddenly she found something.

"Hey, girls, look! I found a wallet," Sherri said, calling them over to her. She pulled out a few cards. One was a credit card, another a learner's permit, but the identification names and places were scratched out. The portrait, though, was still there. "That's him, the victim!" She turned it toward the others.

"You're right!" Chocolate cried.

"But there's no name," Butterscotch pointed out. She fingered through the cards and receipts and found a scrap of paper. There was a series of numbers and letters scribbled in ink on the delicate paper.

"'3042 Pool Street,'" Chocolate read. "Pool Street. Well, well, where's Pool Street?"

"Pool Street!" Butterscotch cried. "That's in southern Detroit."

"Southern Detroit?" Chocolate repeated. "How do you know?"

"Do you remember the lead we got on the case last spring?" Butterscotch tried to jog their memory. They gave no expression of remembering, so she continued to describe the case. "Remember, the victim had drowned, right? The perpetrator was a riddle fanatic, and we got some riddle about the kid drowning in a pool or something. But it was really a clue about a Pool ***Street***."

"That's right!" Sherri exclaimed.

"We should check this address out," Butterscotch suggested. "He might have lived on Pool Street at one time!"

"Wait a minute," Chocolate held up her hand. "What's this?" She reached through the other detectives for an ornate brass frame laying face down on one of the shelves inside the roll top desk. She turned the frame around in front of her to see a discolored black and white wedding photograph of two familiar-looking people.

Butterscotch and Sherri peered over at it.

Their eyes widened and they rushed to the stairs.

Chapter 9

The sun was hot early the next morning. It shined through the windshield of the yellow cab, inside which Dawn was presently on her way to the Sundaes' meeting. She could think of nothing but what Taran had said to her the night before. She thought, at least for a moment, that he may have been right about his "mission." However, Sandy Brown kept coming to mind, more so than the risk involved with Taran's chosen line of work.

How could he be involved with a female co-worker and not tell her?

"How can a taken man get into a working relationship with a woman with an obvious taste for *his* line of work, an obvious threat to our marriage, and not tell his fiancée about it?" She was loud enough for the cabbie to hear, but talking more to herself than anyone. "He should have at least told me. How can he keep that a secret, unless something really was going on?"

The whole situation bothered her throughout the night, and Taran's reluctance to admit what Dawn assumed was happening made it worse. The Sundaes were adamant about keeping her away from Taran. They made so many clear comparisons that Dawn never considered were viable. But with Sandy Brown's emergence, it was clear Strawberry was right. He wasn't being true to her. He was seeing another woman, spending "late nights" at the office. Dawn assumed the worst immediately, and she knew she was right.

But it *was* Strawberry who brought up this Tom Faraday disarray. They got it into her head that Taran wasn't any good, that he was taking advantage of her, but for what? It was their assumption that Taran was creating a bigger mess than either of them could clean up. But realistically, when had Taran ever been unfaithful in the seven years they had been together?

He spent every night after work with her. One late night in seven years, which he brought up two days later, it was either guilt about being untrue, or the guilt of secrecy in his work that led him to tell her about it last night. If it's guilt about her, then she can forgive that, being that he's over her. If it was the innocent guilt about having to cover up his time traveling experience, it was even more forgivable.

"So, what's the problem here?" she whispered to herself.

She was thinking logically for the first time all week.

"You know, he may have been right," she muttered. "I didn't really give him much of a chance to explain things to me, and really, he was just worried about the possible unfortunate consequences. Anything could happen in a situation like this. I didn't trust him. I didn't listen to what he was really saying. What if something *does* happen, and I don't get the chance to see him again?"

A red light was coming up, so when the cabbie stopped the car, he put it in park and turned around to Dawn. "It sounds to me like this guy's just wrapped up in his work. That always seemed like a forgivable offense in my experience," he said, pausing to let her soak in what he had said. "And if you don't mind me sayin' ma'am, what man in his right mind would give up a beautiful creature such as yerself? 'Specially one with her head on straight."

Dawn thought about what this perfect stranger had to say. It was sad, really, that she'd listen more intently to a fat taxi driver who practically lived in his hovercab than she would her own fiancé. *He's the expert, and he doesn't look half-bad, either,* she thought.

"Thanks. I think I'll take your advice… uh, Mr.… ?"

"Mister?" he laughed. "Heck, no. Just call me Paul, Paul Jones."

"Thanks, Paul," she said, getting out of the cab. She closed the door. She then ran down the street toward the Karz building. It was about two blocks away, but she couldn't wait any longer for the light to change.

Chapter 10

It's finally happening, Taran thought. *After more than a decade of my own research and experiments, this job's finally going to pay off. It's* ***finally*** *coming true.* That was exactly what he thought when he first left with Dr. Brown to her unknown destination. Once again, he was at the launch site, just as he had been three nights ago. This time, however, he was alone. This time, he was going in order to find the partner that disappeared in the previous launch. Somewhere between Detroit 4141N8226W-120732348 and Code 2582N6944W-505011841, there was a missing person that no one knew was missing.

There he was, standing in front of his life's work, waiting to find the person responsible for making it work. This time, he would be able to go through time without constraints. It was exciting for him because it was the realization of a dream. His heart started racing as he made the final safety checks. He began making his way back to the compound, beaming.

"Yes," Taran said aloud. "It's almost time." His expression quickly changed to sorrow when he peered up at the tower and only saw two scientists going over the control procedures one last time. There was no one else. She wasn't there, watching over the helipad with a nervous smile and a tear in her eye.

He opened the bunker door and stepped inside. The winding halls inside were plain and white. They led him to a small refreshment room for the employees. There was one scientist in there, eating a bagel and watching the news.

He looked up at Taran as he came in. "Is it almost time?"

"Yeah," Taran said quietly. "Professor Stevens, you should probably get out to the observation tower soon."

"Yeah, okay," Stevens replied. "I'm just gonna finish watching this report. It's very interesting; it's about a murder victim who has been unidentified even up to now. They're releasing new evidence today that was found by Strawberry Sundae Investigations."

"Oh, boy," Taran said flatly.

"You don't sound excited," Stevens responded. "Isn't Dawn a Sundae?"

"Oh no, I'm ecstatic. Can't you tell?"

"Still mad that Dawn won't be here?"

"Well, yeah, wouldn't you want your… well—" Taran paused. He took a donut from the box on the table as he opened the door. "Never mind, Dan. I'm going out there to get ready. I'll see you out there."

Professor Stevens looked up at the HTV screen and saw the reporter interviewing two of the detectives working on the murder case.

"And when we come back from our break," the newswoman announced, "more on the Antique Shop Murder. Also coming up, how are hover travel prices rising? Are wheels now back to being the best deals? And are crystals really a more efficient fuel? We'll have geologist Dr. R. Quartz here with us to talk. More on these stories after this."

Taran was only halfway down the hall when the commercials began, so Stevens knew he could catch up. He hurried out the break room door but stopped short when he saw Taran, now leaning on a wall in the hallway by the stairs.

"Flint," Stevens said. He caught up and put his hand on Taran's shoulder. "Good luck today, buddy. I hope all this works out for ya." He put out his hand for Taran to shake. "And after you find Sandy, when you finish Phase One, don't forget me and the team. This is gonna be an awesome experience, no doubt."

"Hey, thanks, Dan." Taran shook his hand. "I'll see you later."

"If not sooner," Stevens smiled. He hurried back to the room in time for the broadcast to return.

"Hello, everyone. I'm Diane Hannity for Channel 8 News," the woman said.

"Whoops!" Stevens said, reaching for a VD, a videodisk. "I wanna tape this so I can see it again." He checked the disk, but it had an important documentary already taped on it. "Shoot, where are the blanks?"

"In other news, detectives are still investigating the kidnapping of Jean-Claude III," Diane Hannity said. "He's been missing since July of this year. The United Kingdom has been actively cooperative in the search. Our international anchor, Carl Wright, is now reporting live from Britain where the British Prime Minister Alfred Sheridan is about to make a statement regarding the kidnapping updates. Carl?"

Professor Stevens continued to search through the cabinet below the HTV for a disk to no avail. The broadcast continued without him.

"That's correct, Diane, the UK's chief investigatory staff has uncovered some new evidence in the last 12 hours," the overseas anchor affirmed. "Now, nothing has been confirmed yet, but it seems the chances that Jean-Claude survived the assault are very slim."

"Carl, what sort of evidence points to this dark turn from the UK's original view of the French Leader's kidnapping?" Diane asked. "After all, Nathaniel Gordon and his staff were much more optimistic last summer."

"Well, the Prime Minister is going to make a statement shortly regarding just that, Diane."

"Well, thank you, Carl. We'll check back with you in a few minutes," Diane said. "And when we come back, the Antique Shop Murder, here on Channel 8 News."

"Whew! I won't miss it. Good." Stevens sighed. "Thank God for commercials." He spotted the blank videodisks in the next drawer he opened. "Great, just in time." He opened the case, inserted it into the console, and began recording.

"'The Antique Shop Murder,' as it has been called, has baffled police and detectives alike with its unidentifiable victim," Diane began. "But groundbreaking evidence from the Sundaes' detective organization will change the course of this investigation. Among other items, identification cards of several UNA citizens were found in the apartment above the antique shop. Other items include a brass picture frame with the mysterious black and white wedding photograph seen here, and an undisclosed address, which the police will not reveal, they say, 'until further notice.' But let's go to veteran detective and Channel 8 field reporter Gloria Deo on location to interview Sherri Marsh of the Sundaes Detective Agency. Good morning, Gloria."

The camera switched to a young brunette in a home much brighter than the apartment in which the body had been found. It was the house on Pool Street.

Gloria smiled. "Thanks Diane. Good morning. I'm Gloria Deo, and we're here live thanks to cameraman Chip Collour. We're here with our special guest, Sherri Marsh." She turned to Sherri. "Miss Marsh, before discovering this groundbreaking evidence, you and two of the Sundaes came to me with evidence. Did those cards give you any leads?"

"Actually, not any direct leads, no," Sherri answered. "But we still need to search the rest of this house. I'm confident the cards ***will*** tie in somehow."

Professor Stevens continued to record the broadcast, but after he saw the wedding photograph, he stopped paying attention to the HTV and started to think. He was interrupted by another young scientist saying, "Professor Stevens, you're wanted in the Control Tower."

The outside voice shattered Stevens' thoughts, and he left the broadcast to go back to work on the surface. He rushed out to the landing pad where the time machine was being set up.

Suddenly, as Stevens spotted Taran next to the time machine, he remembered the photograph from the news story. He ran up to Taran. “Sir, I—”

“Oh, good, you’re here,” Taran interrupted indifferently. “Now go program the panel for launch, and see if you can’t program that tracker for one last try before we have to launch. Just do it how you’ve been practicing.”

“But, sir, I need to talk to you,” Stevens said grimly.

“Later!” Taran waved him away. “Now go prep for launch, now. That’s an order!”

Stevens turned away toward the tower and argued with himself on the way to it. The tower overlooked the entire helipad and was normally used for air traffic purposes. In this launch, however, there wouldn’t be a need for air traffic control. The tower’s function was to oversee and coordinate the other procedures involved in the machine’s launch.

Chapter 11

By now, Dawn had arrived at the Karz building. She looked around the impressive lobby as she waited for an android to greet her. She didn't have time to look around once again at the elaborate contemporary designs and architecture, but she couldn't help but notice them as she waited for assistance.

When an android finally greeted her, it was a male CV model, one of the original cybernetic models that Karz had designed. He was several years old and still functioned in mint condition.

"Good morning, Miss. I am CV-56," he said. "I'll guide you around today. This way to the lift." He entered the lift; Dawn ran in.

"I'm in kind of a hurry," Dawn explained.

"Where to?" CV-56 asked.

"Taran's office."

"He's not here today," CV-56 informed her. Dawn cocked her head to one side. "He's at the helipad of the Karz Testing Facility outside suburban Detroit."

"How long would it take to get there?" Dawn asked. She jumped up and ran from the lift with CV-56 right behind her.

"I will prepare my hovercraft." CV-56 led Dawn to the building next door. "This way." He opened the mechanical garage door to reveal a parking lot filled with bumper car-sized hovercrafts.

They entered a newer Karz H750. These were designed for higher altitude hover travel and could even fly at faster speeds.

CV-56 was flying so fast that the wind blew Dawn's hair in all directions. She didn't care, though; all she could think about was getting to the helipad before Taran left.

"The Karz Testing Facility is only accessible via Hov-Trak Shuttle," CV-56 explained. "The nearest terminal is over here on the left."

He parked the craft in front of the terminal steps.

CV-56 turned his hovercraft around and headed back to the Karz building as Dawn headed toward the shuttle track. The Hov-Trak system was actually a tunnel in which a small shuttle could travel quickly to another terminal like the one where Dawn stood. She got onto the shuttle, and momentarily, with a warning beep, it launched through the tunnel automatically. The air brushed by her face, and the tunnel was pitch black for the entire five minutes of travel.

When she finally saw a light at the end of the tunnel, Dawn sighed in relief and began breathing again. When the shuttle stopped, Dawn quickly got out and headed for the lift.

Dawn stopped short as she noticed a suggestion box near the door. She quickly wrote up a suggestion and dropped it in the box. It read "LIGHTS!" in large bubble letters.

The lift reached the next floor, and Dawn stepped out into the plain white halls of the Karz Testing Facility Bunker. She found the break room, where the news report had just come to a conclusion. Dawn rushed down the hall to the exit of the bunker. Without noticing the time machine, and not recognizing it if she had seen it because she'd never seen it completed, she headed straight for the control tower.

Taran had already entered the machine, and Professor Stevens activated the control panel.

The machine began to hum and whir, signifying that it was time to activate *the* switch. This was the switch that Dr. Brown had thrown while the machine was in operation, and she'd disappeared. Taran sat watching the switch and knew the window of time he had in which to toggle it was almost over.

He anxiously waited and thought about what he had said to Dawn the night before about the risk he was taking and how it was possible that he'd never return home. But he mostly thought about hurting her feelings and how he wished he'd told her about Sandy from the start to avoid this confusion. He simply wished he could have left 2348 on better terms with his future wife. What if they never saw each other again? He really wanted her to have a good memory of him.

Unable to withstand any more suspense or pessimism, he flipped the switch. The machine began to glow a bright blue. At the last second he glanced at the tower and saw a woman rushing into the top. He recognized Dawn right away. This was his last chance.

Dawn quickly grabbed a pair of binoculars and spotted Taran in the time machine. For a moment, just as he disappeared, Dawn thought she saw Taran look up straight at her and mouth, if not shout, something to her. Now in the pit of her belly, she felt she had seen Taran's face for the last time.

"I love you," she whispered in vain, taking solace in the fact that she had likewise returned Taran's verbal gesture. His muted words reassured her that the events of the night before had not gone unforgiven. She stared at the now vacant helipad as though it were Taran's headstone.

A bright red H encircled in alternately blinking red lights and reflectors was all that was left of the last seven years of her life. It was heartbreaking and uplifting all at once. She knew that if she did see Taran again, they'd be together forever, but when *would* she see him again? How?

"Excuse me?" Professor Stevens said, putting his hand on her shoulder.

"What?" Dawn had been broken from her thoughts, torn from her last sight of her fiancé.

"Oh, you're Dawn!" Stevens said in surprise. "Taran was very upset this morning when he thought you wouldn't be able to come, but I'm sure he's glad you were here now."

Dawn started to sob.

"I'm sure your husband will be fine," he reassured her, patting her back.

"Husband..." She smiled weakly at the thought. She then looked over to him. "No, he wasn't my husband, although he would have been."

"Oh, I beg your pardon," he apologized. "It's just that when I see you two, I could visualize you at your wedding. You know, as if it were a wedding photograph?" He slowly turned back to his work. "That's strange," he mumbled to himself.

Dawn gave the strange man a confused look as she turned toward the exit of the tower. She then saw all of the Sundaes come walking across the landing pad. They ran faster when they spotted Dawn in the tower.

Strawberry shouted, "Dawn, I've got news about our case!"

Dawn climbed down the ladder. "Good news! What?"

"Yes! It's good for you, specifically. We found records at the victim's house, and you, simply put, are going to be the first ***Mrs.*** Sundae!"

"What do you mean?" Dawn said, puzzled. Had she really been staring at the landing site so long that even the scientist in the tower knew more of what was going on than she? Taran was gone; she had seen him leave.

"You and Taran are getting married!" Caramel exclaimed. She started to get excited.

"But I can't be," Dawn insisted. "Taran is gone. He just dis—"

"But look," Fudge said, "look at this picture. Pictures don't lie." She turned a black and white photograph in a brass frame to face Dawn.

There was a flash of blue light from behind her as she recognized the subjects in the picture. Under her breath, Dawn exclaimed, "Oh my gosh!" She turned back to the control tower, but the young scientist was nowhere to be found.

Chapter 12

Dawn stared blankly at the photograph leaning against the lamp on her oak nightstand. The ornate brass frame and black and white likeness of Dawn and Taran was stuck in her mind. That's what the picture was: Dawn, in a beautiful, white linen dress, and Taran, in a white tuxedo, standing under a white arbor with ivy crawling up the sides to the top. No matter where Dawn was, she could only think of how the picture could have come to be. She reached for the diary she had on the nightstand next to the picture.

Dear diary,

Taran left yesterday to who knows where. His new machine is theoretically supposed to send him through time, but I don't think that's possible. However, he did disappear to somewhere. After all, I saw him disappear, so maybe...

I don't know; this whole thing with Sandy Brown, the scientist at the testing lab, and the wedding picture is so confusing. The picture is me and it is Taran, but he looks so different. I don't know how to say this, but he just looks... older.

She put her diary away and picked up her VP. She dialed Strawberry's familiar number and watched it ring.

"Hello?"

"Hi, Strawberry," Dawn said. "I'm sorry I didn't show up yesterday. I was running a couple errands to Lansing, and it took most of the day. Have you made more progress on the case?"

"Oh, you went to see Taran's mom, huh?" Strawberry said.

"Yeah," she answered. "But, anyway, have you made any more progress?"

"How's Mrs. Flint doing?"

"All right, I guess," Dawn answered. "She said she received a videogram from Taran the other night explaining that he'd be away for a while. He didn't say how long."

"I was talking about you, Dawn," she said. She smiled.

Dawn looked away for a moment, back at the picture once again. "I think I'll be all right. I'm just worried about when Taran will come back, how long he'll be gone before I know what happened."

Strawberry looked into Dawn's eyes. "What if he *doesn't* come back?"

Dawn didn't know how to react to this line of thought. She didn't really want to think about it in that way anymore. She just knew that she should keep her mind on her job. "He'll be back," she said with confidence. "Now, is there anything new with this case?"

Strawberry smiled excitedly. "Yes, actually. After you left the other day, we found a few more items at the new house. They're significant to identifying the victim. I think you should come over right away."

"I'm on my way," Dawn answered.

Despite her boss's urgency, after the day she had had, Dawn wasn't in any rush. She ate yogurt and brought orange juice with her, making her way reluctantly to Taran's car, which she was permitted to drive if she took care of it. After all, Taran had always said, it was a Karz. That meant it was much more reliable than the average hovercar.

She drove to the Sundaes' detective office and, after getting the address, drove to the new investigation site. She parked the car and walked up to the large, white, old-fashioned house. As she sipped her orange juice, she noticed the cornerstone was engraved "2108." Dawn's eyes went wide. As she entered the building, she wondered, *how could this building keep standing that long?*

A young officer greeted her. "Good morning, ma'am," he said, holding out his hand. "I'm Officer Paul Murphy from homicide. I moved to Michigan for this particular investigation. You're Miss Vañia, I presume."

"Yes, but you needn't be so formal," Dawn replied. "Call me Dawn, or Vanilla, please." As she looked around the room, she found Butterscotch examining a coffee table, and Chocolate studying a bookshelf in the far corner of the spacious living room. "Where is Strawberry?"

"She was waiting for you in the kitchen last I saw her," Murphy told her.

Dawn ran into the kitchen to find "Miss Strawberry" eating on the job.

She looked up. "Oh," she said with her mouth full, "you're here." She swallowed the small bite of her sandwich and continued. "You're late—"

"And ***you're*** eating," Dawn said, cutting her off.

"Yeah, yeah, yeah. Well, let's get down to business." She picked up a large box that was beside her chair and gestured for Dawn to sit down. She peered into the box and reached in. "This, no… wrong box." She got up and walked over to the counter, where a smaller, shallower box sat. Strawberry reached into it and pulled out a book. "We found this journal lying in a box that was stuffed under the bed. On the cover is the name 'Randy Carr, Jr.,' embroidered in gold."

While Strawberry still faced the counter, Chocolate came in wearing rubber gloves and carrying another small box. She placed it next to the first one on the counter. "I believe we found it, Miss Strawberry."

"All right," Strawberry replied as Chocolate held up a small plastic bag from inside the box and showed it to her.

Strawberry turned around and showed Dawn the journal. The old leather cover was cracked in several places, and Dawn could see the pages were discolored. Chocolate, with her rubber gloves, took a small key from out of the zip-locked evidence bag she held. She fitted it into the lock of the journal and opened it. Without reading any, she brushed by all of the pages carefully and found only one blank page, the last one. The page before only had writing a quarter of the way down the first side.

Strawberry handed the journal to Dawn.

"You don't want to read this?" Dawn asked.

"Not first, no," Strawberry said. She looked at the book regretfully. "We know it will give us some leads, but we wanted you to see it first. We just wanted to wait for you, Vanilla."

"Oh, how sweet of you," Dawn responded; her tone changed quickly. "Now let's get to work."

The other Sundaes came in and sat down at the table with Dawn. There were only four seats, so Cream, Fudge, and Caramel had to stand, or actually, as they preferred, lean against the counter.

Dawn was about to open the journal, but she realized the others knew more than she did. "Do you guys have other evidence that I should know about? That way we'll be on the same level."

"Of course. Oh! We should show you this stuff first," Strawberry motioned for Chocolate to retrieve the box next to the table

Chocolate picked up the box and placed it on the table. "We found several more items in the victim's bedroom. We found a few knick-knacks, but we also found this," she said, holding up a plastic bag. Inside were springs, gears, tiny screws, and pieces of metal, as well as the casing for a golden pocket watch. "It seems as though the victim was repairing this before he died because there was another small box of tools, as well as other watch pieces."

Dawn looked impressed. "Anything else?"

"Yes," Caramel answered. She too was wearing gloves. "You are going to love this!"

Caramel led Dawn to a closet near the house's entrance. She opened it up and reached in. She pulled out a plastic trash bag wrapped around a long, sturdy, slightly curved object. Tape secured the bag to keep the object in. "We found this in the bedroom. This is a very important piece of evidence in this case," Caramel said as she pulled off the tape. She drew the evidence out of the bag. It shone greatly in the light, and its handle wrapped over and around Caramel's hand. It was an antique sword.

"I told you! I told you so!" Dawn jumped excitedly when she saw the saber. Red stains on the tip and most of the blade proved Dawn's prediction.

"This sword," Caramel said, "as you well know and somehow already knew, is a saber. It was found among most of the other evidence like the pocket watch tools. Butterscotch ran some tests and has concluded that this blood is Randy's. This must be the murder weapon."

"I am so right!" Dawn exclaimed proudly, coming back into the kitchen. She then sat down, calmed down, and continued the investigation in her formal manner. "So, does this come to the extent of your investigation?"

"Yes, Vanilla," Strawberry said. "Now we just have to read this journal, find out who Randy is, and learn what may have killed him, if he even had any idea. I'm sure we could dig up something about the people he knew, if he gives us names and such."

Dawn picked up the journal from the table on which she left it. Now they had to decide where to begin reading. Dawn came up with a suggestion. "I think we should read this thing the whole way through, from the first entry to the last. That way we'll know the entire situation."

"We can't; that would take too much time. We have to solve this case as soon as possible," Chocolate commented. "We should just read the latest and find out his story."

"No, we should flip through quickly," Butterscotch said.

"Why do we need to solve this quickly?" Fudge asked.

"Yeah, Fudge is right. If we rush through this, we may miss something," Strawberry agreed.

"Exactly. We should study it thoroughly no matter how long it might take," Caramel insisted. All of the Sundaes were in an uproar and began arguing over how they should approach using the journal to further their case.

In the commotion, Strawberry grabbed the journal from in front of Dawn on the table, and when Dawn grabbed for it back, the leather book fell to the floor. The fighting stopped when they heard the sound of the binding hit the tiles. Fourteen eyes watched the journal hit the floor and open up, the pages flipping to a fate-chosen page.

Strawberry broke the silence when she picked up the book. "Think I should read this page?"

Chocolate nodded slowly as if the book would leap out and attack should anyone move.

Strawberry began to read slowly.

"'Dear journal,'" Strawberry read. "'Today I found myself in a town full of the strangest people imaginable. They look like people dressed for theatre, but they wear clothes like that all the time. There are people that look like astronauts, people who live in a submarine, people who belong in an old western movie, and still others that could possibly be henchmen for Captain Hook. I haven't been through the entire town, but I have met the man in charge. He says he "brought everyone to the island" for some cooperative thing; personally, I think it's too weird. Anyway, this leader goes by Dillon, which is a name he doesn't seem to respond to naturally. I'm under the impression that he's going by a false name. I haven't discovered why yet. I'm planning on—shhh! Don't tell anyone. I plan on sneaking into his headquarters. I think it's located under his house. I'll tell you what I find when I return.' He then signs it Randy Carr." Strawberry placed the journal on the kitchen table.

"May I see that?" Dawn held out her hand. Chocolate opened the journal to the page that Strawberry had just read. Dawn studied the page quickly. "Did you see this?" She pointed to the date at the top of the page.

"Yes, it says 'four, twenty-one, twelve,'" Strawberry replied. "In other words, April 21… 2312?" Strawberry looked up. "No, this couldn't have been written in 2312, could it?"

"No, as a matter of fact, it couldn't, and it wasn't," Dawn informed them.

"What? How do you know?" Caramel asked.

"Strawberry, you looked at it wrong," Dawn said. "It doesn't read 'four dash twenty-one *dash* twelve'; it reads 'four dash twenty-one twelve.' In other words, April 2112."

"Oh my! That's… that's impossible!" Strawberry gasped.

"But it isn't—" Dawn began. "Follow me!" She ran out to the entrance of the house and onto the lawn. She pointed to the cornerstone as the others filed out onto the grass as well. "Look! From 2101 to 2340, all buildings built in suburban or urban areas were required to be dated on the right-hand side cornerstone, and that cornerstone says '2108'!"

"What the—" Strawberry started. She was stunned; she looked blankly at the cornerstone. "You're… you're amazing, Dawn. That's very perceptive."

"Thank you, but—"

"Excuse me, Miss 'History,' but you're forgetting one thing," Chocolate declared.

"What might that be?" Dawn asked, confused.

"In 2310, there was a Demolition Act in Illinois and Michigan," she affirmed. Chocolate was the history buff of the Sundaes. She always came up with an interesting historical fact that led to the completion of a case. "All buildings built before 2300 were demolished and rebuilt in order to meet safety standards. In some instances, however, historical buildings or birthplaces of famous people could choose the alternative of adding 'APPROVED 2310' to the inscription on the cornerstone under the original year. However, the building had to have passed a thorough safety inspection prior to this."

"And this house doesn't have 'APPROVED 2310' on it!" Butterscotch finished. The Sundaes peered over to the cornerstone and then at each other.

"So," Strawberry finally said, "how is this building still standing?"

"There must be records of when this house was built," said Cream.

"Yeah, either in the house or maybe at city hall," Fudge replied.

"There must be some reason that this house was left alone," Dawn said.

"We could possibly find it in the blueprints," Caramel suggested.

"There must be blueprints for this house somewhere," Strawberry added. "We can have Chocolate and Butterscotch go to town hall. They can get the blueprints and find out the history of this house."

"Meanwhile, we'll go back inside and see that Officer Murphy gets back up to speed," Caramel offered. "Those police, they're too dimwitted to figure this stuff out on their own."

"Why's he here, anyway?" Fudge asked. "I thought Detroit was cutting their budget."

"He did mention he was here specifically for this case," Dawn added. "I wonder what that means. Our most complex mystery comes up, and the police want to get involved."

"Yep," Strawberry said. "That's how life happens, girls."

Chapter 13

On the way, Chocolate, couldn't hold in her excitement. They had finally found a good lead. She carried on the entire time about how she knew the history of Michigan would come in handy some day. Chocolate's babbling annoyed Butterscotch to her wit's end. They got to city hall quickly, but not quickly enough for Butterscotch.

Chocolate got out. "Stay here," she said to Butterscotch. "I'll be right out." She went into the building and scanned the lobby. She walked up to the only secretary she found on duty. She was at her desk talking on a VP.

"Umm, excuse me," Chocolate said softly.

The woman looked up and then back to her VP screen. "I'm sorry, Marge, but I'll have to call you back. Bye." The woman turned off the videophone and greeted Chocolate, smiling. "Welcome. Can I help you, miss?"

"Yes, but can I ask you what happened to the staff?" Chocolate pointed toward the lobby.

"Well, after Brick Industries improved their cybernetic designs, all of the local federal buildings added the new androids to the staff," she explained. "We already had androids that could be integrated to the new design, so they were recalled to receive the improvements. Therefore, today and tomorrow there will be a shortage of staff while our androids are at the Brick Factory getting their improvements."

"Oh, all right," Chocolate said, nodding. "Anyway, I'd like to access the local UNA building blueprints," Chocolate told her. "But first I need to know how far back the records are kept."

"We keep all current properties, plots and appraisal values updated on record from 2198 to now," the woman answered.

"Well, I have a particular house in mind," Chocolate explained.

"What region?"

"Michigan."

The woman typed something into her computer after each answer she was given.

"What area?"

"Rural Detroit."

"North, south, east or west?"

"South."

"Street?"

"Pool Street."

"Lot number." The woman looked up at Chocolate.

"I'm not sure of the lot number, but it's beside the house number 3040. There are no other houses on that side until the house at the end of the dead end," Chocolate answered, trying to remember the address to the house itself.

"You mean house 3038?" the woman asked. "A blue apartment, flat roof, L-shape, black shutters?"

"No, no," Chocolate replied. "The other side."

"That would be lot number SIL-402–42," she told Chocolate.

"Yeah, so?"

The woman looked at the detective strangely. "There *is* no building on lot number SIL-402–42. It's been empty since 2310, after the Demo Act. That building didn't meet regulations. Since then it was maintained to keep a lawn, but only up until ten years ago. That street has been uninhabited for eight years."

"What? Are you sure?" Chocolate exclaimed. "There *is* a house there. I was just there!"

"I'm sorry, but you'll have to leave if you raise your voice to me one more time," the secretary warned sternly. "I'll let you talk to the mayor instead. He knows more than I do about that street. You can tell him your situation."

"That would be lovely." She faked a smile and went to retrieve Butterscotch. She filled her in on the way back to the lobby.

"How is there no house there?"

"I don't know," Chocolate answered. "But the records show that the lot where that house was, whatever number it was, is empty. The lady said there's nothing she can do, but she didn't want to deal with me. She's sending us to see the mayor."

"I don't know what kind of help the mayor could really be," Butterscotch said as they approached his door. "If the record says there's no house, then there's no house."

"But there *is* a house."

"I know that."

The mayor was talking to someone else when Chocolate and Butterscotch entered the room. The man talking to the mayor turned around and glanced at the women.

He turned back. "Well, thank you, Mr. Mayor," he said. The man turned around and walked toward the door with rolled up paper and a briefcase in his hand.

Butterscotch eyed the papers.

One suddenly dropped out of the man's grip and unrolled on the floor.

Chocolate rushed over to help. "Oh, I'll get that!" she said. Then she saw the blue side of the paper with white images shaped like a diagram. Chocolate recognized it as blueprints. "Are you an architect?" she asked as she rolled it up.

"Yeah… yes… yes, I am," he answered nervously. "Why?" She handed him the paper. "Thanks."

"I was… I mean, could you…" Chocolate stammered and struggled to get out what she had to say. She had thought about Butterscotch's comments and thought she'd go about the investigation with a different method.

She sighed. "Are you busy today?"

"Umm," the man said. He smiled weakly. He looked over at Butterscotch and then back at Chocolate. "Wha… er, what'd you have in mind?"

"Oh, it's not like that." Chocolate pointed at the door. "We're having a bit of trouble locating the… perfect house. We know what it's going to look like; we just don't know where to find it."

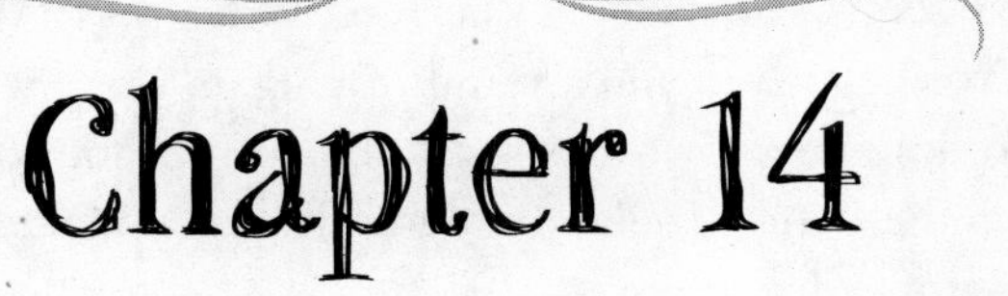

Chapter 14

When Butterscotch and Chocolate returned, Strawberry, Fudge and Dawn were already drawing a conclusion as to what caused this specific building to be exempt from the Demolition Act. Dawn and the others were in the living room when they came in, and Caramel was leading, or rather dominating, the discussion about their idea.

"So that could be how and why they figured out how to slip by," Butterscotch heard Caramel say as she entered. Caramel continued, but stopped short when she saw Butterscotch and Chocolate coming. "The IDD must have seen the inscribed year and—oh, girls, you're back!"

Caramel explained her idea to them. "I think that for whatever reason, the owners of this house wanted to keep this historical building's authenticity, so they devised a way to keep the IDD from demolishing or otherwise. I propose that they created a mask, a plate of cement with a date later than 2300 already inscribed into it, and put it over the original cornerstone. That way the IDD would pass over them."

"That's a very interesting conclusion," Butterscotch admitted.

"Really?"

"But it's wrong," Chocolate declared.

Strawberry smirked. "You girls know what happened?"

"There is no building, on record, built on plot number SIL-402–42, which is this confirmed site," Chocolate explained.

Dawn rose. "That's impossible! We're right here; we can see it. We're in it!"

"Don't worry, we didn't stop at that," Butterscotch said, trying to calm her down. "We went a step further. You see, we talked to an architect whom we met at city hall. We explained to him how the house looks: floors, rooms, and approximate measurements. He was able to draw up a rough blueprint for us. Later, Chocolate and I went onto the UNA Internet and came upon this UNA government website. We found fourteen hundred exact and comparable blueprints of houses throughout the United Nations of the Americas and the former United States of America." Butterscotch took a deep breath.

Chocolate continued, "Here's the interesting part. When we narrowed down the list to the area in and around Michigan, there were about one hundred fifty. We skimmed down that list of blueprints and found one particular house. It was in the state of Indiana and was drafted up for a Randolph Carr, Sr. And get this—it was drawn out in 2107!"

They stared at her in amazement.

"Does that mean this house was once in Indiana?" Dawn finally said. She started to think carefully about how this information would lead to the solution to the case. *If we know all about Randy, we'll probably find out who might have killed him and why,* she thought. *We should find out where this house used to be. The people there may know something about him or his family that we don't.* "Where in Indiana was this house?"

Chocolate took a piece of scrap paper from her pocket. "It was in a city called Tole," she answered. "I have the address right here." She smiled and handed the piece of paper to Dawn.

Butterscotch added, "And if it *was* moved from Indiana, it would have been exempt from the Illinois/Michigan Demo Act of 2310." She paused. "Although technically, they'd have poured a new foundation."

Dawn looked at the address strangely. "'3042 Pool Street,' Chocolate?"

"That's what it said," Butterscotch told her. "But I don't think they could've moved it like Vanilla suggested. They wouldn't have kept the foundation; they couldn't have kept it."

"You mean to say it's the same address, though?" Caramel rose.

"But it's in Indiana?" Cream asked.

"*Tole*, Indiana," Chocolate clarified.

"But it's the same address, anyway, right?" Fudge asked.

"Yes, it is," Butterscotch answered.

"So there are two houses in the UNA at 3042 Pool Street with the same layout and owners named Carr?" Caramel summarized.

"Yeah, I guess so, and that's why I want you and Fudge to go to Tole and investigate," Strawberry answered her. "I think this is one of our best leads so far in solving this case."

"M… me and Fudge?" Caramel asked, sounding a little shaky.

"Yes. I'm sure you guys are excited to finish this case," Strawberry said.

"C'mon, Strawberry, of course we are," Fudge replied.

"And I think this trip to Tole will reveal a significant amount of information on Randy Carr," Strawberry added. "We need to know whether the house moved or they built another one."

"Yeah, but I d… don't fly," Caramel said hesitantly. "You know I'd love to go, but a bus would take too long. And you all know I don't fly."

"All right, fine," Strawberry acquiesced. "Cream, you want to go with Fudge?"

"Sure," Cream said excitedly.

"Tole, here we come!" Fudge exclaimed.

Chapter 15

When they left, Caramel was elected to take over Cream's job. Her job as secretary was to write up reports about the case. They had established the murder weapon: the saber found under the victim's bed. They also had identification of the victim himself, Randy Carr, but in order to find possible suspects, they needed to have some idea of a motive. They needed to find out about his past and anyone associated with it. They also scanned the sword handle for fingerprints. No fingerprints in the UNA database matched those of the attacker, either.

"Girls, let's suppose this house *was* from Indiana originally," Strawberry said, rising. " How and why would it have been moved all the way to this plot of land? It obviously couldn't have been built here. The land is on record as being empty."

"That's right," Chocolate agreed. "So it must have been moved here, and recently."

"Oh, c'mon, girls," Butterscotch replied. "Let Fudge and Cream worry about the house."

"Butterscotch has a good point," Caramel agreed. "We've already got people working on the house problem. Cream had a lot of other stuff that needed to be solved first. She recorded where we got to with the house history so far, but we still haven't gotten to the murderer and his or her motive."

"All right," Chocolate responded, "let's take this one step at a time. What do we have that could tell us who Randy knew and what problems he may have run into with other people?"

"The journal," Dawn answered. "And we haven't really identified him except by name."

"That's another mystery in itself," Chocolate replied. "We can't get further with that."

"Yes, we can, Debbie," Butterscotch corrected.

"How, Donna?" Dawn responded. "The UNA computer system doesn't have him on record, and if he really is from 2108, his records would have already been deleted. The name doesn't do us any more good than the fingerprints and retinal scans."

"That's where you're wrong," Butterscotch argued. She was the computer expert. "You see, every year the UNA computers update the citizenship records for the people who were born in the past one hundred fifty years or who have died in the last one hundred fifty years. The other memory is then deleted. But those megabytes of information cannot be entirely deleted, only from the common user's perspective."

"Wow, that's fascinating," Caramel said sarcastically. "Who cares?"

"Well, I'll have you know that I am no common user," Butterscotch replied. "I know how to override most systems and retrieve lost, stolen, or deleted memory and data. And I happen to know that the files in the UNA system are named by the paternal surname followed by the initial name, not by fingerprints, retinas, or dental records. Therefore, since we have a name now, I can get a full UNA bio on the victim in about twenty minutes. Just leave it to me."

Butterscotch left to get her laptop from her car. While she was gone, the others began to look around and search through the evidence boxes. They rummaged through the living room as well.

"You know, Dawn," Chocolate said as she fiddled with her pen, "we aren't getting anywhere."

Dawn looked up at her suddenly like a deer when it hears a predator stalking it. "What do you mean? We've come a long way, what with Pool Street and the Carr family, and the journal." She toyed with an antique camera from the box she was searching in as she spoke.

"We aren't far enough to solve a murder," Chocolate said back. "Just enough to discover the identity of a perhaps two-hundred-year-old victim. We could be helping someone out there instead of pillaging off of some dead nobody."

Dawn threw the camera back in the box. "But when we find out what happened, we can contact his family or friends that have been wondering where he's been," Dawn explained as she picked up a small HG, or Holographic Globe, from the same box. A holographic, spherical image of the earth was projected over the HG. "This is important to *someone*."

"And that raises another question," Caramel chimed in. She motioned toward Murphy, who was going back up the stairs. "What's *he* doing here?"

The officer had been there ever since their investigation had brought them to the Pool Street address. He had been busy this whole time inventorying the house and its contents.

"Yeah, I see what you mean," Chocolate added. "Detroit doesn't pay for detectives like this anymore, so what's their sudden interest in this case? Especially if it *is* a two-hundred-year-old nobody who was killed."

Butterscotch returned while talking on an AP, an audio only phone. "All right, thank you. Bye." She sighed and placed the phone back into her pocket. She peered over at Dawn.

"Who was that?" Dawn asked, throwing the HG back into the box and getting up.

"That was Sherri," she answered. "The coroner confirmed that Randy Carr died at exactly 12:43 p.m. on Monday afternoon." She sat down on the couch where Dawn had been and sighed.

Chocolate gasped. "But that's only a couple of hours before they found him!" She walked over to Butterscotch. "This case is getting more and more puzzling as we go."

"What did you find in the UNA database?" Caramel asked, rising to go back into the kitchen.

"Oh, I was on it when the call came!" Butterscotch said. "But you'll never believe what it says."

She set up her laptop on the coffee table and uploaded the file she'd found on Randy Carr, Jr. of Tole, Indiana. There was a picture, birth date, hair color and eye color.

"It's blank!" Chocolate cried.

"No, it's not blank, it's… unfinished," Butterscotch explained. "That is Randy's information."

Caramel turned back to the living room.

"So you're saying he never had any information in the database other than his birthday?" Dawn asked.

"Something must have happened to him," Butterscotch said. "Like he was killed or something, and nobody ever found out what happened."

The others stopped what they were doing and gazed over at Butterscotch. Chocolate was on the couch; Strawberry was looking through a drawer in the corner table under the brightest lamp in the room. Caramel was in the kitchen, so she moved over to the doorway. There they were, four adults sitting in the room, lost like little children, unsure of where to go or what to do next.

Chapter 16

THE PLANE LANDED IN Tole early the next morning. Cream led Fudge out of the airplane to see a beautiful grassy countryside to their right. Patches of trees dotted the hills, and there was a large wooded area near the middle. It stretched as far as she could see. There was only one less pleasant and natural area. It was to the left, where there were tall buildings and a smoggy environment much like what she was used to in Detroit. It was seemingly worse when compared to the valley and forest nearby.

"Well," Fudge said, looking over to her partner, "where do we start?"

They walked down the ramp into the airport, which, along with tollbooths and two train depots, acted as a transient between the city and the country. They rented an off-road vehicle from the Brick City/Country Tole Rent-a-Car. The Carr house looked like it would fit in better with the countryside area, so they had decided on a more durable vehicle for the unpredictable curvy back roads.

They drove into the countryside and through the farmlands. They passed large barns and plots of disused land, but there was no significant evidence of a community yet. They approached the wooded area and slowed down as the road got rockier. They were very grateful that they had chosen the off-road vehicle. Soon they saw a partially hidden, orange, homemade sign reading "Caution: Tree in Road"!

"'Caution: Tree in Road'?" Cream read. "How would a tree end up in the middle of the road unless it fell down? And in that case shouldn't they close the road?"

They took a sharp curve hidden by overgrown branches, and sure enough, there stood a small tree, growing in the middle of the narrow road.

Taken by surprise, Fudge, the one driving, didn't have time to react before they collided with the tree. The tree stood as straightly as it had before the crash, but the ATV wasn't in the same boat. The front of the vehicle now looked like a slice of a hot dog bun wide enough for a telephone pole-sized hot dog. They got out of the car and surveyed the damage.

"Well," Cream said, "at least it didn't blow."

Fudge backed up quickly and covered her ears.

"What are you doing?" Cream asked.

She opened her eyes. "Oh, sorry, that's just always the cue for something to blow up." She chuckled softly and turned to leave. After a soft snickering, Cream followed, smiling.

They walked for about five hundred more feet when they found a small village.

The buildings were dark and few people were in the streets. They could see some people scattered on porches. Most of them looked like they'd been working in the fields that the girls had passed on the way into town. The girls also came upon a few stray animals—raccoons, squirrels, feral cats and dogs, and even rabbits on occasion—that were weaving around, in and out of yards. The buildings were all lined up along the sides of the straight road. The road then turned to the left, which appeared to exit the town.

An older-looking man was sitting on one of the nearby porches. He looked like part of an old western movie, with the exception that the rocking chair was designed for several speeds and was controlled by remote. Other exceptions were the air-conditioned porch, the baseball cap he wore, his Brick Co. SR-32 android, his holographic television set, and his videophone. It wasn't that much like a western scene after all, but it easily could have been if he had put away the gadgets and taken off his cap.

The trees near his house leaned toward it as if they were trying to listen through the windows. Ivy crept up the side onto the chimney and stretched itself onto the roof. All the houses in the area seemed very old and hidden by the trees like precious treasure the trees had buried. The roads were dirt, and the sidewalks were beach sand, separated from the roads by a wooden curb. Fudge and Cream felt like they'd gone to the world that time forgot, for this place looked ancient and untouched. The only difference was that the houses, save for the one owned by the older-looking man, looked clean, and the lawns were fairly well cut.

The two girls walked up the sidewalk to the house where the man sat, rocking. They headed up the slate path toward his porch and greeted him.

"Hello, sir," Fudge said with a wave. "Is this Tole, Indiana?"

He looked up, and they noticed for the first time that the man was actually reading a book and had left the HTV on. They also noticed that the older-looking man was actually much younger despite his white hair. "You don' hafta call me 'sir,' ma'am," he replied. "My name's Grant, Andrew Grant. You can call me Andy." He looked over at Cream. "You, too, miss." He got up after disengaging the chair and stretched forth his hand.

"My name is Danielle," Fudge said, "and this is my partner, Delores." She shook Andy's hand.

"Hi," Cream said.

"Howdy, partner!" Andy took off his hat.

"Cute," Cream mumbled to herself as she rolled her eyes.

Andy eyed Cream as he waited for the girls to begin saying whatever it was they meant to say after confirming their location in Tole.

"This is Tole, Indiana, right?" Fudge repeated.

"Yesiree," Andy answered. "I believe you are right." Some locals began to gather nearby. The girls' somber, professional appearances spurred their interests. "Why, what's your business here?"

"Have you ever heard of the Carr family?" Fudge asked.

At that topic more people gathered and began the usual old-time gossiping and murmuring.

"Shh, shh!" Andy put his finger on his mouth. "Keep your voices down!"

"What?" Fudge responded. "Why?"

"Come inside with me, please," he said, ignoring her response.

They willingly followed the curious man. Of course, they would have done almost anything to get a lead on the case. Andy opened the door remotely and led them in. They found the interior surprisingly clean, especially compared to the outside. Andy's appearance would have caused anyone to assume his house would be cluttered and full of knick-knacks, yet everything was neatly aligned in rows on the shelves, on a table, or on a bookshelf.

The sitting room had an old-fashioned HTV. The walls could share some interesting stories, and the room looked as though a lot went on in the past several years. The two sofas, facing each other with a glass-top coffee table between them, looked worn, but the colors remained fairly bright.

Andy gestured for the women to sit down. They sat on one sofa, and Andy on the one across from it.

"Would you like something to drink?" Andy offered. "Coffee?"

Since everything was made with the flip of a switch by this time, the coffee was finished in no time. Andy flipped a switch on a corner of the coffee table, and a coffee machine lowered from a sliding panel on the ceiling. It hovered over the mirrored center of the table.

"I'll have cream and sugar," Delores told him.

Two mugs were raised from the legs of the table, again from hidden compartments triggered by switches. Andy carefully poured the coffee, put the cream and sugar into Delores' cup, and left Fudge's black.

"Enjoy," he said.

"Wow, by the outside appearance of the town, you'd never think that you even had electricity," Fudge said.

"Yeah," Andy said, "that's 'cause we like to keep to ourselves. Lotsa times the census people skip over this area. We aren't in the UNA record for that year, but we usually try and fix that later on. And they usually get us the next year, so the population in Indiana generally seems to fluctuate on average of a one hundred fifty-count-margin each year."

"Wow, this place *is* cut off!" Fudge exclaimed.

"Yeah, now Indiana has the most farmland per square mile in the UNA next to Kansas," Andy replied. "Well, anyway," he said, pouring himself some coffee. "What is it you girls came for again?" He knew fully well, but he wanted to forget about it and waste time so they'd have to leave.

That would never work, he thought. *These girls are evidently cops. They'd stay in town forever if it would give them the information I have in my brain.*

"We wanted to know about the Carr family," Cream answered.

Andy cringed. His face turned pale but he tried to hide it. He put his head down and tapped it as if he had just remembered. He looked back up at the girls but really looked past them, at nothing in particular.

"Now I remember," Andy said. "What do you want to know about them?" He hoped it wasn't what he thought they wanted to know.

"Well, we're from Detroit," Delores began to explain. "We work for a detective agency called Strawberry Sundae Investigations. Our boss, Diane Stroby, is nicknamed Strawberry. You see, we all have ice cream sundae toppings for code names. I think it was kind of clever, actually…" She was going off on a tangent. *Stop it*, she told herself.

"Uh… what're you two… 'detectiving'?" he asked.

"We're *investigating* the homicide of a young man," Fudge answered.

"He was part of the Carr family?"

"We suspect he is," Fudge said. "We indirectly concluded it because we only have a little proof of his real name."

Andy eyed her the entire time.

"His first name was Randy," Cream finally added. *Why is this guy being so secretive? Could he have something to do with all this?*

Andy's eyes went wide and his jaw dropped, his mouth gaping. He sat as if the name Randy struck him and paralyzed his body. "I… I… I can't help… you with that. Sorry, but he disappeared long ago. He… just leave me alone." He got up and left quickly for another room, slamming the door.

Chapter 17

THE TWO SUNDAES APPROACHED the door cautiously. They could hear something inside the door, and they were debating whether they should leave or go after Andy. Once they were in accord, they knocked on the door. They heard his faint reply, and Fudge answered.

"Can we come in?"

"Why, to torment me more? Go away!"

Fudge whispered to Cream, "Maybe we should just leave."

"Good idea," she whispered back.

"We're leaving now!" Fudge called. They crept toward the door. "Sorry, sir. We didn't mean to cause trouble; we just wanted to get to the bottom of this."

The door to Andy's room creaked open slowly.

"No, no," Andy said softly. "You can stay, I just—"

"It's all right; we'll leave," Cream said.

Fudge nudged her. "Delores!"

"Don't worry, girls," Andy said slowly. "I'm all right. Sit down, please." He sat in his spot on the sofa, and they sat in their spots.

"Ya see," Andy began, "the Carrs used to live in Tole. In fact, they lived right 'cross the way in that ol' house out there."

"Out there?" Cream said. Fudge glared at her.

"Yesiree," Andy continued softly. "I remember when I was a young'n, I mean real little, and my folks told me 'bout them Carrs. I never met that family 'cept the kid 'bout few years older than me. But they moved away shortly afterward. I remember goin' over to that house, an' I went to see my friend to show him the new camera I got from my parents 'cause I didn't know they left for the city yet," he said nostalgically. Then his voice turned grim. "And sure enough as I'm an American, I found nobody there… 'cept… I was never so scared since then, 'cause I… I… I saw him…" He looked straight at them now with his deep green eyes wide, visualizing, remembering the sight he had seen.

"He lay there bloodied and all I thought to do was scream. I even… even got a picture of him… and…" He began to sob loudly.

"Who?" Fudge got up and sat by Andy, patting his back. "Who was it that you had seen? Was it—"

"Indeed. It was…" Andy said between sobs. "It was Randy Carr. He'd been missing for years, and now I had stumbled upon him… dead, stabbed by someone so many years ago."

Cream saw the apprehension and reproach in his eyes. "What happened next?"

Andy tried to pass the time by getting up and pacing around. All the time he walked, he was breathing heavily, sighing, and patting his head with a handkerchief. After a couple of laps around the room, he returned to his seat. He had stopped crying, but his sadness and tears were still evident by his expression.

"What happened next will haunt me 'til my dyin' days," Andy finally replied. "I began to leave, but I felt coerced to turn around at the last instant, when this blue light filled the room. Randy's body was gone. So I came to the best conclusion that I knew: he had been killed, I came, then he was abducted. By ethereal or terrestrial, I don't care.

"That was fifteen years ago, and I'm twenty-four now. I was on therapy after that 'cause my parents and the town… no one believed my story… and I just couldn't believe it… but that's what happened… why I can't talk about Randy anymore. No one understands."

Andy's disquieting situation overwhelmed Cream and Fudge, compelling them to show compassion toward the poor man. They rubbed his back and neck to make him feel more comfortable.

"We're sorry, Andy," Cream said. "We didn't mean to cause trouble or disconcert you. We only needed to find out what happened." Cream paused and then came up with something. "What were you told about the Carrs preceding this event?"

Andy looked up and turned toward her. "I was told that the family had a bad history and that a long time ago one of the sons of the family mysteriously disappeared. His name was Randy."

"Disappeared?" Fudge said in surprise. "When did this happen?"

"Prob'ly 'bout two hundred years ago by now," Andy replied. "Th… that's why no one believed me. They said he'd be gone and rotted away by then."

"Two hundred years!" Cream exclaimed.

"But here's the thing. Before I saw the body, I saw a blue light coming from that room, so I think the blue light that took him away made him appear there in the first place. And I got the picture, too. It's in my safe."

He went over to a shelf hanging on the wall. It was holding a bunch of knick-knacks and junk that appeared to be useless. He knocked down one of the porcelain statues on the right-hand side, and it hit the shelf. That's when the girls noticed a small mechanical arm attached to the bottom of the statue. Soon Cream and Fudge could see a cutaway piece of the wall open up and a safe hidden within it. Andy opened the safe and picked through the old papers and coins.

By now the girls had begun to lean over his shoulder curiously to see the picture. Andy picked it up and showed the girls. Sure enough, it was Randy, the victim whose murder they had been investigating. And, oddly enough, the body was in the same position as it was above Forge's Antique Store.

"Oh my! Look at this!" Fudge exclaimed. She stepped backwards several paces. "Delores, come over here a sec."

"Just a second, Andy," Cream followed Fudge back over to the sofas.

"We have to get into that house," Fudge told her. "We got to see exactly what's been going on here. I mean, come on," she began to mumble to keep Andy from hearing, "this guy isn't exactly the sharpest pencil in the box."

"Hey!" Cream scolded. "Easy with the comments!"

They went back over to Andy. "I'd like to, uh, see the house," Fudge requested.

"B… But… I ain't been over there since that day, an' I…" Andy sputtered out. He sighed. "All right… if you girls follow me… I'll bring you 'cross the way to the Carr house."

Andy brought them around to the back of the house, explaining on the way how he'd taken the same route years ago. They walked through the woods along the back of the house. The door to the back had been jimmied open, and the windows were covered with boards and planks. He explained that the building was condemned and was supposed to be wrecked two years ago. However, the crane couldn't reach the town, so they never got around to it.

They approached the door and opened it. Cream walked in and looked around. Her mouth gaped open and she gasped. The sound of her purse hitting the floor alerted a family of cats huddled in the corner. She didn't bother to pick it up.

Fudge hurried to Delores' side to see the stunning reason for Cream's sudden pause. On the inside, the house was filthy, dark, and full of cobwebs, but the Sundaes could clearly see that this house looked familiar.

"What is it?" Andy asked from the doorway, clearly too frightened to go in. But the Sundaes were oblivious to the man's queries.

Fudge was the first to leave her daze. "I've been here before, Andy. Look." She dug into her pocketbook and pulled out a small computer device labeled

"Sundae File: 072." She programmed it for frame thirty-six and showed it to Andy.

His wide eyes grew wider, and Fudge thought they might jump out of his head. Andy lifted the digital photograph to eye level and compared the image of a room to the real room from the view of the entryway. That's when Fudge knew that Andy realized it was a picture of the same house. It was uncanny. The still-shot picture had every knick-knack, every piece of furniture, and every wall decoration that the house in which they stood contained. It was the same house that the other Sundaes were in even as they spoke, only several hundred miles away.

Andy looked at Fudge strangely. "Where did you get this?"

Now it was their turn to tell a story.

Chapter 18

"BUT DON'T YOU GET it?" Strawberry retorted. She and Dawn were in an argument about the wedding photograph. The other Sundaes present were the audience in this matter. "This is a picture of you. Somehow this Randy Carr obtained a picture of you and Taran getting married."

"But we never did get married!" Dawn insisted. "How can he have a picture of something that never happened?" She didn't see any logical explanation for the picture's existence.

"And then this Randy Carr guy from two hundred years ago gets killed in his mid-twenties only five days ago!" Strawberry exclaimed.

"I know, and that's impossible!"

"Well, I have a theory, but it can't be proven yet." Strawberry mentioned. "So I won't tell it to you yet."

"What is it?" Dawn looked up. "Strawberry!"

Strawberry sighed. "I can't tell you just yet. I'll tell you after I get a certain phone call." She looked around for the missing Sundaes from the audience, apart from the two in Tole. "I'll be right back."

Strawberry left the living room and went into the kitchen where Chocolate and Butterscotch were sitting at the table eating leftover Chinese food from the night before. They looked exceedingly tired from their long night of studying.

"Did you find anything yet?" Strawberry asked.

Chocolate came to life with a quick jolt of surprise. "Yes," she answered. "I think—" Her head fell to the table next to her breakfast, and she fell asleep.

The other, Butterscotch, never slept, especially at night, so Strawberry was flummoxed when Donna's head fell right into her teriyaki.

Now Strawberry was mad. It wasn't so much because her best two were asleep when everyone else was investigating, but because no one had told her there was leftover teriyaki. It was her favorite Chinese food, next to pork fried rice with sweet and sour sauce on the side, and no one had had the common courtesy to tell her there was still some left. She was mumbling to herself as she attempted to wake them up.

"Oh, wake up, Donna!" Strawberry exclaimed. She reached over and handed Butterscotch a napkin to wipe her face with. She then walked behind Chocolate and shook her to wake her up.

When the two came to life, Strawberry prepared some coffee and sat down at the table. She cleared the section in front of her, which had been covered with grease-stained papers, pens, plates, and mugs. Butterscotch and Chocolate finally drank some coffee and were wide awake in no time.

"What did you find in the journal?" Strawberry asked.

Chocolate shuffled through her papers. "We found a birth date, parents' names, mother's maiden name, hometown, and just about every tiny detail included in the last four years of his life."

"Good," Strawberry commented. "Is there anything specific that you found that will further us in our case?"

"Absolutely," Butterscotch answered. "We—"

Strawberry's VP rang and cut Butterscotch off. She answered after the third ring as she always did. "Hello?" The other Sundaes could hear an excited voice on the other side of the line even from the other room. There was no video, but it sounded like Cream.

"Yeah… an… this Andy guy… so we found the…" They could hear a few of Cream's words. Strawberry listened for a good five minutes without any responses except the occasional gasp or "oh, really?" Soon Cream hung up, and Strawberry shut off her VP.

"Oh my gosh!" Strawberry dropped into a chair. Her VP fell to the table. "Guys, I think we did it." She looked around at all of the Sundaes. "We solved the mystery of who Randy Carr really is." The others—Debbie, Donna, Dawn, Denise, and Paul Murphy—gathered around to hear what she had to say.

"In Tole, Indiana, Cream and Fudge met a man named Andrew Grant. He knew something about a family across the street. They had had a family member, like a great, great uncle or something, who had disappeared without a trace. But this town, being where and how it was, was so secluded that his disappearance never made the news or the newspapers. But the disappearance became like a legend in the town.

"Anyway, Mr. Grant ventured into the house across the street several years ago and found what he thought was that family's missing relative. By that time the family had moved out. The body Mr. Grant found had been stabbed to death, and he got a picture of him. But when he left, the room filled with a blue glow, and the body disappeared. Grant was about nine years old at the time, so no one believed him when he told them what had happened."

Caramel sighed. "How sad!"

"And he was only nine!" Chocolate cried.

"But that's not the part important to our case," Strawberry pointed out. "Anyway, he took Cream and Fudge across the street, and they found nothing in that house. Just a bunch of regular junk."

"How is that important?" Butterscotch inquired.

"Well, I'll tell you," Strawberry replied. "Fudge, of course, had her handy picture computer with her and showed Mr. Grant, or 'Andy' as she calls him, a picture of this house from the back door entryway. And guess what?"

"WHAT?" the others exclaimed in unison.

"He held it at eye level to see everything in the picture. To their surprise, it was in the same position and place as that entry room in Tole!" Strawberry affirmed. "From every knick-knack to the couch and shelves. In fact, the entire house was literally this house, only that house actually looked the one hundred fifty years older that it really is. *And* the family of that house was a Carr family!"

"Are you trying to imply that this house and the house in Tole are the very same house?" Dawn asked. Strawberry's answer was a nod. "So do you know what this means?"

Strawberry nodded slowly. "Yeah, I do," she replied. The others looked around at one another, exchanging glances. "Congratulations, Mrs. Flint!"

Murphy exclaimed, "That's impossible!" He walked in from the front entryway. He'd gone home for the night, but he was back now and had heard most of the story. "How old is this Andy guy now?"

"I don't know, like thirty," Strawberry answered.

"If Mr. Carr was killed on Monday, and this Grant guy was nine when he saw Randy's body, how could it have gone from Tole to Detroit in twenty-something years and at the same time only five days?"

"Magic?" Sherri suggested. She walked in directly behind Murphy. "Your lights are on, buddy. I'd shut them off before you drain the battery." She winked at him and clicked her tongue.

Murphy ignored her remark. "No, but seriously, what's going on?" He stared at Strawberry, who now had her arm around Dawn.

But Dawn simply smiled, a tear rolling down her face. She knew it. She just had that little hope that pulled her through, telling her Taran was alive, that she'd see him once again and they'd get married. But then she had a strange feeling. Did that mean she could prevent Randy's death?

She knew now that Taran's time machine had worked. All of his hard work paid off. They would get married after all because somehow Randy had gotten involved with the time travel and got a photograph of Taran and Dawn's wedding ceremony, which was yet to take place. She knew they could get to the bottom of this mystery if only she could somehow contact Taran, wherever or whenever he might be.

Chapter 19

DAWN WAS HANGING AROUND the Sundaes' headquarters. It had been another two days since they'd discovered who Randy was and from when he was. It was amazing to her that this machine must have actually worked. It brought a whole new dimension to the case. But it also limited the investigations. How could they investigate something that didn't happen in their time?

She was alone at the office because the others were preparing for their Christmas party. It was only a couple days away, and besides, it was Sunday. They didn't get paid for working on Sunday.

But regardless, Dawn was there. The loose connections between the case and Taran gave her a more personal view of the case. Dawn picked up Randy's journal from the desk and began to read. She was eager to read the entry explaining Dillon.

As she searched for the right page, she began thinking. *Maybe this Dillon is a suspect. After all, if he wanted a secret identity and Randy discovered it*, she whispered, "He'd try to kill him. I know a motive!"

Dear Journal,

I actually got into Dillon's base today. He was at a town meeting, the first since I came to this place, possibly the first ever. It doesn't seem this town has been around or organized for very long. Anyway, I found a secret trapdoor in Dillon's hut today and went down.

It was dark and creepy, but I soon found a switch that lit up a bunker-like cavern. Then I came to a big circular room with a compass rose etched into the floor. There was a door on the wall of the room where each of the directional arrows pointed. That made sixteen doors: north, north-northeast, northeast, east-northeast,

east, and so on. I looked behind me and noticed I had come from the door reading south.

Anyway, in the center of the compass, there was a ladder hanging down from the ceiling. I guess Dillon had forgotten to close the hatch above the ladder because I went through there to learn his true identity.

I climbed the ladder, and at the top was this room with several computers and security equipment. This place was really high-tech! There were concrete walls and no windows. I could see, though, because there was a bright light coming from each corner and the center of the ceiling.

So I found Dillon's desk and I opened the drawer. In it was a book, which I opened up. Guess how it began...

Dawn whispered, "How?"

"'It said, and I quote: "Everything happened so quickly."' Hmm," Dawn read. She paused. *How is that significant?* She continued to read.

That made it obvious; it was a journal of some sort. I skimmed through some of it, but I skipped a few entries. The next one began, 'I've only introduced myself as "Dillon," which is really my middle name.'

So I was right; he was using an alias. This book must have been a journal for that Dillon character, and that's the best way to really find out about someone. I know it's wrong, but there was something fishy about the whole thing. I had to keep reading it.

Anyway, in a later entry, I saw one thing before I had to hide because I heard someone coming. This "Dillon" mentioned bringing a very confused co-worker here. His name was Danny Stevens. But I still can't figure out who "Dillon" really is. I'll be keeping my eyes and ears open, and when I get more I'll let you know.

Randy Carr

P.S. I'll go fix that watch now.

"'Danny Stevens'? Watch?" Dawn said aloud. She remembered the scientist at the launch area. The name tag read "D. Stevens, SC. D. ." She tried to piece together the puzzle. "Does that mean Dillon is Taran?" This thought brought on a whole new wave of emotion, as well as revelation.

"Dillon *is* his middle name," Dawn commented, of course to herself. "My Taran? That would mean Taran… had reason to kill…"

Dawn's voice trailed off as she slumped to the floor, the book falling to her side with her.

Chapter 20

The next morning, Chocolate and Butterscotch pulled up to the Sundaes' headquarters. They parked behind the green Karz H550 in the front of the building. They recognized it as Taran's car, but they didn't expect Dawn to be back to the office so early.

"That's odd," Chocolate said. When she started to put the keycard into the lock slot, she realized the door had already slid freely open when she stepped up to it.

"Should she be leaving the door unlocked if she's here all alone?" Butterscotch asked.

"I know it, but…" Chocolate began as she walked into the building. She suddenly saw the unconscious body of Dawn on the carpet inside the lobby. "Oh my! Donna, help me get her up!"

They rushed over to Dawn's body and set her on one of the easy chairs. These were the chairs Sherri had insisted be put in as a prerequisite to her working in the office. She had refused to use the other "uncomfortable swivel chairs" because they hurt her back. Strawberry knew the chairs would never come in handy since Sherri was only at the office on an irregular, maybe once-a-month basis, but she was wrong, for once.

Chocolate and Butterscotch revived Dawn, and she told them the whole story about how she suspected Dillon to be the murderer because he had motive. She said she deduced Taran was Dillon; this concluded Taran was a murderer. By then, Strawberry, Caramel and the others were all there as well.

"Well, what did I tell you about him?" was Strawberry's remark.

"Diane!" Chocolate scolded. She patted Dawn's shoulder comfortingly. "Don't worry, it's all speculation anyway. Even though he *did* have the opportunity, access to the weapon, no alibi, and a motive, we don't have anything concrete, so don't make accusations."

"Well, it isn't really a motive to kill," Butterscotch said.

"Well, some people are unpredictable," Chocolate added. "And who knows what kinds of things time travel may possibly do to a person. Furthermore, who knows how long it's been between him leaving and Randy dying."

Caramel leaned toward Cream and began to whisper, "Honestly, anything could have happened to Taran, you know, with all these experiments going on. There's no telling what he's been through to get up to this point."

"I don't know, Denise," Cream said. "I see what you mean, but don't you think—" She paused for a moment and looked over at Dawn, who had her head down, leaning on Chocolate's shoulder. She was even softer now, "Don't you think Taran would have sent for Dawn by now?"

"Brought her to wherever he is, you mean? I don't even think he would do that," Caramel explained. "He was always insisting how dangerous it was, according to Dawn. And these are very secretive experiments that even we aren't supposed to know about, so bringing Dawn, if you think about it, would jeopardize the whole thing, wouldn't it?"

"Yeah, I guess that's true," Cream shrugged. Now she started to speak so everyone could hear. "But do you really think that Taran would be capable of killing Randy? Would he do that?"

"Why don't we drop all of this speculation?" Chocolate insisted. "There's nothing to prove it, so let's drop it. There's no way to assume anything about what Taran may or may not be going through at this point, so it's irrelevant."

"Dawn, you need to keep your mind off of this case." Strawberry said. She smiled, which was returned by a half-hearted smile from Dawn. "The Christmas party is coming up. We've got a lot of preparation to do. Why don't you give us a hand?"

Over the next two days, leading up to the Christmas party, the Sundaes kept busy with decorations and kept their minds off of their detective business. That was mainly because they didn't want to upset Dawn. They also figured the murder must have happened many years ago, so three days wouldn't make a big difference.

Chapter 21

The Christmas party at High Street High School was a tradition as old as northern Detroit. It was often hosted by the wealthier families, a responsibility that had been held by Dorothy and Dean Mynt for nearly thirty years. When the task proved too much for the elderly couple, the community gathering was at the risk of shutting down.

The Mynts, along with the town council, petitioned the northern Detroit for aide. With few people willing to put in the time, Strawberry, Dorothy Mynt's niece, recruited the help of her Sundaes to host the celebration. This was their tenth year to be involved with the party, which filled the cafeteria and auditorium every winter.

This year was a big hit. It began in the evening, about six, and ended at midnight. The cafeteria was used for refreshments and dinner. Butterscotch and Fudge hosted games, puzzles, and raffles on the second floor for the younger people. The teenagers and young adults had a dance in the auditorium chaperoned by Caramel and Cream. Later came a huge gift exchange, which Chocolate, Strawberry, and Vanilla had been buying several gifts for since last Christmas. Of course, many people brought other special gifts, too. The party didn't go without incident, however. Not long after most of the guests had arrived at the school, at about seven, Dawn began to hear thunder booming in the evening sky.

"I sure hope it doesn't rain," Dawn said to Sherri, who had just arrived.

"Rain on Christmas?" Sherri scoffed.

"Well, you must admit, it has been a warm winter so far, what with no snow and all," Dawn responded.

"Yeah, you're right," Sherri said. She had been leading a few of her guests in when she saw a dim flash of lightning in the distance. After giving an "I told you so" glance to Sherri, Dawn continued over to the parking lot.

Chocolate and Strawberry were waiting in the auditorium before eating and dancing began at seven thirty. They had planned some pre-dinner entertainment and carols for anyone interested in listening and watching, but they were waiting for Vanilla to return with props. They stood backstage behind a drum set.

"Where did Dawn go?" Strawberry inquired.

"To get the props for the show," Chocolate picked up a drumstick and began tossing it into the air and catching it.

"N... no... give—" Strawberry said as she grabbed for the drumstick. "Gimme that," she said when she finally got hold of it. "We're supposed to be going over the lines here, Chocolate."

"What, for the skit?"

"Yes!" she shouted. "I mean, yes," she said more softly. She didn't want the audience to hear shouting backstage while the comedian presently on stage was performing.

"Don't worry about it," Chocolate patted her shoulder. "Whats-his-face is telling his jokes again. He can stall as long as we need him to."

"Who, Larry?" Strawberry walked over to the curtain. "He's doing his blond jokes now. You know Dawn won't appreciate that."

"Oh, Dawn doesn't mind. You know that."

Finally, Dawn showed up with the props for the skit. "Here you guys go. Sorry I'm late." She was breathing heavily. "I had to run from the parking lot because it started to rain."

"Okay, you rest a while and we'll set these up," Strawberry suggested. "Stage three, right?"

"Right."

The numbered stages were on a machine that rotated four different stages behind the curtain. This way, one stage was on the floor below in a smaller place similar to that of a coffee shop. Another was on the floor above in a spare storage room. The other two stages would be in the auditorium, one behind the other, and behind the back curtains as well. This caused stages one and three to be together on the same stage, and two and four to be together, making changing scenes more quickly accomplished in live performances.

It took five minutes to get the stage ready, and when it was, they had to find some way to get Larry off of the stage.

"Don't worry," Strawberry said. "I'll get him off. It'll be quick and painless." She walked over to the side of the stage, still behind the curtain, and waited for Larry to finish the joke.

"So the blond says, 'Put the blanket down and step away slowly,'" Larry said.

At the roar of laughter, Larry looked over his shoulder to his left at Strawberry, and suddenly his face was pale with horror. The only thing the audience saw was a scared comedian taking a remote from his pocket and pressing a button to close the curtains. Soon afterward, the stage rotated once so that stage three was on the top, the storage room. Strawberry remained on the center floor; she wasn't on the rotating section.

The skit, called Neapolitan Christmas, was performed by Strawberry, Chocolate, and Vanilla. It went well for Vanilla's first Christmas performance. She was stuck adlibbing a few of her longer, poorly-memorized lines inadvertently skipped two lines, but the audience loved the show nonetheless.

After the show, the Sundaes were in the other staged area, behind closed curtains, cleaning up. Vanilla started carrying a heavy box to the back exit when the lights suddenly began to flicker. Vanilla wasn't taken by surprise by this, but the others were.

When the three of them were finally outside in the parking lot, heading to their cars, a flash of lightning struck a tree near the parking lot. The old, tall tree towered over the lot.

Vanilla dropped her box and ran for cover when she saw it begin to give way. Chocolate and Strawberry hastened to meet up with her, but the large, old oak tree fell to the ground, dividing the three of them. The tree's dilapidated and weak branches shattered from the impact.

Concerned, Chocolate and Strawberry raced around to the other side. Chocolate climbed over the tree, and Strawberry ran around what used to be the peak of it. They found Vanilla huddled by a branch holding a magazine over her head.

"Hey, girls!" she said brightly, as if nothing happened.

The others sighed and helped her inside.

Chapter 22

DINNER FINALLY CAME AROUND, and the Sundaes were hosting and waiting on people. The turnout was much better than they'd anticipated. Some people had brought friends and family that weren't directly invited. Because of that, they ran out of the plates that they set aside for the buffet. Cream had handed one little boy the last available plate.

"There ya go, little guy," she said sweetly. "And don't fill up on candy and cake."

Dawn was standing beside her talking to a tall gentleman Cream didn't recognize.

"Yeah, he always knows what I'm going to need ahead of time," Dawn told him.

"I've only gone to Young's Grocer a couple times," the man replied. "But I think I know who you're talking about."

"Well, if it's not a machine, it's probably Joe," Dawn said. "They've only got one other guy, and he doesn't work much, only a couple days a week."

"Vanilla," Cream said softly, "sorry for interrupting, but Sherri and I can handle this food thing for a minute. Would you mind going to get more plates from the storage room?"

Dawn yawned, covering her mouth. "Sure," she nodded at the gentleman. "I'll be right back, Freddie."

Dawn walked slowly to the hall from the cafeteria doors and, with a tired gaze, found the storage room. She opened the door and mumbled to herself. "Why am I always the one they tell every—" She yawned. "I have to do everything." She reached for a large sleeve of Styrofoam plates when the door closed on her. She let go of the sleeve and groped in the dark for the light switch until she hit it.

The room, which she could now see better, was rather large and full of large shelves and bookcases like those you would find in a library. These were full of craft supplies, crayons, markers, finger paints, and odds and ends instead of books.

Suddenly, Dawn felt a rush of wind, and, in a seemingly long instant, she felt herself being pulled backwards. She closed her eyes as if to brace herself for the fall. However, when she opened them, she found she was still standing. She looked around the now thick black room.

Did someone turn out the lights? Dawn wondered. *Or was there another blackout?* She reached behind herself for the door, where it *had* been, but she didn't feel anything. She stumbled over to the middle of the room and encountered a large, soft object that seemed to be firmly attached to a wall and the floor. She found the object to have low walls and decided it was actually a bed. *I didn't see a bed in here. What… where am I?*

Yawning again, she carefully got onto the bed and lay down.

They won't mind if I take a short nap. Freddie will find someone else to talk to. Although, if the power **did** *go out, someone would want to know where I am*, Dawn thought. *Oh well, Cream knows where I am*. Soon she fell fast asleep.

Cream looked over her shoulder toward the exit as she scooped some salad into a bowl. "What's taking her so long?" she wondered aloud. She was tempted to leave Dawn alone and carry on with her own responsibility, but she was compelled to search for her to be sure she was okay. After all, Dawn had been fairly dazed after the lightning incident. Cream decided to leave the responsibility of monitoring the food solely to Sherri.

"Be right back, Sherri," Cream said as she snuck toward the doors.

"Okay, but if you're gone for more than five minutes, I'm gonna go find your party!" Sherri looked at the next person in line for food and smiled. Under her breath she muttered, "It's gotta be better than this one!"

Cream hurried out to the hall and straight for the storage room door. She pushed it open slowly and peered into the black, abysmal room. She flipped on the lights, and, just as she suspected, Dawn wasn't there. A pile of plates were strewn all over the floor, the only sign that she had been in there.

Sherri was getting herself some punch when Cream came in. As casually as possible, Cream ran to Sherri. Now *she* was talking to the tall gentleman. "Sherri," she said softly, "where's Strawberry?"

"Why?" Sherri asked, just as softly. She turned back to Freddie. "I agree, though. Fossil fuels did have bad environmental effects. But for their time, it was a dramatic technological step."

"I couldn't agree more," Freddie replied.

Cream tapped Sherri's shoulder again. "C'mon, Sherri, this is important."

"I'm sorry, Freddie," Sherri said. "I'll see ya in a bit."

"Yeah, no problem," Freddie answered. "I gotta go find Doris anyway."

"Hey," Sherri said, finally facing Cream, "thanks, Cream. That guy was a bore. Now, what's up?"

"Dawn's gone!" she exclaimed.

"What?"

They casually rounded up the Sundaes and headed to the supply closet. There they beheld the scattered mess of Styrofoam plates. Everything else was in its place.

"I found the closet door closed, and the light was off," Cream told the others.

Chocolate ran up to them from the school's entrance. "Taran's car is still here, so she probably didn't leave the building."

"She was too tired to go anywhere anyway," Sherri said.

"She was practically asleep standing up at the potato pan," Cream said.

"Caramel, you search the ladies' rooms," Strawberry commanded. "And Fudge, go and look back through the crowd in the auditorium."

"You got it," Caramel answered. She ran down the hall to the stairs.

"I'm on it, Strawberry," Fudge said before going back through the double doors at the other end of the hallway. A loud buzz of voices came and went with the opening and closing of the doors.

Butterscotch was already exploring the closet, checking for signs of a struggle or anything unusual. "You know what? It looks like she came in here, got the plates, and dropped them. However, it doesn't look like she left."

Strawberry leaned on the doorway, looking around the closet for any other exits. "If that's the case, then where is she?"

Part Two

The Creation of a Culture

Chapter 23

"EVERYTHING HAPPENED SO QUICKLY," a ragged man narrated as he wrote. His light complexion and sandy brown hair were hidden beneath dust and dirt from his surrounding environment. He was in a thick, tropical jungle overlooking a shallow cliff that led to a blue lagoon. He was sitting, leaning against a boulder overlooking the cliff. A small fire and the full moon reflecting off of the water was his only light.

"The machine took me through a bright void and I traveled for a great distance before appearing here. I don't know when or where 'here' is, but Dr. Brown is nowhere to be found. This place looks like the same place that Sandy brought us before, so she should have been right there. The code was accurate, and the jungle looks the same as it was.

"In accordance with Thompson's orders, we arrived to an island—one chosen solely by Dr. Brown herself. Her absence eludes me. Yet I know what my orders are, so I made the decision to move on to the next phase. This would entail reprogramming the machine for subject transmission. My colleagues briefed me on this, and though Dr. Brown was well versed in it, I was on my own.

"The physical damage done to the machine through each of the trips was minimal, but it was obviously worn. The combination of designating an arrival location and a time destination is what must have caused this. We were sent through the dimension of time, but we also traveled forward through the geographical plane. That aspect was handled by Dr. Brown as well.

"Phase Two would have been ready for its launch after I reprogrammed it, but I never reached that point. I was interrupted by a native intruder less than an hour after my arrival."

In a small clearing, outside a thick, green jungle sat a machine the likes of which only a Karz employee would have seen. The front end, with dual seating and a bright electronic control display, would appear to be that of the typical hovercar. The back end would show it was a mechanical device more extravagant than that.

The gray lower panels protruded black tubes wrapping around the tail and connecting to the back of a large clear dome. Inside the dome—when the machine was active—gears, wires, and small flashing blue lights were visible. It was dark and gray within the dome as the ragged man tinkered at it.

In his hand was an arm length tubule device with three blue lights along the side of it. This device, to which he was making an adjustment, was called a Subject Transmission Relay. It was crucial to the ragged man's mission because without it, he'd be stuck on this primitive island and remain there *alone*.

He had not set up a camp yet; he made the machine, his only safety net, his first priority. But the ragged man *had* attempted a small fire, which died down soon after. He left his backpack and supplies on a stone next to the singed twigs and leaves.

"I just need to attach this to 'Dome Quadrant 2' where the original relay is now," he told himself for the thousandth time. "Then the machine should be set to go…"

He heard a rustling in the trees nearby. He turned his head to the side, toward the front of his vehicle. The ragged man suddenly felt he *wasn't* alone. Unsure of whether he had already been spotted, he jumped behind the side wall of the machine, putting it between him and the rustling jungle leaves.

He peered over the side of the dome to watch the jungle wall. After a few tense moments, it spat out a dragon-like lizard. It was the size of a housecat, not like anything the ragged man had ever faced.

Komodo? No, it's too small. He didn't know enough about reptiles to make an educated guess, but he thought a lizard like this one would not attack him unless it was provoked. *I'll let it do its thing.* He whispered to himself, "Go ahead. Sniff around, then go away."

The scaly creature found its way to the remnants of twigs beside which the man's backpack laid. It intermittently popped its tongue out and sniffed around until it discovered the pack. The flap was left open, but the body of his pack was drawn tight with strings, so the lizard's efforts to forage within it were in vain.

It clawed at the straps and pulled the backpack off the stone. Startled, the lizard began wrestling with it, getting its tail entangled in the drawstrings and its claws wrapped in the straps.

Suddenly, it perked up and looked around—not toward the ragged man or his machine but toward the opposite end of the vines and trees. The pack was still tangled on one of its claws.

The ragged man watched as the lizard scurried back from the jungle where it came, dragging the pack awkwardly behind it.

"Hey!" He stood up.

A tall man with a spear in one hand emerged from another side of the jungle. He ran toward the exit the lizard had made, but he stopped when he glanced over to see the mysterious machine.

The ragged man quickly ducked down again and crawled backwards slowly into the woods behind him. In wonder, he watched from behind his natural leafy facade.

The native was dressed in a simple grass skirt and some type of leather belt. He wore a necklace fashioned with red beads and red paint on the right side of his face. Over his left eye, a scar cut from his forehead to the top of his lip. His chest was inked in black and red in symbols unfamiliar to the ragged man.

The scarred native approached the machine cautiously. Wielding his spear ready, he stepped slowly toward it. He was muttering in a hermetic dialect unknown to his secret spectator. What the ragged man *could* see was that this islander began to shiver approaching his vehicle. The closer he stepped, the more violently he shook.

Chapter 24

IN RETROSPECT, THE BOLD decision to face the scarred native was likely my best choice. Though I was hesitant to put myself in that sort of danger, it would only be a matter of time before I was discovered by the tribe that was sure to follow him.

"There was a language barrier between us, so I could decipher very little of his utterances. However, *sign* language was integral in his speaking, and for many of the terms he used, while the words were nonsense, the gestures were the same.

"As it turned out, because of my machine, he looked at me as if I were some type of god. A situation with as many advantages as disadvantages, as it turned out. He led me to his village that night in attempt to parade me around, I assume, but I hastily denied him that privilege. I didn't want to be known to this tribe. It would compromise every phase of this project.

"I only introduced myself as Dillon, which is my middle name. Anonymity, while vain in this case, is key to maintaining success in this project, especially where outsiders like these islanders are concerned.

"Wakna, as I think that was his name, showed me to a place in the jungle sheltered from the weather and still distant from the village. It was a cave overlooking the beach and a small lagoon. He made it clear that if I didn't want to be seen, this would be a better spot for me to sleep than at the machine site.

"After a few moments, he left me to return to his village. I decided I would wait a while before returning to the machine."

Dillon awoke as the sun shined in his eyes, welcoming his first morning on the mysterious island. The trip, the machine, the dragon, and the scarred native all felt like a dream. He awakened to see palm fronds swaying across the doorway of his room which proved otherwise.

Noticing first that he was in a shallow cave and seeing that his uniform was stained and ripped at the ends of his sleeves, the realization hit him like ton of bricks.

"The machine!"

He raced out of the cave and headed north. He was still disoriented from his sleep, but he convinced himself he was headed the right way. He climbed over rocks and crept through the vines haphazardly until he came to the clearing.

Before jumping out of the jungle, he decided to get a peek at what creature—or what people—might be there to welcome him.

From behind the hanging wall of vines, Dillon could clearly see several villagers crowding around his time machine. It appeared to still be intact, but the islanders had erected posts at each corner. They had begun building walls on the front end, which Dillon could see. A platform was sitting next to it as well, on top of which there was what looked like a slain animal and several pieces of pottery and jewelry.

Looks like some kind of shrine. He searched for a better angle, moving slowly to not alert the natives. Dillon looked out again from the vines. He still couldn't identify the animal or any of the natives. The scarred native wasn't with them.

I wonder. Did Wakna tell them about me after all? There was no doubt the islanders saw the machine and had the same reaction as the scarred native. They believed it was a vessel that would transport a god to their midst. It was just a matter to Dillon as to whether they discovered the machine on their own or if they were led there.

Soon another group of islanders joined the builders, carrying more supplies. It became obvious to their audience that these natives weren't going anywhere. Dillon also decided he'd be running a much higher risk by approaching this group, which numbered more than a dozen now. One on one was different odds than being vastly outnumbered.

Instead, Dillon decided to bide his time by exploring. He had seen most of the natives had come from the same direction. That was where he'd find their source. Curiosity overcame him enough to spend his morning searching for the village that the islanders called home.

Creeping through the forest, he searched for a path in the direction of the assumed village. The jungle was thick and twigs snapped underfoot. From the noises he made, Dillon was sure he would be noticed at any time, but somehow he made the trip without incident.

After several minutes of exploration in what he hoped was a straight line, Dillon happened on a great bamboo wall. He searched for cracks and checked for weak points in vain. Looking around, he decided going over or around were the only options.

He made use of his surroundings, the knotty and intertwined tree limbs were an easy climb. Lifting himself from the lowest branch, he hugged the thickest trunk as he scaled closer to the top of a choice tree. Among the fronds of the canopy, Dillon could see over the wall.

On the other side stood what Dillon mistakenly believed to be a humble village. It was in fact a city. Wooden and bamboo huts were scattered throughout the sandy locale. What appeared to be vendor booths were lined up on the far side of the city, leading to a majestic tower.

People were running and playing, buying and selling, lazing around and toiling at the patches of grass, which were few and far between. They all were dressed similarly to the scarred native, grass or leafy skirts, beaded necklaces, and many different colored paints. It seemed very primitive.

He looked around for banners, flags, totems, any sign or marking to distinguish this tribe from other tribes he might have been familiar with. There was nothing.

"I'm not going to take my chances in there," Dillon said softly to himself. "They don't seem violent, but I've heard islander tribes can be very unpredictable."

He shimmied down the tree and landed softly on the ground. He started back by using the path he blazed getting there. Peering over to his right, he spotted a comforting article sitting atop a boulder crawling with vines. It was his backpack, tattered and torn.

He reached over and grabbed the pack by its broken strap. "Least the trip wasn't a total loss." He slung it over his shoulder, holding the good strap. It dangled absently as he found his way back to his cave overlooking the lagoon.

Chapter 25

In my eyes, I have befriended Wakna; to him, he seems to think I have 'accepted' him. This 'god' role I am playing is more uncomfortable than I once thought it would be. I have to maintain an air of power while still trying to figure out how to get back to my project. I believe Wakna is going to play a big part in that.

"I have been teaching the scarred native English for four days now. He's learning well, but it's sort of jumbled up. He insists on saying the direct object at the end of the sentence. The most difficult part about teaching English is figuring out if he really understands, especially since I have no knowledge of his language, though I'm slowly learning it in the process. Then again, he learned sign language somewhere, so I'm going to attempt teaching him English through his sign language. It's funny though, I've been taught several languages and know about many native languages, but Wakna's language is so esoteric that I can't relate it to any other.

"Wakna took me to see his village earlier. The people were out hunting and shopping in a marketplace village on the other side of the jungle, so I got into his family's hut without being spotted. When I went inside his hut, which was surprisingly large, I was in for another surprise. He found a way to keep me hidden from the Kahukah in a place they wouldn't be able to stumble upon as they could a random cave overlooking the beach."

Dillon packed his primitive belongings in the remains of what used to be his pack. He then closed his book and stuffed that in, too. Wakna came in.

"W… What…" He strained to pronounce the English Dillon had been teaching him via sign language. "What arrr doooing… yoo?"

Dillon talked slowly and used his hands to let the native understand what he was saying. "I have to move to another area of the island so Kahukah won't find me," he explained. He had planned on rotating every few weeks to a different location to avoid the tribe, and then he would come back if it was still safe.

"Kahukah no... yoo find," Wakna repeated to understand. "I hide... from Kahukah yoo," he loyally offered.

"Where?" Dillon inquired.

"Waarre?" Wakna was confused; he'd never heard this word before.

"Where, you know, what place?" he clarified.

"I show the place you," Wakna said excitedly.

He led Dillon furtively through the jungle. The leaves underfoot barely made a sound as Wakna ran. Dillon had to concentrate on being more cautious, so he lagged behind most of the way. In a short while they happened upon the end of the jungle, where the south wall of the city stood to keep the outsiders away. It ran in both directions as far as Dillon could see. Wakna knew, however, of a hidden door in the wall that he had constructed for this very mission.

Wakna crept along the wall with his hands in front of him, tracing the bamboo and wooden panels until he found the door. "We go here opens the wall," Wakna said, nodding to Dillon.

Dillon followed his guide through the door at a safe distance. Inside the door, within several feet, was the wall of a crudely built hut. It was fashioned from the same bamboo as the city walls, but the hut was much shorter. Dillon could reach up and touch the straw roof hanging over the edge.

Wakna signaled him to follow, and the scarred native edged along the wall into the hut. Dillon stopped at the doorway.

He watched the door close behind his guide and stared for a moment. Nervously, he sighed. "Here goes nothing."

His misplaced fear subsided as he looked around the empty hut, which had a table, chairs, and a few tools on the side. There were also two other doorways, which he could see led to bedrooms.

"Where do I go so I won't be found?" Dillon asked directly. It was then that he noticed the rug under the table. *The floor under the rug is sand, so why is the rug there?*

"What place?" Wakna said. "In here." He lifted the table and put it to the side. "You go down here, under sands." Dillon had used objects to help teach Wakna some English words like trees, grass, and sand.

Dillon knelt down and helped Wakna dig in the sand. He was curious as to what the scarred native meant, going "under the sands." The sand went down several inches before Dillon's hand hit something hard. He pushed more of the sand away to find a wooden floor. When Wakna cleared the part by him, Dillon could see a large steel trapdoor.

Wakna opened the door carefully. In spite of this, the rusty hinges squeaked loudly. "Safe you be in here, Dillon. You call if need you anything me?"

Dillon climbed into the trapdoor tunnel. There was a ladder leading what he estimated to be roughly six stories into the ground. Before he climbed down, Dillon needed reassurance about Wakna's trust one more time. "Do the others know about this tunnel?"

"I not tell about tunnel the others. I found when tribe built in jungle village," Wakna shook his head. "I still bring down for you every day food."

The scarred native disappeared from the hut. Dillon assumed he'd be back shortly with his first food delivery. From the top rung, he peered around the hut again and located a hanging lantern overhead.

"I'd be lost without this," he chuckled, carrying it down with him into the depths of his new refuge. "What *is* this place? If there's a metal ladder here, and it's sealed by a steel door."

There was no answer for him; he was, after all, alone.

He reached the last rung. Stepping further downward, he was surprised to hit solid ground underneath. It was dark except for the light shining down from the hut above, but that light was less effective than a full moon in the sky.

Dillon began to explore the cavernous-looking grotto. At the bottom of the ladder, he looked around with his new lantern and found sixteen doors in the room where he stood. Three of these, those on the western side, were locked. These doors had keypads beside them that would activate each steel sliding door, but he couldn't find a control panel to open them.

As he searched cautiously, he wondered aloud softly, "Hmm… this can't be a random cavern if there are several steel, mechanical doors." He laughed softly at the thought. "And I wonder where the master control panel would be." He looked around carefully and focused on the keypads. "Technology like this was created in the late twentieth century, however, much of the land mass on earth had been explored by that time. It's bewildering. I don't see how this Kahukah tribe could remain unknown, seeing that this type of technology was once used on this island. Where… when am I?"

He searched around and found a small pile of computer components. They all appeared to be damaged, partly from decay over time, but some components looked scratched and *chewed*. Just as he began to sift through them, Wakna called down.

"Are okay down there you?"

Dillon rose and walked over to the ladder.

"I have for you food," Wakna told him. He was climbing down slowly with a bundle slung over his shoulder. "Is enough all month to last. If want more you, call down me by knock on roof… ing… roofing."

"Wakna, it's not 'knock on "roofing",' it's 'knocking on ***the*** roof,'" Dillon corrected him. "I'll be fine. Don't worry."

"I get back now up." Wakna closed the hatch, and Dillon put the bundle of food next to the control panel.

He pulled some encrusted mud from the computer panel. It was the only apparent evidence of the age of the bunker aside from the rust on the hatch. The mud seemed to have corroded the steel ceiling and collapsed one area of the compound. That was the only area that was visibly unstable.

"If there could be this much decay and erosion inside this bunker—" He attempted to strategically push on buttons. "This can't be right? Right?" The idea confused Dillon to no end. The technology that was once on this island was apparently unknown to the Kahukah. But the Kahukah were historically very unfamiliar to him. "What is going on?"

Dillon finally found the control for the lights. The lights were still operable, so Dillon concluded that the bunker once had nuclear power, which lasts forever.

When the light filled the room, Dillon could see every bit of the lobby-sized area he was in. The center of the floor, which was directly below the entrance, was an enormous etching of a compass. Dillon found that the control panel was on the arrow facing north.

He tried to open the three western doors, but the control panel wouldn't allow access to the locks. He did gain access to the other doors, and found living quarters in the southeast door. He found the bed to be comfortable enough, compared to the floor, at least.

Chapter 26

I'VE BEEN LIVING HERE for a while now and have only accessed the immediate area around the Compass Room. It took me a while to get proper lighting in this underground bunker, or what may have been another facility years before now," Dillon wrote. "I know for certain that the area I've been living in is a small part of this compound. I believe this because there are several halls I cannot access. I ***can*** see through the small windows in the doors, and I've seen long, dark hallways seeming to stretch forever.

"I found an electrical panel the other day. The lights now work; I imagine they must run on nuclear power. Wakna hasn't been down since the morning I moved in, so I don't know what's been going on in the Kahukah tribe. Because of the lights, I've had the opportunity to explore the bunker more, and this idea resulted in an interesting discovery.

"There was a loud noise coming from the northwest door earlier today. Cautiously, with a broomstick in hand, I went over to check out the door.

"I walked up to the wall and looked inside. It was dark and I couldn't see a thing. I quickly ran to the control panel and turned on the lights in that hall. It was the only change I could make on the west side. I then ran from the control panel to the door very quickly. That way, even if whatever was inside ran from light, I might see what it was. But it was too late; the creature was gone.

"From the window, I couldn't see any evidence that a creature had just been in there. I think I was imagining things. I must have been imagining things. I was, wasn't I?

"I finally got back to work and decided to forget the whole thing. I found a room through the south-southeast door that contained some sort of refrigeration system. I took my provisions from Wakna into that room and put the stuff that should be cold into the refrigerator.

"When I got back to the lobby, I noticed something on the floor. It shimmered in every direction. I bent down to look at it. It was directly in the center of the compass rose etching on the floor. But just as I knelt down, I heard a low rumble; it sounded like it came from the northwestern hall. I got up, but before I could turn, I fell to the floor and hit my head hard. The creature standing over me, which looked like a mix of a dog and lizard, breathed on my face. Its slimy face nudged at mine and seemed to be sniffing like a dog checking for fear or trust.

"Just as my questionable trust in this creature began, it slowly backed away and pounced on me. I only remember screaming something after that, and everything went black."

Dillon awoke, unaware of how long he'd been asleep. He found himself on a mound of soft sand in the center of the compass. He looked around the room to see nothing strange except that there *was* nothing… strange. He knew, or at least he thought he knew, that a creature had attacked him the night before. But there was no sign of a creature that size around.

He couldn't shake the fact that he had been attacked and survived through it. If he was unconscious, he shouldn't have stood a chance. He had been unconscious, right?

It seemed to be the same kind of lizard creature that he'd confronted on his first night. Only this time, it didn't seem as though he had been the target, for if he were, he wouldn't have survived.

Dillon finally got up and went to his quarters, where he spent the remainder of the night. He lay on the bed, staring up at the ceiling of his quarters. The walls looked old and plain. There were no pictures mounted. Nor were there any type of molding around the tops of the walls. Nothing significant differentiated the cold, steel walls from the floors or the ceiling.

"It's like a prison."

He shifted his weight to his side and leaned on his arm, looking out into the Compass Room. Staring out into the dim light, he suddenly realized the quiet had surrounded him.

Not for a moment, from the test run with Sandy to the dinner with the Sundaes or the arrival to this island, had there been quiet.

"There's some irony for you. It's disquieting how quiet this bunker can be." Dillon laughed at his dry joke. It was in that moment he realized he missed Dawn more than he ever had.

"Taran, you've been caught up in your own work for so long, you didn't even realize she wasn't here?" he scolded himself. He knew the Karz journal he'd been keeping was for recording pertinent information regarding the progress of Phase Two, so including his personal fraternizations was unprofessional. "But avoiding her altogether?"

His thoughts about his fiancée were beginning to bother him. The argument he had with Dawn before his trip came back to his mind, and he began to get frustrated again, as if it had just happened. He knew his relationship with Sandy was only professional. Dawn wouldn't believe that.

"Why didn't she trust me?" Then he turned it around. "Why didn't *you* tell her?" He had no feelings for *Dr. Brown*; she was just a brilliant mind.

Concentrating on his mission, these things didn't have to come to mind. He would move on without Dawn. The right time to bring her would come, but not until he was ready. He had to move on without Sandy too. Where she was he didn't know; he accepted the fact that he may never know.

"She's gone, and it's *my* fault. I abandoned my search for her, isn't that enough?"

The next morning, Wakna was pacing around the hut waiting for his family to go hunting and to the marketplace. His two sons, who were old enough already to start their own families, were going hunting for the next three days. They were not to return without the largest "zhu-khor," or boar, they could find. Wakna's daughters and their mother were heading off to the market village again. His daughters were young teenagers.

After his family finally left, Wakna closed the door to the hut and moved the table over to the side, off of the rug. He then rolled the rug up and leaned it against the wall. Wakna eagerly cleared the sand from the metal hatch just as a friend of his, Kahlif, entered the room.

"Godatu wak zhu-khor tin bóyin? (You sent hunt boar your sons?)" Kahlif asked. "Gi uatcogu goco kon. (I saw leave them.)"

"Zho, Kahlif, (Yes, Kahlif,)" Wakna answered. He rose and brushed off his knees.

"Mæ gotu? (What doing you?)"

"I'm… I mean, gi gnidi qo, (I nothing do,)" Wakna stammered. He hurried over to the rug and began to carry it over to the place where he had been digging. He then began to kick the sand back into the ditch.

"Gnuat zhodi ti? (Hide something you?)" Kahlif insisted.

"Gni! (No!)"

"Ti gnimot gnuat ok gi'it. (You can't hide from me it.)"

"Zhonin, Kahlif, zhonin, (Okay, Kahlif, okay,)" Wakna agreed. He put the rug back against the wall. He started to unbury the hatch again, but then realized Kahlif would know the whereabouts of Dillon. He looked up at Kahlif.

He told Kahlif to close his eyes and exit the hut.

Kahlif laughed, but he obeyed.

After Kahlif went out, Wakna dug out the hatch and opened it. Making sure Kahlif still couldn't see, Wakna led him over to the ladder and down it carefully. Kahlif slowly descended, fighting the urge to reopen his eyes for fear of missing a rung. Wakna allowed Kahlif to open his eyes at the bottom, but before he did so, Dillon, by pressing a button on the control panel, caused a door to close over where the ladder came down and the ladder to rise into a crack in the ceiling.

Dillon welcomed Kahlif. "Zhomot gotu. (Welcome, literally 'you may come')" He held out his hand but Kahlif hesitated. Dillon turned to Wakna. "What's with him?"

"Mæ? (What?)" Wakna looked confused. "Kahlif understand English does not. Gnimot-zhomot renda Kahlif ti. (Maybe teach Kahlif you.)"

"Good idea," Dillon answered. "Uh…" he said, turning to Kahlif, "okay… zhonin… Kahlif, cazor tin gi codagu. (Okay… Kahlif, friend your I am.)" Dillon didn't have much opportunity to practice this language on real people, so he felt a little uncomfortable. But to maintain his god-like presence for Wakna, he used a powerful voice when speaking Dinokahu.

Dillon was hesitant at first to take on a new student, but Kahlif was eager and excited to learn from this mysterious being. Wakna had explained to him that Dillon arrived to the island using the vessel around which they had built a shrine. This fascinated him even more, prompting immediate lessons of the words Wakna had recently begun using.

When he agreed to teach English to a second native, he realized it would be less troublesome to request his "vessel" back. After Dillon recognized the advantage behind breaking this language barrier, he started teaching them right away.

Wakna and Kahlif started to come to the Compass Room daily to learn English. At the same time, they were unknowingly teaching Dillon their language, 'Dinokahu,' which meant 'language of God.' Dinokahu had a much smaller vocabulary than English, so Dillon picked up on it quickly. There were only words needed to describe places and things on the islands in this area.

It gave Dillon a sense of power to be thought of being a "kahu," or god, or literally holy king in their language. And learning their language seemed to give him more of that power. Simple words would combine to make whole phrases. Kahlif was a name that literally meant "king of life," which to them translated to optimism or good luck. Wakna's name meant "prowling lion," and the king's name—for whom the tribe was named—Kahukah, meant "God-king" or "holy leader."

They held sessions each day for three weeks. It was around the same time each day, when the sun was highest in the sky. Dillon assumed that was an easy time for the islanders to get away from the village without being missed.

At the end of the third week, not long after their daily session, Kahlif came climbing down the ladder, this time alone.

"What is it, Kahlif?" Dillon asked, coming out of his quarters.

"Come down did to invite to audience with Kahukah I you."

"Come again?" The translation took a moment, then Dillon looked at him wide-eyed. "You want me to go to the village to see your chief?" He didn't know what to say. *Should I go with him? And how did Kahukah find out about me?*

Chapter 27

I WAS A LITTLE NERVOUS about the meeting with their king, Kahukah. I'm not sure if I should be concerned for my life, being a trespasser, or if I should approach him as the 'god' the others believe me to be. Furthermore, I couldn't help but wonder if Kahlif had told the tribe about me."

"Regardless, I decided to go see Chief Kahukah, who they revere as if *he* were a god. That made me think of the possibility of a power struggle, that was, if he, too, thought of me as a god. He was in a monument erected at the exact site of my broken-down vehicle. It had only been a month since I left that very spot, and I didn't recognize it.

"A great wall of thick wood and rock surrounded the area with two openings, one in front and one in back. The back led to the sea; there were ships that seemed to arrive every day to trade or meet with Kahukah. The front entrance led to the jungle and Kahlif and Wakna's village. Their village has been built outside to act as a sort of outpost.

"Under Wakna's house, of course, is my inhabitance. But when I went to see Kahukah, I walked around to the seaport and came in from there to make it appear as though I wasn't on the island to begin with. The 'E'fil Kahu,' as I've come to call it, was where Kahukah's monument stood. That means 'Tower of God' in their language.

"I entered through the tall doorway to find a small room that led to two halls, one to each side. A curtain hung at the far wall between the two halls. I was drawn to the majestic purple curtain, but I went down the right side hall instead. It eventually led around in a semicircle until it reached a wall that probably divided it from the left path. To my right was another exit leading to the other side of the tower.

"Instead of taking that right, I turned around to first see where the left hall led. On the way back around, I noticed two natives, who took no heed of me as they came from the left hall and looked joyous as if they'd been with, well, in this case, their gods. I decided my machine must be through there. Needless to say, I went down that hall in haste, but a large native pushed me back as I turned the corner.

"He stood there with his stolid face glaring at me, boring right through me.

"'Gni mot'datu goda ti,' he said shortly.

"It meant literally 'not may pass you,' so, in resignation, I went to the room with the purple curtain again. It seemed that what was behind the curtain might be holy to the Kahukah, so I was hesitant to look within for fear of being caught. But the want was uncontrollable. I drew the curtain just enough to peek in, but it turned out to be too much.

"A native, who stood directly behind the curtain, grabbed me by my shirt. He then yanked me in while saying something in his language. When I could straighten myself out and stand more firmly, I looked up in front of me. There sat the chief.

"He sat regally on a large golden throne. He was a well-built, athletic-looking man with a large red mask over his face that had two holes for eyes. The mask had two horn-shaped projections jutting out on either side. A plume of white feathers finished the look, crowned on top of his head."

Kahukah remained seated as he spoke to Dillon. He was wearing a necklace of small bones and a skirt of green leaves and assorted jungle vines. Wakna and Kahlif stood at Kahukah's sides. Wakna translated the conversation.

"Zhomot goco, gnithudi Dílon. Belgogun a'hu ra'majít ti," Kahukah said.

Wakna said, "Welcome, stranger Dillon. Bow we before in reverence you." The nearby assembly of villagers bowed down humbly. Kahukah himself bowed slightly.

He then continued, "Ok uoy'li bo uatcogun ti. Uat'da gun hu rhi-belbuit doyin ok pfín uéjin uatcogun oy'li tin dil plhu ab'zhodiok'gnidiodgun hu ti huon plhu yhion gun. Gir fhuín, plhu, ok gnibogun a'uatco gocoit tin. Gi mot bo gnimajhudín gen gir hu uatmotait tin."

Wakna interpreted, "At last have found we you. Searching were we among islands these for months many. Found we then your vessel and built we around it an altar and our palace. My apologies, also, for not have we foreseen arrival today your. I will have sorcerers punished my with approval your."

Dillon stepped back, shaking his head. He assumed with a tribe as primitive as the Kahukah seemed that their favorable punishment was death. He did not want Kahukah to kill people on his account. He did realize they revered him, though, so he had to maintain an air of godly presence. He turned to

Wakna. "Tell him that I don't approve of their actions," Dillon responded. "But spare them for another chance."

"Gi gni uéj'mot'da ok kin qoit, gniplhu, boda'meit kin ok oyta meit."

The chief removed his mask to show his respect for Dillon and to show his thanks for such a gracious attitude. Still, his stern face frowned at Dillon. He waited for a long moment before nodding and saying, "zho, phudi, ma uéj'gniboti."

Wakna's translation was, "yes, Master, as wish you."

"Master?" Dillon repeated softly to himself. He assumed that meant that even Kahukah was submitting to Dillon's allegory.

Kahukah continued, "Bo zhodiok'gnidiod kehugun va'on voy'hu ok e'fil ok chuit tin. Gnimot-zhomot uéj'bo ninditu, ra'no Wakna oya'plhu Kahlif. Coda bodagu ok ti kin, phudi."

"Have prepared we a hut nearby to the monolith for convenience your. If need anything you, upon call Wakna or Kahlif. Am giving I to you them, Master," Wakna told him.

"Thank you," Dillon said. *I think.* He turned to leave. "Wait a minute," he said, turning to Wakna. "Can you ask Kahukah if I can enter… the uh… room of the craft, my ship?"

"Of course," Wakna answered. He asked Kahukah, to which Kahukah agreed under the condition that he go in without accompaniment. He clearly felt many of the people were unworthy to be in the presence of the sacred craft.

Dillon was more than obliged. He was led by Wakna and Kahlif only as far as the left hallway. They stopped in the archway past the guard, and Dillon continued on. He found, after a sharp turn, a staircase leading underground. He ran down hopefully, and, sure enough, he found his time machine.

It was set up with a brilliant arrangement of candles, flowers, and gold. Torches were lit all around. The light from the many torches reflected off the metal of the ship despite the dirt and mud covering it, the evidence of its crash a month before.

After checking the switches, buttons, and particularly provisions, Dillon left for another audience with Chief Kahukah. When the chief agreed, Dillon requested a new village be established outside of the walls of Kahukah's fort, near Kahlif and Wakna's hut. He also requested that Kahukah have his ship moved to the village he wished to begin.

Kahukah was reluctant, but he did agree, for a price. He knew he couldn't demand anything from a god, but instead he begged him to give the people some other evidence of his coming to them. Dillon didn't know why, but he decided it couldn't hurt. He gave Kahukah a microcomputer panel in return. It was a handheld piece Dillon had used for navigation, but it had malfunctioned. By the time Kahukah had the craft moved from its original spot to where the new village would be, the navigation panel sat on a golden platform in the place where the craft had been in the tower.

Either way, Dillon knew that he had everything he needed. The Kahukah tribesmen had put the craft in Wakna's hut. It took Dillon three days to transfer the craft piece by piece into the compass room, with the aid of the two henchmen. Now Dillon had everything he needed to continue with his long-awaited plan.

Chapter 28

We finally built my hut," Dillon wrote. "Wakna was reluctant to let me leave his hut, but it's only a short walk away. I didn't tell Wakna or Kahlif this, but the hut we built is directly above one of the hatches to the bunker. I found it in the south hall. I'll dig to that on a free day when I'm not busy with them.

"I also toted my machine into the small room in the southeast door of the bunker. It needs some minor repairs, but I'll get to it after I build enough stable huts for several people to live in. For some reason, Kahukah reveres me as some sort of god, but I think it would be a sacrilege to be the usurper they seem to want me to be and take Kahukah's lofty place. That's one reason I'm staying in a hut outside Kahukah's walls. I'll stay out of their affairs and have my own work separate from them, with the exception, of course, of Wakna's and Kahlif's families. "In the few days I was in the Kahukah village, I realized something. This island, however small it is, is large enough for me to develop a township, even a society, outside of the Kahukah village. I would be able to keep the natives *in* the village, and, if necessary, I wouldn't even have to present the Kahukah to any community I develop.

"The jungle surrounding much of the Kahukah walls will aid in keeping whomever I bring to this island away from the dangers that may exist in the Kahukah village itself.

"I don't believe dismantling the machine in its move from the Kahukah altar will have an adverse affect on its operation since I'll be able to accurately reconstruct it. I'm only afraid the programming may glitch when I finally get it running again.

"After I have completed the repairs and scanned for errors, I'll be able to move on to Phase Two, only a month or so behind schedule. This will be the exciting part, yet it will be a tough task to bear. Once I have the Subject Transmission Relay calibrated, I'll begin transporting from the list of subjects my Karz crew compiled and programmed into the machine's console.

"I read the files on some of my future 'citizens,' but I'm still unfamiliar with many of them. According to project guidelines, I am to transport subjects singly, that way maintaining control never gets out of hand. Best way to do that, as my crew had agreed before I embarked, was to transport law enforcement first.

"With luck this really will work; the machine is yet to be tested in this way. It's a component Dr. Brown designed. Theoretically, the flow of time can be more easily manipulated to transport people with the machine than for it to receive targets. I guess I'll find out when this thing does or doesn't work."

Dillon worked night and day to reconstruct his vehicle. On a slower day, he found a mechanic's repair bay in the east-southeast door. He earnestly moved the vehicle into there, where he had tools to do the tougher work. After several more days, he got it running.

Soon, the only thing left to do was push that button once again. It was set up and ready for receiving. Dillon pushed the button while observing the staging area the subject was programmed to appear on.

He could hear a soft rushing sound after he pressed the button. The test, so far, seemed to be successful. In a long, anxious instant, the back of the figure of a middle-aged man began to form. In a bright blue glow, it looked as though black, peach, and brown grains of the man fell into place to paint his figure. He stood up straight and still. He had dark hair and wore a black long-sleeved shirt, which, even from the back, resembled a Detroit police uniform.

"He turned around and examined Dillon head to toe. Then he lifted his hand and pointed in his direction.

"You… you…" he said, pointing, but not accusingly, more in a vague recognition.

Dillon playfully turned slightly around and then back to face the mustached officer. "There's nobody else in the room, so you must be referring to me."

"You…" he said again. "You're that… I've seen you before…" He paused. "And… I just forgot where from." He eyed Dillon suspiciously, his eyes seeming to bore right through him, forcing Dillon to look away. They weren't in Detroit anymore, but this officer's persona still kept him alert, the same way teenagers often feel when a police car drives behind them on the road.

"My name, people around here call me Dillon." He extended his hand. As the mustached officer took it, Dillon read the Detroit police badge pinned to his chest. "Welcome, Chief. You *are* the chief of the DPF, right?"

"Yes, I am," he answered. 'The name's Murphy, Chief Paul Murphy." He stopped and backed away, letting go of Dillon's hand. "This may sound stupid, but where did every—" The bewildered look on his face made it obvious he hadn't realized until then that he was no longer where ever he thought he was only minutes before. "How… where in the world… am I?"

"I…" Dillon left his mouth open, but paused. "Good question."

"What?" the chief replied. "That doesn't make any sense. You mean to say you don't either? Who are you? Why am I here? And *how* am I here?'

"You forgot one question,' Dillon told him softly.

"What?" He shook his head.

"No, when."

"WHAT?"

Chapter 29

MURPHY HAD HEARD ME the first time, but it was hard for him to believe. After all, real time travel is relatively new, though the idea is older than anyone alive. Anyway, I soon found out who Chief Murphy was. He was from the year 2349. He succeeded Jack Palmer as the Detroit "C.O.P.," as he calls it. He transferred from Chicago only days after I left Detroit to join the homicide division. However, when Palmer stepped down, Murphy was offered the job.

"Working with Murphy didn't seem like a tough prospect. I was straightforward with him about my goals for the island town, and he seemed more than eager to be involved. It didn't take long for us to become good friends. After all, we were the only people on the island outside of the Kahukah village, save for Kahlif, Wakna, and his wife, Jaza.

"In one week, we built several huts. One for the planned general store, another for a possible bank, one for a town hall, and several for residents. We had help from the islanders, of course. Wakna and Kahlif showed us ways to design the huts to withstand harsh winds and rain, which won't come often."

"Although Murphy has taken to them quite easily, they are the only Kahukah people that will meet Murphy if I can help it. I don't want to get the Kahukah tribe involved. It would likely be disastrous. Of course, Wakna and Kahlif understood; they were elated to be given secrets from their 'gods' about their ethereal plans."

Soon, four men weren't enough. Jaza and her children kept to themselves, even the boys didn't help with a lot of the construction. Wakna's family spent a lot of time going back to their village during the days.

Dillon and Murphy tried daily to cooperate with the Kahukah in building sturdy huts. They needed better support and more careful design. Dillon got to the point where he had to bring more people to the island to help out. Besides, Murphy had been begging him to bring his partner, Chris Miller.

"Why are you so hell bent on not bringing anymore help?" Murphy finally asked him. It had been bothering him that anytime he suggested bringing more people to help build, Dillon was quick to refuse him.

Dillon had to think for a moment. "Mostly, it's because I think people would adjust more quickly if they had somewhere to stay first, a sacrifice I made in your case."

"Gee, thanks."

But after another couple more hours being short-handed, Dillon finally gave in. He agreed to bring *one* more person.

He took Murphy to the repair bay, and Murphy watched as Dillon made a reference check on Miller against his subject list. "You're in luck. Your buddy is approved for transmission."

He punched in the reference code attached to the profile for Chicago's Officer Chris Miller. After a bright blue light and a rushing sound, Officer Miller stood inside the dark repair bay of the bunker.

"Murphy?" Chris called. He seemed to be searching around. He finally turned toward Murphy. "Hey, there you are. You know that house up on Maple—" He saw Dillon standing next to his partner. He gave him a strange look and turned back to Murphy. "What happened with the lights in this place? Did you—"

He looked back around at the room and noticed the equipment at one end and the staging area that was now behind him. "Where… did I go through the wrong door or something, because I've never seen this room before…" He then turned back to Dillon. "And who are you?"

"Ta—er, Dillon."

"What's going on?" the officer looked to his comrade.

Murphy caught his friend up on everything that had been going on with the island. All the while, Miller sent suspicious glances in Dillon's direction.

Dissatisfied with Murphy's explanation, the despondent officer nudged him with his elbow and pulled him aside. "Are you nuts?" he began, when he was out of the whisper range of their alleged captor.

"No, Chris, this guy is legit," Murphy assured him. "Trust me. He's working with Karz on some sociological experiment. He first needs to develop a sort of society, and I'm helping him out. I asked him to send you too; thought you might be interested."

"What's in it for you?" Miller argued. "You're a successful homicide detective. We're *partners* in Chicago, buddy. You're the best cop I've come across since I lived there."

"Thanks, but I'm done with homicide, man. I've climbed the law enforcement ladder to the top already. My job consisted of managing unprofessional, rookie investigators and bugged androids." He shook his head. "I don't have any family around, so what's *not* in it for me?"

Murphy pointed to the badge pinned to his chest.

The officer squinted. "Detroit?… When?"

"*Chief* Paul Murphy, reporting," he said flatly. "I was going on seven months in Michigan when July came around. Detroit is headed down hill; there *is* no future for me in our present. My future's here now… in the past."

Adding up the time in his head, Miller decided Murphy's transfer would have come in only a few weeks. After *he* left the force, who would the officer get stuck with on duty?

He shook his head doubtfully. "This is incredible."

Murphy placed his hand on Miller's shoulder. "It's an adventure, man."

The reluctant officer glanced at Dillon again. "Are you for real?"

Dillon sighed. "Do you have another explanation for this?" Motioning toward the machine, Dillon slid open the door to the Compass Room, drawing its wonder into Miller's eyes.

Chapter 30

The second subject, a hesitant Officer Chris Miller, was a tremendous help to the progress we were making in securing the huts. He and Murphy worked well together; it was easy to see they were partners on the force.

"After his arrival, I spent some time sorting through the subject list more thoroughly. I spotted a name I thought I had recognized that according to the code would have placed him in the mid-twentieth century. Curious, I decided to bring him to the island as well.

"He was an archeologist and historian with very few details recorded about his life. The biography was incomplete, leaving little to go by but his profession. Still, he was my next target subject, Daniel Stevens."

A rather young man appeared on the staging area. He wore a leather hat and goggles like that of a World War I pilot. When he turned to face Dillon, Dillon saw that he had a monocle over his left eye and a scar on his right cheek. He also had a hook on the end of his left arm, where a hand once rested.

"Excuse me," the man said, "my name is Stevens. I am, or was, on an expedition in Egypt with my crew to find rare gems." He didn't seem at all surprised about the turn of events that would have brought him from the deserts of Egypt to an underground bunker. He was nonchalant as he extended his hand to the man he found in the dark.

"Welcome to the island named Ailiokahu." Dillon shook his extended hand, obviously the right.

"Ailiokahu, huh? Is that Hawaiian?"

"No, it's Dinokahu, actually," Dillon answered. "It literally means the 'Island of the Time God.'"

They talked for a while. The man's name was Danny Stevens, a professional jewel and precious stone appraiser.

"So you were a jewel appraiser prior to coming here?" Dillon asked him.

"Yes," Stevens confirmed. "For almost a year now I've been accompanying several African expeditions through Congo and the jungles there. Back, or excuse me, later on in 1941, I went, or will go, or whatever, to Egypt, and that's when I ended up here."

"So, you're from 1941," Dillon concluded.

"Yes. Well, actually, no," was Stevens' reply. "I'm from a later time than that, but I was sent through time to 1939. Now I'm in 18 what, 40s?"

"Exactly, 1841," Dillon answered. He stepped back for a moment. Then he started to think. "So this isn't your first time traveling experience?"

"No, not in the least. I ran a few tests with a scientist named Taran Flint."

Taran Flint? Dillon thought. *Whoa… this guy… I know him.* "T… T… Taran… Flint?" Dillon's jaw dropped. "That's… that's not… not… possible… Wait, what year did Flint begin these experiments with you?"

"That would've been 2350."

"2350." Dillon paused. *So I must have brought Stevens from 2350 to 1939 after, in my view, what's happening now but before this event in Stevens' life… Wow, this is confusing.* "That means you *are* Professor Stevens!"

Stevens immediately thought it was ridiculous that he hadn't recognized Taran right away. "Wow, so… well, I know what you're going to be up to…" he said under his breath. "So I guess, I should say, how are you?"

"I'm doing all right," Dillon answered. He wasn't sure what to say; he wasn't expecting someone from his own time who would know what he was doing here. "Uh… I'm starting a little town here, and—"

"Yeah, I know, you're gonna—" He stopped short. "On second thought, I shouldn't say anything. It wouldn't be good."

"What do you mean?"

"Well, I already know about the town. When you came back for the Time—well, no, just drop it."

"No. C'mon, Danny, just tell me."

"I can't tell you, buddy," Stevens insisted. "You know it'll mess everything up. Just do what you're gonna do. Pretend I didn't say anything."

Dillon sighed. "All right, Stevens. You win." He had to admit it; he knew the potential of "changing the past" or future or whatever would happen. "And, don't call me Taran up there, Danny. It's Dillon right now."

"All right, I know." Stevens made his way to the end of the south hall. "Oh, and Dillon, good luck with everything. Don't worry about not bringing me the first time. It's gonna be an awesome experience, no doubt."

Dillon smiled as Stevens proceeded up the ladder. *That's… what he said before I left Detroit… He remembers that? Three years later?*

It had only been three months since Dillon had last talked to his colleague in Detroit, yet to Stevens it had been much longer. It was a strange experience that Dillon knew only time travel could convey on someone's life.

He looked at Professor Stevens as a different person at that time. He never bore the scar, wore the monocle, nor had he the hook on his left arm when Dillon had known him. All of his characteristic traits didn't exist in 2348.

The monocle covered Stevens' blind eye, which had been badly burned from an explosion. He had lost his hand in Egypt; it was crushed by a brick of an Egyptian obelisk his team had been sent to dismantle. The scar was caused by the knife of a Saudi marauder that he encountered in northern Egypt six months prior.

Soon after Professor Stevens was brought to the island, Dillon couldn't help but bring more people. He knew he was restricted to the researched list, but from those names he chose randomly. He started bringing anyone, from anywhere, and anywhen—that is, any*time*. In the beginning, most of the people came from the Detroit area. He wanted to see if other people could change as much as Stevens had.

The first was Kelley Longley, a cook from Lansing. Raymond Caldor was from Detroit, so Dillon knew him. He and his wife, Jayne, were police officers there. They and their son came next. Others included: Joe Young, the supermarket clerk; Mr. Owner, an auctioneer; Erik O'Connor, Jacob Brown, and Isaac McNally, a submarine crew from 2021; and Timothy Talbiss, a reformed pick-pocket who would become the owner and operator of the town's general store.

Dillon met with each of them personally when they came, but only briefly, continuing to transport others immediately. The guys didn't have a problem helping Dillon create the island town. For many of them, their own lives didn't compare to the possibilities this character proposed to them. Kelley, on the other hand, didn't do a lot of the heavy lifting. She helped Wakna's wife, Jaza, braid ropes to use in lashing the huts together.

Later, after many of the huts were near completion to their standards, Murphy met Dillon with an idea.

"Hey, Dillon." Murphy approached Dillon as he was preparing to set his time machine to stand by. "Looks like your *one* extra set of hands did a good job building huts, huh?"

Dillon laughed. "Very funny." He turned back to his invention. "You'd be surprised at how addicting this experience can be, Murphy."

"Yeah, I get it." Murphy nodded. "You worked your whole life on this one project, this one toy. Now that it's operational you gotta play with it, right?"

Dillon's response was just a nod.

"Anyway, I came down because I've got an idea," Murphy said, changing the subject. "I think it would be better if we had a professional construction crew to build real buildings. I mean, in time—"

"Why didn't I think of that?" Dillon exclaimed. *And supposedly I planned for everything.* He shook his head in disbelief at his own negligence. *A real crew could make more permanent homes, instead of huts.*

"I know a great construction crew from rural areas of Michigan," Dillon told him. "I'll bring George Sullivan and his crew: Nathan Brick, Justin O'Brien, Sean Formann, Ian Jones, and Brian White."

So, before shutting down the machine, he had to transport the last six people. Right away, Justin was put to work drawing up plans. Sean was sent to get strong tree trunks, and Ian was sent to the "real" world to get construction vehicles, equipment, and supplies to build a lumber mill of sorts. The others were sent out to get better support for the huts that were already built.

Chapter 31

It was hot and sultry the next day. Kel, as they called Kelley Longley most of the time, prepared some lemonade for the crew for later in the afternoon. In the morning she had prepared eggs from Wakna's and Kahlif's huts. Their families had begun a small chicken farm after leaving the Kahukah town, from which she'd gathered the eggs. There was hardly enough to feed the whole town.

Dillon was eating in his own hut when Kel came in. "Hey, good morning, Kel. What can I help you with?"

"I—" she began, but Tim rushed in and bumped her accidentally.

"Mr. Dillon, did you get that order for the—oh." He saw Kel on her hands and knees, trying to get up. "I'm sorry about that, Kel. I'll help you up." He reached down to her.

"Thank you," Kel said. Tim pulled her up and she turned to Dillon. "I've got a couple of things I'd like to address. That is, if you have the time."

Dillon looked over at Tim, who nodded back, which to Dillon meant he had time to wait for whatever Kel needed.

"Sure, Kel." He walked behind his desk. "Have a seat, guys."

They pulled up two chairs that were sitting by the door to the hut.

"Careful with that one, Tim. It was Murphy's first, so I'm not sure if the knots will hold," Dillon warned.

Tim chuckled. "I think I'll stand."

Kel sat down anyway, but carefully. She sighed silently, as the chair did not collapse and send her tumbling to the sandy floor.

"Umm, listen, I think this island thing of yours is really great," Kel started off, not with a grave undertone, but with a complimentary quality to initiate a request. "But I've been thinking about what my life was going to be like before you brought me here…"

"And?" Dillon cringed a little, as he thought he may have inadvertently jeopardized his mission.

"Well, I had these plans of starting a restaurant back home, you know," Kel said. "Home-cooked meals and fresh foods would have been my specialties. It's something my neighborhood really needed at a time like this, that is, now, or then…"

"I know what you're saying." Dillon sighed on the inside. "I think that's a great idea. You should open up one here; it'll be a good social place for the town as we start developing a society."

Kel was excited now. "Really? You mean it?"

"Of course!" Dillon stood up. "I have a system already set up that can get you anything you need from produce to cookware."

"Wow, that's so cool!" The phrase revealed her character and age. Kel was only twenty-one when Dillon brought her to the island. And now she was going to be able to run a restaurant like she'd always dreamed, without the cost of starting a small business. "It would have taken me forever to pay for a place in Lansing."

"I'll show it to you guys." Dillon motioned for the two to follow him. He led them down the tunnel he had made that ran from his hut to the hatch leading to the bunker compound. "I hooked up my time machine to the R.S. I designed and tested before coming to the island. I know we were talking about establishing a 'store' last night. That's what you came for, right, Tim?" he asked at the end of the south hall.

"Yes," Tim answered.

"What does R.S. stand for?" Kel asked.

"Replenishing System," Tim replied, leaning toward her. He generally didn't expound on his answers. He could have added that he and Dillon had gone over all of these details the night before and that Dillon needed to program it, which is why he didn't have his own supplies the night before. He could have also informed her that he'd written up a list, per Dillon's request, of the stock he was getting for his "store." He could have gone on about the fact that the store was simply a place where people could get the food they would need for the day for free (at the moment). He could have gone on about everything else he had discussed with Dillon the night before, but he didn't.

"Replenishing System" was the only answer that escaped his mouth, leaving Kel in the dark about the semantics of his own business operation.

"How does it work?" Kel questioned, looking over the strange looking machine. It looked like two twenty gallon drums, each hooked up to three large hoses and hundreds of colorful wires braided together in a clear rubber casement. They all connected to the very same control panel Dillon had repeatedly used already.

"At a set time of day, which is controlled by this dial here," Dillon explained, pointing to a numbered dial displaying one through twenty-four, "the time machine activates and transports whatever is inside this corresponding drum to 2348. The next dial is set for a time to receive food or supplies *from* 2348, or the year set, from the counterpart machine which is in the Karz building. The machine has been designed to parallel its counterpart, so if, for example, it's May 3 here, it's May 3 there when the transfer takes place. Got it?"

"I've got the basic idea, yeah." Kel nodded. "How do you know what you're getting, though?"

"We type in the order and send it to 2348," Dillon answered. "It's that simple. However, just because we have to make it more complicated than it is, any item you should want is logged in this book and on this computer." Dillon pointed out a monitor off to the side of the contraption. "Everything has its own twelve digit assigned number combination, each beginning with one letter. Any special orders or items you'll have to type in, but the people at Karz will be stubborn if you type in 'popcorn' instead of…" He flipped through the massive book with three inch thick binding, first to the index, then to some page in the middle. "There. 'P15–456–771–9099.'"

"Okay," Tim replied.

"Oh, but don't type '9909,' because that's parsley, not popcorn." Dillon smiled. "Just be careful when you type; you never know what you could get if you type in the wrong numbers."

"What about costs?" Kel asked, ignoring Dillon's comment.

"What do you mean?" Dillon asked. "Oh, right, it isn't free. The company I work for supplies all of that. They take it out of my checks, which are going to my, well…" He sighed and avoided that conversation. "Yeah, 'real-world' money isn't an issue."

"That reminds me," Tim said. "How are we going to set up an economic system?"

"I'm planning on getting a mint of sorts built in combination with the bank…" Dillon's voice trailed off. "Well, we'll deal with that when we get there."

"You got it," Tim answered. "No rush."

"You were saying you needed some supplies now, right?" Dillon asked them both.

"Yeah, I've written up the list right here," Tim said. He handed it to Dillon.

"I could use a couple things," Kel added. "The workers are getting hungry, as well as me. I figured I could make something for lunch."

"Do you already have a list of what you're going to get?" Dillon asked her.

She pointed to her head. "My list is up here."

Dillon handed the list back to Tim. "Well, I'll leave the two of you to handle this. I've got more important work to finish up with. I'll be back in a few minutes to finish up." He left through the hall from which they came.

Chapter 32

THE SEARCH THROUGH THE book lasted nearly half an hour for the page full of items Tim needed. Kel read them off as Tim searched through the book. Everything was listed alphabetically with sections and subsections, most of which didn't make logical sense to either of them.

Kel looked through the list of items that filled Tim's page. The lines of the paper were filled out first, and then wherever Tim could fit it, he wrote sideways, upside down, and in tiny letters. "This is crazy, Tim. There's probably more stuff on here than in the book."

"That, th… well, there's another side… too, Kel," he stammered. Kel glared at him when she turned it over. "But, really, I don't think," he said, clearing his throat, "that there's any more on the list than in the book. Look at this. There must be a thousand different cheeses! I'm just looking for cheese, and it fills three, four, five… no, six and a half pages! There's Swiss, Brie, Colby, Havarti, Ardrahan, cheddar… and then, they can all be mild, sharp, extra sharp, 'seriously sharp'? Is there a difference? White cheddar, yellow cheddar, white American, yellow American… it's not even really yellow! It's orange!" He was yelling out of frustration.

"Okay, okay, Tim, calm down," Kel said. Now she was nervous. "I'll search and you look at the list. I've crossed off everything that you already punched in." She handed the paper to him and stood over by the monitor where he had been.

Needless to say, Dillon made it back before they finished. Their order went through, and in seconds the hoses radiated with a bright blue light that instantly filled the drums.

"Order up." Dillon smiled.

"All right, I'm outta here," Tim said. "I'll take my drum full of supplies to the store and then begin setting up the displays." Tim unhooked one of the large metal drums from the machine and unscrewed the tube and wires from it. He carried it out toward the steep stairs of the south hall and toward Dillon's hut.

"Well, when Tim gets back, I'll lock up, Kel," Dillon told her. "Do you want me to help you carry yours up?"

"No, I can get it," Kel answered. "Thank you, anyway, but... umm... I have a question," Kel said. "Before you leave could you bring a friend of mine here? I would hate to be left here alone. No offense to Jaza, but we don't really connect, and she's the only other woman."

"Yeah," Dillon said. "No problem."

"Besides, Lindsey's always wanted to help me out with the restaurant; it was kind of *our* thing."

"Of course," Dillon answered. He was excited. Not only did he find people that enjoyed being here despite leaving their entire lives, but Kel wanted to refer a friend as well. Dillon thought this was the greatest thing. Simple as that, his dream was coming true.

So Dillon brought a certain Lindsey Fowler to the island from Kel's neighborhood. She was happy to see Kel, scared but excited to be on a time "twisted" island. When Kel told her the plan for the new restaurant, she was elated.

The two headed back to Kel's hut. They decided they would practice their cooking skills and test out new recipes there for the others to try. When the construction crew was ready to build what they decided to call "Kel's Place," they would be prepared.

Murphy entered just as they were leaving.

"Is this supposed to be the busiest part of your island?" Murphy commented, referring to the "secret" bunker Dillon was running.

"No. Actually, I didn't want many people to know about it," Dillon answered. "But that's a difficult thing to accomplish when it's the first place anyone sees when they come here."

"Well, I can assign the crew to build an addition to either your hut or the town hall where we can store this thing," Murphy suggested. "Or we could move it and build around it."

"I like the first idea better," Dillon replied.

"I'm getting bored. There's nothing here," Murphy said.

Dillon looked up. *That's not a random thought, right?* Dillon thought, but "I see..." was his only reply.

"I just... thought I'd put it out there," Murphy said.

"No, you're right. I should vary my citizens a little. Otherwise, living here would be just like living back home; there'd be nothing magical about this place at all. They may as well stay in 2348," Dillon said. *Besides, it wouldn't prove anything that my experiment is supposed to be based on*, Dillon thought. "So what I have to do is get people from diverse times."

"Hey, great idea," Murphy exclaimed. "It's not that I want hate crimes and a ton of other problems that arise from diversity, but as long as it doesn't get really bad, I've got something to do, right?"

"Uh... yeah, sounds like a plan," Dillon answered. "I'll bring someone from..." He typed four random number keys without looking. "Just to make it interesting..." The numbers came to one, eight, seven, and two. "1872 sounds like a good year." Dillon peered over at Murphy, then noticed the drum sitting on the RS nearby. "Oh, shoot."

"What?" Murphy jumped.

"Kel forgot her drum of food and supplies for her restaurant," Dillon informed him.

"Oh," Murphy was relieved. "I'll take it to her," he offered as he lifted the metal drum. "I'll meet the newcomers later. Just go on with what you do without me, it's all right."

"All right." Dillon pressed the button as Murphy left the room. The machine hissed on one side, and Dillon heard a pop as four men formed in a blue light on the staging area. The one in back appeared to be chasing the others, or had been until they came there.

Dillon leaned over, grabbed a hose that one of the components to the R.S. was connected to, and reattached it. When he looked back up, he was just in time to see the four men run out the door. He ran to chase them, but he was too late. They had run right out of the bunker.

Chapter 33

DILLON LOCKED THE DOOR to leave so he could chase down his most recent prospects. As he approached the south hall, he heard a loud crash. He ran to the hatch and found two storage drums lying on the floor, two covers to the drums, and Murphy and Tim behind them, lying on the ground. They looked like they'd fallen down the stairs.

"What in the world?" Dillon helped Tim up as Murphy stood up the drums. Murphy's head was bruised, but he wasn't badly hurt. Tim brushed himself off. "What happened, guys?"

Tim moaned. "We were carrying the—" Murphy handed him his sunglasses. "Thanks... the RS drums back down when this stampede of people bumped and pushed us to the wall," he replied. "I lost my footing in the commotion. Since Officer Murphy was in front of me, I took him down the stairs with me."

"All right," Dillon said. "You guys can clean up and attach the drums to the tubes. Use my keycard to lock up. I'll go after those four."

"How will you know who you're going after?" Tim asked.

"They're the only ones here that look like they performed in movies with John Wayne," Dillon clambered up the stairs. The sight he beheld at the top was a nicely dressed man sitting on the ground, propped against the corner of the room.

He looked unconscious, so Dillon checked his pulse. He was alive and his pulse seemed normal. Dillon picked him up and put him onto the bed. His dress shirt was blue, and he wore a brown leather vest over it. His gray hair matted his head with sweat, and his hat lay on the floor near the stairs to the bunker.

"I don't want to let the others run rampant. I'll just have to leave him here," Dillon said after checking the man for any cuts or abrasions. There was only one small bump, which Dillon assumed was from bumping his head on the wall.

Dillon then ran outside.

Out in the middle of the street in front of the Island Inn, he found a strange, heavy-set man in gray, facing away from him, looking around at the town. He wore a brimmed hat similar to that of the man in Dillon's hut. When the man turned around, Dillon saw he had a black, bushy mustache, an unshaven face, a star on his hat, and a sheriff star pinned to his chest.

"Excuse me, sir," Dillon said. He suddenly saw the revolver in the man's right hand. "Whoa! Hey, put that away, will ya?" He put his hands out like a shield, as if it would help deflect the bullets.

"All righty, I'd be happy to, but who're you?" The sheriff put the gun into his holster, much to Dillon's great relief.

"My name's Dillon," he said.

"Mah name is West, Sheriff Wyatt West," the sheriff replied. "Nice to meet you, Mr. Dillon."

"Heh, heh, that's pretty funny!"

"What? What's funny?" He reached for his gun.

"Huh? Oh! Nothing. I forgot," Dillon raised his hands again. "You're about a century too early… sorry. I just… you know, put… sheriff and… Mr. Dillon." He shook his head. "Never mind. What were you saying?"

Wyatt put his hand down. "I was wonderin' what you do here in town."

"I am… I guess, what you could call the mayor," Dillon answered. "The whole thing is probably a little bit too complicated for you to—"

"What's that s'posed to mean?" Wyatt cut in. He pulled his gun out once again. He didn't appreciate the insult to his vanity.

"Oh, no!" Dillon cried. "No, you've got the wrong idea. See, I'm trying to find some gangsters that headed this way. I… it looked like you were… you were chasing them, right?"

"Yeah," Wyatt said. "Yah know 'ere dey went?"

"Well, pl—could you put the gun down?"

"Huh-uh." Wyatt shook his head. "Where'd dey go?"

"Put the gun down."

"Are yah skeared uh guns er somethin'?

"Yeah, all right, and I'm in charge in these parts. Put the gun on the ground before I get the local sheriff on you," Dillon threatened him. "He'll get you to put the gun down."

The sheriff cautiously lowered to put the gun on the sandy ground.

"Kick it over here now!" Dillon commanded.

"Can't," he answered.

"Why not?" Dillon shouted.

"It won't slide over tuh ya through the dirt."

"Then... then pick it up and toss it lightly over to me!"

West did so.

Dillon caught it. "All right. Now, who..." He threw it into his hut. "That was a real gun, too." He shuddered, his voice shaky.

"Well, what good does throwin' it in there do ya?" West inquired.

"I can't talk that well at gunpoint; it's not something I've become accustomed to doing, all right?" Dillon answered. "Now, would kindly tell me who it was that ran by me earlier?"

"The ones I was chasin'?" Wyatt said. "Wow, I chased 'em farther than I 'spected."

"Wh... what," Dillon stammered, "what does that mean?"

"They were the Trickster 'n Flatfoot Thompson, the two most notorious bandits in Laredo!" Wyatt said. "You never heard of 'em?"

"No, I can't say that I have."

"Well, there's no use jawin.'" Wyatt looked around again. "Let's find these bandits before it gets too late." He turned toward the town, but Dillon caught the sheriff's shoulder by his jacket to stop him.

"You know... wait, why are you after them now?"

"No reason in particular. It's just cuz theys bandits," Wyatt replied. "We don't need a reason no more."

"Yeah, well, you're not in Laredo anymore," Dillon pointed out. "Now we're playing my game by my rules. They are fine until they cross me or the rules in my town. But until that time, you leave them alone. 'Theys' not bandits yet."

The sheriff ignored Dillon's derogatory mocking. "If I ain't in Laredo," Wyatt replied, "where am I?"

It took some time, but Dillon got Wyatt used to the fact that he was on an uncharted 1841 island. He did have one request after that, however. It was for Dillon to bring one more person: Wyatt's best and most trusted deputy, Bubba. Bubba didn't have a normal reaction, though. He had a bad history of paranoia and broke down when he reached the island. He had to be contained for a while.

Chapter 34

SOON, THE TOWN HAD calmed down, and everyone was out and about meeting people and making new friends or enemies. Dillon had put using his time machine aside and refused to bring anymore people at others' requests. He needed to get to know the people he was already responsible for before bringing anyone else, especially if they were potentially dangerous or unpredictable.

A couple nights later, during what had become a nightly vigil for Dillon, he was watching over the man who he had found unconscious in his hut. The man finally woke up and introduced himself as Aaron Richmond. He said he'd been working in the Laredo General Store when he and the sheriff began chasing Trickster and Flatfoot. That's when they all suddenly ended up in the bunker. He ended up running into the wall when Flatfoot pushed him to the side at the top of the stairs.

Dillon and Aaron were sitting outside Dillon's hut in two chairs opposite each other at a small table. A torch was lit, hanging on the side of the doorway, illuminating the night's darkness by their site.

"So, these gangsters, Trickster and Flatfoot," Dillon asked, "are they dangerous?" He needed to know how he should address this situation, if he should send them back to their own times before they learned too much.

Aaron scoffed at the question he was asked. "You obviously don't know who you're dealin' with. Trickster and Flatfoot are notorious for startin' trouble wherever they can find it, *whenever* they can find it."

"So, I should find them and get them back to Laredo as soon as possible, then," Dillon said.

Aaron immediately changed his tune. "Well, to tell you the truth, they mayn't be misbehavin' too bad, what with the Wolf Pack Gang not bein' around here. They's always fightin' with them for territory outside Laredo."

"So they won't be a problem?"

Aaron straightened up. "So, Dillon, you say you're from the future, right?"

"Yeah, about five hundred years after your time," he replied.

"Don't they got crooks where you're from?"

"Well, where I'm from, you sometimes can't tell the crooks from the cops. The crooks don't even have to leave home to rob a bank. The innocent don't usually stay that way for long, I guess." Dillon leaned back in his seat, being careful not to break it. It was, after all, the first chair he'd ever built from bamboo culms.

"And gangs, they rule entire cities from the ghetto ground up," he continued. "We might have your time to thank for that. People in your towns, even in your government, are going to become corrupt. Things will change. Some for the worse, a lot for the better, but your country is in for a long, painful journey to prosperity.

"I wouldn't even say America has reached that in my time. We still have crime, and we still have murder. There's so many people, we don't know them by face anymore. You might know everyone in Laredo, Mr. Richmond, but I don't know *anyone* in Detroit."

"America don't sound like it *did* get much better," the general store manager stated.

"Well, don't get me wrong," Dillon recanted. "It's not just America. Corruption took on several forms over the years. Everything has been about money, and that's how things have turned out. But, if you think the Transcontinental Railroad you guys have is impressive, you should see some of the things we've created for ourselves."

"Like time machines." Aaron stood up.

"Yeah." Dillon stood up as well. "Among other things. Most of it recreational. A lot of it is scientific discovery. Children in your time are going to be the leaders in your next generation, and they've got some wild imaginations at work."

Aaron sighed. "Well, Mr. Dillon, I think I'll have a look-see at this town tonight. I'll come around tomorrow."

"All right. I'll see you around." Dillon pointed to a nearby hut. "There's free room and board at the Island Inn, right up there if you need a place to stay."

"Thanks."

The communal hut that the people had stayed in for the first night was now the Island Inn. It served the same purpose, but like Kel's Place and Tim's Shop, Danny Stevens ran the Island Inn. Dillon retired to his bunker shortly after. Aaron had gotten him thinking about a number of things that never really crossed his mind in the past. He'd learned about the grafting in the nineteenth and twentieth centuries, and about the gangs of the past, but he had learned about it in a school atmosphere. Learning about something was a lot different than seeing the past face to face and interacting with it.

Chapter 35

I'VE GOT AN IDEA!" Murphy exclaimed, running into Dillon's hut. He sat down in a rugged chair in front of Dillon's desk, behind which Dillon sat. "See, we can get these blocks of—"

Dillon looked up. "Whoa, whoa, whoa. Wait a minute!" He rose from his chair. "Murphy, do you always start off your conversations this way, in mid-idea?"

"What do you mean… oh… like that," Murphy replied. Dillon nodded. "Sorry about that. What I was referring to was the safe for the bank."

"Okay, go right ahead." Dillon nodded. "Now that we all know what we're talking about."

"We can get these blocks of concrete, see." Murphy separated his hands to show the size as he talked. "And we can construct the entire interior safe wall with these. We can make the outer walls still appear to be made of wood, you know—"

He turned around be sure no one could hear what he was saying. Aaron Richmond walked in. Dillon looked at Aaron. "I'll be with you in a minute, Mr. Richmond, if you wouldn't mind just waiting outside."

"Oh, all righty." Aaron walked out and closed the door, but he didn't leave. He hung around to the left of the doorway where Dillon and Murphy couldn't see him. He then listened in, trying to look as casual and inconspicuous as possible for people passing by. He took out a pocket knife, produced a piece of wood, and began whittling.

"Anyway," Murphy continued, "if the vault looks like wood and is made of concrete blocks, it would fool the criminals, you know, should there be an attempted robbery. Then we can install a metal vault within the concrete structure and build a wooden-looking secret door to the vault as well."

"So the vault is completely hidden?" Dillon asked.

"Exactly. Only you, myself, and the banker will know it's even there."

"And the builders," Dillon added.

"Well, yeah," Murphy replied. "And then, I know what you're thinking, 'where do we put the money while customers are there,' right?" He didn't wait for a reply. "Well, during the day, the banker will keep a small amount of money in a safe that can be seen by everyone, you know, in front of the vault wall. Then at night most of the money can be transferred into the big vault."

"Oh, that's a great idea," Dillon said. "Kind of like a security precaution. That's very good. I can go and retrieve the supplies that we'll need for that job right away. I'll send Ian for a list of supplies: lumber, cinder blocks, metal, a vault, countertop, and—"

"Cinder blocks?" Murphy looked at Dillon quizzically.

"Yeah, those blocks of concrete you referred to are called cinder blocks," Dillon explained. "They used them for construction a few centuries ago, before they developed the supplies for what we use now, or will use, in, you know, 2348."

"Oh. Anyway, it was Kel's idea," Murphy added. "She told it to me last night. She said she thought she saw someone hanging around the construction site last night while she was closing her restaurant," he explained.

"Really?"

"Yeah, do you think that's a problem?"

"Well, with those old west guys I just brought..." Dillon's voice trailed off. "It shouldn't be a problem. And we've got your guys and Jayne, so just have them keep an eye out like Kel did."

"Yeah, sure, Dillon," Murphy answered. "Just so long as we're prepared."

He began to walk toward the door, but suddenly he turned back around. "Oh, yeah, I forgot. One more thing." Murphy reached into his pocket and pulled out a small piece of paper. "Kel asked about this." He tossed it to Dillon.

"A neon sign?" Dillon asked as he read the paper.

"Well, she said any sign would do, but neon or lights were best," Murphy replied.

Dillon sighed. "We'll get lights, and we can hook them up when we actually get electricity here," Dillon answered. "Of course, George said he could recommend a couple of electricians. We'll get them sometime tomorrow."

"Mr. Brick said that Sean and Ian could do electrical stuff," Murphy pointed out.

"All right, whatever works," Dillon answered. "I'll send Ian to get lights, wires, junction boxes, and the other electrical stuff tomorrow along with the bank supplies. Then you can get someone to make Kel's sign." *I would imagine the compound's nuclear power could power the town*, he thought.

"Okay," Murphy said. "Is there anyone you could suggest in particular?"

"Yeah," Dillon answered. "Joe Young and Mr. Owner are looking for jobs right now until Mr. Owner's "Auction Block" is built. Then there are the divers: O'Connor, Brown, and McNally, who also came in today looking for jobs. Of course, they suggested deep sea fishing and scuba diving expeditions, or at least a fish market to start."

"I'll suggest that to Kel." Murphy opened the door to leave. Aaron saw this, so he ran around to the back where no one was looking and casually walked back in the direction of the door. "You know, I'll never get used to having to turn these… these knob things to open doors," Murphy said as he held the door open.

"I highly doubt that we'll have electronic sliding doors anytime soon," Dillon remarked as Murphy walked out.

Murphy saw Aaron Richmond walking by and caught his attention. "Hey, Mr. Richmond!" Murphy waved. "Dillon's all set and ready to see you now."

"Yeah, I'll be right there," Aaron said. He then added an excuse so he wouldn't lead any suspicion to himself. "I was on my way to the store. I'll be right back." Then he was off.

Chapter 36

AARON MADE HIS WAY to the other side of town, where a hut had been sloppily built. It had been Dillon and Murphy's second hut, but it had been partially blown over by strong wind only days after being built. Aaron ran to the back and grabbed a shovel.

He came upon two other men who looked as though they had been digging for quite a while. They had already started a wide hole and had shoveled the excess dirt into the hut. This served two important functions. One was to dispose of excess dirt without other people knowing what was going on; the forest behind the hut also aided that. The second function was to keep the hut from collapsing, which would also expose their secret hideaway.

One of the workers wore a green tuxedo, vest, collared shirt, and pants. He wore a black top hat with a small tear in the rim and a black tie tied in a bow, and he had a golden tooth where an upper canine should be. He snarled as he worked and growled softly whenever he hit a large rock. Then he looked like he wanted to throw it at somebody.

The other worker had a torn, red, buttoned shirt. It was partially unbuttoned, not because of the unbearable heat, but because most of the buttons were no longer present. His ragged appearance was opposite that of the visage displayed by his neat, formal-looking partner. His pants were ripped at the right knee. The leg was liable to get torn off anytime now. This man didn't have a golden tooth, but he could use one, two, or about a dozen. Most of his back teeth were black from smoking, and some of his front teeth were missing from getting into brawls.

Aaron Richmond didn't fit in with either of them physically. He was dressed up more than the others, with more expensive clothes. Nevertheless, they were a team. His real name, in fact, was Aaron Thomas, but his fellow gang members called him "Lefty" because he was left-handed. The man in green's name was John Smith, also known as "The Trickster" because of his "magical" talents. The one in red, of course, was "Flatfoot" Thompson, the leader.

"Hey, how long is this gonna take?" Trickster threw the spade shovel down to the ground.

"It's gonna take as long as it takes to get a decent-sized tunnel," Lefty explained, "which doesn't have to take a very long time, that is, if y'all will dig when yer s'posed tuh dig an' talk when yer s'posed tuh talk. And dis is diggin' time, awright?"

"Keep yer voice down, Lefty," Flatfoot commanded gruffly. "We gotta all stay low here, else we might as well give ourselves in. Now get in here and start diggin,' or I'll come up and get ya m'self."

"Good idea," Lefty replied, jumping into the dirt with the shovel ready. "Finally, yer makin' some sense." He looked over at Trickster, who had stopped working. "Now dig, Trickster, DIG!"

They continued digging for a while when Lefty began to tell something new. "Hey, guys, I got some good news."

"What is it?" Flatfoot didn't even look away from his work.

"I was outside Dillon's hut earlier," Lefty told them. "Ya know, the mayor of this place. Anyhow, he was talking about the bank and how it was going to be built. I heard them mention exactly how they'll store the money and everything!"

The gang made little progress during the duration of the night, mostly because they were listening to Lefty's strategy of infiltrating the bank. However, they did finish a good sized hole by the next morning when the sun came out.

Progress at the bank went even better. Lefty visited occasionally to see the progress, but no one was allowed inside the building since they were building the vault. But restricted access didn't stop Lefty; he checked into the bank routinely every two hours by peeking through the windows or between doors.

Chapter 37

By the next morning the safe was finished, and Murphy and Dillon were working on their next priority: a banker.

"I met with Murphy today," Dillon wrote. He'd been writing since he landed on the island in order to document a log for Mr. Thompson when he got back. He was growing hesitant, however, since he wasn't following the proper objectives in his mission. The log might then be solely for his documentation. "He wanted me to get more police forces, but I reminded him that we needed to get down to business with the completion of the bank. We needed a banker.

"We were discussing the matter when the sheriff came sauntering in to voice his opinion. He suggested we get a banker who had been in the field and experienced a robbery, or the prevention of one. We needed to get someone who "knew the potential burglars personally." Of course he was implying that I bring a banker from his time, so I checked out the history of his friend, Banker Reuben Milton. He seemed like a strict but decent fellow, so I brought him here to look after the vault and do all that teller and banker stuff.

"I'll need to get someone else, too, but I'll get him later on when Mr. Milton settles in. I'll probably get someone from my time. That way Milton can benefit from the technology and security we can supply. The money and Milton will be safer that way.

"As to the money itself, I hadn't even given a thought. I mean, Wakna told me of the mines where Kahukah got the gold they used for the altar, but Kahukah insisted gold was too valuable for the village to use outside of tribute to their gods. That gave me an idea, which Wakna helped me follow through. He and I went to the Kahukah village yesterday to address it. When I'd finished talking to him, Kahukah had two of his strongest palace men continue the mining. The gold and other ores were to be brought to Wakna's hut, where the center entrance to the compound is located. They were instructed to leave the ore in a small shed that was used for storing chicken feed.

"So, that said, minting the money is going to be another process entirely. After it's been refined, I'm simply going to store the gold in the vault that is to be built. Milton and I can go over the details later."

Dillon placed his journal in the drawer and locked it as Wakna entered with Kahlif following close behind him. They looked impressed with the progress of the town, but they liked it. That was the problem. They wanted to live and interact with the strange new people.

"Want we to live with these 'Kel's' and 'Joe's,'" Kahlif said. "To not mention the food guys have here you." His mouth began watering.

"What do you mean?" Dillon responded.

"No live we in town your," Wakna answered.

"Of course you do." Dillon shrugged.

"Farm our of chickens is away far from town this," Kahlif explained. "Almost is like not are we part of town. Have we to walk long so that, zho, almost like not are we part of town, far so it is."

"You know what?" Dillon said. "You're right. You guys live too far from the town to really feel like a part of it." Then he added, almost to himself, "Besides, you guys would make the town even more diverse, being in town more often."

"Zhonin," Wakna answered. "Good does sound it. Jaza and family my will be happy. Daughters the food like they, and sons bring want them their wives in time."

"I'll have some people help you build a new chicken farm for your families near mine," Dillon suggested. "That way you'll be right near the center of town." Then Dillon got an idea. "Actually, you guys could stay in the other rooms in my hut," he offered. "That is, until your new farm is built."

"Oh, could oppose not we," Wakna said.

"*Im*pose," Dillon corrected. "And it wouldn't be any trouble. Make yourselves at home."

The natives then left to get their families and personal belongings. Meanwhile, Dillon prepared not for their arrival, but for their departure. He escaped down his hatch, which the natives still didn't know about, and closed it. Then he hurried to the central hatch and opened it. He climbed up and peeked through the trapdoor. The rug still remained over it, so Dillon couldn't see inside the hut. He could, however, hear the Kahukah families talking amongst themselves.

When they finally left, he opened the trapdoor and climbed out. He closed the door to the hut and checked to see if the islanders had forgotten anything. No, only the rug. He installed a makeshift lock on the door.

He covered the hatch up with sand on the floor, rolled up the rug, and placed it neatly outside by the window. He planned to make this hut a secret above ground base. He could have his computer station here. The ceiling hatch was the one place in the compound the people had not yet seen. He might have some privacy yet, as long as he was careful about when he visited.

He crawled over to where the hatch was and began to descend. Suddenly he heard voices, so he quickly unlocked the door and jumped into the hatch, shutting the trapdoor behind him.

Dillon didn't get another opportunity that day to steal away from any of his citizens, so he didn't have time to return to his base or finish with the third priority, especially with the potential opening of the bank and mint building.

Chapter 38

The grand opening had everyone there, including the gangsters, which was no big surprise because the bank was giving out one hundred gold pieces to each person attending. Dillon planned the giveaway to jump start the island economy. It didn't cost him too much; the money was made from the gold that Kahukah had given to him as a tribute. Furthermore, there were hardly thirty people living in town.

Before the day was over, Joe and Mr. Owner had finished Kel's sign. They had hung it above her door, and they had been hired to Kel's Place as waiters. Additionally, plenty of people enjoyed Mr. Milton's free banking.

But the day wasn't without a bad event. Joe had spilled orange paint all over one of Kel's more popular outside tables. Erik O'Connor bumped his head on one of Kel's tables when reaching down to get a fork. Bubba suffered from a panic attack and thrashed out at Lindsey, followed by extreme and sincere apologies. Mr. Owner broke a bottle of milk at the store while checking the price and expiration date. Finally Murphy ran into Wakna, knocking them both down while Murphy was chasing a wild monkey that had gotten hold of his Detroit Police badge.

Nightfall fell soon enough, and the town was quiet and peaceful again. Dillon was too tired to work, so he didn't make any progress in his plans. However, he did manage to run one last errand. It was to put up a phone in each of the businesses. Each business also got their own four-digit numbers to connect lines.

That night, Kel was closing up Kel's Place at a late hour. Once again, Tim had closed up earlier than she had, and he came over to help and walk her home. They got into a small conversation this time, but Kel looked over Tim's shoulder intermittently at the street candle that had been erected the day before. Under it she noticed a shadowy figure.

Guess it may be a good thing when Bubba doesn't remember to put out the street candle, Kel thought when the shadows caught her attention once again.

"C'mon, get over here," the figure whispered. She was wiping the top of a table and could barely see the contour of a hunched person whose voice she could hear. Another figure, also hunched over, ran to the street corner. The man's apparent idea proved inexpedient, assuming he'd been trying to hide his identity, because Kel then recognized the figure.

"It must be Flatfoot," she said softly to Tim. "We never should have trusted him. He looks like he's attempting to rob the bank with that other guy." She reentered the restaurant and picked up the phone.

"They sure don't waste any time. First day, too." She looked at the paper by her phone. "Let's see, the list of numbers is… aha!" She dialed Dillon's number and he answered right away.

"Hi," Kel said. "I found a man sneaking around outside. Could you get some of your police on him right away? I believe there are two of them."

"Did they do anything illegal?" he asked.

"I don't think they have yet, but they're sneaking around the bank, which doesn't look good."

"All right, I'll send the officers down there immediately." Dillon hung up and went to Murphy's house next door. Murphy was still awake, so it took no time. Miller was already with him. They'd been playing cards.

Dillon quietly led them to the Caldor house.

They knocked on the door and Ray's son, Thomas, answered it. "Hey, what's up?"

"We need to talk to your dad," Murphy said.

"I'll go get him," he answered. "Come in."

The Caldor house was the biggest of the residential huts because an entire family lived there. The other huts were small and were made only for small groups until more supplies could be used to construct bigger huts.

"Hey, Chief," Ray said as he came out of his room, rubbing his eyes. "What can I do for you now?"

"We have some trouble near the bank," Murphy said quietly. Ray nodded. He went over to a small table and picked up his gun and badge. "All right, now get your wife up and let's go," Murphy said. "I'll be outside when you're ready."

Jayne and Ray were ready within minutes. They met Murphy and Miller outside, all of them armed, and snuck over toward the bank. They then split into pairs, Jayne with Murphy and Ray with Miller. That way, Ray and Jayne wouldn't get distracted and Miller and Murphy wouldn't get distracted. Murphy accompanied Jayne instead of Miller because Miller was unpredictable. As long as Murphy went with Jayne, he felt he knew she was safe, and Miller most likely wouldn't try anything with Ray.

All the while Dillon felt it best to leave the police to their job. Even so, the responsibility remained that he was to monitor his subjects, so he kept a safe distance out of sight.

From their posts, the police moved in a couple yards and stopped. They watched the gangsters move around. There were two, just as they suspected. One was wielding a long object that appeared to be an ax or rifle; it was hard to tell in the darkness. The other went around to the front of the bank where Murphy and Jayne couldn't see him. Miller had his eye on him just the same.

Soon the man wielding the long object lifted it up like a baseball bat, and the police could identify the object. The man began to hack away at the building. Splinters of wood went everywhere, so they were sure it was an ax.

Just as he did this, a third man carrying a box of supplies came from a direction out of town and placed it near the front of the bank building.

"Hey," Murphy whispered to Jayne, "I think we should move in now, since there's now a third. Go signal your husband to move in."

She walked slowly about halfway to where Ray was. She blinked a small flashlight with her hand over the head and her fingers parted in one spot to let out very little light, signaling Ray without alarming the robbers. She ran back over to Murphy, and they moved in swiftly. The keener third wheel saw the light, though, and ran off. It was Lefty, but they didn't see him when he ran off; Trickster and Flatfoot didn't even see him leave.

Flatfoot was still waiting for a signal from Trickster when he heard the click of a gun cocking to load a bullet. He turned slowly, but when he saw Ray, he swung his arm, hit Ray, and ran to Trickster, only to find him at gunpoint by Miller. Then he was being held at gunpoint by the other Caldor officer, Jayne.

"You have the right to remain silent," Murphy said.

They booked the Trickster for attempted bank robbery, and they arrested Flatfoot for aiding and abetting and assaulting an officer.

Flatfoot's sentence was only two weeks, while Trickster's was a month. They were given mild punishments for two reasons. One was because there wasn't a jail building built yet. They had to be confined to a small room branching off of Dillon's hut with at least four guards on duty, twenty-four hours a day. The second reason was because Dillon was too gracious. He felt they should be given another chance. The stunt didn't even end up on their town records.

Seemingly soon the two weeks were over and Flatfoot was released. He laid low until Trickster was released for two reasons. The first reason was because he was all alone and had no way to support himself. Secondly, until he located Lefty, there were no brains in the gang, or lack of gang, so it was.

During the remaining two weeks after Flatfoot's release, there were no new arrivals in the town. The people who had already come there made an attempt to live life smoothly and get settled into a habitual lifestyle.

Some of the people had jobs, but many decided to take the once-in-a-lifetime chance to enjoy the island breeze, the tropical sun, and the warm, sandy beaches. Apart from the citizens feeling like they lived in a theme park with a bunch of strangely time-twisted people, it still seemed like a paradise. That sense proved to ease a lot of the tension that would have been brought on by such a diverse society.

Chapter 39

Ailiokahu, as the island town was called, was always quiet, especially with the mingling of such adverse cultures. The people, after a while, refused to associate with each other, so there were hardly any public gatherings, either. This wasn't satisfactory for Dillon. Lack of interest in associating with the other townspeople wasn't Karz's plan for time travel, but the opposite.

Karz's intentions with their Time Twister Program were to first make it safe for historians to travel through times and get the facts firsthand for their studies. Their next object was to intertwine people from diverse times and circumstances to create a society. The final step would be to create an interchronological traveling depot to bring past, present, and future together. Therefore, time would no longer be a boundary or obstacle.

Dillon's urgent circumstances, along with his eagerness to see the phenomenon for himself, had caused him to skip the first step, so historians hadn't yet come. There was *some* research, done by his associate, Dr. White, but it wasn't nearly as extensive as they'd intended at this point. There was no place for the historians in what Dillon had planned now; he no longer saw a need for them.

Dillon's intention now was to develop a society out of the island town. It would be one that overcame the walls built up by coming from different times and historical backgrounds. It was essentially what was necessary to create the depot Karz was striving for, only using a different method. It was easy for Dillon to find the slightest variation of the truth to convince himself that he was doing the right thing. After all, *this* method could work, however, it was his responsibility to report to his boss.

Dillon made his way back down to the compass room. He was alone, as per usual, and like before, he was headed to his time machine. He intended to fill up the empty Island Inn rooms that had recently been emptied due to the construction of the newest homes.

There was more than enough room for Dillon to bring more people. Even if he decided on ten, they could have their own rooms at the Island Inn. Really, maybe eight could have their own rooms. After all, the second floor wasn't finished yet. The rooms weren't incredibly big, either. In fact, they were quite the opposite: there was only room for a bed and a table. "Well," Dillon said aloud, "I've brought people from my time, and people from the twentieth century, as well as people from the 1800s. I think I'll get people from different parts of the country, too. I have Detroit and New York, Texas and… well, Egypt." *Although that wasn't exactly what I had in mind, Stevens* was *brought from Egypt.*

"Speaking of Stevens, he wants me to bring his expedition buddies now?" Dillon mumbled as he approached the east-southeast door. "What was his name… Larry something; then there was… Charlie? No, someone like that." He shrugged. "I have the list somewhere."

He had agreed once again to take requests for new citizens. He had compiled a list, and he planned on taking some people from it. However, in the interest of developing a more challenging diversity, he would only accept a few requests. Others would have to be made using his randomized databases.

Karz had supplied him with a database of persons living throughout history. Some of them had minimal to no historical relevance. Some played a part, having one or more personal biographies over time, and many names and profiles were that of more famous figures, such as Julius Caesar and Thomas Alva Edison.

It was this list of profiles that Karz was determined to update by sending investigators through time to monitor each subject. The latter list was especially critical for their search for historical accuracy. The former list was the list Dillon would focus on for bringing people to the island, apart from the requests, of course.

The first subject on the list was Fred Cramden. Actually, it was a pair; his wife Alice was to be brought with him. They were both attorneys from Dillon's hometown. He thought might as well start with his *own* requests. They were good friends of his through his mom.

That transfer went without incident. In fact, Fred wasn't even the least surprised went he turned toward his wife in mid-sentence to realize the lights had gone out and his buddy Taran Flint was standing directly behind her. They were ecstatic. Fred had had suspicions from the start of Taran's career that he was involved with a major transition in modern technology. This incident simply confirmed them.

His next few subjects were requests. Tim had requested the Scott MacKensie he'd been talking to Kel about. Professor Stevens had requested a couple of guys from his Egypt expedition, Harry Cane and Mike Porter. Dillon brought

Harry, but decided against the other because his profile made him seem a bit too dangerous. In Mike's place, Dillon decided to bring Chuck Jones, another member of the same expedition.

He brought the three mechanics on a whim. Dillon knew that if the construction equipment were in need of repair, there would be a need for a good mechanic. So, he had researched a team from 2122. Their names were Steve Carter, Coty Clark, and Don Reynolds.

Finally, there was Lindsey's uncle, Harry. Dillon found his profile and realized he was *always* with a certain woman; they did everything together. He couldn't see separating them, so he brought her, too. The woman, whose name was Gloria, was oblivious to the entire event, but Mr. Angel was overjoyed to see his niece again.

The last subject was another randomized pick. He was a stand-up comedian from 2141 who was still rough around the edges. His profile seemed extremely vague, which interested Dillon. It seemed as if he'd gotten to a point in his career as an entertainer and then suddenly dropped out of the public's eye altogether. That was where his profile ended. His name was Randolph Carr, Jr.

Chapter 40

"Where in the—" Randy looked confused when he finally realized his circumstances. He was standing on a platform, as he had been only moments ago, but the spotlight was gone. It had been replaced by a single light shining in from the open doorway across the room.

In front of him now stood a man he'd never seen before, standing in a room he'd never set foot in before now. The rows and rows of chairs he had once thought were filled before him became a single pedestal in the shape of a computer console facing the opposite direction. The strange man was leaning on it.

"I look down for a second and they cart my people away." Randy stepped off the platform and approached Dillon. "'Cept for you, what'd you do with them all?"

"I didn't do anything with them." Dillon laughed. He led Randy out of the room and into the dimly lit compass room. He had his arm around Randy's shoulder. "I couldn't afford to 'cart all of your people away.' So I just brought you away."

"You couldn't have brought me away. I would've… no." Randy looked around and was stunned to see that he wasn't in the auditorium. He looked down and lifted one foot. There was a strange compass carving on the floor.

Dillon then carefully explained the situation to Randy.

"So, you brought me through time to entertain people." Randy tried to get the story straight in his own brain. "Am I really that good?" he added sarcastically.

"Yes and no, but actually that's the point," Dillon answered. "I needed someone fresh and new. I need someone who can conform his act so that a lot of different people would… enjoy your act, kind of to bring the people together. I've got a few plans for a theater of sorts."

Randy sighed. "I see." He looked around the empty room. Then his eyes widened, and he looked directly at his "captor." "What about everything back home? My mom, my dad, my town..."

It was an idea that Dillon had always realized. The people in this island town would miss and would be missed by the people in their real lives, but it was a topic that he never really planned on addressing. Since it hadn't come up yet, in so much that many people chose to accept it, and Kel embraced it, he had ignored the concept. He assumed Randy would move on as well.

"Well, Randy, I have another job for you," Dillon said. "Just think of this as being on the road. You'll perform for the people of this town and get paid to bring *them* the joy of comedy."

"Well, at least let me call my folks to let them know where I am and that I'll be fine."

Dillon didn't like where this was going. "Uh, you can't talk to them about this, Randy. This is a top priority, top secret developmental exercise. I can't allow you to inform any outside individuals about this at this stage of the operation. And on that note, since you are now here, you may not leave for any reason until I've completed what I'm trying to accomplish here."

That wasn't good enough for Randy. "That's not just like being on the road, then! I *have* to tell my family where I am. Otherwise they'll worry themselves sick, and I don't want to leave them. If I can't go back whenever I like, then I want to go back now. Get me outta here!"

"Randy."

"Stop callin' me that as if you know me, man," Randy snapped. "Only my friends call me Randy, got it?"

Dillon sighed. "Listen, Mr. Carr, I'm not trying to agitate you or ruin your life, or anything like that," he said calmly.

"You ain't tryin' to ruin my life?" Randy shouted. "You just *pulled* me away from my life! You brought me to a place I can't get back from and told me I can't go back to where I just was five seconds ago!"

"Just calm down, Ran—" Dillon stopped himself. "Keep your voice down, all right?"

"You can't tell me that I can't leave, that's called kidnapping. How can anyone trust you with that thing? You can take anyone from anywhere and bring them to anywhen that you want." Randy started to shake. "Just send me back, man. I want to go back to Tole and forget this happened, like a bad dream."

"But Randy, there's so much to see, so much you can learn here. Just give it a try."

Randy slumped to the ground and sat cross-legged on the "N" etching. With his head down, he mumbled, "I can't stay here, man. I've got to see my family again; I've got to go back. You brought me here. Just send me back. I won't say anything to anyone."

"Randy, I can't do that." Dillon kneeled down to be eye level with Randy. "I do have a way to send you back, back to the exact time and place I took you from." Randy looked up at him. "And I promise you I'll send you back there if you give Ailiokahu a real chance and still decide that you want to leave."

Randy thought about his options carefully, including the option where he would kick the weird man as hard as he could in the shin and make a break for it. He knew he couldn't get far, so he decided to give in. "Yeah, I'll do it."

Chapter 41

Randy was led around part of the town that morning. Dillon let him stay in the Island Inn, for free until he could make his own money from his comedy acts. Dillon finally allowed him to explore on his own after about noon. By then it was very bright and sweltering hot in the clearer part of town.

Randy walked along a newly paved sidewalk. When he turned a corner, there was a bright glare in his eyes. He put his hand above his eyes like a visor, but there was still too much glare to see ahead of him very well.

Not known to Randy, because of his impaired sight, another individual was coming along straight toward him. He was dressed in all green and wore a black top hat. His concentration, however, was on his pocket watch, so, though the sun was behind him and he could see clearly, he didn't see Randy until he tripped over Randy's shoe and fell to the ground.

"Hey." Trickster groaned and began to shout as he rose to his feet. "Watch where yer goin'!"

"Oh! I'm s… sorry, sorry, sorry," Randy stammered. "I'm so sorry!"

Trickster glared at Randy until he entered the general store. Randy looked down shamefully as he walked away slowly. He then noticed a pendent lying on the sidewalk. It was a golden pocket watch with a poker hand engraved on the front cover.

"Ooh, what's this?" Randy picked it up and studied it. He opened the cover and discovered a small piece of paper inside. Shards of glass then fell to the ground. Looking down at the glass and then back at the watch face, he noticed the watch hands didn't move either.

"Hmm… must belong to that man. I guess it broke when I bumped into him." In the interest of maintaining a good image in case he decided to remain in town, he decided to help out this stranger. "I'll fix it," he said to himself aloud. "That way next time I see him, I can give it to him."

After a few minutes, Trickster came out of the general store. He noticed a small, golden chain link glistening on the ground. "Hey, it's a golden… wait a sec…" He picked it up and checked his pockets. "Holy… golden pocket watch! My watch… it's gone!"

He looked around himself and ran down one side of the road. "It must've been that clown outside the store."

For the next few hours, Trickster kept his eye out for Randy, but to no avail. The next day, he decided to take a more active approach. He planned to scour the town one building at a time, starting with the Island Inn.

However, he wasn't allowed to go searching through the hotel. So, to get access, he posed as a safety inspector and "borrowed" a costume for the part.

Each room now consisted of a bedroom and a small living space. After the Island Inn received more funding, they planned to expand. The residents, or "inmates" as they often called themselves because they were on the island without their consent, lived on floors and in rooms dividing them into like times and jobs.

Randy's room, therefore, was located on the newly built second floor, classified as 2000–2300 because he was from the 2140s. All of the rooms were identical, and few were empty. The walls were all white with hardly a poster or painting hanging on them.

The inn also had a communal bathroom, which was very primitive. It was similar to an outhouse and was in a fenced in area at the back of the hotel. A door at the end of the hall on the first floor led to it. It was planned to be temporary until they could develop a plumbing system.

The costume Trickster donned, one he wore because he knew he couldn't snoop around overtly, was white and, in his mind, futuristic looking. It was made of a durable, hard material, and with it he had gloves, a white hat, and big-lens sunglasses so he wouldn't be recognized. He had been practicing his line quietly outside the Island Inn before entering. "I'm with the SSB. I'm Agent Smith. I need to inspect the entire premises for any safety or sanitization violations."

"I was not aware of such an inspection," was Stevens' reply when Trickster had worked up the mettle to put his facade into practice.

"Mr. Dillon informed me that you had been discussing… methods of maintaining safe living… conditions." Trickster had trouble remembering the technical terms. "He sent me to inspect what… things… would need altercations."

"Alter*cations*?" Stevens asked.

Trickster leaned toward Stevens. "Did I stutter?" He gritted his teeth together, displaying his radiant golden tooth while he talked.

Stevens cleared his throat. "Do you mean alterations?"

"That's what I said," was his stern reply.

His intimidating look caused Stevens to hold in his next comment. "All right, you can inspect for any violations. Be sure to leave a list of what 'things' I'll need to make improvements to." Stevens led Trickster to the lobby that led to the residential areas.

After he was given access, Trickster began to search as Stevens returned to the front desk. Trickster looked into each door carefully, all the while running over the line he'd been rehearsing. By the time he reached Randy's room, the line was well rehearsed. He'd said it several times in such a preemptory way that he'd enter rooms even without a reply.

At room 201, he didn't even think to knock. He barged in, but the tiny, dark room was empty. Angrily, he shut the door.

Room 202 was right across from it. He impatiently knocked, again without the intention of waiting.

Trickster was about to open the door when it was opened for him by a man behind him. "Excuse me, sir. This is my room." It was a man dressed in a red jumpsuit, embroidered with what Trickster believed to be a strange-looking yellow craft over a blue patch on the left of his chest. Underneath it was a word. "Brown."

He saw two more walk by him into the room, also wearing jumpsuits like the first. One, with glasses and a red cap, had "O'Connor," and the gray-haired one had "McNally" where the first had read "Brown."

Jacob Brown remained in the doorway. "Is there something I can help you with? Are you looking to find *your* room, or…"

"Uh, just the three of you live here?" was all Trickster wanted to know.

"Uh, yeah," Erik, the one with glasses, answered. Then he laughed. "Couldn't really fit anymore in these cells, could you?"

Trickster peered into the room past Jacob and the others. "True, true," he said. He laughed as well. *Yeah, whatever, freaks. They're gonna ask, anyway, so I should set it up now.*

"Well, I'm working for an agency to ensure the comfort of our clientele here at the inn," Trickster lied. "Today I simply needed testimonial regarding the… the general comfort… of the people staying here. Thank you for your time, fellas. You're sure to be seeing me again."

He walked away without response, and the divers merely stared at each other in confusion.

"What was that all about?" Isaac turned to Jacob.

"I still have no idea," he answered, scratching his unshaven chin and turning back to his diving team.

Chapter 42

IGNORING HIS LAST VENTURE, he proceeded to the next door, 204. This time he knocked slowly, and he awaited an answer. He could hear a faint mumbling, but that was all. He knocked again, with another indistinct answer.

"C'mon, open up!" The door was locked, so he began to pound on it.

Another response came, but what the man said, Trickster couldn't tell. He pounded again.

The door finally swung open, but it wasn't the clown from outside the general store. It was a man Trickster had never seen before, his hair askew and wearing only shorts. It appeared Trickster had woken him up.

"Can I *help* you?" he asked, annoyed.

"Uh, sorry, sir, I uh… umm," Trickster stuttered and looked down a bit.

"Who is it, Fred?" A redhead came into view and leaned on her husband's shoulder. "Who is this?"

"I don't know. He still hasn't been able to spit it out," Fred answered, still glaring at the interloper.

"Sorry to disturb you folks," Trickster said with a little more confidence. "I'm looking for a resident here, and I was told he resided in room 203."

"That's right over there." The woman pointed.

"Ah… I'm terribly sorry about that folks." He nodded. "Have a pleasant day." He turned away immediately and approached 203.

The man closed his door, muttering under his breath. His wife cuddled him closely and urged him back into bed.

Trickster knocked impatiently on the door that now stood before him, across from 204. He was getting frustrated at his lack of good fortune in finding his prey. *How could such a small town with so few people have so* ***many*** *people living in it?*

When no response came from the room, he checked the knob and found it to be unlocked. He looked around the drab, empty room and found a table on the side with odds and ends on it. Among the odds and ends, he spotted it:

a small, shining pendent with a short chain attached. Getting a better look, Trickster knew that it was his stolen pocket watch.

"This must be that guy's room," Trickster whispered. Then he came up with a brilliant solution for revenge. That is, the most brilliant in his eyes, being a nineteenth century gangster. Revenge might seem like a brilliant solution to anything, and yet turn out quite the opposite.

Meanwhile, Randy was wandering around the island. He was searching, as he often did. For what he was uncertain, but upon stumbling on whatever it was, he would know. He, looking left, right, and then left again, crossed the street to where Dillon brought him when they met earlier.

He walked in and came upon the trapdoor. He found it by the feel of the floor. When he walked behind Dillon's desk, the dirt floor, because the trapdoor was covered in sand, was softer, as if it had been recently moved around. He dug through and lifted the trapdoor, though not with the greatest of ease.

After a short, dark walk down the hall, Randy reached the compass room, the first sight he had seen in this strange world. His path a small circle around the center, Randy looked all around. He strained to see with the single dim light, which cast eerie shadows on every nook and crevice of the walls.

The only difference in the room since he'd been here before was the presence of a metal ladder hanging from the ceiling. It led to a hatch of some sort, which was brightly lit from where Randy stood.

As he began to climb the ladder, he could hear the metal moaning under his weight. He peered cautiously into the room above, which previously was the hut of Wakna's family until Dillon made a couple of adjustments.

"Look at all this stuff!" Randy whispered. He was trying to be careful not to be heard by any others that he feared could be present. He picked himself up off the ladder and set foot on the concrete floor. He stood up straight while still in awe of the technology.

The far side of the room was covered in large monitors. The middle and biggest monitor was black, void of any projected images. The screens to the left displayed the familiar images of the town; each screen focused on specific places, buildings and halls, like those of the hotel. The four screens above displayed four hallways of the bunker. Those screens were void of any movement or people, unlike the screens on the right. The right-hand screens displayed a village unfamiliar to Randy. It was that of the Kahukah tribe.

Below the black screen were four more monitors, each with a blue screen that flashed through slides of schematics and diagrams of different vehicles, buildings, and ships.

These proved especially helpful in solving the enigmatic puzzle of who "Dillon" really was. It was the screen furthest right. It displayed a holographic three-dimensional image on a technological grid atop the console.

"What is that thing?" Randy whispered. He was intent on discovering everything he could, so he logged onto the computer system, something he was somewhat familiar with.

He located the files quickly and found the mysterious diagram he was looking for. The file name it was under was "Tmmchn01." He commanded the computer to print, and though it began to hum and whir, he couldn't locate the source of the noises: the printer. He exited the files of the diagram and logged off so he could search for it.

He searched through a couple of cabinets, most of which were empty. However, one he found had a book lying on the top shelf. Piquing his curiosity, the book reached out to Randy, and he returned the gesture, picking it up slowly and opening it to the first page.

Reading the first few lines, he closed it again as he noticed a voice coming from below. It was coming from the compass room. He ran to find a place to hide.

Chapter 43

SUDDENLY, A LIGHT POUNDING on the ground seemed to approach the ladder from the far side of the room. Soon, he heard the soft and steady clang of metal to metal. *Most likely, by the soft tap proceeding, a person going up the ladder*, Randy decided.

Dillon entered the room, rising after climbing up the ladder. He looked around the apparently empty room. The lower screens, for some reason, were out of the screen savers. Two unseen eyes watched Dillon as he approached the computer with a strange expression. They peered out into the room from under one of the computer terminals. There was a sliding metal door underneath. It had a small crack from which someone could probably see most of the room.

"What's this?" Dillon said aloud, as if talking to the watchful eyes that he could sense were there. *Hmm, but who could it be? Who knows my secret? Where is he? And who would want to know it?*

Dillon turned to leave. Luckily, the printer had turned silent before he came in. With a shrug, he climbed down the ladder to continue with the rest of the day's business.

When the intruder was finally gone, Randy crept over and obtained the papers from the printer, which he'd found while underneath the console. Then he walked back over to the cabinet containing the mysterious book.

He spent what must have been only a few minutes skimming through the pages beginning, "Everything happened so quickly."

Some of the information he'd come across seemed to be better than the simple schematic he'd printed moments before. If this Dillon wished to remain the enigma he appeared to be, he wasn't doing a very good job. His life was unraveling rapidly in Randy's perspective.

"Now," he whispered. "Back to my room."

He was on his way to exit the bunker, just dropping off the ladder, when he stopped short. He looked in all directions for the door he'd entered before to get into the compass room. Too confused to care, and running low on time, for he didn't want to be caught as he'd almost been before, Randy ran through a random door. Above the doorway, the letter "N" was etched into it.

Through the door was a short hall that led to another door. The door was half open and wouldn't complete a circuit either to close or open fully. Still, he could squeeze through. Inside the door was a small, dark room. There was a platform in the center and another futuristic computer console on one side of the room. On the other, there was another door. A glowing green light hovered on the right side of the door. It beckoned Randy over to it, and, discovering it was a button, it begged him to depress it. So, of course, Randy gave in, despite knowing it wasn't the exit he initially sought.

The door softly whished open. Inside there was an intense darkness beyond that of the previous room, with no light reaching from the compass room. Randy searched the wall for a switch to no avail. The door closed automatically when Randy approached the heart of the darkness. His eyes gradually adjusted to see blurrily in the dark.

He saw a large object protruding from the far side of the abysmal darkness. When everything came vaguely into focus, he could see a slight rising and lowering on it. He approached it and discovered it to be a woman on a strange-looking cot.

Randy looked at her with a sad expression. *She's probably lost like me. Probably hasn't seen the outside world yet. Looks as though she could've been down here a long time. In the deep darkness and all alone, she must be frightened. Poor lady. Maybe, just maybe I can cheer her up…*

Chapter 44

DAWN OPENED HER EYES to realize she was still in the dark. She still lay on the mysterious soft bed she'd discovered in the supply closet of Northern Detroit's High Street High School. She looked around her when suddenly she sensed movement along the side of the bed.

"What's that?" she said softly into the dark. She rose and sat up on the bed. She picked up a square object that lay next to her and held it against her chest as her feet dangled over the edge of the bed.

"Don't be afraid," she heard a man's voice say. It was soft and sweet; soothing would be a more accurate term. "I am here to help."

"Who are you?" Dawn asked him. She could only see a blurry, dark figure, but he seemed to have a compassionate air about him. He seemed to be genuinely innocent and very curious.

"My name's Randy," he answered softly.

Dawn gasped and dropped what she'd been holding. Randy could hear glass shattering. "Oh no!" she said. But the shattering glass and gasp rang together, and Randy was unsure which was for what.

Dawn now had a dark feeling in the pit of her stomach.

"I'm sorry. I didn't mean to wake you."

It's him, isn't it? she asked herself. *I must be dreaming. He can't be alive again.*

Randy picked up the picture. "The light is too dim," he said. Just then the lights turned on to a dim glow. *Hmm… it appears the lights are voice activated.*

Now Dawn could see his face. She saw his deep brown eyes and his brown hair; it was so real and alive. It was the living flesh of the victim she knew to be dead. She began to feel an awkward sensation and couldn't withstand his presence without words spoken.

"I'm Dawn," she said finally. *Even if this* **is** *a dream, what could it hurt to live it?*

"You're the one… in here." Randy pointed to the photograph that he could now see clearly. "And this man right here… he… he looks familiar."

"He's my fiancé."

"F… fiancé?"

"That's right."

"But this is a wedding picture, right?" he asked.

"I suppose so," Dawn answered. "Actually, I'm more surprised than you are. We never got married. He…" Her voice trailed off and she paused for a few long moments. Then in a trembling voice, she continued. "He was gone before we had the chance… he disappeared and… he…"

She couldn't tell him what she knew, or not really knew but had presumed. She loved Taran and couldn't betray him; she didn't even want to admit it to herself. She fell down onto the bed again.

"What's wrong, Dawn?" Randy sat beside her.

Dawn wiped her eyes and looked into his. "Do you know a man named Dillon?"

Randy's eyes widened. "That's the man in this picture. Why do I get the feeling you haven't been in town long?"

"Huh? What do you mean?"

"Dillon is the self-proclaimed leader of this town."

Dawn wasn't surprised by his answer. She knew that from the journal, and that's when she noticed a book sticking partway out of Randy's back pocket. "What's that?" she asked, pointing to the leather book. She knew what his answer would be, for she'd already read that book. There wouldn't be many more entries written in it after this day.

"That's my journal," he answered shyly. In order to circumnavigate the journal subject, Randy asked the question he had held back. "How is this a picture of something that hasn't yet occurred?"

Dawn was relieved; she didn't want to stay on the journal subject either. "My fiancé…" she began. *How do I say it?* "He…" *Just say it!* "He invented a sort of time machine."

"I knew it!" Randy exclaimed. "Does it look like this?" He pulled out a folded paper from his journal and showed it to Dawn. It was one of the blueprint diagrams that had been flashing as a screen saver on the computer. "It's weird, but I kinda thought he was pulling my leg."

"That's it," Dawn said when she saw the schematic. She could remember the last time she had seen it in real life. It was on the helipad for mere seconds. She should have run to it instead of to the tower. What was she thinking?

"Well, congratulations, then. You're getting married." Randy smiled. "Be sure to get me some pictures of you in your gown in case I'm not there to see you when you get married."

Dawn looked down. "Some things aren't worth it, you know? Some people..." She sniffled. "They do the wrong thing, even if they know it's the wrong thing."

Some dream, she thought to herself. *What does it all mean... Randy, the photograph... a dark room?* She could remember being at the Christmas party. She could remember a lightning strike, the tree falling, and paper plates.

She's got a morose expression again. What's wrong? "What's wrong?"

She looked at Randy's eyes again. This time she had red, teary eyes and couldn't stop sniffling.

"Dawn," Randy said gravely, "what's going to happen to me?"

"Taran is my fiancé," Dawn said. "*He's* Dillon."

"Yeah..." Randy replied. "And?"

She dropped her face into her hands.

There were several moments of silence, but Randy knew what she was saying. He'd seen the movies, read the books. Tole might be in the middle of nowhere, but they still got the newspapers on most days and still had TVs. He had dug too deep.

"Will I see my family once more?" Randy asked. He looked down at the picture, which he still held in hand. He already knew the answer before Dawn could breathe a word.

He read my mind... how did he know? She looked up at him. *But of course he did. He's the dream, remember? It's you who don't have any control. But shouldn't I? That is, after all, what lucid dreams like this are for...*

"Will I?" He looked into her eyes.

She shook her head, but she couldn't bear to stay in the room. She ran out. She didn't know what she'd find beyond the walls of the darkest room, but it didn't matter where she went. She just couldn't face her fiancé's victim.

"Dawn, wait!" Randy ran to the doorway. "Dawn!" He stopped at the doorway and looked down the hall at the fleeing woman he'd only just met. He couldn't follow her, though; it didn't feel right.

Part Three

The Island Sundaes

Chapter 45

DAWN WAS NOW FILLED with mixed emotions as she ran down the hallway. That was the very same man she had been examining the corpse of weeks before, and she was talking to him. He lived and breathed; he was alive. The hall seemed to last forever. She felt like she couldn't run away from what was at the door, as if it drew her in closer the further she ran from it.

Finally the endless halls came to the compass room. This was the compass room in his journal. That was the dead author of the journal, and not too far away was the killer. Not only a killer, but her fiancé, whom she'd been dying to see once again and know he was alive. What had happened, and how did it happen so fast?

This was either a lucid dream or a dream come true. Could the machine have worked? And was she now there, in the journal entries of the deceased she'd authorized an autopsy for? The Sundaes were gone, as if they never existed, or maybe they didn't exist yet? Her world had been turned upside down in a matter of one nap. Everything happened so quickly…

She thought she saw a shadow float by into one of the doors, but she couldn't be sure. She looked up and down at the dark room, at the sixteen doors in the room, at the eight doors facing her. She'd just noticed they each had directions above them. Only three doors were open. Four other doors seemed calm and peaceful, but the eighth door appeared darker than the others. It wasn't darkness like that of shadows in the bunker, but rather the shadows of evil.

Dawn decided immediately to avoid that door and studied the open doors. *Which will lead out of this place?* she thought, for that was what she wanted: to be out of the darkness. She didn't know the way through to get outside, but she found a light coming from the end of one hall, through the south door. She thought that she also saw a figure climbing up a ladder directly into the light source. Racing to the ladder, she called for the person to stop and then shouted for help.

The man climbed down most of the way. When he jumped to the ground and turned toward Dawn, she knew him right away.

"Taran!"

"Dawn?"

They ran to each other and held each other tightly for a long time. They were both overjoyed and had tears in their eyes. Dawn was a sight that Taran hadn't seen in a long time. She still looked just the same as she had when he left her several months before. Taran, for Dawn, looked much different. When he left, he had been younger-looking, untried, and innocent.

"I missed you so much," Taran whispered. "How'd you get here?"

"I…" She let go and looked into his face, an unshaven and strong face shaped by experience. She could almost see, by the scars, the hardships he had been through. He was stronger and somehow different in ways she still didn't know.

But he was too real. She could see him, hear him, and feel him around her. It couldn't possibly still be a dream. Still, she had mixed feelings tangled inside. "I… I knew it would work!" she boasted.

"I… you knew it would work?" Taran repeated back.

"Yes… I had… total confidence in your machine's capabilities," she restated. She smiled as best as she could, though it was a weak smile.

"That's all you have to say to me?" Taran asked.

She read his face and thought about Randy's murder. "For now…" She had to double check with his eyes. "Yes."

They proceeded up the ladder and eventually into the town. It was around mid-afternoon now, so they spent the rest of the day touring the town. Taran led Dawn around the more popular places: Kel's Place, the Island Inn, and Tim's Shop. All the while, they tried to keep away from the marriage topic or anything else that would lead the people to assume they were engaged, at Dawn's request.

Randy found an easy route out of the bunker that led to another ladder through one of the directional doors, the east. It came out at the end of the hall on the first floor of the Island Inn, much to his surprise. Peering around the empty hallway, he stopped short to process what had happened back in the bunker.

How did this strange woman know so much about me? If she was from the same place as Dillon, is it safe to assume that she's involved with his work as well? If that's the case, it would make sense to assume she's upset at… this turn that leads to my… well, whatever it is. It would explain her sad demeanor, mostly after discovering who I am.

Randy went back to room 203 and opened the door. He went over to the table full of odds and ends and reached into his back pocket, instinctively pulling out the small, leather book. He then sat at the table and began to write. About what, he would never tell, but he worked at it for an hour or more.

Chapter 46

A shadow outside Tim's Shop paced around the front, avoiding the display window. It walked toward more shadows to the side of the building, between Tim's Shop and Kel's Place. Both were dark, closed for fifteen minutes now. Finally, as the wait became unbearable, a bulky-looking shadow awkwardly stumbled over to the first.

The latter threw down half of his shadow and began to search for the right one inside its counterpart: a flaccid and obscure shadow. When the right shadow was found inside of it, the first pulled it out. It appeared long and thin; it almost appeared as though it were an outgrowth of the latter shadow's arm. The flaccid shadow was soon left next to the building and not recovered for a while.

As the two moving shadows disappeared into the building across the street from Tim's Shop, another shadow came onto the scene. It had been waiting in front of this spectacle, watching.

It floated toward the flaccid shadow for inspection. Finding it to be nothing but an empty shell, the third shadow turned toward the building as the others had. It then followed the shadows into the building. The all-too-familiar Island Inn lobby was inside. The two shadows could be hazily seen edging along the walls to the stairs.

The shadow in pursuit better resembled a person than the first two. It was furtively led to the second floor, the same floor on which Randy lived. It continued on until they reached room 203, the same door behind which Randy lived. The first two peered into the small window of the door.

Inside, Randy was leaning over his desk, busy at work with what the shadows assumed was a letter he was composing. But regardless of what it really was, they planned for it to be his last.

The leading shadow, holding the shadow that the pursuer presumed was lethal, reached for the door knob. It stopped at half-turn, not because the door was locked, but because the shadow had felt something sharp on its back.

It appeared to turn around slowly, but, noticing the sharp feeling wasn't caused by its partner, the lethal shadow met with the stranger. The pursuer went down to the floor with a soft groan.

After the episode was over, the two remaining slid quietly into the room. However, the lethal shadow had been traded for another, one that the pursuer had originally wielded.

The dim light of the room, created by a dim desk lamp, was hardly enough to give a face to the intruding shadows. They approached where Randy was sitting. The new lethal shadow was soon lifted. Just then there was a glimmer in the face of the leading shadow, the one wielding the lethal extension of its arm. That was the end; no more light shone from the room.

Back in the view of Tim's Shop, outside the Island Inn, the latter shadow returned to the flaccid shadow. It made its best attempt to fold it into as compact a shadow as possible and carried it inside. A complexity of shadows returned after a short while; this time, there was a new shadow, a lifeless, unmoving shadow that appeared to be lifted and carried by the other two. It was now merged with what used to be the flaccid shadow, now rigid and dead.

They continued across town, westward. The hut in which they ended up was dark as well. Once inside, the weight of the still shadow was so overwhelming that the two intruder shadows had to let it gently down.

A part of the floor was opened, a rope was tied around the rigid shadow, and the leader shadow descended into the opening of the floor that was opened. The second shadow then lowered the still shadow into the floor after its boss.

When the shadows finally reached their dark destination, they sealed the door. The only lights here were in the form of several digital numbers on the right side and the spotlight over the center platform.

The rigid shadow dissolved into the spotlight. Randy's body seen within a clear bag was in its place; it was a motionless, lifeless Randy. The other shadows avoided this light. It would be their end, so they slid the body onto the platform without touching the light.

Now the shadows stumbled around in the cluttered darkness; the second headed for the number lights. The shadowy touchboard was visible below the numbers, visible only by the light of the platform.

It seemed unsure but was told that the last numbers, one-eight-four-one, should be changed to something, anything completely different. When the shadow touched the board, a flat screen lit up next to the console. The shadow couldn't just randomly type a code; he had to find it.

The screen continuously flashed different objects and pictures. Finally, the user found a chart filled with a log of a random series of numbers and letters. He haphazardly pressed on one reading 3851N8630W-120732333. There was then another code that appeared. Thinking nothing of this six character code, TI-PS-42, the shadow ignored it and activated the machine. Within seconds, a blue light flashed and lit up the entire room, and then, the body was gone.

Rid of the evidence, the two shadows turned to leave the room. Then suddenly, the blue light returned and the body reappeared.

"What in the—" the shadow spoke in a soft growl. He hurriedly ran to the console and clicked the number code below the one ending 120732333, which was 120732348. "The code must not have worked," he grumbled. He then changed the TI-PS-42 code to another random code, DM-DA-02.

After a third blue light, the body was gone.

"That was strange," the other shadow whispered.

"Let's go."

The shadows left.

The room was soon empty, and the two shadows carried the empty bag out to the dark. They fled the outside scene, and soon, from that very direction, a man in green and black came strolling by the light outside Kel's Place.

He had an upbeat appearance and passed by the street lamp, seemingly intentionally, to perhaps show off the rich green color of his jacket. He walked straight into the Island Inn. After talking to the man behind the lobby desk, he walked down the hall and up the stairs. On the second floor, near to room 203, there was a glint of light reflecting from the open room.

He looked inside and found a strange man, sword in hand. Though he'd been in such a small town, he'd never seen him before.

He wore a musty, blue shirt and gray, torn pants. On his flat, brown, triangular hat, which lay next to him on the floor, was a thick white feather, decoratively stuck in the top of one corner. Over his left eye was a black patch sewn onto his face.

Chapter 47

THE PATCHED STRANGER LOOKED at Trickster quizzically. He held the sword loosely, peering at it, and then back at the man in green. It appeared to both parties that they were equally shocked at this spectacle.

"What happened here?" Trickster questioned him. He saw the sword and took it away. "Well? What happened, and what—" He then noticed a thick red liquid dripping slowly to the floor.

The stranger looked straight at him. "I… I have no idea what you mean…" He looked around again at the room.

It looked like someone had been looking for something and trashed the place while doing so. The chair was knocked over, tiny pieces of metal and shards of glass were scattered on the floor, and an assortment of books was strewn all over the desk.

"What did you do?" Trickster said accusingly.

"It wasn't me… that is, whatever it is you mean," the stranger declared defensively. "But I think someone was killed in here." The voice of this strange man was also unfamiliar. Trickster assumed he was from England by the accent. Then again, having been in town long enough, he could be from anywhere.

"No kidding…" was the gangster's mordant reply. "But the question remains. Who was killed, when, and why would you do such a thing?"

"Y… you're accusing me?" he asked in his gruff voice. He knew how these rich conmen worked. They would twist anything he said to mean something completely different. He knew this swindler had something up his sleeve, and he assumed Trickster was rich by his fancy suit, the golden chain across the belly of his vest, and the shining shoes.

"There really is no one else to blame," Trickster told him. "You were found here, with the weapon… I mean, clearly from the blood on it, the resident of the room is gone, and everyone else is probably asleep. Not only that, this sword looks like something that someone of your t—someone like you would have with you."

"You've got some good points, but I can tell you exactly what happened. I think I know who killed whoever used to live here," the stranger said. He sat down and motioned for Trickster to sit. Trickster prepared for a long story.

"I got where we are by boat," he began. "My captain weighed anchor offshore by the cove back there. He sent me and another to find somewhere to stay before we uh… well anyway, Johnson left to look at the southern side, and I was on my way to the northern side. On the way, I found this pair of people lurkin' around over by here, this building, so I watched them.

"They took something out of this bag and left it outside the door. When they went in I looked in the bag, but it was empty. I, from a distance, followed them into that hall," he said, pointing to the doorway. "They were outside that door, and I thought they were going to hurt someone. I tried to stop them, drawing my sword, but the other one, I think, clubbed me out."

"And then you woke up, the door was open, the sword was near you on the floor, and you looked around, shocked by the blood. You were stunned, looking dumbfounded until I came in," Trickster said, looking at him sideways.

Now the stranger had an eerie feeling in the pit of his stomach. "You're absolutely right. I couldn't have said it shorter myself."

"A likely story…" Trickster replied. "I could've written this story myself. You think your supposed Good Samaritan antics can save you from what you've done?"

"What?"

"I hear it all the time from the people who usually done it," Trickster explained. "So there's no way I'd buy that story."

"But it's TRUE!"

Chapter 48

Murphy looked around the room. "This room is number 203, right? Yep. This room definitely belonged to Mr. Randolph Carr." He turned to the suspected stranger, who had been detained in the room all night with a police guard.

Trickster had been there, too. He had insisted on staying because "if his friend Randy was involved, then he had to be there for him." On a couple of occasions, the guard had to separate them, but Trickster's fury had subsided since then.

This was Murphy's first opportunity to come down and interrogate the pirate that Trickster had discovered in the inn the night before. Dillon was on his way, but he had a previous commitment to which he needed to attend.

The dripping sword was sealed in a bag on the table. Ray, who was the overnight police guard, was presently inspecting the other contents of the table, including what turned out to be tiny watch parts and gears that he'd found on the floor.

"What was your name again, sir?" Chief Murphy asked the pirate.

"Blackbeard, *Captain* Luke Blackbeard."

"When was the last time you saw Mr. Carr, Captain?" He held his pad ready to jot down anything that Blackbeard had to say.

"I told *him* already." Blackbeard pointed at Trickster. "I don't know who you're talking—"

"Ah, yes. You had just arrived… I remember," Murphy confirmed. "You have never visited this island before, sir?"

"No," he said flatly. "Well, actually, yes… once," he admitted.

"Mr. Blackbeard, you admit, then, that you've been to this town before?" Murphy said. "When was this?"

"No. I've never been to this town before. I came to this island several years ago," Blackbeard clarified. "None of this was here."

"Yeah… right."

"It wouldn't matter either way," Blackbeard insisted. "I told him what happened, too." He motioned toward Ray, who looked up and shook his head.

"Yeah, same thing you told me," Trickster added.

"Exactly," Blackbeard replied. "I came here following these two men into that hall. One hit me on the head. When I woke up, the door was open, my sword was bloody, and nobody else was around. It was probably two minutes before that man came in and started accusing me of murder."

Trickster leaned toward Murphy and whispered, "Pirates like this one can't be trusted."

"Neither can magicians, Mr. Smith," was Murphy's soft reply. "Magicians have a way of disappearing. If his story is true, and your story is true, then you're just lucky that he didn't find you in his place had you shown up here first."

"What's that supposed to mean?" Trickster was taken aback, as though Murphy was turning the tables, accusing *him* of this atrocity. "What… do you think I could've had something to do with this?"

"What were you doing here anyway, Mr. Smith?"

"I came back to pay Randy for fixing my watch," Trickster took out the golden pendant and showed it to Murphy. "He had dropped it and wanted to fix it. He did, and I couldn't pay him at the time. Now that I can, I came back last night, but he wasn't here…" he started to ramble frantically.

"Try to calm down, Smith," Murphy said.

"Well, you don't understand, sir." Trickster began to tear up. "He's the only almost normal person that would accept me after I was released. He really believed I could turn my life around…"

"Well, Smith, try to calm down. It hasn't been proven yet, but we think Mr. Carr has been stabbed," Murphy said. Trying to be more compassionate, he added, "I won't know until I get a positive blood sample on the sword and find a way to match it to Mr. Carr's. But it is possible that he wasn't here. It's possible Blackbeard murdered someone else here, not Randy. We'll know when we find the body."

"This—that's impossible!" Blackbeard rose to leave.

"Sir, I'm sorry, but you cannot leave this room!" Murphy firmly gripped the suspect's arm. Blackbeard shook free and ran to the door, only to find it locked. "You're not leaving; even if you could open the door, I've assigned several guards to stand outside that would apprehend you at once."

"This system doesn't make any sense!" Blackbeard sat back down reluctantly. "Just let me back to my ship. I didn't kill anyone!"

"Then you should have nothing to worry about with a trial," Murphy said.

"That is, if you really are innocent. Then when the perpetrator has been jailed, you'll be set free."

"But... how long will that take?" Blackbeard asked.

"It can't be determined. Anywhere from a week to several months."

"All right, fine," Blackbeard said. "But I'm still not going to be helpful; I told you everything I know."

Dillon approached the door from behind which he could hear an argument taking place. "What's happening in there, Caldor?"

Jayne, who was guarding Room 203 from the outside, answered quietly, "Well, I guess someone really *was* killed." She unlocked the door. "Murphy's expecting you."

"Thanks." Dillon entered the room to see Murphy setting Blackbeard down in the chair against the pirate's will.

"Sir," Murphy addressed him, "the suspect has informed me that he will do his best not to help us with this case."

"Did he?" Dillon glared at him with a penetrating stare.

"Well... kinda, in his own way," Murphy answered nervously. "Well, actually, he gave me this story about what happened last night, or what he says he saw last night, and I don't think he's telling the whole truth."

"But we have to believe or at the very least consider his story, don't we?" Dillon didn't really need confirmation, but he felt Murphy should agree, being from the UNA and living by certain laws.

"I... I guess so," he answered. "But who can we tie to the homicide?"

"From what you have written here," Dillon said as he glanced over the notepad Murphy held, "you don't even have a homicide case to tie him. Just a bl... bloody... pirate sword." A light bulb came on in Dillon's head that no one else could see. Murphy could still tell by his tone that Dillon had an idea of what was going on.

"What? What?" Trickster asked.

"Yeah, what?" the other insisted.

"Step outside, Chief." Dillon opened the door, and they began to talk as the door clicked shut. "Hey," Dillon began. "All right, now this pirate didn't get here by me, so how did he get here ?"

"He claimed that his captain's ship brought him here last night. Then he left his ship off-shore a ways," Murphy answered.

"Hmm..." Dillon sighed. *This can't be good. There wasn't supposed to be any interference from outsiders. It's bad enough that the Kahukah tribe turned out to live on this island. Whatever happens, this pirate cannot go back to the outside "real" world. He can't get a chance to tell his friends about this place. Shoot... what am I going to do?* After careful consideration, Dillon finally asked, "Did he say anything about other pirates coming ashore as well?"

"Yes, a man he referred to as Johnson," was Murphy's answer. "Johnson, I assume, is a cabin boy from the ship. He came with that guy to search for something around the island."

"Search for what?"

"He wouldn't say."

"Well then, we should be able to find this Johnson and pump him for information," he said to Murphy. "His testimony would back up or discredit the pirate's story about last night. It may prove helpful as the case develops."

"Yeah, but then again, it could be both."

"How so?"

"The same occurrence may have happened last night, but if Johnson is here, the characters of the pirate's story could be switched. That would make Johnson and Blackbeard the crooks and the other guys the ones who were knocked unconscious, unless the victim himself was—"

"Wait!" Dillon interrupted.

"I know. He could still be living."

"No, what I mean is what you said about Johnson and the other..."

"Blackbeard?"

"Exactly. That proves it," Dillon said. Murphy naturally didn't catch on. He didn't say anything, but he looked very confused. "I'll explain it to you later, but first I need to talk to someone."

"You can't withhold evidence from me, even if you are the leader of the town," Murphy warned.

"I'm not withholding; I'm delaying. And probably only for an hour or so."

"Wait up, Dillon," Murphy exclaimed. "I'm coming with you." He ran after Dillon, leaving Ray inside with the suspect and con man. Jayne was left guarding the door alone.

Chapter 49

DILLON KNOCKED ON THE left side door inside his hut, behind which Dawn had been staying. Chief Murphy was right behind him.

"Yes?" was the reply, clearly Dawn's voice.

"I need to talk to you."

"Who is it?"

"It's Dill-" He looked around the empty hut. Then he glanced at Murphy. "It's me, Taran."

Murphy mouthed, "*You're* Taran?" inaudibly.

They'd gotten to know each other well over the past few months, but the subject of Dawn and her friends had never come up. Murphy never would have guessed that Dillon was the Taran who the Sundaes had been talking about all along.

"C… come in," she called.

Taran walked in and attempted to smile at her. "How are you doing?"

"I'm okay, I guess…" Dawn smiled as she sat on the cot. She noticed Officer Murphy in the doorway. "Officer, what are you doing here?"

"Dawn?" Murphy looked very confused. "I haven't seen you in quite a while."

"But I just saw you last—or no, I guess not really to you." Dawn stopped. "But to me, I just met with you at the house on Pool Street. The Carr case in December, remember?"

"The Carr case…" Murphy tried to think back. His eyes widened when he remembered all the "facts." "Oh… the Antique Shop Murder? And this is Taran?"

Dawn's smile turned grave quickly.

To Murphy, the Antique Shop Murder was history. The case had been filed as unfinished and all but forgotten since the Sundaes had stopped returning his calls. It was as though they just disappeared one day.

"I have something to tell you about that, Dawn," Taran said grimly. "I'm not sure if this would come as a relief for you or not, but I have to tell you about this." Dawn's expression was grim as well, but she still couldn't look him in the face anymore. " I've figured out who your victim is."

Dawn gasped, then began to sob.

"What, what's the matter?" Taran sat down beside her, rubbing her back.

"Nothing… nothing." She wiped her face. Now she needed something to occupy her mind. She had to come up with something, anything, some bit of conversation that would steer away from the investigation. Then again, she needed to find someway for Taran to bring the Sundaes to the island to help her out, in order for her to investigate more easily. This had to be done without alerting Taran. "Don't worry Taran, we're… done," she lied. "We solved the murder."

"Really?" Taran looked surprised. "Who did it?"

"Umm…" Dawn looked down.

"What is going on, Dawn?" Taran asked.

"What do you mean?" she replied. "We know it occurred a long time ago, the person who did it couldn't still be living in our time, and the pirate's sword was definitely the murder weapon." *No!*

"Yeah, about that—"

"But I don't want to focus on that anymore," Dawn said. "Especially without the others…" *Shoot! It slipped out! I linked them openly to the case, and now he'll know I want to bring them in order to find enough evidence and probably convict him. Oh no.*

Dawn was caught up with the possibility of Taran being guilty. She was flustered by the fact that the man in front of her could have just killed, plotted to kill, or planned to soon kill a poor young man.

"If I brought the others here, would you continue the case?" Taran suggested. "Find out who did it?"

"The case is… finished; we don't need to continue," Dawn still insisted. She was confused now. Why would Taran have them brought here to continue the case? She knew Randy would be murdered here, but she didn't want to let him know she knew. And how did he know? She never addressed him by name before with Taran. *What is going on?*

"How could we possibly finish the case here anyway?" she questioned. "This place has nothing to do with the case. We don't have any evidence here."

"We sure do," Taran answered. "He's here."

"What?"

"He's here on this island."

If he killed Randy, why would he let it be known that he was here, reveal that he had opportunity, and want the Sundaes to investigate? Of course, motive was appar-

ent from Randy's journal, but has Taran read it? For an instant, she felt a little relieved, forcing herself once again to consider Taran's innocence.

"Where… is he?" she said, assuming the worst.

Taran looked down. "He's dead."

"Wha—he died here?" Dawn tried to act surprised. Really, she was saddened. Randy seemed to be such a sweet guy; she regretted not trying to find him over the course of the afternoon the day before. She just didn't know she had such a limited time.

"Yes, I'm sorry," Taran said. "I had no idea he'd be here when he died. If I had, I would have tried to do something to prevent it. I didn't even recognize him when he came. It was the sword that showed me the connection to the two murders."

"Even so…" Dawn wondered, "how—" *Where's the body? How did it end up in our time? Is it still in this time now?* "Where is… can I see the body?"

"That's what I came here for." Taran shook his head. "We can't find it; it's missing. I don't have time to search for it because I have other things that take priority, and I don't want it publicized right now. So to keep this quiet, I figured I could get you and your friends to comb the island for the body."

"Great!" Dawn exclaimed. "I mean… well yeah… that narrows down the suspects to the people on the island—"

"Actually," Taran stopped her, "I've produced a prime suspect. And it would coincide with the case you guys had before I left, a stabbing. We found Blackbeard's saber, and we found Blackbeard with it. That was how I knew Randy was the same victim as yours."

"Randy…" Dawn looked down again. "All right, I'll talk to the suspect, but I think you're right. The girls should come with me."

Chapter 50

Dawn followed Taran down to the bunker and into the platform room under the east-southeast door. The machine was already set to the correct time, 2348, and it was set to "send." Taran accessed the computer and set the codes to the corresponding date, December 29, 2348.

Before long, the images of all six of the Sundaes and Sherri appeared on the platform; they appeared the same way as Murphy had, the first Taran had brought to the island only three weeks or so before. Their candid faces were classic; Dawn wanted a camera by this point, so much that she laughed out loud.

"Butterscotch, is that…" Chocolate stammered. "It is!"

They all ran over to rejoin their lost comrade.

"Where did you go last night?" Cream asked.

"Last night?" Dawn repeated. "What? Oh, the party. Sorry about that, Cream. I ended up here. Oh, and sorry about the mess of plates that must have ended up on the closet floor."

"That explains it," Caramel said. "Except where *is* here, exactly?"

"Oh, I apologize." Dawn walked over to her fiancé. "You girls remember Taran." She put her hand on his shoulder. She was slightly behind him so that he couldn't see her waving her hands, signaling the Sundaes to avoid mentioning Taran's involvement in the murder.

"Of course." Sherri held out her hand. "How have you been?"

Taran shook her hand. "I've been doing just fine, thank you."

He greeted them all and left them to Dawn for whatever business she had planned out for them. Dawn then showed them upstairs and led them across to the Island Inn. She led them into the room in which they would be staying. It was a room much larger than the others, but clearly not spacious enough to comfortably house seven people.

"There's a communal kitchen on the first floor and an outhouse out—"

"An outhouse?" Strawberry exclaimed.

"Yes," Dawn answered. "There isn't any indoor plumbing yet. Most of the people don't like it, but the plumbing won't be finished for a while. So for now, there are several outhouses around the island town. One of them is behind the inn in a fenced yard at the end of the hall on the first floor."

"Whatever," was her disappointed response. The others had similar reactions, too.

They all entered the room and sat down on whatever they could find that looked comfortable. Chocolate, Sherri, and Butterscotch were on one bed. Strawberry, Cream, and Vanilla stood in front of the door. Fudge sat in a wooden chair in one corner of the room. Caramel leaned against the wall on the far side of the room.

"I suppose you are all wondering why I brought you here today," Dawn began, trying to sound like a movie detective about to reveal the most critical piece of evidence in the entire film.

"Skip the show and get on with it," Cream scoffed.

"Okay, fine." Vanilla gave in, but she did start to pace around in a straight line in front of her audience for effect. "As you know, or have very well assumed, Taran brought us here with his time machine. This island, all of us, and many more people are all in 1841. Taran has, for whatever reason, brought together an ensemble of people from different times and walks of life to inhabit this primitive town."

"I don't follow." Fudge looked up at her. "Why'd he bring us here?"

"Did he miss us?" Caramel asked with pouty lips.

"I'm getting to it," she replied. "Taran doesn't want people knowing his true identity for one reason or another, so he's going by an alias: Dillon. That's what you girls are to call him from now on in public."

"All right," Strawberry agreed.

"Okay," was Cream's reply.

But, just like Sherri would, she exclaimed, "But who cares? Why wouldn't Taran want anyone knowing who he really is? Would anyone honestly even care who he really is?"

"It's a Karz thing," Vanilla answered. "It doesn't have to make sense; they just want to be able to cover this whole thing up if something goes wrong."

"So..." Butterscotch concluded, "we were right. Taran is a bad man. He's one of those twisted freaks who would stop at nothing to rule the entire world."

"Oh, come on," Dawn said. "You're overreacting."

"Yeah, you guys get carried away too easily," Caramel added.

"Do we, though?" Sherri turned to Caramel, then back to Dawn. "She could be right. Who knows what someone could do once he can control time itself?"

"He could even cover up a murder," Fudge blurted out.

Everyone gasped, but they received a bigger shock when they heard Dawn's next response.

"Unfortunately," Dawn began to explain, "she's right." She drew in a deep breath. "And Sherri was wrong. There is, or I should say *was*, someone who cared about knowing Dillon's true identity: Randy Carr."

Now everyone was slack-jawed, with gaping mouths and wide eyes. This included Chocolate, who broke the silence with her own conclusion. "Dillon... the Dillon from the journal is Taran..."

Dawn explained the situation about Randy being on the island and getting killed. Of course, there was really no way to determine the time of death because of everything that had happened. "But we do have one undeniable piece of evidence." She reached into a drawer in the desk beside the door. She pulled out a clear bag, from which she pulled out the evidence.

"*This* is the evidence linking the case to here." Dawn lifted the sword for them to see. "It looks exactly like the antique that we found at Don's place in 2348. The man murdered here was killed the same way, and the people's primary suspect here is..." She waited for the others to give the obvious reply.

"L... Luke Blackbeard," Chocolate walked over to the sword and, with her gloves, lifted it gently from Dawn's hands. She saw it was true. "It's the very same sword, only 500 years before we found it!"

"Exactly. Randy was killed here, by one of the few suspects here, and the body was sent into the future," Dawn explained.

"Do you realize what you've just said, Dawn?" Strawberry asked. "You've given enough evidence to incriminate Taran..."

Dawn looked down gloomily. "Yeah... I know."

"But at the same time we opened the door for numerous suspects, none of which we've had the pleasure of meeting," Butterscotch informed them

"I agree. Taran may very well have killed him, too," Sherri responded. "But Butterscotch is right, the time machine is here along with all the evidence we had in 2348. The difference is the people who actually have access to the weapon, victim, etc..."

"It's possible, I guess," Dawn responded. "But Taran *is* the only one who knows how to operate the time machine."

"That we know of, yes," Caramel added. "But circumstantially, we *do* have Blackbeard to consider, girls." She looked over at Dawn. "I mean, pressing some random buttons on the time machine couldn't be too hard. And he's already their suspect."

"But still," Strawberry said, "we have to be able to prove it somehow. So, really, girls, it's possible he's not our man, anyway. There are several other people on the island capable of getting access to the machine and sending a body randomly through time."

So they started the full island investigation. They planned to find any and every piece of evidence from this town's version of the murder. The Sundaes knew it would fill in any gaps time travel left in their original conclusions.

Cream, Dawn, and Strawberry went to the general store, where they looked for people to talk about Blackbeard. Their main goal was to find out if anyone around town had seen or heard of him prior to the night before. Most of the customers and employees still hadn't seen or heard of Blackbeard, so they really weren't that much help in finding out about him.

Sherri, Chocolate, Butterscotch, and Fudge kept busy nearby at the beach. They split up and talked to several people who were sunbathing, playing Frisbee, swimming, and burying each other in the sand. Sherri was talking to one of the two lifeguards who were on duty at one end of the beach. Butterscotch and Chocolate were scanning for people to question. Finally, Fudge was at the edge of the water talking to somebody who was swimming.

Chapter 51

VANILLA WALKED OUT OF the congested general store building to look around the town and breathe. She wanted to relax and soak in the calm, warm sunshine.

Meanwhile, inside the store, Cream got distracted by some colorful tropical fruit laying in one of the tight wall aisles. When she reached for a papaya, she looked left and right. She noticed a heap in the corner. It appeared to slowly move as if it were breathing in and out, breathing steadily as if it were asleep. She suddenly realized that it was in fact a jacket and that a new-looking hat was on the top.

A tag hung from the hat that caught Cream's attention. She bit into the papaya and softly chomped away at it. She walked over slowly to the jacket heap that she assumed was a poor person who could find nowhere to sleep the night before. It was definitely a person; upon closer examination, she saw a muddy, old boot at the bottom and a finger or two peeking out behind the sleeve of the jacket that was thrown over him.

The owner of the store, meanwhile, saw Strawberry interviewing some of his employees. "Hello there, miss." He shook hands with Strawberry, who had been talking to a black haired man in blue jeans and a white dress shirt. "If you'll excuse me, Scott, I need to talk to her just for one second."

He took her away from the people in the store and lowered his voice so that even Strawberry had trouble hearing what he was saying. "You're a detective, right?"

"That's right."

"Well, I didn't tell anybody this because I didn't want to cause a scene, but there is a man by the fruit stand in the corner," Tim explained. "He was there this morning when I came to open the store. I thought he was homeless so I gave him a jacket to cover up with without waking him. But I heard something earlier about a..." He said the last word softly.

"A what?"

"A..."

"I can't hear you."

"Murder" escaped his lips.

"I... a rumor about it or heard about it?" Strawberry asked.

"I guess it was just a rumor, but this corner guy looks like what you just described to Mr. MacKensie."

"This man's a pirate?"

"See for y—" He looked over Strawberry's shoulder and saw Cream leaning over the clothing heap eating a piece of papaya. "Hey!" He ran up to her. "Get away from there!"

Cream looked straight at him like a deer looks at an oncoming car. "What... what did I do?"

"It's all right, sir." Strawberry ran up to intervene. "She works with me. She's also a detective. They call me 'Strawberry' and they call her 'Cream.' If our nicknames are too distracting, just call me Diane and her Delores."

"I guess all you need now is Vanilla and Chocolate," Tim joked.

"Actually, we've got them, too."

"Anyway, what is it you had to say about this man again?" Strawberry asked.

"I think he may have been involved in the occurrence last night," Tim whispered, now looking at Cream.

"So he's a pirate?" Cream asked.

"Yes," Strawberry answered. "Do you know what this means? Blackbeard very well may have been telling the truth about what happened last night."

"So there *was* a murder!" Tim shouted.

The customers and clerks all looked in his direction with shocked faces. With his face beet red, Tim laughed weakly and returned their stares, not in shock as theirs were, but in embarrassment.

"Well, of course!" Strawberry said loudly, devising a plan to make Tim's exclamation more inconspicuous. "Otherwise, why would the object be to... to find the weapon, place, and murderer if there wasn't a murder, you know? It wouldn't be much of a game."

"He'll never understand this board game," Cream said, also loudly, to back up her friend. Then the customers continued their business, realizing there was nothing to be worried about.

The detectives dared not arouse the man under the heap of jackets until there wouldn't be as many witnesses, in case the man ended up getting upset or dangerously violent.

By that time, Dawn had come in and led them to Kel's Place for something to eat. They hadn't eaten all day. Since the restaurant hadn't been running very long and there were few customers, there weren't any extensive choices. Despite this, they were all happy with chicken sandwiches.

Chapter 52

DID YOU SEE A large boat or ship sail past here today?" Sherri asked a lifeguard, dodging a Frisbee. The lifeguard was holding a red life preserver and wearing dark, reflective sunglasses.

"No, not that I remember," he answered indifferently.

"You must have been watching the water all day, right?"

"Yep."

"Nothing?"

"Nope."

"Gee, thanks for your help."

"No prob… really." He still stood staring at the waves and the people swimming. He stood stolidly, as if she wasn't still standing right next to him, looking at him with a disgusted look on her face.

Sherri scoffed and walked away.

Butterscotch looked everywhere at the rocky shore along the sides of the beach. She couldn't locate a ship or dinghy that would prove Blackbeard's story. She'd just ended a meaningless conversation with a swimmer who had been at home at the time and never went to the beach beforehand, so he couldn't aid them in the investigation anyway, having no clue about the situation.

She mumbled to herself as she sauntered over to the forest on the side of the beach. Now she stood facing the forest with the waves to her left. She reluctantly stepped into the slimy, wet sand, just enough to peer past an outcropping of trees, but she couldn't spot a beached ship. There wasn't even an anchored ship, for that matter. Then she heard the other three walk past her into the forest along a path. Before long, Butterscotch darted onto the dry sand and ran to join her comrades.

They walked briefly and stopped at an unnatural-looking bush. Fudge and Sherri fumbled through the brush and twigs. Surely as the weather was hotter than blazes, the "bush" had no roots. Under the camouflage was an overturned canoe. It was painted red and appeared to have been hidden for sometime. The paint was worn, and the blue and white painted markings and symbols were smudged and worn as well.

Chocolate and Butterscotch inspected the boat closely. Butterscotch found a small hole in the bottom near the front of the canoe. Chocolate, however, was more interested in the history of the boat; the most telling of features were the blue and white painted markings.

"I've never seen this type of writing before. It must be an ancient cryptic language that was lost somewhere," Chocolate explained. She would be considered the expert, given her extensive historical background of dead western languages and tribes. "This symbol looks almost like a mask with horns and a carved face with eyeholes. It's probably a tribal canoe belonging to the natives of this island. It… you know, it almost appears to be similar to the style of ancient Bermudan tribes, perhaps eighteenth or nineteenth century."

"I think that's what year Dillon hypothesized as well," Butterscotch agreed. "Dillon was telling me about the village on the other side of the forest. He offered also to show me the islander palace and all around the center tower, which is some sort of shrine or something. Anyway, the way he described it, the palace must have had similar symbols and markings as this canoe."

Sherri didn't care about the history of the canoe or about the mystery of the symbols and carving. She just wanted to take advantage of the practical use of it. "Why don't we just take that canoe out and find the ship?"

"Very direct, Sherri," Fudge said. She turned to Butterscotch. "I agree. Let's take the boat out and look to see if Blackbeard's story has any truth behind it. It will help us along with this case."

They ripped away the smaller, loose vines and worked at unburying the rest from the thicker, denser vegetation. When the canoe was finally cleared off, all four carried it to the edge of the woods, where it met the beach. They pushed it smoothly through the sand into the water. Chocolate and Butterscotch volunteered to stay ashore as the others threw their sneakers onto the beach and steadied themselves in the old craft. Realizing they had no tool with which to steer, Sherri sent Chocolate to locate an oar near to where the canoe was found.

It took some searching, but, sure enough, she found two short red oars under the brush and carried them over to the others in the canoe. "There you go." She handed one to Sherri, in the front, and one to Fudge, at the rear of the canoe.

The two on shore watched as the canoe crept slowly away from them toward the horizon. When it left the cove, they saw the canoe head to the right and disappear behind an outcropping of branches.

Chapter 53

It grew darker as Vanilla was filled in with the details about the store corner pirate, and they all shared their suspicions about him. The entire time that they ate, Strawberry had kept her eye on the entrance of the store, suspecting the pirate would want to leave sooner or later. By then they had all polished off their plates and were ready to leave, but Cream and Vanilla engaged in an extensive conversation about nothing.

"I see what you mean, Vanilla," Cream said. "But you have to admit the resemblance…"

Dawn was about to argue a point she'd kept in the back of her mind since Cream had started her argument. However, she was interrupted by Strawberry tapping lightly on her shoulder.

"I'd hate to interrupt at this critical juncture in your ever important conversation, but the pirate is on the move." Strawberry couldn't help but point out the window at a man leaving the general store.

At the same time the other two came to see this. In a rush, they went down the stairs and ran out the door, nearly knocking poor Kel flat on her face. But even in the rush, Strawberry apologized and made sure Kel was still standing.

The restaurant door swung open and 'the who' that the Sundaes presumed to be Johnson heard a loud slam and looked in their direction. Realizing the three women must be running toward him for one of two reasons, he decided also to run.

"Hey!" Strawberry shouted. "Wait up, it's all right!"

Still he ran, and at first much faster than they did. His path wasn't favorable for the Sundaes, either. He zigzagged through the streets, turning left at the first and turning right down the second. He circled the Inn and turned back down the street toward Kel's Place. Then he hid in the forest around the back of it.

When the Sundaes reached the restaurant, the branches were dead still, making finding him nearly impossible. Nevertheless, the attempt was made.

Vanilla stayed outside the trees, and the others circled around Kel's Place in opposite directions until they met Vanilla. They never spotted any movement in the dead streets, so they concluded that their suspect had fled into the jungle.

"Did you see anything move in there?" Cream whispered to Vanilla.

"No."

"This is hopeless," Strawberry exclaimed. Still, she assumed they'd have seen something if the pirate hadn't merely dropped into a prone position just behind the brush. "Listen, if there is any movement, even the twitching of a small branch, we move in immediately," she commanded as softly as she could. "He's not getting away."

Sherri steered the craft swiftly around, and they headed back toward the cove. They had had no luck on this end of the beach, so their next destination was the other end, where, if Blackbeard's story was true, there should be a massive pirate ship waiting for them to spot it.

But neither girl was paying attention. Sherri was more interested in surviving the waves constantly threatening the canoe's stability. Fudge was concentrating on her one-person conversation, which she thought Sherri was listening to. So when the red and white sail came slowly into their view and a Jolly Roger was staring at them with his hollow eyes, they were taken by surprise.

"Oh, good gravy!" Fudge exclaimed. "It's really there! It's a… pirate ship! Isn't she beautiful?" Fudge was just as amazed as Chocolate with historical things such as the canoe and pirate ship.

The ship, massive as it was, was a small ship for its day. It could be well managed with a mere skeleton crew and had only three sails. The front sail was smaller and had thin red and white vertical stripes; the back sail was similarly designed. It was triangular and designed for steering, secondary to the rudder. The main sail was massive and had thick red and white vertical stripes. There were several tears in this sail, and in the center was the Jolly Roger, who also appeared atop the main mast on a red and black flag waving in the wind.

The rest of this piece of history wasn't as glamorous. The hull was composed of rotting, wooden boards that were peeling and warped. In discolored white paint, *Atlantic Gemini* was written along the side wall under the rail. The crow's nest had been taken down, and the flag was torn. The deck was falling apart, with warped, arched planks. The rudder was bent, and finally, the helm's wheel had taken too many turns against the currents. Three spokes were missing, and it creaked with every movement.

Regardless of these minor details, Fudge was fascinated, so much so that her eyes would have jumped out of her head if they weren't connected.

Finally, Sherri steered the canoe toward one last wave and straightened it out. She then looked up and saw the ship. "Fudge!" Sherri tapped her shoulder. After she got no response, she shook Fudge violently. "Fudge, the ship!"

But Fudge's fascination with the ship was too intense and too distracting. It was too late when either of them realized how close they'd ended up to the ship. They were close.

TOO close.

Chapter 54

Through all of this investigation and exploration, Caramel held the fort. She kept their hotel room secure and searched thoroughly throughout Randy's room. Just after Vanilla led the second group from their room, Caramel locked the door and went to room 203. She was looking, unsure for what, but nevertheless desperately for something on the junk table. The scene seemed to revolve around it. The weapon was under it, there was blood next to it, and blood stained on it.

The junk table seemed to be covered in random shards of metal, springs, gears, and other shiny bits and pieces. But, upon closer examination on Caramel's part, there was a recurrent theme. She found that all of the pieces were certain parts of clockwork and clock casings. There were faces and hands in one pile, gears in another, springs and screws in another pile, and underneath some casings and glass was a booklet.

She picked it up and opened it. Inside were diagrams and pictures of several types of analog clockwork and watches, many of which were small pocket watches.

"This is interesting. Did Randy fix clocks for a living or something?" Caramel was thinking out loud, of course with no one to listen to her. "Let's see here…" She flipped through more of the book.

It was fascinating to her that people had once used these as time pieces. "How could they possibly get used to deciphering an analog image?" she wondered aloud. She was contemplating that when she turned another page, on which she found a slip of paper.

It read "the green man" in a scribbled and rushed writing, as if it may have been in despair. The writing was definitely the same as that in the journal, only less neat and less carefully written. The paper was on page 173, which showed a close, detailed picture of a nineteenth century style golden pocket watch. Engraved on the cover was a winning poker hand. Just under the picture, handwritten, was "It's uncanny!" in blue ink. It was in the same writing as the "green man" bookmark, but not as desperate.

"'It's uncanny'?" Caramel read. "What does this mean?" *There's probably an identical watch to the one in the picture and he found it? Maybe. Maybe the one who had possession of it was involved in something he'd kill to keep secret. Maybe the watch is worth a lot to him…*

Her thoughts began to go wild with theories that could answer the question of motive in the case. *Was it an insider, a government scandal? Wait a second! "The green man"? Who is that? And is he significant? He must be!*

Caramel left the hotel room to seek out the answers to these questions. Her first stop was the Sundaes' hotel room to get her notepad. She would want to jot down some notes and some questions, allowing her to stay on task more easily.

She started down the street, turning left out of the inn, and walked around the northern part of town. She was keeping her eye out for any large mass of green that may resemble a person. Searching the northern area, a more residential section, was a failed attempt, so she came back around past Taran's hut and toward the store. Soon she saw, from the front of the store, a man wearing all green.

Is that him? It was Trickster that Caramel had spotted, standing in front of Kel's Place talking to another man. He, Flatfoot Thompson, was another man Caramel didn't recognize. She approached the two cautiously, watching from across the street to be sure they wouldn't notice her watching them. She couldn't hear what Trickster was saying, so she stressed her eyes to read his lips.

"Are… sure… rid of…" she whispered, reading what Trickster said as she watched. She sat down on a bench, conveniently placed beside where she stood. It had been made to someday become a bus stop. She wrote down on her pad exactly what she could be sure he said. After a few minutes, the latter in the conversation looked around and sneaked away. Trickster then casually left the scene.

He proceeded down the road that was to Caramel's right and walked past the store. After he was quite a way down the road, Caramel quietly followed him. After Trickster repeated the same trail for two laps around two blocks, Caramel lost her patience.

He's probably not actually going anywhere. Either he has nowhere to go or he's just wasting time, Caramel thought. She caught up to him and tapped on his green shoulder.

"Hey, you," she greeted him.

He turned around. "Hi, can I help you?" Trickster looked confused.

I'll try to lead him into talking about the watch. "I was wondering if you'd been in town long or not."

"Only a few months. Why?" Trickster asked, now suspicious of the strange woman's motives.

"Well, I can't find a pawn shop around here," Caramel said. "Can you help me find it?"

Why not? Trickster thought. *If there is one, may as well help out, got nothing better to do. Besides, she's kinda cute and well, a pawn shop is an* easy *place to hit.* He nodded.

Trickster continued walking down the road, only this time Caramel was right beside him. As they walked, she and Trickster talked. About what, Caramel never even caught onto; she just said what came to mind that would seem to make sense. Mostly, the conversation revolved around antiques.

"What are you looking for a pawn shop for?" Trickster asked. All the while he looked at her keenly, with an obvious infatuation.

Not responding to Trickster's stare, Caramel answered shortly, "I'm looking for a collectible for my uncle. He collects all sorts of trinkets and odds and ends."

"Are you looking for anything in particular?" Trickster asked. He pulled a golden pocket watch out of his vest pocket and flipped open the cover, checking the time. He was about to put it away when Caramel grabbed his arm.

"Wait!" *That's it, I think.* Caramel asked more gently, "May I see that watch? It may be a perfect addition to my uncle's collection." She didn't mean to imply that particular watch, but that was what Trickster inferred.

"No! Not *this* watch!" Trickster shouted defensively.

"No, no, I mean this style; it looks pretty neat," Caramel said. "I—"

"You can't have this one!" Trickster insisted.

"I meant I'd look probably for something like that at the pawn shop," Caramel reassured him. "May… I see that one now… for a second?"

"Oh…" Trickster sighed and acquiesced. "Sure."

As they continued to wander—for that's what it was, Trickster knew there was no pawn shop, and Caramel certainly didn't want to go to one—Caramel studied the watch intently, and Trickster studied Caramel in the same way.

Meanwhile, Caramel was explaining the situation to herself. *All right, I've got the watch. This must be it. It's uncanny. But now, what did Randy want with this watch? Hmm. I wish I had—oh, what is this? I can feel… I feel weird. Is he looking at me?* She looked up slowly and smiled weakly. Sure enough, he was. *Oh no. I've got to get out of here. He doesn't seem,* she swallowed hard, *safe.*

"Wow, this is an extraordinary design!" Caramel exclaimed.

"Yes," Trickster said indifferently. "It's a poker hand. I had it custom made."

"Really?" Caramel looked up. "You play cards?"

"Oh, yeah," Trickster said. He pulled out a deck of cards and started a showy shuffling routine common to that of a magician's. "Poker is *the* game." He held the deck and fanned out the cards, face down in front of her. "Are you a gambler, Miss... ?"

"I've been known to take a few risks on occasion," she said as she opened up the watch to check the time indicated by the golden plated hands within. "Oh my, is that the right time?"

"I believe so," Trickster answered.

"Well, I'm sorry, I've got to go then," Caramel said nervously.

"Oh, come on, just one card," Trickster enticed her.

She reluctantly drew a card from the middle of the fan. When she turned it slowly to look at it, she was surprised to read what was written on its face: "Kiss me" in red marker. *Huh?*

He leaned toward her, when she went to stop him. "I'll, I'll be late." She turned to leave.

"B... but," Trickster said, grabbing her arm, "what's the rush?"

She shook him loose. "Excuse *me*! I have to go!"

"Hey, hey, hey." Trickster held up his hands.

He could see fear creep into her eyes. He let her go, and she backed away from him slowly, toward the road.

She then said, "I'll find my own way to the pawn shop." She finally turned around after she felt she'd gone a good, safe distance from him and ran toward the Island Inn.

As she left his sight, Trickster thought. He wondered, *Why, why did she abruptly leave? What did she suspect him of? Could he have read her that wrong? Besides, she couldn't have been only looking for a watch for her uncle. There was something deeper, right?*

Finally, he continued to walk through town again, trying to forget about the entire episode. He concentrated more on what his comrade from his earlier conversation had found out during the day.

Caramel began to pick up speed. She could no longer see Trickster behind her, and he obviously wasn't following her. Still she ran. She made it back to the Island Inn in no time. She, more calmly now, headed to Randy's room and entered. Once inside, she peered around, looking for more evidence of the intruder, whom she suspected was that gambling, punk magician.

She was thinking about the preemptory way he assumed she liked him, his crooked smile, his enticing but evil eyes, and his penetrating stare. That was when it caught her eye. It glimmered on the floor, sitting mockingly next to the leg of the junk table, laughing at her for not having seen it sooner.

Chapter 55

Cream and Vanilla still kept their vigil between the vast mass of forest and the back patio of Kel's restaurant. It was nearing midnight and Vanilla was slowly drifting away. The pirate had been hiding for nearly four hours without even rustling, so Vanilla couldn't help but let herself go… back to Detroit, back home.

Cream soon followed, only she'd decided to go to the park downtown and wander aimlessly. It was a beautiful day, and the sun was bright, but not too hot. The warmth of it was soothing as she came upon the bench in the center of the park.

But the sandman's lead was interrupted when someone tripped over the both of them, causing the sandman to disappear. They heard Strawberry shout their names and yell for them to follow "that man!"

"Cream, Vanilla! I need you!" They heard her, along with a rustling in the woods, as she also came into view. "He's over there, girls. Come on. Dawn, Delores, follow that man!"

Still dazed, they followed Strawberry, who was now sprinting down toward the street lamp at Kel's Place, then turned left onto the main street. The pirate, they could see, turned sharply left again and headed for the beach. They followed and soon came to the sandy beach, which was now completely empty save for the silhouette of a man running along the woods on the right side of the beach.

Cream, Vanilla, and Strawberry darted after him, running as fast as they could. Vanilla, who was faster than her friends, had only a fifty foot distance from him when she suddenly slipped, landing face first in the sand.

Strawberry stopped to help her up, and Cream, seeing now that the man was carrying something that was very heavy, something he'd retrieved from the woods, stopped to help Vanilla as well. She figured he couldn't go far, assuming he was planning on carrying what looked like a boat to the placid water, still several yards away.

They swiftly helped Dawn along just as the boat was placed into the water. Cream took the lead and followed the boat into the water, now knee deep. She grabbed the pirate's arm, which reached for an oar, and hurled him over the side. She then took the bandana from his head and tied his hands together, jerking him up to stand.

Impressed by the improvisation, Strawberry followed suit. She removed the towrope from the boat and restrained the pirate's arms. Along with the rope, she found a sword fastened to the floor of the boat.

They brought him on the beach to dry off, leading him to a log to sit down. He calmly gave in and sat down willingly. Without any delay, Strawberry began to question him. She looked directly at him, through him. But he didn't notice; he wouldn't look at her. Even in his responses, he kept a firm watch on his feet.

"What's your name?" She pointed at him accusingly. "Well?"

"Whaddya want tuh know fer?" the pirate responded.

"Tell me, now!" she commanded. "Is it Jonathan Johnson?"

No response.

"Are you Johnson?"

He still wouldn't say anything.

"Listen, Strawberry," Cream said, taking her arm gently, "you're being too… come here for a second." She led Strawberry aside and spoke softly so Johnson couldn't hear. "You're being too aggressive. The guy's probably scared to death, after us chasing him like that without any apparent reason, especially if he didn't do anything."

"Then why would he run?" Strawberry insisted.

"Because he's a pirate, he—"

"Exactly, a pirate, you can't trust pirates."

"But he's used to people not trusting him, so he assumed we were chasing him, which we were, and ran. Listen, I'll talk to him about his captain and stuff, *calmly*, and that way he'll know the price he'll be paying by keeping quiet."

Coming back over to him, they found the pirate was still looking down.

"All right, Mr.… Sir," Cream began. "I don't know if you're this Johnson or not, but either way, since you are a buccaneer of sorts, what I have to say pertains to you." She paused and then began to pace, never looking at the accused.

"Last night, a young man with his whole life ahead of him, in more ways than one, I suppose…" she said, beginning to go on a tangent, "because his death came physically before his own birth. He even had his birth ahead of him. Then again, he'd have been dead by the time we were born, had he been murdered or not…"

"Oh my gosh, Cream." Vanilla shook her head. "Get to the point."

"Hmm?" Cream looked over at Dawn, and then at Johnson, who had a confused look on his face. "Right, sorry. He was killed, stabbed. Stabbed with a sword like that one." She picked up the sword in Strawberry's hands. "And a man, similar to you, was found with the sword, in the same room… and yet a different room… anyway, and only minutes later. Or is it many years before?"

"Ahem." Strawberry glared at Cream.

"I know." Cream nodded. "It's just a very confusing concept, that we could find him dead and then Dawn could find him living and then dead again, years before. Anyway," she said, shaking her head, "the man found with the sword claims to be Captain Luke Blackbeard. Sound familiar?"

The pirate started to look up when the name was said, then back to his feet.

Without waiting for a reply, Cream carried on. "So, Mr. Blackbeard claims he has an alibi, but no one else can vouch for him. So, unless someone can truthfully tell us where he was when the murder occurred, that would be the only thing that could legitimize Blackbeard's story and save his butt. Otherwise, Blackbeard's going to jail for murder."

The pirate was clearly interested in Cream's story, but he tried to hide it. "So what if this Black… beard you're talking about needs an alibi…" He looked up, but not at any of the Sundaes. "What could I do to help? There's nothing I can do."

"Sure you can," Vanilla answered. All you have to do is tell us what you and Blackbeard did last night, or what you were doing, and legitimize Blackbeard's story. You know, prove it's true."

The pirate, Johnson, knew he was figured out, but he continued to lead them on anyway. "What did Cap—Blackbeard claim to be doing last night?"

"He said that he and another pirate landed last night and came to this island to search for something," Strawberry said. "He said it has been a long time since the last time he came to this island, said he was looking for something valuable, so he and the pirate split up to search. He took the eastern side, and the other took the west side. If you can back up this story, we really can't hold him unless we get better evidence to convict him, like a motive."

"Aye." Johnson sighed. "I guess, then, I'll have to say yes. My name is Jonathan Johnson. I'm Captain Blackbeard's first mate. He and I *did* land here last night, and he brought me to find something buried. The island is very different, so he wanted me to look for a specific land mark that was near to it. It would have been very easy had this village and these strange roads not been built here. Anyway, I went that way." He pointed toward Dillon's hut, which was barely in view, at the top of the inclined beach. "And then the captain went that way." He pointed this time toward the right turn near Dillon's hut, in the direction of the Island Inn.

"Thanks, Johnson." Strawberry smiled.

Chapter 56

While sipping some juice through a straw, Chocolate looked across the table at her friend. She then looked through the window to her left, into the dark night. "It's getting kinda late."

Butterscotch nodded in agreement, her mouth stuffed with food that Taran had prepared for them. They had decided to wait in Taran's hut for Fudge and Sherri to return. From there, they had a clear view of the beach. Taran had to prepare food for them; otherwise, he'd be branded by them forever as having the worst manners. So to redeem himself, he whipped up some of Wakna's recipes. He left shortly afterward to talk to someone in the native's village.

"I think they should have been back by now," Chocolate said again. After no response, she sighed heavily and looked out the window. "Oh! There they are!" She pointed and ran outside. She had seen the outline of four people running outside, on the beach, toward the water, tackling each other, and then returning from the water. One of them was restrained by two of the others.

Chocolate stood watching the spectacle from Taran's doorway. Butterscotch still ate and nodded. Chocolate dashed in the direction of the beach. She looked back for Butterscotch, who wasn't there. She returned and looked into the hut through the window to see her comrade. She stomped over to her and shouted.

"Are you even listening to me?"

Butterscotch now looked up at her. "Oh…" She put her hands up to her ears and tapped what looked like the entrance to her ear canals with each of her index fingers. "I'm sorry, did you say something?"

Chocolate scowled at her.

"What?" Butterscotch said innocently. She'd been listening to music in her communication earpiece. The earpiece went right into her ears and blended in to look almost invisible.

"Follow me." She sighed and walked out of the hut. "They're ba—" she began. Then she got a closer look at who was on the beach. *That looks like Strawberry, not Sherri or Fudge.*

"No, Chocolate." Butterscotch swallowed. "That's Cream, Vanilla, and Strawberry, all talking to a man with the outward appearance of a buccaneer sitting down on a log."

"Thanks for clarifying that; I don't know what I'd do without you," she quipped.

They headed down and heard Strawberry say something just as they came into her view. "Hey, girls!" Strawberry looked up. "There you are. Guess who we have here, Chocolate and Butterscotch?"

"Is that who I think it is?"

"It's Jonathan Johnson, Luke Blackbeard's cabin boy."

"For the last time, I'm not a cabin boy, ma'am." Johnson rose and added, "I'm a first mate, only me and me cap'n don't have a ship anymore, so we're travelin' with another cap'n." He turned and shook Butterscotch's hand and then Chocolate's. He could be a gentleman when he wanted to be. "Nice tuh meet y'all."

"So is he going to cooperate?" Butterscotch asked Strawberry.

"He says he's going to," Strawberry replied. "But I'm not sure if we can trust him."

"Well, he does want to get his captain back," Cream said.

"He seems all right to me," Vanilla added.

"We'll give it a go," Butterscotch agreed.

"I wonder if he really *is* missing an eye," Chocolate chimed in.

"What?" the other Sundaes all exclaimed.

"Anyway, are you sure he—" Cream started.

"You all know I can hear you, right?" Johnson looked around at them. "I'm still here, and I can still understand yer English. I've heard every word you guys said. And to respond to yer doubts, there is no reason for you to not trust me. I'll help you guys clear me captain's name."

"Right… anyway." Chocolate walked around the log to Strawberry's side. "Fudge and Sherri left over five hours ago in a canoe to find the ship. I'm kinda worried. You don't think anything could've happened to them, do you?"

"Don't worry," Strawberry replied. "We've got Johnson's boat." She turned and pointed down to the shore. "We can just use it to go find them. If they encountered the ship, it can't be too far."

"She's right," Johnson said. "If they found the ship, they've probably been captured. I know exactly where the ship is. I can get your friends if they will help you in yer plan to get me cap'n back."

"That would be great." Cream patted his back.

They went down to the boat and Johnson brought it further ashore. Strawberry sat in the front with Vanilla. Chocolate sat on a plank in the middle, and Butterscotch sat in the back. Cream was standing between Butterscotch and Chocolate, but she couldn't sit down. There wasn't enough room.

"I could sit on the floor of the boat. That way Johnson could sit over there." Cream pointed to a spot between where Strawberry and Butterscotch sat. "Right in there."

"No, that won't work," Strawberry said. "Sherri and Fudge need somewhere to sit after we get them. We can't overload the boat. You guys are just going to have to draw straws on who goes and who stays. The short two will stay."

"Wait, 'you guys'?" Butterscotch repeated. "What about you?"

"Are you kidding me?" Strawberry scoffed. "I'm the boss; I have to go. It's an obligation for me to be with my girls in any case of severe danger. I think cutthroat pirates qualify as danger."

"That's a bad excuse!" Butterscotch complained again. "You're so mean!"

"C'mon," Strawberry said, "you're acting like you've already lost. Quit complaining!"

Everyone piled out of the boat and went over to the log. Strawberry found a twig there that she broke into three pieces of equal size. She then broke one in half. She put all four into her left hand, where she let each stick out of her fist about an inch and a half.

Finally she allowed each of the Sundaes to pick, in alphabetical order, a makeshift "straw." First Vanilla (Dawn) got a long stick. Next Chocolate (Debbie) got a short stick. Third was Cream (Delores), who left Butterscotch (Donna) with a short stick.

"Oh, man!" Butterscotch threw the stick to the ground. "Well, at least I'm stuck with Chocolate again!" She sighed and led her friend toward Taran's hut. "We'll be in the hut should you need us," she called to Strawberry.

"All right!" Strawberry sat again in the front of the boat with Vanilla beside her. Cream took the back, while Johnson put the oars on his bench in the middle of the small, red rowboat. It was a bench similar to that in the front and back of the rowboat.

Johnson then pushed the boat into the sea and took his position. Facing Cream, with the oars in hand, he rowed as hard as he could. When they finally got going smoothly, he instructed Cream to navigate.

"What... wha... how do I do that?" Cream stammered.

"Aye, it's very simple. Just tell me when we're headed for a wave or a tree or a rock; that way we can prevent a crash," Johnson explained. "It's an easy job once you get used to it."

"Oh, okay, sounds simple enough," Cream replied. "Good thing I brought my flashlight with me. I can see anything with this, even at this time of night." She turned on her flashlight and beamed light out in front of the boat.

With that, they sailed off on the calm, black water in search of the pirate ship Sherri and Fudge had sought after that afternoon. Soon they disappeared from Butterscotch's sight into the night.

Chapter 57

"THERE IT IS!" STRAWBERRY pointed. The massive ship was anchored among a group of overgrown trees overhanging the mouth of a cove. The water was calmer here, but still very dark. Strawberry could see a treacherous lamp among the trees, which gave away the ship's refuge.

"Aye, ma'am," Johnson confirmed. "And Cap'n Redbeard is on the deck up there with his first mate, the ones in blue, see?"

The deck on the stern of the ship was the highest part of the bulk of the ship, second only to what used to be the crow's nest atop the main mast. A golden-colored rail made for the perimeter of the deck was crafted into intricate patterns, and on the back was a lamp that shone brightly across the sea. On the deck stood a well-trimmed man in black with brown shoulder pads and dark red hair. The traditional patch was over one of his eyes, and where his left hand would have been, there instead was a sharp, metal hook.

Next to the man in black was a man wearing a blue bandana with a blue, light coat. He appeared young, but he had a beard and mustache that were prematurely gray. He didn't have a patch like his companion, and he had both of his hands as well. Next to him was another man that looked exactly like him. He wore the same clothes and had the same face. The only difference was the latter's hat; it was a black triangular hat, similar to Blackbeard's except for being black and not having the feather.

"Which one is the first mate?" Cream asked. "There are two in blue."

"They both are," Johnson stated. "They're twin brothers, and they both act as first mate for Cap'n Redbeard. The one on the right with the bandana is Joshua, and the one on the left, Caleb Stone. The one in black is the Captain."

They neared the ship, so one of the pirates threw down a rope ladder from the starboard side. Johnson steadied the boat as Strawberry led the others up the ladder. The one who lowered the ladder was at the top to help them up. She too had a triangular hat over her dark brown hair.

One of the Stones, the one in the bandana, stepped down from the stern deck to investigate, on behalf of the captain, why these strangers were on the ship. The captain and first mate soon followed.

"Aye, who is this, Johnson?" Joshua Stone asked. "More to imprison? Only this time ya got 'em yerself?"

"No, not at all." Johnson got up from the ladder and stood beside Strawberry. "These girls are going to help us get Cap—uh, Blackbeard back."

"Why?" Redbeard stepped in. "What happened to 'im? Where is he?"

"He's been thrown in jail or somethin,'" Johnson answered. "The runner of the town thinks he killed someone illegally."

"Ha!" Redbeard burst out. "That yella, he'd never kill a man in cold blood, the coward." He changed to a more grave tone. "And *if* he done killed someone, he deserves the punishment fer it. I sent ya over there to retrieve—" He looked over at the Sundaes. "Well, if we got an audience I should be careful what I'm sayin.' We're outta here. We'll leave 'im."

"But he didn't do it!" Johnson said.

"Listen, I will not tolerate insubordinate behavior, 'specially by someone not even in me own crew," Redbeard chastised. "If it's so important to ya, go. Get 'im back as soon as possible. You've tried me patience enough on this voyage. We aren't waitin' too long, or we'll shove off without ya!"

Johnson turned back toward the ladder, but Strawberry stayed.

"Aye, more to ask for, missy?" Stone asked.

"Yes," she replied. "I'd like to bring the others back with me."

"Who?"

"The others to whom you earlier referred."

"You mean the other two women?" Stone asked.

"Yeah," Strawberry repeated, "the other two women."

"All right," Stone said. "Take 'em. We have no useful purpose in leaving them on the ship." He turned to the only female pirate. "Miss Smith, show them to the brig and release the other two prisoners."

Miss Smith, as Stone called her, brought the Sundaes to the bow of the ship and released Fudge and Sherri, who willingly went with them to return to the island even though it was the dead of night.

Unfortunately, Sherri and Fudge had little to report, since they assumed Cream, Strawberry, and Vanilla knew enough now about the ship. All that was said on the way back was Vanilla informing the two that the man rowing was the Johnson that Blackbeard mentioned.

"Wow. So this means we could be pretty close to solving this mystery," Sherri said after they lowered themselves and the boat into the dark water and everyone was seated as comfortably as possible. "Right?"

"Well, not really," Strawberry replied. "We can only supply enough evidence to justify Blackbeard's innocence, not determine anyone's guilt. We're only halfway home." She peered over at Dawn, who took no heed to what they were saying; she was dozing off. Her head soon fell to rest on Strawberry's shoulder.

"But still," Sherri insisted. "Blackbeard could very likely have more knowledge to incriminate whomever he claims he saw. Maybe there were some distinguishing characteristics or something."

"That's true, but we still have to go back to the Island Inn first," Strawberry answered, now quieted to a whisper. "That way we can get Caramel in on this. She's missing out, and I don't think it's fair."

"She won't find anything good just lying around in our room," Sherri added.

"Yeah," Fudge agreed, and then she dropped her head onto Dawn's shoulder.

"Besides," Cream added, "I'm tired."

Chapter 58

THEY LANDED ON THE beach for the last time that night; it was about two o'clock in the morning. Strawberry led everyone up to Taran's hut. There they met with Butterscotch and Chocolate. They all drifted tiresomely without much conversation. They reached the inn in the same manner and climbed up the stairs to their floor. All the while, Johnson followed. They got to their room and opened the door.

Caramel was waiting by the door.

"There you girls are!" she greeted them excitedly.

Strawberry only moaned something, and then she dropped onto the sofa. Butterscotch collapsed on the bed. Fudge and Sherri slumped into two chairs, and Chocolate had passed out in the doorway. Vanilla didn't even make it down the hall.

"Well, I guess it's been a long day for all of us." Caramel sighed. She stepped over to the door, over Chocolate's body. Then she noticed Johnson standing near Dawn's body. "Oh!"

"Hi, I'm Johnson," he said, holding out his hand. "Well, that's what these girls call me, anyway. My name's Jonathan. I'm with Mr. Blackbeard."

"Oh, I see!" Caramel exclaimed. "So you're the pirate. Oh, so they did find you… hmm." She sighed again. "But I'll have to tell them *my* news later. They're, umm, way too tired right now."

"Aye," Johnson agreed. He smirked. "They've been 'running around' all day." They talked for a while, and he left soon afterward to find a room to stay in on the first floor.

When the next morning came, the Sundaes were all fast asleep. That is, of course, except for Caramel. She got up early to fix a healthy breakfast for the girls and run a few errands. She left the waffles, sausage, and eggs in the oven of the inn's kitchen. She left a note by the door explaining where she was going and about the breakfast.

Then out she went. It was another bright and beautiful day. She headed down the road to the temporary home of the police station, the hut built by Miller and Murphy several weeks ago. It was a mere hut, but it did stand sturdily, withstanding a lot of the elements. Across the street from it was an empty lot. That site was where the new and permanent police station was going to be built.

Caramel opened the door and found Murphy inside at his desk, just as she suspected he'd be. He was talking to an officer that he had had Dillon bring to the island that morning. They both looked distressed. That is, until Caramel came in. Then Chief Murphy smiled brightly.

"There you are." Murphy got up. He took a small plastic bag from the drawer on the left side of his desk. "Where did you say you got this again?" He held up the bag. Inside was a golden tooth.

"It was next to one of the legs of the junk table in Randy's room," Caramel told him. "And after a long talk last night with the right person, I think I know just who it belongs to."

"Good, because if this guy is the one who did it, you can't fool around," Murphy warned. "Dillon told me Blackbeard's trial is today, and he said one trial is it." He looked up at her and then at the bag. "He said it begins and ends today, to get it over with. So, if whoever owns this tooth did it, you've got only a few hours to figure out who it is and prove he killed Randy Carr."

"Yes, sir!" Caramel replied. "I'll get the others, and we'll meet you, with my suspect, at Kel's Place in one hour."

Murphy waved her off. "See you then."

When Caramel reached her room, it was empty. She assumed everyone had gone to the kitchen to eat, so she went down there. Sure enough, they were up and heartily eating her food.

She approached Strawberry first, who had a stack of waffles smothered in raspberry maple syrup. She peered up at Caramel and swallowed, waving her hand to signal to her that she had something to say. She then licked her lips and nodded.

Strawberry said, "We have got quite a bit to catch you up with, Caramel. The pirate, the ship, every—where is he, anyway?"

Ignoring Strawberry's rambling, Caramel began to tell *her* what *she* had accomplished. She had already heard from Johnson what the others had done. "Strawberry, I've got a favor to ask you."

"Sure." She swallowed. "Anything." She put more food in her mouth.

"I need you to talk to someone," she began. "I met a man yesterday—"

"Oh," Strawberry scoffed, "you didn't fall in love with him, did you?"

"No!" She laughed. "Oh, gosh, no! This guy's a pig!" Caramel shook her head disgustedly. "Just listen and let me finish what I have to say."

"All right. Shoot."

"I met this man yesterday while I was walking around town," she said again. "He wore this green suit with a green vest, green pants, and a black top hat. Now, he's a gruff man, and he looked like he was a gangster from Gunsmoke, you know, the traditional Dodge City bandit. Anyway, he had this disgusting smirk on his face I could never shake off. Now I think it's a good thing he did.

"His name was John Smith, a 'magician,' so he says. Anyway, he had one tooth missing on the right side of his twisted smile, if you want to call it that. And I didn't think much of it, but then, after I kinda scared him off, I got back to the room and found this."

Caramel held in her hand the bag that Murphy had given her. "It's a golden tooth," she told Strawberry. By then the others had woken up enough to be interested in the conversation. Soon, there was a crowd, everyone except Vanilla.

Strawberry gently handled the bag and inspected the precious token that could very well solve the case for good. "Oh my… go…" Strawberry gasped. "Taran's innocent! He… I mean, he must be. Well… wait a second, who cares about this crummy old tooth?"

"Oh, I was getting to that part." Caramel took the bag carefully and handed it to the others. "I found this tooth directly beside the leg of the junk table inside Randy's room, 203."

"Really?" Sherri looked at the tooth closely.

Butterscotch inspected it. "How could we have missed it?"

"I don't know." Fudge chuckled and passed it to Chocolate.

"But we did." Chocolate eagerly took it.

"Who'd you say this belongs to?" Cream had it next.

"A man I met," Caramel answered. "And Murphy, the Police Chief, told me Blackbeard's trial is this afternoon. Any evidence we have needs to be submitted today. One shot, one trial, is all he gets. If he's convicted, he goes to prison for an undecided amount of time. However, if someone else can't be implicated with stronger evidence as the killer, then—"

"That's the end," Strawberry finished. "But Blackbeard's innocent!"

"Well, we have until one thirty to prove that." Caramel looked at her holographic watch. She then put the evidence into her pocket.

"Well, how?" Butterscotch desperately asked.

"I'm getting there, I'm getting there!" Caramel insisted. She looked up at everyone. "I found something in room 203. That's how I got on the guy's tail in the first place. Watch, girls. Follow me."

She led them up to room 203. On the way she explained how she found a note written in the book saying "It's uncanny!" and the bookmark reading "the green man," both in the same handwriting. She then explained how the picture in Randy's book, next to which the note was written, was the exact pocket watch that the "green man" had with him when Caramel met him.

"Wow, Caramel." Strawberry, wearing protective gloves, picked up the book of pocket watches and studied the photograph of the watch. "Fantastic job! And this poker hand design is perfect for a magician."

Butterscotch was hunched over the junk table looking at assorted gears, springs, and pieces of watches. "It looks like Randy was building a pocket watch, or perhaps repairing one."

"Was the book open to this page?" Chocolate asked.

"I believe so," Caramel said. "*I* think Randy was repairing Trickster's watch—oh, Trickster, Murphy said, is John's nickname, by the way—and for some reason, Trickster came to this room to beat up Randy. On the way, though, Blackbeard stopped him at the door. Trickster clubbed out Blackbeard and stole his sword; with it he could do one better. He could kill Randy for destroying his favorite watch. At the time, he probably didn't realize Randy was trying to fix it.

"Anyway, Trickster went into Randy's room, sneaked up to Randy, and stabbed him." All the while, Caramel acted it out. "Then they got into a struggle while Randy was still alive, and he punched Trickster's tooth out. Trickster probably didn't realize his tooth was missing, so he just bagged the body and dragged it from the scene of the crime.

"That's when, if Blackbeard was being truthful, he woke up by the doorway. He noticed his sword was bloody and on the ground, and he picked it up. Realizing he'd left Blackbeard in the room, Trickster figured he could easily frame the bewildered pirate by returning to the scene later, after disposing of the body, catching him with the weapon at the scene."

"Brilliant story," Sherri said.

"So wait, where's the body?" Butterscotch asked.

"Yeah, if we find it, we can prove the case, right?" Cream said excitedly.

"Right." Strawberry peered over at Cream. "But we already found the body… in 2348. So Trickster would have had to use the machine to dispose of it, but how did he know how to use it? And why did he set it to 2348? You know, specifically *our* time?"

"We're going to have to assume he learned," Caramel answered. "Or just assume it was a random setting like we suggested before. Besides, unless that issue comes up in court, it's irrelevant. I think the evidence we *do* have will be enough."

"Furthermore, this theory supports Blackbeard's story." Fudge nodded.

"Exactly." Chocolate smiled. She looked over at Strawberry, giving her a "Dawn really needs to know about this" look.

It was returned with a nod.

"So… what are we waiting for?" Butterscotch asked.

"Yeah!" Cream nodded. "Let's get that little 'green man'!"

They all laughed.

Chapter 59

The first stop was Taran's hut. They figured they could get Dawn so she could help them out. She'd been there the longest. She was thrilled with the news, mostly because she finally knew for sure that Taran was innocent.

They all headed to Kel's Place. There they filled Dawn in with the rest of the details about how Trickster looked, and they discussed the issues that Taran wouldn't have liked to hear, about how they suspected him earlier. Murphy was there, too. He didn't appear surprised at all that Trickster became the prime suspect.

Finally, they discussed a way to trap Trickster. Caramel led this plan, but she decided that she couldn't take part actively, considering her last encounter with him. But, just the same, it would be simple, via her plan, to make him present at the court hearing.

They were sitting at the outside table. It was the only table big enough at Kel's Place to fit all nine of them at once. The only thing that any of them had to eat or drink, however, was coffee.

"Here's what we do," Caramel began. "This Trickster is one macho guy. He acts really tough, but he's also cavalier. He goes for a lot of ladies for shallow reasons, so here's my plan. We spread out around town and find him. That is, save for Murphy." She turned to the chief. "I don't think you'll have to worry about that. We ladies can handle it." She continued, "Whoever finds him has to pretend to like him, you know, *really* like him.

"In whatever way possible, get a date for a nice picnic or something at the lot across from the police hut. It has to be around one thirty because that's when the trial starts. And it's going to be at that lot, so get the date before the trial begins, around one o'clock. Start the date, and it will be interrupted by the trial.

"Now, we—" Caramel stopped. She noticed a familiar man at the front counter of the restaurant where the hostess and owner, Kel, sat. It was the man Trickster had been talking to when she found him the day before.

"Guys," Caramel said. She lowered her voice and leaned toward the table. "Don't look now, but that guy at the front desk—Fudge, I said don't look!"

Fudge whirled back around. "What?"

Caramel continued much more softly now. "He works for Trickster." She looked to her left and right. "I think they both did it. He probably helped Trickster move Randy's body."

Now the Sundaes felt it was safe to look, so they, one at a time, glanced over at the gruff, dirty, Billy the Kid rebel hunched over the front desk. He wore a cowboy hat and a red shirt. He was also missing some teeth, and it looked as though he was hitting on Kel, who was obviously disgusted and turned him away.

"Fudge, go out with *him*," Caramel said softly.

"What?" Fudge cried. "Oh, no!"

"Well, you're the one that looked," Caramel retorted.

"Th... th... th... that..." Fudge stammered. "Th... that's not right! They all looked, too!"

"But you started it!" Caramel argued.

"Listen, listen!" Strawberry took control. "I'm the boss, and I say Fudge goes out with that hideous slump of muddy creature over there! And I don't want any argument. Got it?"

"Yes, Strawberry," they all said quietly.

Strawberry took on a sweeter, gentler tone. "Don't worry, Fudge, it's not as if it's a real date. Just fake it. You don't have to kiss him or anything."

"But why do I have to?" Fudge whined. "We don't need him for anything substantial. We've got all the evidence we need."

"Yeah, but there's more to it. If we can make a deal with this guy for even more proof, the jury will definitely convict Trickster," Caramel explained.

"B... but—"

"No buts, Fudge," Strawberry responded. "You gotta do this, for Blackbeard."

"Oh, all right," Fudge said. "When do I start?"

"Now, if you can," Strawberry told her. "And since Caramel can't go out looking for Trickster for some reason, she'll stay with you for safety. Caramel, try hard not to be interested in this flat-footed monster, as," she said, pausing with a cough, "appealing as he is. Meanwhile, we'll all go off and get a date with Trickster. Just remember girls: think 'green.'"

Part Four

A Trial and Closure

Chapter 60

VANILLA, BEING ENGAGED, SOUGHT out to find Trickster, but only to help locate him. She planned to notify the first Sundae she encountered, if she found him, that was. *Hmm… if I were a nineteenth century gangster magician, where would I be on a time twisted island?* As ridiculous as the idea sounded, she came up with an idea.

I'd go to a saloon, or at least look for one, she thought. *But do we have any building similar to a bar? Kel's Place, Island Inn, Tim's General Store, Stevens' Jewelers… I can't think of anywhere.* She'd given up on the saloon idea. *Well, plan B: Where would I be hiding?*

Then she remembered the hut she'd seen on the northeast outskirts of town, near the jungle. It was broken down and unused. It had been built before the town was organized and dirt roads were created. It was then abandoned when the owners built a better hut in town.

It's worth a shot.

Butterscotch was lost from the start. " Chocolate, where should we start?" she asked her friend. They were walking by Tim's Shop.

"Listen." Chocolate stopped walking and turned to her. "I didn't agree to go find him with you. I'm just getting you started; you know what I'm saying?"

"No, I don't," Butterscotch said innocently. She looked into Chocolate's eyes with a look of bewilderment. "What are you trying to say?"

"I'm breaking up with you," she replied sarcastically. "We have to find him separately. I don't want you to be tagging along on our first date." Chocolate laughed. "I mean, how would it look?"

Butterscotch whimpered. "What, are you afraid he and I won't get along?"

"C'mon, Butterscotch," Chocolate replied. "You knew this day would come. I just can't have you there with me. I need to be alone with Trickster so that he feels like we have something special."

"I suppose you're right." Butterscotch looked down glumly. "But… not if I find him first!" She sprinted away down the street toward the empty lot and the eastern outskirts of town.

Chocolate just sighed and went into the store.

Sherri had a different idea from everyone else. They all had strategies for finding Trickster. She figured she'd just walk around town, up and down every street, walking laps around the town. That was, until she met with Trickster, or the time came to meet outside Taran's hut. The time had been determined to be noon. She wasn't too keen on finding Trickster, however, so she didn't put a lot of effort into finding the green man.

"A theater, of course!" Cream exclaimed.

She ran down the street to where Stevens' Jewelers was built. This side of town was set apart from the other businesses. She thought it would make for a better hiding spot. Furthermore, an amphitheater of sorts was in construction next to Professor Stevens' house. They planned to have drama, theater, concerts, and magic shows, as well as other possibilities. That would attract a magician, right?

The construction crew had not yet begun work for the day, so Cream had easy access to the site. She crawled under the rope barrier and carefully stepped down the rickety stairs held up by braces. They descended at a gradual slope until they reached the empty space and the pile of wooden planks that would eventually become a stage.

Strawberry decided to take a more lax approach; she decided just to check the hotel. The desk clerk, she assumed, had a list of all of the residents. Since few people had their own hut, it was likely that Trickster lived there. It seemed logical to her.

"Mornin,' ma'am," the young clerk greeted her. "Can I help you?"

"I am a detective working on a—" She paused, not for effect, but to reconsider exactly what she'd say. "A case of… tax evasion. Yes, that's it. A man staying here isn't caught up with his taxes. I just need to talk to him."

The clerk eyed Strawberry suspiciously. "Can I see some identif—"

"Chuck," said a man who came through the office door behind the counter.

He was the owner of the inn. "Can you come here for a minute?" He disappeared back behind the door.

"Yes, Mr. Cane," the clerk replied. "Excuse me, ma'am. I'll be right back." He followed the short walk to the door through which the man had gone and shut the door behind him.

There was a book open on the desk that appeared to have a list of information on it. Of course, Strawberry eyed the book. She could see that there were several names with personal information listed with each. She just couldn't resist. She quickly grabbed the book and skimmed as swiftly as she could, looking for… *What was his name? John Smith, right?*

Her attempt was to no avail, but when Chuck, the clerk, returned, the book's pages were blowing from the wind. It faced the opposite side of the desk. The door was wide open, but the room was empty.

Chapter 61

OF THE FIVE, THE one to find Trickster was Vanilla. Of course, she didn't interact with him. As she approached the broken down, abandoned hut, she saw some motion in between two planks covering the front window. She then ran to hide behind the left wall of the hut. Sure enough, a man in green emerged and headed into town. Vanilla was even close enough to hear him grumbling to himself softly, but angrily.

"Where… Flat… go? Stupid… lazy…"

Having discovered the only thing she wanted to, Vanilla took a route around the perimeter of the town to find the others. It was a short search because the amphitheater construction site was located just south of where she stood. She had come upon the back of the stage, which was approximately twenty feet below her, separated by a rope barrier that surrounded the site in its entirety.

For fear of falling, she remained a safe distance from even the barrier as she glanced over the side. She saw somebody behind a pile of wood. It appeared as though he or she were hiding, probably kneeling. Now curious, Dawn walked alongside the rope and found one of the staircases on the opposite side.

She walked down and found an unfinished stage area.

Cream could see Vanilla from where she hid. *What's she doing here? She'll blow my cover if I'm found. I've got to wait for Trickster. Well, I've got to get rid of her or he'll never show.*

"Vanilla!" Cream called softly. "Psst, over here!"

Vanilla found her. She was the one Vanilla had seen from above, and she was still hiding behind a pile of neatly stacked plywood. It was beside a pile of folded cloth, enough probably to be the curtain.

"Cream?" Vanilla moved toward her. "What are you doing?"

"Shh!" Cream pulled Vanilla's arm until they both ended up behind the pile. "I'm waiting for Trickster," she whispered. "I figured he'd be here; it's going to be a theater, after all."

"Well, I already found him," Vanilla informed her. "We've got to hurry though, otherwise I'll lose him."

"You know where he is?"

"Yes," Vanilla said. "But we've got to hurry. I think he was headed toward the store."

Vanilla led Cream back the way she came and ran down the street. Sure enough, Trickster was in the street, but he wasn't headed for the store. He was walking back toward the broken down hut.

"Here," Vanilla said, formulating a plan, "just go knock on the door and talk to him… like, pretend… pretend you're selling something. Yeah, try to sell him something, Cream." She nodded.

"Well, I don't know… I… I think I'll wait until he comes back out," Cream said. "After all, you said he was grumbling about someone before, right? Evidently he hasn't found him, so he'll be back."

The door swung open, and the girls remained where they stood by the edge of the forest to the right of the hut, just out of Trickster's view. Trickster once again started down the street.

Vanilla pushed her comrade to follow him.

"Just be inconspicuous," she advised.

Cream nodded and hesitantly anticipated where Trickster was headed. She walked about one hundred feet behind and watched as he passed the theater site. Cream ran in the opposite direction from the hut, past a residential hut, and turned at that. She planned to cut him off on the road just after the construction site. She stood beside the next hut, which was located at the corner toward which Trickster was headed. She cautiously checked around the corner. Seeing him coming, she walked out casually and turned in his direction.

Neither of them was watching where they were going, so when their paths met, Cream walked into Trickster and fell to the ground.

"Hey!" Trickster shouted. "Watch where… you…" He looked down at her, sitting up and leaning on her arms. "Hey…" he said softly to himself. *Two in one week, huh? I could get used to this.* "Are you all right, ma'am?" He held out his hand.

"Umm… I'm fine, thank you." She took it and got up. "My name is Delores Crém."

"Uh… John…" Trickster responded. "John Smith."

Well, he doesn't look ***too*** *grungy*, Cream thought.

Man, she is hot! Trickster lightly brushed some of the gravel from Cream's back. "I'm so sorry about that, Delores." *Say something nice; don't scare her off like the other one.* "Delores, that's a pretty name." He smiled his crooked smile.

"Thanks." Cream tried to blush and look shyly down. *And John's a very... original, boring, probably made up name. Coincidentally, so is Smith... so boring.* Looking away, she rolled her eyes in secret.

"Where are you headed to?" Trickster asked her.

"Umm... over to..." She searched through her brain for the places on the island. It had to be somewhere they could go to and go out. *I know. I'll buy some picnic lunch at the store, like Caramel suggested.* "I'm... going to the store to buy lunch."

"Really?" Trickster replied. "I was headed for lunch, too."

"Really? For what?" Cream asked.

"I hadn't decided."

"How about a picnic, John?" *This is too easy. Caramel was right; he's a pig.*

"Sounds great!"

"I thought I'd go to the grassy hill right over there," Cream told him. As it turned out, she'd caught up to him across the street from the vacant lot, the opposite side of the police hut. "I was going to get sandwiches and juice, then I was going to eat at that lot and read my book."

"But..." *The store is in the opposite direction,* Trickster thought. *Maybe she got turned around; I don't know.* "Oh... well," Trickster said, looking into her eyes, "I'll join you, if you don't mind, and we can get to know each other better."

"Sounds good to me," Cream replied. *Yes! He bit the bait! I thought I messed that one up when I mixed up where the store was. And I didn't think my flirting was going so well, either.*

They went to the store and Cream bought ready-made sandwiches. Then she and Trickster went to the empty lot. Cream had also picked up a blanket from the store and laid it out on the grass. They were in the lower corner of the lot at the top of the hill, away from the street. On the other side there were two people who were talking while making signals with their hands, as though they were surveying the land.

Cream checked her watch. *It's eleven thirty. We should eat in a few minutes. Then we can stay and talk. We just can't leave until after one o'clock. He needs to be present at the trial.*

She took out the sandwiches and the grape juice. She then offered Trickster a sandwich and poured him a glass.

"Thank you." Trickster lifted the glass in the air between them.

Cream met his glass with hers. "To us," she toasted.

"So, do you like cards?" Trickster put his arm around her back.

"Oh, yeah... yeah!" Cream tried to sound convincing. She tried to perk up and tried very hard not to shake his arm loose. *Maybe we could even start a game of cards... a very long game, like rummy... no! War. Yeah, war takes forever.* "I love... cards. Blackjack is my best."

"Oh, yeah?" Trickster responded. "I *love* poker."

They enjoyed their lunch for a good hour, talking about their times. Cream did most of the talking, however. Trickster didn't want her to know too much about his being a gangster.

It would turn her off, he assumed.

Chapter 62

THERE WAS STILL PLENTY of time before the trial, but Taran still paced across the floor of his hut. Dawn was the calm one of the two, which was odd because she'd always been the anxious one of the Sundaes, and she proved it by sitting patiently at the table while Taran was restlessly pacing.

"Calm down, T... Dillon," she said, still not accustomed to calling him that.

"I can't. I have to contact Mr. Thompson about this," Taran explained. "But I want you guys to solve this mystery first. It's going to be tough enough having killed someone because of this experiment. We have to know for certain what has happened."

"Couldn't you just go back to that night with your machine and see for yourself?"

Taran stopped and faced his fiancée. "No," he said, "it would be too dangerous. Going through time like that can theoretically create a paradox. If I should somehow be caught by someone, or if I can't return to the exact second I left..." he started mumbling. "Anything, really, that would bring two of me into the same... well, really anything that..."

"All right, Dillon, all right." Dawn got up and held his shoulders.

"Don't call me that." Taran looked down to his left.

"What?"

"Say it," Taran begged. "Call me Taran, please. There's no one else around."

"Of course, Taran," Dawn said. "What's wrong?"

"I... I'm lost in this." Taran shook his head. "I'm not me anymore. I've only become the ruler of this town. This experiment has made me a man called Dillon, not Taran Flint. I'm... I can't do this..." He began again to mumble. "I need Thompson, but this crisis has to be over with."

"Listen, Taran." Dawn tried to force him to look into her eyes by looking into his. "Listen, you have to calm down. I'm here for you, Taran." She hugged him tightly as tears came to both of their eyes. "Listen, Taran," she said, still holding him, "you have to go out there and finish this case for us. Taran, if you need to just move up the trial, just have it now, if everyone's ready anyway. Then it will be done sooner."

Taran wiped his face. "I'll talk to the lawyers and the construction crew. As soon as they're ready with the vacant lot, we'll be able to begin," he concluded.

Dawn began to leave.

"Dawn," Taran said softly.

"Yes, Taran?"

He was unsure as to why Dawn wouldn't kiss him before, and now he was unsure whether or not she wanted to until the case was over. That's how it seemed to him, so he just said, "Thanks."

A couple more people joined the two across the lot. They both wore red hardhats and blue jumpsuits. The one on the left was very tall with dark sunglasses. The other was of medium height with a small mustache.

Cream could see they were measuring the area to fit an apparently large object. *I think they're setting up now! It looks like that truck they are with has furniture in the bed. It's probably the judge's bench and the attorneys' tables.*

A big, blue pickup was parked next to the lot. It was the only automobile that Dillon had brought to the island. It had to be brought in manageable pieces in order to bring it out to the surface from the bunker, so it was too much of a hassle to bring cars for everyone. The construction crew, the four surveyors, had already agreed beforehand to rebuild the truck themselves for easier transportation.

The four of them moved the bench out of the truck and placed it gently in the grass. Next came two small tables set up facing the bench, and two chairs behind each, also facing the bench. Then they added a chair to the left side of the bench. After those were arranged, the four men arranged two rows of eight chairs along the left edge of the lot facing in, probably for a jury. Last were the chairs for the audience, easily seven rows.

"What's going on over there?" Trickster raised his head with interest. *Hmm… that arrangement looks… somehow familiar.* Then a once-hidden fear could be seen in his eyes again, but with a mixed confusion of hopefulness as well.

"I… hmm…" Cream copied his motions. *That's weird; it's starting early, isn't it? Not that I'm complaining. Or… maybe it isn't early, it's… no, it's still more than an hour before one. Strange.*

She then saw Dillon coming out of the police hut, followed by an older man dressed in a black cloak like that of a judge. They were conversing as they walked across the street to the lot, now a simulated courtroom.

Trickster eyed the man in black as he inspected the courtroom. He sat behind the bench, got up, and thoroughly scanned each rock and chair in the lot. *What in the world is that?* Trickster thought as he remained with Delores, his arm still around her uncomfortable shoulder.

"What do you suppose that place is supposed to be?"

"I don't know. What?" Cream followed along idiotically.

"It kinda reminds me of—" Trickster stopped.

"Yes?" Cream urged. "What does it remind you of?"

"Like a, a—"

"This court is now in session," Trickster heard the man in black say, just before hearing the slamming of the gavel onto the bench. "The prosecution will present case #1 of this island town, the case of Ailiokahu vs. Blackbeard."

Chapter 63

RAYMOND CALDOR ACTED AS the bailiff next to the witness stand. Chief Murphy stood behind the audience in the aisle to escort witnesses to the stand if need be. The jury consisted of eight randomly selected citizens: Scott MacKensie, Tim's only shop employee; Kel Longley, owner of Kel's Place; Jayne Caldor, Ray's wife; Tim Talbiss, the store owner; Sheriff Wyatt West; Sean Formann, a construction crewman; Professor Stevens, proprietor of the Island Inn during the day; and Sherri Marsh. Sherri was elected by all of them to be their speaker, representing all of their opinions in court. When there was to be a recess, they would adjourn to the police hut to deliberate the case.

Blackbeard's defending attorney was the lawyer from 2348 named Fred Cramden. He had been filled in on the case a few hours earlier and had decided to take it. The acting prosecutor on behalf of the town was Fred's wife, Alice, also a leading attorney in twenty-fourth century America.

"I would like to open my case against Blackbeard with this statement." Alice rose from her chair and stood facing the jury. "Mr. Blackbeard is a ruthless, cutthroat pirate from the real, historical, nineteenth century. He is legendary for being greedy, black-hearted, and… black-bearded. He is fully capable of killing an innocent man, whom he may have presumed was in the way of his precious treasure.

"He was found with the weapon at the scene," she continued. "He had no real alibi, only a false, trivial, and hardly believable 'shadow story' testimonial that is truly a shadow in itself, one that will disappear in the right light. That's the light that I intend to illumine for you folks this afternoon."

She gracefully sat back down and glanced at her husband, chuckling.

"How long did you rehearse that bit in the mirror?" Fred muttered. Then to the judge, he said, "Your Honor, if I may present my opening statement?"

"Please." The judge welcomed him.

Fred rose and addressed the jury just as his wife did.

"Ladies and gentlemen of the jury," he said, "Ms. Cramden is misleading you." He pointed at his wife. "There is no concrete proof to incriminate my client. Sure, he's a cutthroat killing pirate, a lying seadog; he *was* found with the weapon and at the scene at the wrong time. But that is all circumstantial evidence, completely inconsequential and irrelevant to this case. This 'evidence' my opponent claims to have is speculation and analysis of only classical and stereotypical characters."

"*We* have evidence that we've brought to this court that not only proves my client's innocence, but evidence that could quite possibly incriminate another," Fred continued. "During this trial, Alice—uh, my opponent will have you eating out of her hand with seemingly incriminating evidence, flawless in appearance. But beware, because I can see through her tactics. I will change your minds by the end of this day. My client *is* innocent."

Fred dismissed himself back to his table and sat next to Blackbeard.

"Is this true?" Blackbeard whispered to Fred. "Do you really have such evidence?"

"Not a bit," Fred whispered back to him, rubbing his forehead. "This case is almost definitely hopeless. There's nothing that could, at this time, prove your innocence. Not yet, anyway."

Chapter 64

"PROSECUTION WOULD LIKE TO call Paul Murphy to the witness stand," Alice declared.

Chief Murphy proceeded to the stand and sat down.

Ray approached the stand. "Would you please state your name for the court?"

"Paul Murphy," he stated.

"Please state your occupation."

"The Det—the chief of police in this town."

"Raise your right hand," Ray commanded.

Murphy obeyed.

"Do you swear to tell the truth, the whole truth, and nothing but the truth so help you God?" Ray asked mechanically.

"I do."

Ray then resigned to his place on the opposite side of the judge as Murphy lowered his hand. Alice approached him.

"So, Mr. Murphy," Alice said, beginning her normal routine. "You seemed hesitant in answering the question about your occupation. Could you clear up that mere hesitation for the court?"

"Well, I'm accustomed to testifying in court," Murphy answered. "I used to work for the Detroit Police Force. That is what I stopped myself from saying in mid-sentence earlier."

"I see," Alice said. "As I understand it, you weren't the first officer at the scene of the crime, correct?"

"Right. Officer Caldor was the first to get to room 203."

"Because of his volunteering as bailiff, you've been briefed on his testimony, is that correct?" Alice asked.

"Yes."

"So what exactly happened there, according to Ray?"

"He got there about three o'clock that morning," Murphy answered.

"Some man was in the room with the defendant and Harry Cane, the night shift operator at the Island Inn. The man was in green and a black top hat. He had contacted Harry about finding the defendant with a saber in his hand.

"When *I* got there, the defendant was sitting near the wall, and the green man—"

"Excuse me, but before you go on," Alice interrupted, "who is this man in green?"

"I believe his name was John Smith," he answered slowly. He chuckled.

"John Smith?"

Murphy nodded.

"Is Mr. Smith present in this courtroom?" Alice asked.

Murphy looked around. "I don't believe so."

"All right," Alice insisted, "go on."

"Well, the defendant was sitting down, and Mr. Smith was talking to Harry Cane. I went at that time to question the defendant:

"Aye, sir, what're we all doin' here?"

"I'm Chief Paul Murphy, local law enforcement, sir," Murphy told Blackbeard. "A man has been murdered here, or so Mr. Cane has told me."

"But, why am I here then?" he asked.

"Have you ever seen this sword before?"

"Aye, it's mine," he answered. "But I didn't get that blood on there; I didn't kill no one with that sword."

"Did anyone borrow this sword?" Murphy asked.

"No, I had it all night 'til I came here."

"What were you doing here?"

"I came ashore down at the beach with me cabin boy, and we came lookin' all over the island."

"For what?"

"I'm not 'lowed to tell ya."

"Well, you have to tell me."

"I can't. Me Cap'n told me tuh keep it secret-like."

"So it's a treasure, so what?" Murphy replied. "What did you and this cabin boy do when you came ashore?"

"We split up. I ended up by this place here, and I saw two people doing somethin' out there an' followed 'em in. They seemed unfriendly, so I tried to stop 'em when they got to that door there. But they clubbed me out. When I woke back up they was gone, and my sword was bloodied up and lyin' on me chest."

"So who was it that clubbed you?"

"I dunno."

"So that's the story *he* gave you?" Alice pointed at Blackbeard.

"Yes, so I talked to John Smith after that," Murphy continued. "He was upset, loud, and, to put it lightly, skeptical of Blackbeard's story:"

"Sir, as I understand it, you found Mr. Blackbeard here holding the weapon." Murphy walked over to the distressed man in green.

"Yes." He began to sob. "He was… had th… that sword in his… he… I think he killed him."

"Who? Who is it that he killed?"

"Randy. He's dead… dead." He was hysterical now.

"All right, Mr. Smith, calm down," Murphy said.

Harry patted the man in green's back.

"Did you see exactly what happened?"

"No… when… when I came in…" the man said, swallowing hard, "he was pacing around with… *it* in his hand."

"Where is th—" Murphy began to ask, but he changed his wording. "Did you see a body at all?"

"No… he, he must've gotten rid of the b… body…"

"Well, until a body is found, I don't see that we can penalize him for anything, really. He could have had that blood on there long before he got here; he is a pirate, after all."

"But he k… killed him!" the man insisted. "I saw Randy only hours ago. He said he'd be here in his room… an… and he's gone!"

"Well, regardless, I have to leave," Murphy told him. "I'm having another officer come, whom you guys can talk to, and he'll keep you guys in line. Mr. Cane, come with me. You'll have to stop the flow of customers in and out of the inn. One, so we'll find the body, and two, so we won't miss any other evidence."

"So then you left?" Alice asked.

"Yes," Murphy replied.

"Did you ever verify the victim's death?" Alice asked him gravely. "Did you find the body going out of the hotel?"

"Well, yes to the first, and to the second, no," Murphy answered. "The body was never found, but we verified the DNA in the blood sample from the sword. That sword was definitely inside Randy Carr at one time."

"And who is this Randy Carr?"

"The tenant of room 203."

"Thank you, sir," Alice responded in a satisfied tone. She then turned to Fred. "Your witness, honey."

Fred approached the stand slowly. He looked back at Blackbeard as he leaned on the judge's bench. Then he turned back toward the police chief.

"Well, Mr. Murphy, I trust your story *is* accurate, but I don't see how it even slightly incriminates my client. Would you please tell the court where my client came up? Precisely why was my client singled out as the culprit over the others?"

"There was simply no evidence to point blame on Mr. Cane or Mr. Smith," Murphy replied. "However, your defendant, Luke Blackbeard, was found with the sword in hand."

"But the body wasn't there?" Fred added.

"Right."

"So you would assume that the body was moved?"

"Right."

"So why did Blackbeard return to the scene?"

"I don't—"

"Objection, your Honor," Alice shouted. "Mr. Murphy can't possibly assume to know the mind and methods of the defendant; it's merely speculation."

The judge answered quickly, "Sustained. You'll have to find a new line of questioning for your cross examination, Mr. Cramden, unless you have something concrete that Murphy can present to us."

"All right, all righty," Fred replied.

Murphy straightened up in his chair.

"Mr. Murphy, I didn't intentionally presume that you should know the mind of this pirate," Fred apologized. "Sorry. Instead I'll ask you this: at any time at all did you suspect this Mr. Smith, not even only from his given name, of the murder?"

"No… well, actually, when I got to the scene," Murphy said, "my immediate presumption was that Mr. Smith had an active involvement in what had transpired in room 203—"

"Could you tell the court why?"

Murphy sighed. "Uh… yeah, Mr. Smith, or 'Trickster' as he's known in his time, was recently released from the island prison for robbing the bank."

"So he's a convict," Fred clarified.

"Yeah, a gangster."

"A gangster?" Fred repeated. "So, just as Blackbeard is a pirate who must be vicious, greedy, and murderous by nature, Smith is a gangster who kills people for kicks and robs banks to be richer. Yet, out of the two, the *only* person present at the scene who was prosecuted for this atrocity is my client?"

"He's a pirate." Murphy shrugged and motioned toward Blackbeard.

"And this Trickster isn't even *present* at this trial, though he should be suspect, *and* he's a material witness?"

"Well, *he's* a pirate."

"No further questions, your Honor," Fred responded disgustedly as he returned to his table. "No significant basis whatsoever," he mumbled as he sat down. He turned to his client and whispered something.

"You may step down, Chief," the judge told him.

Chapter 65

BLACKBEARD WAS NOW ON the stand. Fred had called him as his next witness. Blackbeard had just finished relating his story to the court. "As I understand it, Mr. Blackbeard," Fred said, "you say you followed the alleged shadows. What urged you to do that?"

"I saw them outside with a big bag," Blackbeard answered. "That interested me. An' when they went inside the place, Ah had tuh look in tuh see what it was fer."

"What was in there?"

"It were empty."

"And where's this bag now?"

"It were gone when I went back to look for it again."

"How very convenient for you, as well as the killer," Fred said. "Sir, how large was this bag? Large enough for, say, a body?"

"Aye."

"Objection!" Alice rose again. "This is speculation, a fictional bag. There's no relevance."

"Do you mean to say my client's testimony is irrelevant?" Fred turned to his wife.

She sighed and ignored the remark.

"Overruled," the judge said. "Continue, Mr. Cramden."

"So, just a quick recap: two shadows enter the building, leaving a bag outside. You, Blackbeard, are clubbed unconscious. When you wake up, your sword is bloody and the bag is gone. But the only blood on the scene is the sword," Fred said. His next comments were directed to the jury. "And I don't see how that story cannot parallel Murphy's story. Mr. Smith just walked in at the wrong time. Otherwise, there might have been a different defendant here."

Fred walked back to his table. "You can cross-examine the witness, Mrs. Cramden."

"Thank you." Alice rose. "Mr. Blackbeard, we have three witnesses who can confirm Mr. Murphy's testimony and at least one other who can confirm Harry Cane's story, whom I'll later call up, but can anyone else verify *your* story?"

"Only those who clubbed me out and me cabin boy, only he left before anything else happened," Blackbeard answered.

"Those? There was more than one?"

"Aye, there were two," Blackbeard answered.

"Oh, but where did they go after the incident?"

"I've already told you, ma'am," Blackbeard answered. "I was knocked out cold. I didn't have the chance to see where they went."

Alice began to pace back and forth from her table to the stand as she spoke.

"Okay, then." She began what she felt was a more productive line of questioning. "This treasure that Murphy alluded to, were you actually coming to the island for that reason? To find a buried treasure?"

"Yes," Blackbeard admitted.

"Where is this treasure?"

Where? Blackbeard thought. *I can't say where. It might… no, I would definitely be hung for murder if they knew.* "I'm not sure. That's why we split up to look, but we believe it's in this area of the island."

"Not under the Island Inn itself?" Alice asked. "It doesn't happen to be buried under that plot of land directly under the inn? You didn't believe it was directly underneath what used to be Randy's room? That's not why you killed Mr. Carr, because he was too close?"

"Objection! Your Honor, the prosecution is harassing the witness." Fred rose swiftly.

"Sustained."

"But—"

"Butts are for ashtrays, Miss Cramden," the judge interrupted her.

"All right," Alice said. "Mr. Blackbeard, I have no more questions for you. You may step down."

Blackbeard returned to the table, and Alice called for her next witness: Harry Cane.

"Mr. Cane, you say you've been running the Island Inn since its opening, correct?" Alice asked Harry Cane; he was sitting rather uncomfortably on the witness stand.

"No, just for a couple nights now," he answered.

"So there haven't been any other incidents on your land of this magnitude? Of any magnitude, for that matter, that would attract police attention?" she asked him.

"No, there haven't."

Alice nodded slightly and continued. "Okay, then, Mr. Cane. When did you first find out about the murder? Where were you and what were you doing at the time?"

"Well, it was pretty late," he answered. "I was about to lock up the door and other things in preparation for closing. That is, the lobby; we stop letting people get rooms about midnight. Then, umm… the Mr. Smith that Murphy mentioned ran up to the front desk:"

"Mr.… whatever…" He ran up to the counter. "Mr.… umm, Cane, there's trouble in room 203." He began to sob. "I think he killed him. Quickly, follow me!"

Mr. Cane followed him down the hall and up the stairs. The door to room 203 was wide open. They saw Blackbeard sitting nervously against the wall on the side of the room.

"I… I'll get the police, sir," the man said.

"No, sir, just relax and make sure he doesn't leave," Mr. Cane said. "I'll get the police down here right away."

The man turned quickly and walked cautiously to the pirate, who had just dropped the bloodied sword onto the chair by the table in the center of the room.

"Just… don't touch anything," Mr. Cane warned as he turned toward the stairs and went back to the inn desk. He dialed a number on the phone.

"So you got the police to the scene, and then what happened as Murphy testified is exactly what occurred?" Alice asked, just to be sure.

"Yeah, exactly," Mr. Cane answered. "It happened just as he said."

"All right, Mr. Cane." Alice began another question. "Did you at *any* time see this Mr. Smith enter the inn before the episode you just described of him running for your help?"

"Well, yes," he answered. "He came in minutes before and went in the direction of the rooms. He said he was going up to see somebody in room 203."

"Did he give a reason why or his relation to Mr. Carr, whom I assume resided in room 203?" she asked.

"That's correct," he answered. "Mr. Carr lived in room 203. And yes, Mr. Smith told me something about a pocket watch."

"A watch?" Alice repeated softly. *Interesting…*

As Fred watched his wife ask questions, he considered the testimony that Mr. Cane was giving. There hadn't yet been any information that would contradict what Blackbeard's testimony implied. Therefore, there was nothing Fred had to ask him, and so the Trickster scene could commence any time now. If he needed to, he would call a recess.

"And you were at your desk at all times that night?" Alice asked Mr. Cane.

"Yes, of course," he answered.

"At no time did you leave your position?"

"No..." He stopped short. "Well, actually, yes... yes. I left for a few moments to check on one of my tenants. It's a nightly routine I keep; it was just before Mr. Smith arrived to go to room 203."

"And who might that tenant be?"

"That's confidential information concerning two of my tenants. Knowing who they are has no relevance to this situation."

"For your sake, I hope not," she said under her breath. "Well, then, Mr. Cane, how long was this trip?"

"Only a couple minutes; the room is one of the first in the hall."

"Did you ever see anyone at any time come into the inn carrying a large bag or anything?" Alice asked him.

"No, nothing of that sort," he answered.

"But in your opinion, do you think you were gone for a long enough period of time that someone could bring this alleged bag to room 203 and back before you returned?" she asked him.

"I... uh, suppose so," he answered. "Maybe."

"Thanks, sir," she said abruptly. "Your witness, hon."

Fred rose and approached the stand. "So, Mr. Cane, it is possible then that the story my client told is true? There's nothing that could, in the slightest way, contradict that?"

"Not that I've seen or heard," he answered.

"Then I won't trouble you any further by wasting more of your time." Fred walked back to his table and picked up a few papers. "If it pleases the court, I would like to call up my next witness."

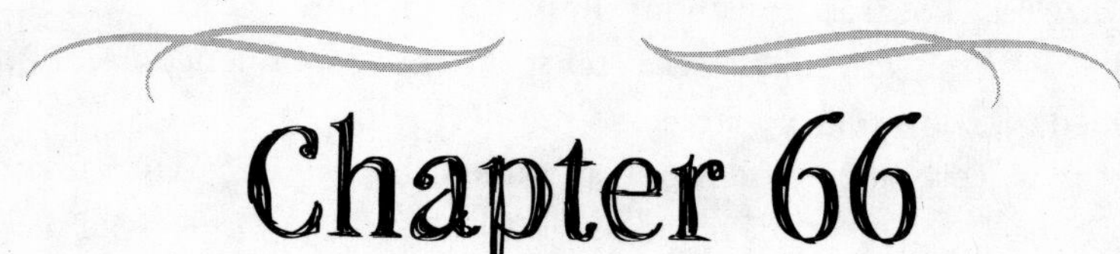

Chapter 66

THE DAY WAS GOING by quickly, and the sun was beginning to set. Winds began to blow softly around the courtyard lot. It was a soothing feeling for even Blackbeard.

Trickster and Cream were still talking and watching the trial. From their position, they could only hear bits and pieces of what the people were saying, but they both realized it was Blackbeard's trial for Randy's murder.

"Let's go, Delores," Trickster suggested. "I know a nice part of the beach where you can see the sunset. It's beautiful."

"It sounds really nice, but..." Delores answered nervously. *I can't let him leave.* "But I want to sit back and relax a while longer."

"But it'll be too late if we don't go now," Trickster said calmly. He was agitated but held it in. "I mean, too late to see the sunset, that is."

"Uh... all right," she looked around desperately. "Could you just help me pick this stuff up first?" *And what else? Oh, perfect! The inn is over there. We'll walk by there, and they'll see him from the court and ask him to testify.*

"All right, but quickly."

"Then we'll put it back in the inn so we won't have to carry it with us later tonight," Cream told him.

Trickster put the last glass into the basket as Delores rolled up the blanket. "Okay, Delores. Let's go." He sighed.

He quickly led her near the courtroom arrangement. Delores then linked her elbow with his and hesitantly cuddled his shoulder as they walked.

Fred walked back over to his table to call his next witness. He habitually looked over to the top of the hill where Cream and Trickster had been. They weren't there. He saw them walking by the courtroom.

"That's him!" Fred pointed at Trickster. "It's the man in green to whom everyone earlier referred!"

Trickster's immediate reaction would have been to run, but Delores' elbow prevented that. Instead, he turned unassumingly toward where he heard the voice from. "Say what?" he said, looking puzzled.

Fred walked over to him.

Alice rose. "Your Honor, is that right? He can't leave the courtroom."

"Mr. Cramden," the judge agreed with the prosecutor, "over here. You may not leave the courtroom without my having called a recess, which I didn't."

"Uh... your Honor," Fred said. "If it pleases the court, I'd like to call Mr. Smith to the stand. He's obviously an invaluable witness."

"W... what's going on?" Trickster asked.

"This is the trial between the town and Blackbeard," Fred explained. "I just need you to testify about what you and Blackbeard discussed, and what transpired between yourself and Mr. Cane. Your testimony would clinch the case."

Not realizing that Fred was the defense attorney and that he was misleading Trickster to think he was home free, he agreed to testify.

"Do you swear to tell the truth, the whole truth, and nothing but the truth so help you God?" Ray recited mechanically once again.

"Uh... yeah." Trickster put his hand down.

"Please state your name for the court." Fred walked up to the stand.

"Umm... John Smith," he answered.

"And your occupation?"

"Currently nothing, but I... umm, do some magic tricks and stuff for small audiences," Trickster answered, rolling his eyes.

"All right, Mr. Smith." Fred picked up the bag that lay on his table that held the sword in it. "Do you recognize this sword?"

Trickster winced as though it brought up a bad memory. "Yeah, I do. That's the sword the man sitting over there had when I walked... into Randy's room that night... two nights ago."

"Can you tell us exactly what happened?"

"Well, I was walking to the inn to see Randy about my watch. He had borrowed it so he wouldn't be late to a meeting that afternoon.

Trickster walked casually past the lamp post to the inn door. He entered and saw Harry Cane at the front desk. He walked over to the desk and leaned on it nonchalantly.

"Hey, my friend stays here and he borrowed my watch," Trickster explained. "I was just wondering if I could go get it now. Which room is he staying in?"

"Who is your friend, sir?"

"Randy. Randy Carr," he answered.

"Hmm, yes, he resides in room 203," Mr. Cane replied.

"Yeah, thanks." Trickster walked down the hall and up the stairs. He came to room 203, the second room on the left, but the door was wide open. "Oh my G—"

There was a man in the room, holding a bloody sword. He was dressed raggedly and had the classic appearance of a buccaneer. He gasped in surprise when he looked up and saw Trickster.

"What did you do?" Trickster gasped and covered his mouth. "Where's Randy?"

"Aye, don't know what ya mean. I've been awake for only a couple seconds now," the pirate answered. "I'm not sure where I am or even what this place is."

"You stay right here," Trickster said. "I don't know wh… what you did, but I have to notify the clerk."

"So I went to tell the clerk—" Trickster said.

"Yes," Fred interrupted him. "We've already heard that story from Mr. Cane himself, thank you." Fred paused. "But, where were you, exactly, before going to the inn at about closing time for the businesses?"

" What do you mean?" Trickster asked defensively.

"Where were you before you decided to see Randy about the watch?"

"W…" He sighed. "Wh… I was with a friend of mine."

"Can he verify that?"

"Yes!" Trickster said quickly. "Wh… you're not meaning to accuse me for this now, are you? 'Cause I didn't do it!"

"Oh, no, no, no!" Fred shook his head. "Listen, there is no reason to lose your head. There has not been *any* evidence brought to this court's attention that would associate you."

"Good." Trickster crossed his arms.

Fred walked back to his table. *Two shadows… could've been him and his friend… borrowed his watch! An ineffable claim. I need a recess.* He sat next to Blackbeard and whispered to him, "I've got this case pretty much closed; I just need to do one thing." He then rose and walked back toward the stand. This time he addressed the judge. "Your Honor, the defense would like to request a recess."

"Is the defense finished with this witness?" the judge asked.

"No, sir," replied Fred.

Alice barged into the spectacle. "What's going on, Fred?"

"Fred's requested a recess, Miss Cramden," the judge explained, "if that's all right with you."

"What for?" she asked the judge. She turned to her husband and whispered, "What is going on? If you have some information I don't know about, you need to tell me."

Fred glanced over at Trickster and quickly looked back at his wife. "I need to talk to you before we continue."

"Okay, okay." Alice had been working with her husband long enough to know he had an ace in the hole. "A recess will be good. It's been a long trial."

The judge nodded.

"Very well," he answered. "We will take a recess and resume in half an hour. Meanwhile, I would like the jury to go to the police office building. I want you, Mr. Smith, to stick around."

"Yes, sir." In all of the aggravation, Trickster had forgotten about Delores and the sunset.

"And *I* will be over at Kel's Place getting a bite to eat." The judge slammed his gavel and headed to Kel's Place with Taran, who had been standing near Murphy behind the audience, watching.

Meanwhile, Murphy led the jurors to the police office.

Chapter 67

Many of the people got up to walk around the town as the recess went on. Some of them, like Taran and the judge had, went to get something to eat. The best place in town for that was Kel's Place. So at this "half-time" break, they had plenty of customers lined up on their lot. With Kel in the jury, Lindsey was rushing around so much that Joe and Mr. Owner decided to help out and do the waiting as Lindsey worked in the kitchen. Occasionally, Lindsey helped the boys cater to the customers; there she could at least get some air.

"So, Judge Stone, what do you think so far?" Taran was sitting at an outside table at Kel's Place. "It's pretty impressive, huh?"

"Yeah, I'd have to say it is." The judge nodded. "It's really remarkable how far our technology has been able to evolve. Never in my life did I imagine time travel was possible. I'm not surprised, though, that it was the guys at Karz that made it happen. You guys have always been on the cutting edge."

"Yeah, I've got a good team." Taran looked over at the town. It wasn't much, but only weeks before it had been nothing. He had built this community from nobody to the thirty-odd people before him now. All of the huts that he and the construction crew built, such as the Island Inn and Kel's Place, were really nice. Tim's Shop was good, too. A theater was in the process of being built. Stevens' Jewelers, even, although there wasn't much demand for such a nonsensical facility. *A jewelry store built on a tropical island where even a monetary system is virtually obsolete? C'mon, Danny. What were you thinking?*

"Hey, how do you explain this to your boss?" the judge asked. "In the UNA, you'd *technically* be responsible for Randy Carr's death since, of course, you created the hostile environment, which was bound to lead to confrontation."

Taran sighed. "Yeah, I'm working on that one right now, judge." He sighed again, this time more heavily. "Honestly, judge, Thompson doesn't even know about the town yet."

"What?"

Lindsey, who was passing by with a plate of food, turned to the judge curiously.

"Geez, keep your voice down!" Taran scolded. He turned to Lindsey. "Would you mind getting me some more water, Lindsey?"

"Uh, sure, Dillon." She took the fisherman's platters to Jacob, Isaac, and Erik, who were at another outside table, before returning to the restaurant building.

The divers were enjoying a bountiful meal with three of the Sundaes: Caramel, Butterscotch, and Chocolate. Butterscotch had stumbled on Jacob and Erik while looking for Trickster earlier that day. While they had been talking, Chocolate had joined the conversation, and they landed a double date.

Afraid of leaving the third man out, Erik asked if there was another topping available. Since Caramel happened by on her route, she landed the third party for the triple date.

Dawn was eating at Kel's Place as well, but she and Strawberry were eating inside by the bay window, of which Kel was so proud. There, she and her boss had a perfect view of the triple date and Taran's encounter with Judge Stone.

Fudge's experience with Flatfoot was less than enjoyable, and they managed to stay out of sight, eating on the side of the restaurant away from the crowds. She didn't want to be seen publicly with him, which was fine with him. Flatfoot wasn't one to attract attention without being armed.

Cream stayed out of sight as well after her date was taken into custody. She joined Strawberry and Vanilla inside Kel's Place.

"Hey, girls," Cream greeted them.

"You did good," Strawberry told her. "We were even able to move up the trial, so your picnic was perfect."

"Easy for you to say," Cream said. "He wasn't touching *your* back. Eww!"

"Sorry, Cream." Strawberry glanced at Dawn, who was still staring at her fiancé as he talked outside the restaurant.

Taran proceeded to tell to the judge many of the details of his journey, including the details that were supposed to be undisclosed until he was debriefed at Karz. In any other situation, this would have been a dangerous move, but realistically, Taran had the only equipment that could reach the island at this time. He felt safe because of that.

"So you haven't given up on finding your lost comrade, right?" the judge asked him, eager to learn more about the web that Taran had woven.

"There is absolutely nothing I *can* do, judge," he answered. "Believe me, I've double and triple checked all of the logs in the machine's databases. If Sandy Brown wasn't where I appeared, *when* I appeared, then she's gone for good. I have no way to track her—"

"Here you go, Dillon." Lindsey set the glass of water carefully on the table. "And I'll take those dishes, too. Then I'll come back and get your orders."

She started to walk away but stopped short. She turned back toward the judge. "Oh, did you want something to drink, sir?"

"Yes. Water, please."

Lindsey went back to the kitchen.

"That's a technology that I would invest in, then, Mr. Flint," the judge advised. "That is, before you bring anymore people that could get killed or lost in time. You will need to know where everyone is at all times, in *this* time." He chuckled softly. He shook his head and changed back to a grim tone. "You *are* solely responsible for these people's lives, Flint."

One more sigh.

"You know, judge," Taran said, looking over at Dawn, "you're absolutely right."

Chapter 68

SHERRI LED THE OTHER jurors into the building, and Murphy waited outside. All of them sat down at a long, wooden table set up inside. Sherri sat on one end. Kel, Scott, and the sheriff were on one side. Sean, Jayne, and Tim sat on the other side, and Stevens was on the far end. They were there to share their thoughts, feelings, and opinions about the case.

"All right," Sherri said. "I guess we'll start with a vote to see where everyone stands. First we'll do a secret ballot to judge whether we think that Mr. Blackbeard is guilty or not guilty. This isn't final, now. I just want to see where everyone stands and how each of us sees this case. We'll tear up a piece of paper into eight pieces. We'll then put them in a hat, and I'll draw them out one at a time and see what the majority rules."

She passed all of the papers down to everyone, and they quickly jotted down "guilty" or "innocent." Sherri then looked around the room.

Where is there a hat? "Aha!" Sherri exclaimed. She spotted the sheriff's big cowboy hat. "Mr. West, do you mind if we use your hat for this?"

"Sure, ma'am," he answered. "There ya go." He passed it down the table until it reached Sherri. Each person placed their vote into the hat as it passed them.

"All righty, let's see what we've got." Kel gave the hat to Sherri.

"'Guilty,'" Sherri read aloud, placing each piece of paper on the table face up in two corresponding piles. "'Innocent,' 'Guilty,' 'Guilty,' 'Innocent,' 'Innocent,' 'Innocent,' 'Innocent.' Wow, that's three votes guilty and five votes innocent," Sherri declared.

"Well," Kel said, rising, "I think we should find out who said what. Pass the hat back around, and everyone take one of the papers that matches what he or she wrote down before. Then everyone lay it in front of themselves."

Tim laid down his first: innocent. Next was Professor Stevens: innocent. Third, Sheriff West: innocent. Next Scott laid down guilty, then Jayne with guilty, and Sean with guilty. Finally Sherri and Kel laid theirs down; both read innocent.

"Hmm..." Sherri peered over at Sean, Scott, and Jayne's papers, the guilty voters. She planned to ask each of them to present their opinions first. "Sean, why did you say Blackbeard was guilty?"

"Well, I can't see how he has any alibi for innocence," Sean said. "He was found with the weapon, it belongs to him, and no one else was seen passing by Mr. Cane's desk. It had to be him."

"So, because of overwhelming evidence against him, and no evidence working for him but his own testimony," Sherri concluded. "He had the opportunity and access to the weapon." She turned to Scott. "What about you, Mr. MacKensie?"

"For the same reasons," he said shortly.

"How about you, Jayne?"

"Well, although Mrs. Cramden didn't go about the questioning in a justified manner, I think she was onto something with the treasure," Jayne explained. "It could very well have been his motive."

"But *was* it?" Kel asked rhetorically. "That is the question that we have to use our best judgment to decide on. Is Blackbeard's search for the alleged treasure a valid motive to use against him in this trial?"

Some murmured softly and nodded in agreement.

"Sheriff," Sherri said, turning to Wyatt, "You said 'innocent.' Why?"

"'Cause I think Fred was gettin' somewheres with his witness, Mr. Smith," Wyatt explained. "I believes Fred's got somethin' up his sleeve that will put Trickster in jail for a long time. I knows Trickster; he prob'ly done it himself."

"I said innocent because of the evidence Fred does have," Kel added. "When Fred requested a recess, it looked like he had something formulating in his brain. It was as if he wanted to check on something Mr. Smith had said. I don't think Mr. Smith is quite as innocent as they claim."

"I agree with Kel," Tim said. "I think 'Trickster,' as Sheriff West called him, did it. I've seen these TV shows before; Fred called him up on the stand so that he would confess when Fred introduced new, overwhelming evidence against him."

"All right, all right." Sherri rose from her seat. "I guess you guys all have something against Mr. Smith. I do, too, but that's a different story. I just found Blackbeard's testimony more believable. He *was* hiding something, like Jayne said, but Mr. Smith definitely had something to hide. He sounded so phony with his story. Besides, he *is* the only person to have been arrested and confined for a felony, or even a misdemeanor. He robbed the bank a couple months ago, so he's already got a record."

"Wait, now that's not fair!" Scott said defensively. "We've already agreed specifically not to use Blackbeard's past to sway our decision because it's irrelevant. It would hardly be right to use Trickster's against *him*."

"Yeah, you're right." Kel nodded. "But Sherri's also right. I was thinking the same thing. Trickster's story is phony, and I can't see convicting Blackbeard with only circumstantial proof. He was found at the scene with the sword, but he could have been investigating for himself. Had Mr. Smith walked in first, I'm sure the roles would have been switched, and Mr. Smith would have been charged. Blackbeard was just in the wrong place at the wrong time."

"You are absolutely right, Kel." Sherri nodded. "Only, Mr. Smith would have been convicted as well, because he *can* be linked with motive, opportunity, and access to the weapon. There's also some tiny evidence that was overlooked."

"How?" Kel was surprised.

"What do you mean?" Stevens looked puzzled.

"Oh, I forgot," Sherri said. "I'm a detective. I've been working on this case, and we have substantial evidence against him."

"Is that even right?" Scott asked. "You shouldn't be a juror if you're working on the case yourself. You have a biased view."

"Hardly." Sherri laughed. "My friends were mistreated both by the pirate and his crew, being captured, so I wouldn't side with them. Trickster indecently approached one of my partners, so I wouldn't take his side, either. There was a third party involved, someone close to my friend; still we had to investigate objectively, even if the evidence leaned to his conviction. The way I see it, I just know the facts better from firsthand experience, that's all."

"Whatever." Scott shook his head now. "Why didn't you tell us this before?"

"Because I wanted to know the take that you guys had on the same situation, being outside of the investigation. After I knew your take, I was going to tell you," Sherri explained.

"Whatever." Scott crossed his arms and rolled his eyes.

Everyone then sat down again, waiting with anticipation, looking directly at Sherri. The wait lasted for several minutes as Sherri looked down, around, or at the others. She was waiting for them to continue talking or for them to finish their opinions.

"Well?" Sean said impatiently, looking at Sherri.

"What?" Sherri jumped and turned toward Sean.

"Are you going to tell us what happened with Randy and Smith or not?" he answered, crossing his arms as Scott had.

"Oh, yeah," Sherri said. "Well, the Sundaes, a detective agency, and I have discovered some evidence at the scene that points directly at Trickster."

"You said that already. What is it?" Kel asked excitedly.

"The books Randy had on his table were open to a page that had a picture of Trickster's exact watch. You know, the watch he mentioned earlier, during the trial," Sherri explained. "We also found several notes written in Randy's handwriting about a 'green man.'"

"Those just verify that Randy had Trickster's watch!" Scott scoffed. "He already claimed to have been friends with him and said Randy was repairing his watch for him."

"Yes, but I have more evidence to announce." Sherri began to walk around the table. "The Sundaes have presented Mr. Cramden with a very incriminating piece of evidence. A tooth was found next to the table. There was blood on it, and it was made of gold."

"A tooth?" Kel exclaimed. "Was it Trickster's?"

"Have you seen his smile lately?"

Chapter 69

Everyone proceeded back to the courtyard. It grew to be nighttime, and the lot was soon illuminated by an array of torches. The judge waited patiently at the bench as the others took their places once again.

Trickster was between two police officers, Miller and Ray Caldor. They were guarding him from leaving the courtroom, and he was calmly waiting, just hoping they'd use the evidence against Blackbeard and not him.

"There's nothing I can do at all. Man!" Trickster said softly. "Where's Delores now?"

She was nowhere to be found. It was the same with Fred. Alice looked all around and couldn't locate him as she sat down at her desk.

"Where is he?"

Without any further delay, Fred returned from the direction of Kel's Place. With him were Delores, Dillon, and Dawn.

"I sure hope you're right." Taran sighed as he walked along.

"Don't worry, it's all set." Dawn grabbed Taran's arm.

"Yeah, don't worry, Dillon," Fred added. "This thing is going to be a blast. I have everything I'm going to need. Just be sure your police officers are in position in case he tries to escape."

The trial resumed with Trickster in his place on the stand. The lawyers took their places, and the audience sat back down. Delores joined them, and the jurors were the last to sit back down in their seats.

"You may proceed." The judge waved his hand at Fred permissively.

"Thank you, your Honor." Fred rose once again and approached the stand. "Now, Mr.... Smith, where did I leave off before?"

"You... uh... accused me of killing Randy—"

"Oh, that's right." Fred walked over to his table and flipped through a stack of papers. "I was going to check on your alibi…" he mumbled. "Who was this friend to whom you earlier referred?"

"Huh?" Trickster gave him a weird look.

"You said you were with a friend before deciding to retrieve your watch," Fred told him. "Who was your friend?"

"W… Why does that concern you?."

"Answer the question, Mr. Smith," the judge commanded.

"Uh… his name's…" Trickster looked down, hesitated, and then stopped.

"It's Tom Thompson, isn't it?" Fred asked.

Trickster looked up. "What? No!"

"You weren't working together up until that time?" Fred asked. "It isn't true that you and he, two infamous gangsters, have just recently been released from prison for a felonious conviction?"

"Uh… yeah," Trickster answered as if it were public knowledge.

"Yeah," Fred repeated. "He and you go around together committing crimes back in your own time, right? In a gang? Do you see what I'm getting at here, Mr. Smith?"

"Getting at?" Trickster shouted. "You're not 'getting at' anything! You've already stepped in it! You're accusing me of this murder, and it's a lie. A lie, I tell ya!"

"Perhaps you don't see this the way I do," Fred explained. "This is my hypothesis. You and Mr. Thompson went to the inn because it fits the evidence. You went to the inn intending to teach Randy a lesson, and Thompson was there to help you carry it out. You had a bat in your hand, and you were going to knock him senseless. Then you planned to drag him outside, for what I don't know. But when you got to his door someone stopped you: my client. He hit you, but you clubbed him out causing him to drop his sword. So you got a better idea, to stab Randy instead."

"What? A lie!" Trickster shouted again.

"It isn't true that you were going to 'teach him a lesson'?" Fred asked.

"Who… who said that?"

"I talked to Thompson during our break," Fred explained. "He graciously filled me in for a decreased punishment of merely aiding and abetting if he agreed to testify. He is ready to testify in this court, with the exact story I told you."

"Well, he's lying just to get back at me!"

"So it isn't true that you were going to club Randy out? Teach him a lesson?" Fred repeated. He was leaning toward Trickster and getting louder. "And isn't it true that you found my client's sword when he dropped it? Isn't it true that you were so upset from all of this that you decided to stab him right there? So you took the saber and stabbed Randy, killing him! "

"Objection! Now *he* is harassing the witness!" Alice shouted, rising from her seat.

"Proof! I have proof, your Honor," Fred shouted back, holding up his finger.

"Let's see it, Mr. Cramden," the judge said sternly.

Fred walked back over to his table, next to which his briefcase stood. He placed it on top of the table and fiddled with the lock.

"You *did* stab Randy." Fred was quieter and calmer now, trying to decipher his combination. "But that really wasn't enough to kill him. He fought back, or tried to fight back. In the struggle he punched you, right in the mouth," Fred explained, peering at the briefcase with a confused look.

"How… how could you… say that?" Trickster stammered. "Me and him… we're like this." Trickster crossed his fingers and showed Fred.

"Oh, yeah." Fred's gave an expected reaction. Then he muttered, "What is wrong with this thing?" Realizing he'd said that aloud, he glanced at his wife.

She uttered four numbers under her breath and motioned for him to get back to the case, pointing at Trickster.

Fred shook his head as the locks snapped loose. He cleared his throat and looked back at Trickster. "First of all, it's 'he and I.' Secondly, I checked that story out."

Trickster adjusted his position, more a reaction to Fred's statement than to the uncomfortable wooden chair. Just the same, he turned a little away from the judge.

"You and Randy didn't know each other," Fred stated. "You bumped into each other on the street one day and had a huge confrontation; I have witnesses. You guys weren't friends. He destroyed your antique watch, and you were furious and despised him for it."

"It's a lie," Trickster insisted, in a weaker voice. "I have my watch. It's right here, alive and tickin'!" he said more desperately. He lifted his golden watch to show the court and especially the judge.

"That's because he fixed it for you," Fred continued. "That's one thing you didn't realize until after you had killed him. Like I said, you stabbed Randy and struggled with him."

"And I told you that's a lie!" Trickster yelled. "There's no proof." He sighed. "None at all."

"That's where you're wrong," Fred responded gravely. As he opened up his briefcase and pulled out the plastic bag, he said, "This was found at the scene right next to the 'junk table,' as it were." He walked back to the stand

and displayed it in his open hand. “Would you tell the court what this is, Mr. Smith?”

He shook his head. “I don’t know what—”

“Now, now, now, before you answer,” Fred said, holding up his hand to stop him. “ Remember that you are under oath. Also, I have to tell you that we found some DNA on here that verifies what I will say this is.”

“Listen, I don’t know what DMA is, but—”

“D*N*A. Deoxyribonucleic acid,” Fred interrupted. “It’s something inside of you, in every cell, hair, and part of your skin, which is so unique that it can differentiate between your hair and blood from anyone else’s in the world.”

He paused to let the reality sink in the Trickster’s head. Trickster slowly rubbed his cheek to search for the absence in his mouth, the deceitful absence that gave him away.

“So I’ll ask you again, Mr. Smith, will you please tell the court what this is?” Fred moved the bag closer to Trickster’s face, and Trickster cringed.

“It’s… a tooth,” Trickster said hesitantly. “*My* tooth… that is, my golden tooth that I got a long time ago. I… It must’ve fallen out when he punched… when he punched my jaw…”

“Who?” Fred asked quietly. “Who punched you?”

“Randy,” Trickster said. He snarled, then merely looked down in defeat. “Right after I stabbed him.”

Alice rose from her seat again. “Your Honor,” she said, more relaxed now, “the prosecution would like to move to dismiss all charges against Blackbeard.”

Murphy and Miller approached the stand as Ray stood next to Trickster.

“Sir,” Ray said, taking Trickster’s arm, “you have the—”

Trickster obstinately ripped himself loose of Officer Caldor’s grip. Knocking over his chair, he ran out of the courtroom, chased by the three officers. He ran as fast as his feet would carry him, his hat flying off of his head. Not seeing the hat, Ray slipped on it and hit the ground. Murphy grabbed Trickster by the shoulders and tackled *him* to the ground.

Chapter 70

TARAN SIGHED AGAIN.

Dawn did the same. It was the morning after the trial. They were sitting together in Taran's hut, just relaxing and discussing the complicated, confusing events of the previous few days. The Sundaes had just left the hut after sharing a big breakfast with them, which Kel had helped Sherri prepare by allowing her to use the restaurant kitchen.

Strawberry was the last to leave. She was still hesitant, but not because she'd be leaving Dawn with the man she had never had respect for before now. It was because the last time she had left Dawn alone, she disappeared.

"Well, I'm gonna be..." Strawberry turned to Dawn. "I'll be over at the Island Inn. The girls and I have to figure out what we're gonna do from here." She looked over at Taran and smiled. "See you guys."

"Bye, Strawberry." Dawn waved.

"Where was I?" Taran looked back at his fiancée. "Oh, yeah." He yawned. "That's right."

"Wow," Dawn suddenly said. *And to think I once suspected Taran of killing Randy because it seemed to tie together. Hell, I didn't just suspect him. I convinced myself so well that he'd done it; it was terrible. And now it just seems so ridiculous.*

"What?" Taran looked up at her eyes. "What's wrong?" *She has been acting very strange since coming to the island. I don't know what it is, but she seems like she is hiding something.*

"We've got a lot still ahead of us, a lot of planning to do," Dawn told him.

"W... What do you mean?" Taran asked. *Oh, duh, of course, the wedding. She's been waiting a long time for that, too. How did she not get fed up?*

He got up and led Dawn over to one of the side rooms. They sat on the cot that he had built after meeting up with Murphy. It was hard and uncomfortable, but he felt better when Dawn sat right beside him.

"Well, Dawn," Taran said, peering down at the ring on her left hand, "you've been waiting a *very* long time for this… and, as I promised, the time is now… or then, whichever."

They both laughed, loudly at first.

But Dawn's laugh faded as she stared down at the same object Taran had. She fiddled with it nervously, turning it each way and pulling it up and down in position on her finger.

First things first, Dawn thought.

Back in the other room, Dawn had been referring to the wedding. But remembering what Taran had talked about before, she knew he had to speak to Thompson first. "You should go tell Mr. Thompson about this stuff now, don't you think? Now that it's over?"

Feeling almost rejected, Taran's smile faded. "Thompson. Yeah, the trial *is* over. Things are going to get back to whatever we're going to have to accept as normal around here. And the social cooperation has, in some ways, failed."

"It hasn't failed."

"Murder on Randy's second day isn't a failure?"

Dawn sighed this time. She had gone to the house on Pool Street. She had read through the journal of Randy Carr. She had learned about his family, his town, his likes, his dislikes, his neighbors, and everyone involved with the discovery of his body. The trunk, the roll top desk, the photograph, the Christmas Party, and the skit, all of these ran through her mind right now. When she remembered everything that happened since Taran disappeared at the helipad, Dawn realized one simple truth.

"He *had* to die, Taran." His eyes met hers again. "Don't you see? *My* detective agency already knew about the murder before *you* went back in time. Although *you* brought Randy here, he was already dead to me. So after he came, there had to be some way for his body to end up in 2348 for me to find.

"Historically, Randy had already disappeared. Andy Grant had known that since he was nine. And because *I* came here and met with Randy alive, even I couldn't save him. If I had, I wouldn't have…" She stopped when she realized the conundrum she found herself in. She then had to explain it to herself to understand.

"If I saved him, he wouldn't have died, and therefore I wouldn't have thought to save him," she restated. "So, he *had* to die."

Taran stood up.

"You're right," he said. "You're absolutely right, although Thompson won't see it that way."

"That doesn't matter, Taran." Dawn shook her head and stood up as well. "What matters is that those pirates are enjoying a very twenty-first century meal over at Kel's Place right now. My friends actually have potential boyfriends, despite the fact that they'd have died *years* before we were even born!"

Taran nodded.

"And Joe Young is having a ball interacting with Tim, who happens to run the same business Joe did, four hundred years earlier," Dawn added. "Kel has her dream job with her best friend by her side. The Caldors have a son who can stay home since Lindsey and her uncle can home-school him. There are so many reasons this thing worked out."

Dawn leaned in and finally kissed him. "Your dreams have finally borne fruit. Don't let Thompson get in the way of that."

Taran simply smiled.

They stood in silence for a little while. Taran was enjoying her company, something he hadn't done in a long time. Something had always gotten in the way, which was what he realized was happening again when Dawn finally spoke up.

"Well, you've got to do it," she said. "Get it over with."

"Okay, babe." He smiled again. "I'll be right back." He went over to the trapdoor and descended on the ladder. Dawn closed the door behind him and waited there.

Chapter 71

"I WENT TO TALK TO talk to Mr. Thompson today," Taran began to write as he sat in his computer hut. "I had to tell him about Randy's murder. Randy's… murder. My fiancée's most challenging case followed me here. It's ironic. We solved it. The problem was to deal with the killer, the 'Trickster.'

"So I had a jail built. Actually, it had been built for his first offense: robbing the bank only a couple months ago. Anyway, he and an accomplice killed Randy and disposed of the body, which I plan to bring here to bury it on this island.

"Dawn and I decided the best way to end this whole circle of murder was to plant the evidence that led us here. We had ID cards from the thirty or so residents. There's some personal effects that were in the trunk Dawn told me about. The saber would have to go along with the watch parts and everything that was in room 203, save for the tooth, of course.

"Randy's body has no doubt already made it there. I checked the logs on my time machine. It was transported for less than thirty seconds to some town in southern Indiana. I assume that's where the Andrew Grant character I was told about would discover it in 2333. It was then transported 'randomly' to Detroit. Apparently Trickster didn't know how to adjust the destination points.

"Everything was set, but I still had one more errand to run, which I was more afraid of than anything else. I had to go tell my boss about all the things that went wrong with his multibillion dollar mission.

"I couldn't communicate through time since the technology isn't yet available, nor do I know if it ever will be. However, I was able to transport back to my office and avoid seeing Thompson face to face. From my office, I was able to talk to him via video feed… much, much safer for my sake."

"Where the hell have you been, Flint?" were Thompson's first words when

Taran appeared on his office screen. "And don't give me a wise remark this time, Flint. I know you were on a run. Just tell me what you have to report."

"Well, sir, the time machine ended up on an island somewhere in the nineteenth century," Taran explained. "It turns out that a small tribe of natives live there, however, I've had minimal contact with them."

"Go on."

"Well, I have already established the experimental group for our social exercises as well." He cringed a little, awaiting his verbal thrashing.

"Excellent!"

"Huh?" He was a bit more than confused by Thompson's change in tone. "Is everything all right, sir?"

"You tell me, Flint." Thompson chuckled. "You're ahead of schedule. You probably should have reported to me after the completion of Phase One, but that's forgivable."

"Well..." He was supposed to tell him about how the STIM method had actually been altered for this case, but the Randy news came out of his mouth first.

"There's more, sir..." Taran said, slowly and sadly. "Randolph Carr, one of my citizens, has been killed." Taran rested his elbow on the table and cupped his face in his hands shamefully.

"What?" Mr. Thompson said. "Who did it?"

"'Mr. John "Trickster" Smith,'" Taran read from one of the computer screens. "'Number 1872–338–140.'" He sighed. "What do I do now, sir? As far as dealing with the morals that will arise, I mean."

"First, you must terminate this operation," Thompson said quickly. "This is way out of your control, Flint. I can't believe you made those moves without my say so."

"Terminate?" Taran responded in shock. "Isn't that being a little harsh? I... I mean, do you realize what terminating this project would mean? Not only would the people here have no place to go to, we'd have to start time experiments all over!"

"What do you mean 'no place to go'?"

"Well, they can't go back to their own times," Taran replied, "and tell people what they've been through over the past few months. It would make this situation worse."

"Of course we can't," Thompson agreed. "If this got out, Karz would have a terrible scandal to deal with."

"So you agree we can't terminate the project?"

"I didn't say that." Thompson shook his head. "We simply need to proceed to the emergency stage. Use a dose of the K3 serum on each of the people and send them home."

"Sir, we can't use that; it's hardly been tested," Taran urged. "We don't know if there could be any side effects, especially after time travel. The results could be disastrous."

"Then what do *you* propose we do?" he replied. "And keep in mind that the UNA government is breathing down our necks constantly. The lives of your people are in your hands, just as many of them have been for the past few months; they are your responsibility."

"Then, we..." Taran stammered. "I, we... I suggest we go on with this operation... follow through. We've simply bypassed a couple of the STIM steps, which can easily be made up."

"And what about Dr. Brown?"

"S... Sandy?" Taran replied nervously.

"First name basis now?"

"Umm, no, sir," he responded, shaking his head. "That is, Sandy has already returned to Miami Tech. She had completed her analysis, and she's gone back to work on one of their assignments."

"Good." Thompson sighed. "Now, what about this murderer?"

"We place Mr. Smith in prison."

"Have you arranged for a prison to be built?"

"Yes," Taran answered.

Thompson drew in a deep breath. "Well, what then for Mr. Carr?"

"I don't know. I didn't plan for this contingency," Taran answered.

"*I* did, Mr. Flint," Thompson retorted. "It was to use the K3 memory faltering serum, send the people back to their times, and eliminate the clones. And even that could have been avoided had you proceeded using the proper steps we had discussed."

"There *are* no clones," Taran responded.

"What?" Thompson shouted. He looked like he was about to jump through the screen and strangle his rebellious employee. "You mean to tell me that people have been disappearing left and right throughout time?"

"Oh, come on, sir, people disappear every day without any explanation." Taran crossed his arms.

"And you think it's okay to make even more disappear without a trace?" Thompson asked rhetorically. "I was right before; this is totally out of hand. You cannot, within *any* bounds, do what you're doing without questioning the dispute of your morality in this circumstance."

"Thompson, you have to—"

"No, *you* have some choices to make to straighten out this whole mess before the UNA government comes after you for overstepping our laws and Karz gets involved in a scandal. What you are doing is no more than kidnapping people, with a much more complex MO. Simply put, it's illegal, Mr. Flint.

"If you want my advice, I think you need to end this project immediately until we have worked out the bugs. It's time you stopped playing God," Thompson added. "Thompson out!" The screen turned black, and Taran hung his head.

"Needless to say, I was pretty upset," he continued to write. "So I had to figure out a solution, some way to keep the island, to keep the people who are there, and to clear this Karz thing to avoid a scandal."

Chapter 72

"WELL, I TALKED TO Mr. Thompson," Taran said as he climbed up the ladder to his hut. Dawn stood watching him from her doorway.

"That was fast," she answered. "What did he say?"

"He insisted I 'stop playing God,'" Taran quoted Thompson mockingly as he put a book into his desk and locked the drawer. "So he wants me to terminate this whole project and go home. It's too dangerous to keep this program going, endangering people's lives like Randy's."

"So what are you going to do?" Dawn led Taran to a comfortable chair and patted his back.

"Well, I can't just ignore him," he said, then he added, "although he really can't do anything about it until he builds his own time machine. " Taran sighed. "So, I suppose I'll have to compromise on something, you know, in order to fix the problem and still keep the island."

"Well, couldn't you develop a law enforcement… I mean, better than just Murphy, Miller, and Ray?" Dawn asked.

"Yeah, but that still wouldn't solve the problem of someone actually coming and killing someone," Taran replied. "It would just punish the killer." Taran paused. "Anyway, I don't think that was what Mr. Thompson had in mind for the 'UNA government scandal' thing."

"How do you mean?" Dawn asked.

Taran sighed again. "I never exactly explained to you the process that we use for time travel, huh?"

"I'm still lost." She shrugged.

"Well, the Safe Time Travel Method, or what my co-workers call 'STIM,' has three primary essentials. It's what's in the books for a sort of loophole in UNA laws. One: an isolated test area. Two: the time travel itself. And the third is how to keep everything in line, a way to cover the whole thing safely."

"Well, what is it?" Dawn asked.

"We planned to research everyone, each person independently, and… program a clone to live their life in their place so they wouldn't be missed," Taran said hesitantly. "But that's not—"

Dawn gasped. "Oh, Taran!" *That's a felony!* "If the UNA ever found out, you guys at Karz would be shut down, and they'd confiscate your time machine and all the schematics and everything!"

"Not to mention I'd be thrown in jail."

"That too." Dawn nodded.

"So you see, I didn't actually clone all of the people that came. In fact, none of them were cloned, exactly," Taran told her. She was more confused, which Taran could clearly see. "Well, it's hard to explain really, but I was supposed to get historians going and all that stuff. There are so many complications with strings we had to pull to get people here."

"You're making absolutely no sense." Dawn shrugged again.

"Well, you see, in order to continue, I would have to… I would have to set up a different way to bring people here," Taran said. "I would have to basically issue each… I don't know. I don't know how to cut out the cloning process." Taran got up and walked around the room.

"An isolated area," Dawn repeated. "What do you need that for?"

"That's to keep the experiment from interference from the outside world," Taran explained. "And this may sound confusing, but it prevents everybody from encountering themselves. You know, if the 'me' from 2341 found the 'me' from 2348 walking down the street, who knows what could happen."

"Oh."

"Also, so that the people I bring can't change the future by changing the past and creating a paradoxical cataclysm," Taran went on. "That definitely wouldn't be good."

"So, Taran, this island *is* isolated, right?" Vanilla asked.

"At the time being, yes."

"Then how did the pirate get here?"

"Pirate?" Taran asked. "Oh, and the Kahukah tribe, too."

"Kahu-what?"

"They're the native tribe to this area, I suppose," Taran answered. "They're called Kahukah, and they live in a palace on the other side of the jungle."

"Well, this island can't be in the middle of nowhere, I mean, literally," Dawn answered. "It would have to be somewhere, but Kahukah? It doesn't sound familiar. I don't think that's a real tribe."

"Real?" Taran replied. "They have to be real. I mean, they're here; they have to be real. I didn't imagine them. But still, why *are* they unheard of?" he asked, not really expecting an answer. "What about one of your Sundae friends? Isn't one of them a historian?"

"Yeah, that's right," Dawn answered. "Chocolate could help you figure out who the Kahukah are."

"Good," Taran said, "Because, if we can identify the tribe, then we can locate where we are geographically."

Chapter 73

IT DIDN'T TAKE DAWN long to drag Chocolate away from her room at the inn, especially since there was nothing to do along the line of detective work.

"All right, all right," Chocolate said as she opened the door to Taran's hut. "Good morning, Taran," she greeted him.

"Hey, D… Debbie." Taran rose from his chair. He was getting better at putting the right name to the right Sundae.

"So, what is it that you needed me for?" Debbie asked as she sat in the chair across from his. She already knew, but she didn't want to make it look like Dawn had filled her in with everything. She hadn't paid attention to half of it, anyway.

"I understand you know a lot about ancient history and ancient customs of many dead civilizations," Taran said. "Am I right?"

"Absolutely," Chocolate answered. "And if I don't know it, I know just where to find it out."

"Well, I just got to thinking—"

"There's a first." Chocolate sighed.

"I just got to thinking," Taran repeated, "that I don't remember the history of a particular tribe in this area. It's a primitive tribe from the 'modern era,' just before the end of the second millennium. They're called the Kahukah."

"'Kahukah'?" Chocolate repeated. "That does sound familiar. I believe the Kahukah were an ancient race of nomadic islanders in the Caribbean. Not much is known about them because they disappeared from the records in the mid-nineteenth century."

"That's… very interesting," Taran replied. "What events led up to their disappearance, do you know?"

"No, I'm not sure," Chocolate answered. "But if I had access to a major database or a computer system, I could find what you're looking for."

"All right." Taran sighed. "Follow me."

"W... well, wait, wait a second, Taran." Chocolate rose. "I could really use some help from Donna. She's really a whiz at this computer stuff."

"No," Taran said sternly as he reached for the trapdoor.

"Oh, come on," Chocolate begged. "She's right outside the door; we'll be done in no time."

"Fine," Taran agreed.

"Debbie," Taran said as he reached for the ladder in the center of the dimly lit compass room, " don't say anything to *anyone* about this place. Either of you."

Butterscotch and Chocolate both looked around at the sixteen doors, then to the compass rose on the floor, then to the ceiling hatch, which Taran was opening. Dawn was standing in the doorway leading back to Taran's hut.

"Of course, of course," was Chocolate's reply. She and Butterscotch were staring at the dark door, the door marked "NW" at the top. A cool breeze blew by them that gave them a chill.

"What was that?" Butterscotch jumped. She looked nervously to Taran.

"It was just the vents and the door opening, circulating air from the outside world to down here," Taran told her. Still, they stared at the door. "Donna, Debbie." Taran was now at the top. "Come on."

Butterscotch began to climb up the ladder. "Oh, yeah, just point me and Debbie in the direction of the computer so that we can—oh my!" She looked around at the bright room where Taran's computer systems sat.

The screens still flashed different displays. Some were still shots of different portions of the island town, some were blueprints of vehicles and buildings, and other screens merely listed names and numbers along with short biographical information.

"I'll set up the computer for you," Taran offered. "You girls have a seat."

"You don't just use a standard operating system?" Butterscotch asked.

"Oh, yeah, I do," Taran said.

"Well, which monitor?" Butterscotch asked impatiently.

"Right here."

Butterscotch sat down at the keyboard. Chocolate sat beside her in another chair.

"We're going to look in the UNA database for information on a tribe of the nineteenth century," Chocolate told Butterscotch.

Butterscotch quickly accessed the site and located files on ancient cultures. Different unpronounceable symbols and names appeared on the screen. Butterscotch typed in "Kahukah" and found two files.

Chocolate touched the icon on the second file, and it revealed a historical article. "According to this article, Taran, the Kahukah tribe, 'led by the tribe chief after whom it was named, lived in peace with a second tribe, the Ja'it,'" she read. "'Kahukah led his followers on a quest to locate their gods. In the 1840s, they left the Ja'it tribe alone on the island they called Wazafíon to begin their quest.' They weren't heard of for a year, but a messenger aptly named Zhorenid, meaning "good news" in the Kahukah language, was sent to them with a message that their god was found. 'The Ja'it tribe was said to have followed the Kahukah tribesman to their god's island, but they were never heard from again.'

"Also, according to this, the island, Wazafíon, was found later on in 2206 near the Bermudan islands. It was fifty feet under the water, and several artifacts were recovered from a diving expedition later that year."

"So this story involves two tribes from the nineteenth century who disappeared completely with hardly a trace," Taran summed up. "So how did the writers get this information?"

"Apparently," Butterscotch answered, "among the artifacts found on the sunken island, there was a 'journal presumably kept by one of the natives or a visitor to the island. It was in a watertight chest and written in broken English.'" Butterscotch looked up at Taran. "All of this information came firsthand from that journal."

"Who was it?" Taran leaned into the screen. "Does it say? 'A man named "Leon Hunt"'? Who is that, and why haven't I ever heard of him?"

"This is pretty interesting stuff, Taran." Butterscotch nodded. "But what's the real reason that *you* wanted to know about this lost civilization? How does it help you?"

"Well, Donna, on the other side of this wall," Taran said, knocking on the cement wall by which the computer lay, "*is* the Kahukah village."

"What?" Chocolate exclaimed excitedly. "Are you kidding me? This is amazing! The village you told me about before on the other side of the jungle is the Kahukah village? No way!"

"Yes, it is," Taran said proudly. "But back to business, Chocolate. What is *this* article about?" Taran pointed the cursor to the other file. "The first one from the search."

"Let's find out, shall we?" Butterscotch opened the file. "It looks like an update to the first article. It says, 'Further investigations performed by the diving teams conclude that "Leon Hunt" was a pseudonym.' Hmm... 'In the journal, he explained his background. He was a tribesman from the Kahukah tribe who learned English from Dilón, the god found on the island. His real name was Wakna, the literal translation for "hunting lion" in Dinokahu, the Kahukah language.'"

"'Dilón'... Taran?" Chocolate smiled and looked up at him. "You're the god? The god Dillon?"

"Yep." Taran smiled and peered down at Chocolate.

"So that means we're living this history?" Chocolate asked excitedly.

"It would appear so," Taran answered.

"Well, actually, Chocolate," Butterscotch said, turning to her friend, "Taran created this history by landing on the island. Apparently, this island has never been found, even by the UNA government in 2348. The Kahukah tribe landed here, found a futuristic man named Dillon, and assumed he was their god. That is, the god they moved to the island to seek out."

"Yeah, she's right," Taran replied. "When I landed here, the Kahukah found my ship and thought it was a flying transport that would bring them their god. They even built an altar for it. I showed up one day and befriended one named Kahlif and one named Wakna."

"Wakna!" Chocolate exclaimed.

"Yes. I taught him English, and he allowed me to stay in this very hut, where his family lived," Taran explained. "Underneath his hut was the bunker down there; that's where I stayed. Then I taught his family English as well."

"He lived in a concrete hut with a metal, power-sliding door?" Chocolate pointed to the door on the opposite wall from the computer.

"Don't be ridiculous—"

"No, wouldn't want that," Butterscotch said.

Taran sighed and smiled. "I refurbished this hut and built concrete walls inside this room. The door used to be behind this computer," Taran explained. "This door leads to the other rooms of the hut, which remain authentic even now. I also made a door in there that is the new entrance to the hut."

"So you disguised a concrete computer room with straw to make it look like a hut?" Butterscotch summed up. "What about the sliding door? Do straw doors slide open now?"

"Well, first of all, the door wouldn't be stable at all if it was made of straw," Taran answered. "It's bamboo. Secondly," he started as he opened the sliding door. The bamboo door stood in the doorway now. "The door opens inwardly, but it's locked when the sliding door is closed. No one goes in there anyway; this hut is left unused as far as Kahukah is concerned."

"Wow, this is ingenious," Butterscotch said. "But still, why did you need this information about the Kahukah tribes at all?"

"I needed to find out exactly when and where we are," Taran explained.

"Oh, so we don't mess up history?" Chocolate asked.

"That," Taran answered, "*and* because Mr. Thompson wanted to terminate this whole project."

"What? He can't do that!" Butterscotch exclaimed.

"What would he want to do that for?"

"Yeah," Butterscotch added. "This place is great. Almost like a paradise."

"Well, his reasons are mostly because of what happened with Randy, but don't worry about it. We're all set now," Taran reassured them.

"How come?" Chocolate asked.

"We're in an isolated area in 1841," Taran exclaimed.

"How can you be sure that we're isolated?" Butterscotch asked.

"And that it will stay that way?" Chocolate added.

"Well, because by this evidence, we're in the Bermuda Triangle," Taran answered. "We must be. Why else would the Kahukah civilization have been lost? No one can track people that come here. It's a strange phenomenon."

"That's right," Butterscotch said. "Even when planes and technology *are* invented, the people here will be safe from outsiders. Planes' systems jam in this area, and boats get lost forever. No one knows why."

"Not only that, but we can set up our own defense from outsiders to ensure that they won't get in," Taran told them. "And since we're in the Triangle, it won't interfere with history at all."

"Well, not as far as we're concerned," Butterscotch said. "When we set up this defense system you're talking about, we'd be *causing* the disappearances in the Triangle."

"Either way, we're all set," Taran responded. "I've got to kick you out now."

It was a statement that was followed by groans. They didn't want to leave. Chocolate was infatuated with the "new" history she could learn, and it had been too long since Butterscotch had gotten her computer fix.

"We've got to get going anyway," Butterscotch said.

"Yeah, I want to see the Kahukah people," Chocolate cried.

"Oh, and you better let me use that computer again sometime," Butterscotch demanded as she got onto the ladder.

"All right," Taran agreed. "Hey, thanks a lot, girls. I owe you one. And Debbie," Taran said as he went over to the ladder that Chocolate was already halfway down, "Debbie, don't go in the village alone; be careful."

Taran sat down at his desk in the hut and explained everything to Dawn. She was, to say the least, relieved; everyone truly enjoyed being on the island. Besides, they could now go on with their own plans and even get married. As Taran removed the book from his desk, Dawn left to make arrangements with Strawberry and the others.

"So now I have to leave this island and discuss our plans with Mr. Thompson," he wrote silently. "I discovered today that this island is in the Bermuda Triangle, probably the island referred to as Devil's Island. That's the basis for my new plans. This island is completely safe now, with the most certainty I've had in a long time.

"We can develop technology to hide the island from radar, satellites, or other equipment the people of this island may encounter down the road, in the future. In fact, I've got some ideas already that I'll tell Mr. Thompson about, like an EMP shield. Electromagnetic Pulse would disrupt electrical signals in the area.

"And because we're in the Triangle, I don't have to worry about this place being discovered. One more thing actually caught my attention. It said that divers discovered the island underwater in 2206, and that they found a 'lost civilization.' Well, that civilization is my civilization. In time, this 'island of time' will eventually cover itself up and historically never be found, an assuring discovery. My own civilization will probably last a long time, long after the people here now. It's going to go from a mere experiment to a successful civilization. It will be a second Atlantis that historians will investigate for years.

"Anyway, Debbie, Donna, and I looked up a lot of information; that's how we discovered where we were. After they left the room, I contacted Mr. Thompson. He told me he'd hold a staff meeting. There I'll go over my plans with him and the new Time Crew, which I will arrange tomorrow."

Chapter 74

The corner office on the ninth floor of the Karz building was lit brightly by the sun flowing in from the window. In the corner of the office sat a large bookcase, next to which stood a filing cabinet. On its opposite side was a potted plant that hadn't been deprived of water despite the inactivity in the office room over the past four months.

The desk stood a comfortable distance from that wall. Atop it was a stack of papers, a pencil holder, a closed laptop computer, and a telephone. On the front center of the desk sat a plaque reading "Taran Flint."

Presently, a blue light filled the room and Taran appeared within it. Without delay, he purposefully walked to the door opposite the desk and exited the room, turning left. The halls were empty except for the small paintings or plants along the walls, just like they'd been when he left.

It took him about half an hour, but Taran successfully rounded up a group of five people who would oversee or work with him to maintain order on the island and control the use of time travel: the Time Crew. They had already been in the works for several independent studies and research on time travel. Taran felt it was time to bring them all together officially.

First was Dr. Laura White; she was the crew's micro-technician. She had long black hair and blue eyes. She was tall and a stickler for attention to detail. She specialized in designing micro-technological machines. Her primary goal was to one day safely manipulate time with a device the size of a diamond stud earring, specifically one of the ones she always wore.

Dr. Bruce White, Laura's husband of eighteen years, was also tall and had brown hair and brown eyes. He had a better sense of humor than his wife and was very easygoing. His primary job on the crew was serving as historian. He could tell anyone what happened in any country in practically any decade since the eighteenth century when the United States began. This era was known as the more modern era of Earth's history.

Dr. Tony Black was the third crew member. He had black hair and brown eyes. He worked hand-in-hand with Dr. White, or Laura, that is. Black was the Time Crew's specialized computer programmer.

Dr. Randy Grey had brown eyes, gray hair, and a gray mustache. He worked systematically and procedurally. He oversaw small operations and functions in his specialized field, which was behavioral psychology. He was mostly involved with the effect of trauma concerning suppressed emotions and dissociated memories. He aimed to disprove time travel having any effect of the said disorders.

Last was Dr. Dave Sanders. He wore glasses and had black hair, a black mustache, and gray eyes. He had the fun, but fairly odd, job. Testing was his skill. He tested anything and everything that the others produced or programmed. That wasn't the fun part for him, though. His favorite part was the demolition. If something didn't test satisfactorily, or if it endangered people's safety, he would dispose of it, usually with an isolated explosion.

"All right, Dave." Taran shook his hand. "Welcome aboard. Let's head down to Thompson's office." Dave Sanders followed Taran and the four others down the halls of the Karz building.

"It's good to see you again," Laura White said as she walked beside Taran, who led the others. "I know it's only been a few months, but it seems like forever. We have to, well, get started on the project."

"Tell me about it." Taran sighed.

"Oh, and I *have* been," Laura said, leaning toward Taran, "working on that project with some new materials since you left." She nodded. "It's going very well. This micro-technology works well with your time machine. The research documents your Dr. Brown left have come in handy as well."

Taran nodded.

"Where is she anyway?" she asked. "I figured she'd be here."

Taran didn't have an answer for his associate. He didn't know where she was, when she was, or how she was. Frankly, he didn't care. She was out of the picture, lost in time, perhaps, but perhaps that could only be blamed on her. She set the codes, and she had made the rules that day. He searched for her the only way he knew how and couldn't find her, end of story.

"She's on her own assignment," Taran answered.

"Really? Does Thompson know about this?" she asked.

"No, it's through Miami Tech," he answered.

"But—"

"Don't worry, Laura," Taran assured her. "Sandy's gone back to her own work. Karz won't have to deal with her anymore."

"Pity. She had some valuable time travel insight."

"Tell me about it."

They reached the elevator shortly, and Taran pushed the down button. When the doors slid open, everyone entered.

"So, guys, did you figure out yet why Mr. Thompson's office is on the first floor?" Taran asked them.

"Oh, yeah, Flint," Bruce White answered. "That's actually all we were working on these past months while you were gone: why Thompson is on the first floor."

Everyone chuckled.

"Yeah, all we can come up with is that he's afraid of heights!" Sanders told him.

"Or that he couldn't operate the elevator," Dr. Grey added.

"He doesn't know up from down," Dr. Black chimed in.

"Perhaps he's too old to walk up more than a flight of stairs in the morning!" Bruce White added.

Everyone except for Laura laughed.

"Or maybe he wants to stay on the first floor because it's easier," Laura snapped. "Easier to get here, easier to leave, easier to talk to customers, and easier to help clients so everyone else doesn't have to travel far to talk to him!"

They all sat in silence for a moment.

"Nah," Taran and Sanders said in unison.

"No, not likely," Bruce White said.

"Probably not," Dr. Black replied.

"Uh-uh, no, that's not it." Dr. Grey shook his head.

They proceeded down the first floor hall, and Taran led them into Thompson's office. He was sitting at his grand desk perusing papers, files, typing, and working on his computers, just as he always had.

"Hey, Mr. Flint!" Thompson rose, leaned over his desk, and shook Taran's hand. "How are you doing? I haven't seen you in… how long? 450 years?"

"Actually, it seems more like 408 years," Taran answered.

"Wow, it's still been a while." Thompson walked around the desk and patted his worker's shoulder. Then he became more serious, not grim, but serious. "So what's the new plan with our operation?"

"Oh, right," Taran began. "You know Dr. White, Dr. White, Dr. Grey, Dr. Black, and Dr. Sanders." They each shook Thompson's hand. "They have been exclusively chosen as the new Time Crew."

"'Time crew,'" Thompson repeated in confirmation.

"That's right. Each one specializes in a particular function, and they're the best in their corresponding fields," Taran explained. "Now, I've been consulting with these guys, and I think we've come up with a solution to avoid a scandal with the UNA government."

"Go on." Thompson sat back down.

"It's very simple," Taran said. "All we have to do is take our primary essentials to safe time travel, you know, STIM, and omit one. We can, I believe, omit the cloning aspect—"

"How?" Thompson asked in anticipation.

"Simple," Taran repeated. "We have our isolated area, and our method of time travel, thanks to Dr. White, can be altered."

"How is that, Laura?" Thompson asked her.

"Well, Mr. Thompson," Laura said, peering over at Taran, "over the past few weeks I've been researching new technology and have produced a prototype of a device that can track people inter… chronologically."

Thompson raised an eyebrow at the impressive technological advancement as well as Dr. White's improvisational lingo.

"We've done quite a bit of research," she continued. "Each individual who goes through this process, who we choose to go through time, has a certain signal that can be tracked through time because of this device." She glanced at Taran intermittently as she spoke. "This way, we can be sure they're on the island or where they should be at that time as they should be."

Thompson nodded to show he understood.

Dr. White then continued with more confidence. "A final changed aspect of our process is a time allotment, which will be prearranged. Each person will have a device to be worn that will bring them from their time. Let's say if you were to use one, Mr. Thompson." She pulled the tiny device from her pocket and showed it to him as she continued to explain. "We would set this device to today's date, April 24, 2349, to the time and place. Then we would set it to the destination, time and place. Finally, we would set the device itself for a time of duration.

"At the end of the duration, which I'll set for, let's say, five minutes," Laura set it as she talked, "you would return to now. It will be, to us, as if you never left. But to you, you would have been gone for the entire five-minute duration."

"Let me see that, Dr. White," Thompson held out his hand, and Dr. White pinned the device to her boss's collar. She straightened it out. "Okay, now what?"

"Just press this button." Dr. White tapped next to the green button in the middle.

"Wait, what will stop me from reprogramming this thing after I go?" Thompson asked.

"There's a twelve button sequence on the inside of that pin," Dr. White explained. "And besides, with the micro-technology, a needle would need to be used to press the buttons. Furthermore, every programming requires specified codes. Even Taran doesn't know them." She pointed at Taran with her thumb. "Bye. See ya in five!"

She pressed the button. Thompson glowed in a blue light, and then immediately his shirt was torn, his eye was bruised, and his lip was bleeding. When the light died away, he fell to the ground.

His body didn't move for several seconds as the Time Crew stood there in shock.

"Sir, are you all right?" Dr. Grey ran over to Mr. Thompson and picked him up by his shoulders. He held him up, but soon Thompson shook his head and looked up at the others.

"Dr. White…" Thompson shook Dr. Grey off of him. "I ought to kill you." He walked up to her.

"Why?" Dr. White chuckled. "Did you see that, too, sir?"

"You do know where you sent me, right?"

"I'm sorry, we didn't know it would be *that* rough," Dr. Grey apologized.

"But it wasn't supposed to do that," Dr. White insisted.

"Wha… What? Where did you send him?" Taran asked.

"She sent me to a saloon outside of El Paso in 1840," Thompson told him. "I have to admit that I'm glad you only set it for five minutes. You see, I was brought into the middle of a very violent bar fight. This one guy belted me in the face and knocked me onto the bar. Last I saw, he came at me with a knife!"

"Wow," Dr. Black exclaimed. "How do you get so lucky?"

"It really didn't even seem like you even left," Sanders said.

"We just need to find some way to get rid of that blasted blue light," Dr. Bruce added.

"That's what I think," Laura added. "The programming glitch must be caused by a miscalculation in the sequencing. It's just a nanosecond off, a slight delay where the light is still fast enough to show through."

"Listen, guys." Thompson patted his lip tenderly with a tissue. "This time travel thing is remarkable. It really is. And that test right there, Dr. White, proves, on my life, that this new system really works better than your original method, Taran."

"Thanks." Dr. White took the pin off of Thompson's collar. She then began to reprogram it by unlocking it and opening it to reveal a small keypad. She used the pin sized laser key to press the buttons. The others continued to talk as she worked.

"So, Mr. Thompson," Taran said, leaning on the desk as Thompson sat down and put a cold patch onto his left eye. "I have an idea. The Time Crew and I have decided to continue research with time travel and possibly other manipulations of it, if you will," Taran explained. "However, I'm bogged down in managing the people in the island town and keeping them happy until they become more independent and prosperous…"

"So you want me to lead the Time Crew?" Thompson assumed. "I don't think so, Flint. I'm not caught up on the technology you guys have developed. I don't really have the credentials needed to lead the Time Crew. I think you're perfect for that."

"No." Taran smiled and turned his head, chuckling very softly. "I was thinking something else. For a little while, would it be possible to get… you have the perfect leadership qualities, Mr. Thompson. My idea was to step down as leader of my island to become the Time Crew leader and give you leadership of my town. You could give Sean what's-his-name the position of president of Karz—"

"You mean my son?" Thompson asked. "My vice president?"

"Yeah, and you can come to the island and lead the people for a couple years until a real government is established," Taran answered as Dr. White handed the pins out to each of the Time Crewmen. She gave Taran two. Taran handed Thompson a pin, and he received it willingly.

"Wait, wait, wait." Thompson peeled the cold patch from his now healed eye and looked at the pin. "I thought this island was really important to you, Flint. But you're going to willingly give me your town?"

"Sir, the town is what I've always dreamed of accomplishing," Taran explained. "Watching the people interact with each other despite temporal differences is what I've always been passionate about seeing and experiencing."

He turned toward the Time Crew.

"But, honestly, I can't settle down," Taran said. "I mean, I *am* going to settle down, with Dawn as my wife, but I'm not going to settle down in the island town and become consumed by the responsibility of the people's lives."

"That's something I can respect, Flint," Thompson answered. "You're right. There is nothing that would please me more than to join you in going to this 'Island of Time.' And, despite the burden of responsibility governing over these people may be from time to time, it's sure to be an unforgettable experience."

Chapter 75

The cool breeze and the calm sea were a refreshing cure for the rocky road that the town found itself on in its development over the past two months. It was May 1 at last. The trial had been over for a week, and the town had quieted down.

Still, there were people cruising around the streets. Men and women walked along by Tim's Shop, the usual midday customers were enjoying hot food and cool lemonade outside Kel's Place, and groups of people were collected in the areas of the still vacant lot. Some of them were checking out a row of stands selling goods at small prices. Many of them were arranging chairs and tables in the lot once again; however, this was under hardly the same circumstances than what had occurred the week before.

At the first of each month, Taran had arranged for a town meeting. That was the purpose of the chairs. There were flowers arranged in pots along the sides of the lot, and a white carpet created a path down the center of the chairs. All of these faced a white arbor at the end of the carpet.

There was also a platform to the right of the arbor. There sat a lectern, also decorated for the occasion. On the other side of the arbor stood a table, on which there was a semicircular object hidden underneath a white sheet. Under the table was a trunk.

Taran was across the street from this display, on the opposite side of the police office building. There he was patrolling the new arrangement of refreshment stands. Each stand, except for Gloria's and Mr. Owner's, sold different foods. Also, each was run by one or two people.

The bakery, on the far right, was run by Miss Smith, the pirate woman who had been with Redbeard's crew on the pirate ship. The pirates decided to keep port at the beach, where currently they worked at building docks. Redbeard decided they would stay for a while. At the bakery stand, Miss Smith baked breads, pies, and other pastries.

The stand next door to the bakery was a fruit stand, where Tim sold apples imported from the UNA, bananas, coconuts, pineapples, as well as other exotic fruit. He was continually checking the fruit for blemishes.

Gloria Deo ran the next stand, a newsstand, where she sold newspapers that were written in town, by hand for now, each week. She named the newspaper "The Oracle."

Next to the newsstand was a seafood stand. This was the only more elaborate stand in the row, dead in the middle of the others. There were three people who ran it, the divers: Jacob Brown, Isaac McNally, and Erik O'Connor. They sold lobster, crab legs, scallops, fish fillets, clam chowder, most every seafood imaginable. These things were all caught offshore from the island. The pirates allowed the divers and the divers alone to board the ship to go out fishing and diving on occasion.

Their stand also had hot dogs, also imported from the UNA, for the people who wouldn't eat seafood. What made this stand appear more prominent than the others was that it had two tables out front for people to sit and eat. Also, it was twice the length of the other stands.

The small stand to the left of the seafood stand was Mr. Owner's. He had many antiques, trinkets, and figurines set up on a table. He also had small paintings, posters, and other art displayed for sale.

Sodas, juices, and lemonade were sold in the next stand, which was run by Harold Angel. He sat patiently behind his counter with portable R.U.s to keep the drinks cold. He had three of each bottled drink on display, along with large bowls of ice and disposable cups.

The next stand was the ice cream stand. On the center of the table under the stand's red canvassed roof, there was a sign: "Build your own sundae." There were bottles lined up of chocolate, butterscotch, and strawberry sauces. There were pots of hot fudge and caramel next to those, then marshmallow sauce, walnuts, and hand-whipped cream. At the left end, next to the bottles of sauces, were three drums of strawberry, chocolate, and vanilla ice cream. At the far end sat two bowls, one full of rainbow sprinkles and one full of chocolate sprinkles. Next to those were the cherries. However, there weren't many because the proprietor of the stand couldn't keep her hands off them.

"Sherri!" Cream slapped her colleague's hand. "Keep out of the cherries! Those are for the sundaes later on." She knelt down beside the stand and lifted a jar filled with more cherries. She poured them into the bowl until it was full. "If you can't handle managing the ice cream stand without *eating* anything, I'll do it myself."

"All right, all right," Sherri answered. "Calm down. I'll wash my hands and..." She stopped to lick her juice covered fingers. "Get back to preparations." She headed to Kel's Place as Cream rejoined with Fudge, who had been talking to Chief Murphy. They were both standing outside the police office building.

"So then what are we going to do for him?" Cream heard Fudge ask. "We need to tie up the loose ends."

"Yeah, Fudge," Murphy agreed. "Yeah, Taran said everything is going to be resolved after this meeting. He said there will be a lot of changes and developments. He's planning on sending this town down a new road to—"

Murphy was cut off by the sound of a whistle. Professor Stevens was the source of it. At that time, he was calling for all of the people to gather around and take seats in the lot.

"Thanks very much for coming, everyone." Taran stood behind the lectern on the platform. Everyone was in attendance. Joe Young, Mr. Owner, Kel Longley, and Tim Talbiss were in the front row on the left. Dr. White, his wife, Dr. Grey, Dr. Black and Dr. Sanders were in front on the right. Everyone else sat further back, including Luke Blackbeard, Paul Murphy, the divers, Aaron Richmond, and the Caldors.

"We have a lot of ground to cover today," Taran started. "First, I'd like to begin this meeting with an overview of today's events. I hope you guys all cleared your schedules because it may take all day. Our first order of business, however, is to pay our last respects to Randy Carr."

The audience remained quiet as Mr. Milton approached the table to the left of the arbor. He pulled the trunk out from under the table; as he did this, Taran moved under the arbor. Milton then dragged the trunk out in front of Taran.

"Ladies and gentlemen, Mr. Milton here, our own banker and mint manager, has activated the mint and has just officially released the very first 1841 edition silver coins," Taran announced. He took a small pouch from his pocket and opened it. Inside were dozens of coins. He pulled one out to show the people. "These are going to replace the gold coins we handed out previously. Those coins will be melted down and re-minted. The new coins are gold as well as silver and have been given several denominations. This one is the smallest."

The coin was one inch in diameter with the likeness of Randy's side portrait on the front. On the reverse side was an outline of the island, engraved with the words "ONE TOLE" beneath it.

Mr. Milton took a handful of pouches, with which the trunk was filled, and carried them into the audience. He handed out a pouch full of coins to each person there.

"Inside these pouches is a sum of two hundred and fifty 'Toles,'" Taran explained. "All of them were minted last week after the mint became operational on Tuesday. The Toles are in denominations of one, five, ten, twenty-five, and fifty. These will become the official currency of our town as of today."

Taran then took out another coin; it wasn't silver like the first, but golden. "Only our fifty Tole coins will be pure gold. All of the other coins will contain silver. For now, the first year, Randy's likeness will be on the front face of the coin. And as a memorial, his likeness will ever after remain on the fifty Tole piece."

"Let me tell you something," Taran continued. "Randy Carr was from a town in Indiana after which we named our currency: Tole. So the currency will remain as such in honor of him for as long as this town is around."

After Milton had finished distributing the money, he stood patiently next to the table, eyeing the semicircular object sitting on it under the sheet.

"All right, Mr. Milton." Taran turned to the banker.

"All righty, in commemoration of our lost friend, Randy," Milton said as he pulled the sheet off, "we have engraved this piece of granite with his name, date of birth, and so on. We've arranged for this to be placed in the new town hall tomorrow night."

Taran walked over and opened the trunk again. He took the few pouches remaining in the trunk out and put them on the table. "And finally, as our final tribute to Randy, I would like each of you to turn in your ID cards, the ones given to you several months ago. I would like to send this trunk, filled with all of your ID cards as well as some personal effects belonging to Randy, through time to be lost forever, as his body was."

Everyone was willing to do as he said, in remembrance of Randy. One by one, each person dropped in their card and found a new one on the table in front of Randy's stone. The new cards were designed differently, and this time each had a designated spot for each person's signature.

"These cards make each of you official citizens," Taran explained as the people proceeded to exchange their cards. "Any other people who may visit or come to this island to stay will be required to register for these."

After everyone was seated again, Murphy came up with a box full of stuff belonging to Randy. In it, there were a couple books, a small key, some papers and notebooks from room 203, and finally a leather-covered book with "Randy Carr, Jr." embroidered in gold.

Chapter 76

After the memorial service, Taran announced his plans to marry Dawn Vañia. As she shyly walked up to the podium from the back row where her friends sat, her simple but beautiful white lace dress proved to the crowd what was going to happen next.

"Uh… after several months' wait, Dawn and I are finally getting married," Taran declared. "And we obviously didn't want to return to our own time to do this when our new life is right here with all of you… very interesting people." He laughed softly and stepped aside as Dawn stepped up to the microphone.

"Good afternoon, everyone," Dawn greeted them nervously. "As if you haven't guessed already, the wedding ceremony will take place momentarily. We, uh… wanted to do this today because of the significance of today's date. First, it was a day that everyone would be gathered together for anyway, the first of the month. Second, today was already planned for Randy's memorial service, and a lot of changes have occurred and are yet to occur today. Third, on May 1 of 2341, exactly 500 years from today…" She began to cry and wiped her face with a tissue.

"I'm sorry." She cleared her throat. In a stronger voice, she continued, "Exactly 500 years from today, May 1, 2341, is the day Taran and I first met."

On that note, Dawn stepped down, and, after hugging his bride, Taran stepped back up to the microphone. "All right, ladies and gentlemen, I know what you're thinking: we can't get married without a priest. Well, I've talked it over with my superior, and we have a qualified person for the job already on this island. It seems that an ordained minister has the legal power or whatever to wed two people, but so does a ship's captain."

There was certainly shock in the crowd when Luke Blackbeard stood up and approached the platform. His ordinary rugged self had been transformed into a clean-shaven gentleman with neatly combed hair and a black suit. His patch, of course, remained; it was the only pirate part left.

Taran shook Blackbeard's hand, leaned toward him, and whispered in his ear. "From killer to clergyman in just two weeks," Taran whispered. "That's, that's… impressive." Then Taran stood behind the microphone and continued to speak to the crowd.

"All right, there's been a slight change in schedule for today," he announced. "Now, I know you're all excited to see us get married, but I think it's way too much excitement to follow up with anything else," he said with an air of sarcasm. "So before the ceremony I want to make my final…" He glanced over at Dawn.

She nodded in approval.

"My final announcement as mayor, or governor, or whatever my so-called title was in this town," Taran declared. It was an affirmation received with a hum of murmuring. "Well, whatever you may have called me before doesn't matter. I want to introduce you to a very fair and respectable leader whom I think can help this town greatly. He's a little strict, but entirely just. Please welcome Mr. Patrick Thompson."

There was some applause, but it wasn't overly joyous, as it wasn't expected to be anyway. *Well,* Taran thought, *change isn't always welcomed with open arms, but I think this change is a good thing.*

Merely an hour later, there stood Dawn, holding her groom's hand and looking into his eyes. Behind her, or to the left as seen by everyone in the audience, stood Diane, Debbie, Donna, Denise, Danielle, Delores, and Sherri. They wore dresses of alternating colors, starting with white, then a light green like that of the leaves of the ivy crawling up the arbor. On the right side stood Murphy, the best man, and Dr. White, Dr. Black, Dr. Grey, and Dr. Sanders. They all wore black suits, but their vests alternated similarly to the girls' dresses with silver and green.

As Taran held Dawn's hand in his, Dawn could feel him trembling slightly. She was trembling as well as Blackbeard said his final lines, the only life-changing words of the ceremony. *Of course I do,* she thought. *I do, I do.* She looked into Taran's eyes and he looked into hers. *Taran, you fool, what are you thinking right now?*

Dawn, you know I'm thinking about how beautiful you look, Taran thought as he too awaited her answer, though he already knew it. *I love you, Dawn Vañia. I always will.*

I love you, too, Taran Flint, she thought. *I never want you to leave me again, you hear me?* "I… I do," she finally said with a short and quiet sigh of relief.

"Aye, aye, ma'am," Blackbeard said. "Then by the power vested in me by the town of… of…"

"Zíon," Taran whispered.

"Of Zíon…" Blackbeard finished, "I now pronounce you man and wife."

Mr. Thompson, Dawn, and Taran were now sitting outside Kel's Place at her best table. The wedding was over and the reception had been short. Everyone was back in their more routine lives, or as routine as Zíon would allow.

"Taran?" Dawn reached for his hand. "What will we do now?"

"Life as usual, Dawn." Taran smiled.

Mr. Thompson put a piece of steak in his mouth. "Just out of curiosity, Flint, where did you come up with the name Zíon for the town? You never told me that name before."

"It's short for Gnico-Zíon," Taran answered. "I learned the word from the local tribe. It means paradise, or 'place of everlasting joy,'" he explained. He looked over at his wife. "I can't think of anywhere else, or with anyone else, I'd rather be."

"And to think, Mr.… and Mrs. Flint," Thompson said, almost regretfully, "that at one time, I wanted to get rid of such a remarkable, and I must say, diverse, paradise."

"Well, sir," Taran said, smiling, "you're right, at *one* time: 2348. But *this* is 1841!"

Epilogue

Ailiokahu was separated into two divisions, the Kahukah village and Gnico-Zíon. The Sundaes, particularly Donna and Debbie, acted as mediators between the two villages in order to maintain peace. They informed Kahukah that Dílon had returned to the heavens and that Gnico-Zíon had been founded by him in order to create the paradise its name implied. The Kahukah tribesmen were thereby permitted to go to Gnico-Zíon, and the citizens of Zíon were permitted to go to the Kahukah village. During the first few months, however, the Sundaes had to accompany any visitors until they earned Kahukah's trust.

Wakna and Kahlif continued to learn and study English, and even changed their names to the English translations. Wakna took the name Leon Hunt, and Kahlif took the name Lucky Fortune. They continued to document the occurrences of Ailiokahu in texts, both virtual and on paper.

The Time Crew claimed the northeast extension of the underground compound as their own quarters. They took trips to the surface to mingle with the citizens, make friends, and so on. However, they didn't take an interest in much of them for the long term. They had a careful focus on their work, which didn't focus on the people of Zíon. That is, except for Dr. Grey; he made a point to see the people in order to take note of the psychological effects this experience was having on them.

The Sundaes fully enjoyed the benefits of a Caribbean setting. They spent hours at a time at the beach every morning. Some of them met a few good career men they could spend their time with, namely the divers, Jacob, Isaac, and Erik.

Joe Young and Mr. Owner became good friends. Joe helped Owner keep his Auction Block up and running on the island. He in turn became the inventory manager, as well as the supplier. He would comb the island for rare-looking junk that Owner could sell for whatever people would bid on it.

Kel and Lindsey still ran Kel's Place. They even expanded to accommodate the growth that Thompson planned on having. They added a seafood buffet line, as well as a bakery. Both were thanks to the divers and Miss Smith's bakery, respectively. Lindsey also home-schooled the Caldor's son, Tom.

Gloria Deo and Harold Angel worked for the "Oracle," which became a five Tole paper that included interchronological comic strips corresponding to the date in several different times. Harold also wrote his own strip, but his favorite remained Peanuts.

Paul Murphy stayed on as the C.O.P., and he finally got an official police station with an exceptional police force. It consisted of Chris Miller, Ray and Jayne Caldor, Crystal Gates, André Stone, Wyatt West, and Bubba. Of course, they counted on the Sundaes to investigate the tough stuff.

Tim still ran the general store. In time, however, he planned to make it a full supermarket as demands needed to be met. In the meantime, however, he and Scott MacKensie simply maintained the store they had.

Sean Formann and the construction crew still had plenty of work ahead of them. They would be building for years to come, whether they liked it or not. Along with their regular crew, Justin, George, Ian, and Brian, they had also hired "Flatfoot" Thompson to help out. He had vowed to turn his life around.

Danny Stevens still ran the Island Inn. It was reserved for new citizens of Zíon. Nearly everyone else had their own homes built by the time the money was circulated. Harry Cane was still the clerk. Since Stevens spent most of his time at Stevens' Jewelers, Chuck Jones had resumed the day shift responsibilities.

Finally, Banker Milton enlisted the help of Blackbeard, Johnson, and the Stone Twins to help run the bank and the mint. The pirates were experts with money and treasures. Their input into the value of coinage was important. Furthermore, the other pirates helped by mining on the northern end of the island, on the other side of the jungle. There was talk that Blackbeard might begin an insurance venture.

Without a doubt, Ailiokahu flourished on its own. Thompson had little involvement except for political or civic concerns. He was able to enjoy the island along with everyone else.

Taran "Dillon" Flint was all but forgotten by the people in the political sense. He still took walks around the town on occasion with his wife at his side. He often went to Kel's Place to visit and eat dinner and made a few appearances at the amphitheater where all town meetings took place, as well as movie nights imported from any time that there were recorded motion pictures. Most of the time, however, Taran was lost in his work.

Only four short months before, he had been struggling to understand the methods of time travel. After ten years of research, he had finally built a machine that could prove successful in transporting someone through time. Out of the blue, a woman by the name of Sandy Brown had shown up at Karz. She studied the machine, made two adjustments, added a single component, and it finally worked after only working with him for a week.

They had "test driven" it one night, and she had disappeared, suddenly lost in time. Taran, with no way or any know how as to how to find her, had gone back to Karz and worked on his own to redirect the machine back to the initial destination. Somehow the code had been wrong, or Sandy had changed it, or she had fled from the island because Sandy hadn't been seen since. That was behind him now, though. Taran had all but forgotten about her when he began Phase One of his social experiment.

It had gone well, but when he brought one particular Randy Carr to the island, things had heated up. Randy had been killed, and the Sundaes had solved a case 500 years in the making. Dawn and he were finally married, and life was good. Taran had work, family, and paradise all at once.

However, curiosity got the better of him. With the power of time travel came the dreams of what could be, what should've been, and what if. His Time Crew was there to facilitate answering those questions, beginning with Dr. Laura White's project, Operation: Ice Age.

Only weeks after the wedding, Taran returned to work and extensive research in his reclusive bunker. He proceeded to the compass room and, followed by his wife and Dr. White, began to work on his machine. He was making an important adjustment to his invention in order to incorporate the technology Dr. White had been working on, what she had begun weeks ago.

Dr. White was holding a small device. When she approached the machine, it began to hum and whir. It was a gray, tubular device with several green flashing lights and a counterpart that Dr. White wore as a pin; it had one green light matching the ones on the device.

"What is that?" Taran looked down at the device. "Is it supposed to do that now?"

"Oops." Dr. White started to shut down the device, which had been inadvertently activated. Suddenly, the whirring became a rapid beeping, and it startled Dr. White. She dropped it in surprise, and an explosion filled the room with an ethereal bright green light. The explosion sent Dr. White hurtling to the ground by the door.

She woke what seemed to be only moments later. Groaning, she painfully turned onto her back and peered over toward where the time machine had been, but she beheld a strange sight. The machine was still there, but it glowed in a motionless green light. Bursts of flames coming from it were suspended in an inanimate explosion that remained motionless in the air. She felt as though she was looking at a three-dimensional photograph, but it was all too real.

Then she saw Dawn. Dawn's body was arched, like she'd been attempting a backward flip but had never finished. She too was inanimate. Her body lay suspended in the air, her arms looking as though she'd been flailing them.

That's what it was... frozen, Dr. White decided. She now realized Dawn had been in the area of the explosion, and the blast had sent both of them flying back. She had landed and Dawn had somehow stopped partway. *Dawn's there, and I'm here. What about*—"Taran! Is he all right?"

She rose slowly and painfully and walked around the explosion. It was amazing. The billows of smoke and flames were motionless on the platform, but no... no, Taran was gone, nowhere to be found.

Dr. White proceeded to leave to get help from her crew, but as she approached the door, she heard the familiar beeping begin again. She glanced down at the pin on her chest, the source of the beeping. The green light flashed consistently with the beeps. Still, she walked up to the door, but as she reached for the keypad, she noticed the green light was now solid and the beeps had become a high pitched tone. She heard an explosion again.

She whirled around immediately to see Dawn hit the floor, gasping for air, and the time machine up in flames. These weren't the inanimate flames, but real, licking, burning flames...